Henry Allen Tupper

Around the World with Eyes Wide Open

The Wonders of the World Pictured by Pen and Pencil

I0592135

Henry Allen Tupper

Around the World with Eyes Wide Open
The Wonders of the World Pictured by Pen and Pencil

ISBN/EAN: 9783337190606

Printed in Europe, USA, Canada, Australia, Japan

Cover: Foto ©Andreas Hilbeck / pixelio.de

More available books at **www.hansebooks.com**

Around the World
with Eyes
Wide Open

•

The Wonders of the
World Pictured by ⚜
⚜ Pen and Pencil ⚜

. . . BY . .

H. Allen Tupper, Jr., D.D.

Author of "Armenia : Its Present Crisis and Past History," "Columbia's War for
Cuba," "Uncle Allen's Trip Through Palestine," Etc.

Published by
THE CHRISTIAN HERALD
Louis Klopsch, Proprietor
Bible House, New York
1898

DEDICATION

To my wife

MARIE

and

my children

ALLENE, KATHERINE AND TRISTRAM

This volume
is lovingly dedicated

H. ALLEN TUPPER, JR.

HOW IT ❧ ❧
···HAPPENED ❧ ❧

IT happened in this way. In the spring of 1895, a handsome map of the world was presented me by a friend at Baltimore; and while glancing at it, hanging on my study wall, I arose from my desk-chair, one quiet midnight hour, and traced with my pencil a route from Baltimore, over the American Continent, to San Francisco, thence to the Hawaiian Islands, Japan, China, Malay Archipelago, Ceylon, India, Assam, Arabia, Africa, Palestine, Syria, Asia Minor, Europe, and back again to the Monumental City. This was only on paper! But, day by day, as my eyes turned wistfully toward the map, which now became increasingly fascinating, the desire of my life to visit the countries of the world, and study the peoples of earth, grew into a determination to start upon this circuit of the globe at the earliest practicable moment. Difficulties which seem insurmountable, frequently fade away as you approach them. Distance not only lends enchantment to the view, but oftentimes it disenchants, by seemingly magnifying the obstacles that lie in the pathway of our goal. The only way to do a thing is to do it. Events conspire to lend a helping hand to a determined purpose. A few months after the pencil-tracing on the map was made, I waved farewell to my loved ones at the Union Station, Baltimore, and was off—moving toward the setting sun. While I expected to receive much pleasure from the extended trip before me, this was not the supreme motive that actuated me. I decided, in my journeyings, frequently to turn aside from the usual route pursued by the globe-trotter: to rough it while studying the customs and characteristics of natives far from the treaty ports; systematically to record my impressions and the results of my study, on the ground, day by day, while they were fresh in my mind: to illustrate these strange scenes and interesting studies both by the pen and the photographic art; and to present to the public a book on travel that would be somewhat unique in its character. If I have enabled others to share with me the pleasures and profits of

my visits to many lands and among many peoples, and if I
have evoked or strengthened a desire for travel in the minds of
the readers of these pages, my pen has not written in vain.
In the words of the "Two Gentlemen of Verona," we find
nothing wiser than this :

> " I rather would entreat thy company
> To see the wonders of the world abroad,
> Than, living dully sluggardized at home,
> Wear out thy youth with shapeless idleness."

H. ALLEN TUPPER, JR.

CONTENTS.

(9)

CHAPTER VI.

LANGUAGE AND LITERATURE IN THE MIDDLE KINGDOM.

CHAPTER VII.

IN THE MALAY ARCHIPELAGO.

CHAPTER VIII.

THE SPICY BREEZES OF CEYLON.

CHAPTER IX.

FIRST IMPRESSIONS OF INDIA.

CHAPTER X.

IN THE HIMALAYAS.

CHAPTER XI.

THE WONDERS OF INTERIOR INDIA.

CHAPTER XII.

THE QUEEN OF THE EAST AND INDIAN MOSAICS.

CHAPTER XIII.

FAREWELL TO INDIA, GREETING TO EGYPT.

CHAPTER XIV.

THE HISTORIC NILE AND THE EXCAVATOR'S PICK-AXE.

CHAPTER XV.

THE GREAT PYRAMIDS AND THE ANCIENT EGYPTIANS.

CHAPTER XIX.

THE EYE OF THE EAST.

CHAPTER XX.

IN ASIA MINOR.

CHAPTER XXI.

A REIGN OF TERROR.

2

CHAPTER XXII.

AMIDST THE CLASSIC RUINS OF GREECE.

CHAPTER XXIII.

A GEM OF THE SEAS.

CHAPTER XXIV.

THE CITY OF THE CÆSARS.

CHAPTER XXV.

GENOA AND GIBRALTAR.

ILLUSTRATIONS.

(21)

PAGE.

ILLUSTRATION 31

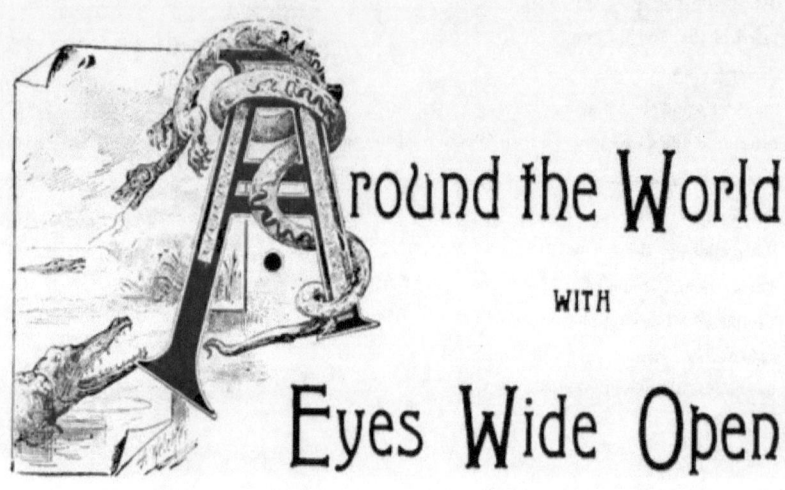

Around the World

WITH

Eyes Wide Open

Around the World &
With Eyes Wide Open.

CHAPTER I.

ACROSS A CONTINENT AND AN OCEAN.

DR. H. ALLEN TUPPER, JR.

ACROSS the continent in five days and nights, crossing eleven States and covering 3400 miles! Every imaginable panorama passes before the eye during this trip from the Atlantic to the Pacific—the cultivated fields, the quiet hamlets, the crowded cities, the homes of cliff-dwellers, the rushing rivers, the snow-blanketed mountains and the sparkling bay opening into the great sea. West of Chicago, until we reach the ocean, Denver attracts the attention of the tourist more than any other city. Like white-plumaged sentinels, the snow capped peaks stand guard over this pride of the West.

The Denver Carnival.

Fortunately we happened in her streets while the brilliant "Carnival and Festival of Mountain and Plain" was in full blast. The city was bedecked in yellow and white (gold and silver), the procession, composed of symbolic floats, moved through the streets, United States troops, cowboys, city officials, Indians, members of local and national orders, school and college youths fell into line, and, under the thrill of stirring music from string and brass bands, every one caught the spirit of the festival, which is intended to lift the shadows and rift the clouds of financial depression that have cast gloom over the State of Colorado for the last years.

Two hundred and seventy miles from Denver, at an elevation of 10,200 feet, we reach the unique city of Leadville, one of the richest placer camps in Colorado, known to fame in 1859 as California Gulch, where $5,000,000 in gold were worked out during five years. As we dash out of this picturesque State we are reminded of the exclamation of Joaquin Miller: "Colorado, rare Colorado! Yonder she rests; her head of gold pillowed on the Rocky Mountains, her feet in the brown

PIKE'S PEAK FROM COLORADO SPRINGS.

grass; the boundless plains for a playground; she is set on a hill before the world, and the air is very clear, so that all may see her well."

The Garden of the Gods.

The ride from Denver to San Francisco can never be forgotten by the lover of the beautiful in nature. The wonderland of the Rocky Mountains opens, hour by hour before him, the most enchanting scenes. In the Garden of the Gods are seen vivid suggestions of Athens and the Parthenon, Palmyra and the Pyramids,

Thebes and her crumbling columns. While riding upon a plateau of over 10,000 feet above the sea you look from your car window and there, standing outlined against the clear azure background, gigantic portals rise hundreds of feet above you and flash with the bright splendor of carnelian. The obliging conductor points out "Statue of Liberty," "Cathedral Spire," "Dolphin," a "Bear and Seal;"

WITHIN THE GATES, GARDEN OF THE GODS.

but these names seem quite inadequate to express your inexpressible admiration of the marvelous forms which nature assumes in these mountainous contortions.

The Cheyenne Mountain.

As we pass near the Cheyenne canyon, the scene changes. Down the side of the gorge leaps and foams a series of cascades—seven falls pouring the water from the melted snow above in the echoing chasm beneath. It will be remembered that on the eastern slope of the Cheyenne Mountain was the grave of that sweet American poetess, Helen Hunt Jackson ("H. H."), whose rhymes have covered these barren slopes with fadeless verdure.

Sierra Blanca is the giant of the Rockies, and is the loftiest mountain, with one exception, in the United States. It is a triple peak and springs from the valley 14,469 feet—over two miles and three-fifths of ascent. As you watch the varied beauties of "Wagon Wheel Gap" the train plunges into the blackness of Toltec Tunnel, which pierces the summit instead of the base of the mountain. When you emerge from the tunnel a thrilling sight greets your eye. From a trestle-bridge you look into a tremendous gorge, whose sides are splintered rocks and huge crags and boulders; below are the white waters of a

THE "MOUNTAIN OF THE CROSS," COLORADO.

foaming torrent, above the deep-blue sky; and on either side the majesty and mystery of the mountains.

Space forbids me to speak of the homes of the cliff-dwellers in picturesque ruins, or to dwell upon the wonders of Royal Gorge, Fremont Pass, the Black Canyon, Marshall Pass and Castle Gate.

The Holy Cross.

But the Mountain of the Holy Cross cannot be passed unnoticed. From the crest of Tennessee Pass, many miles away, you can plainly distinguish the snow-white emblem of the Christian faith gleaming with bright splendor against the sky. The cross is formed by canyons of immense depths riven down and across the summit of the mountain. Eternal snow fills these canyons, and this " sign set in the heavens " is a silent sermon of the greatest fact of all the ages.

THE EAST SIDE OF EAST TEMPLE STREET, SALT LAKE CITY.

Our new sister, Utah, contains one of the most mysterious inland seas on the globe. The lake's surface is higher than the Alleghenies, and its dead, tideless waters remain an unsolved enigma. One cannot sink on account of the density of the water, which contains 22 per cent solid matter, or 16⅔ salt —greater than the Dead Sea of the Holy Land. In the early morning we leave the train, and, sailing over the beautiful San Francisco Bay, we reach the city of the Golden Gate, situated at the north end of a peninsula thirty miles long, separating the Pacific Ocean from the bay.

At the Golden Gate.

San Francisco is pre-eminently a cosmopolitan city. Its buildings display every style of architecture and its population is composed of every nationality.

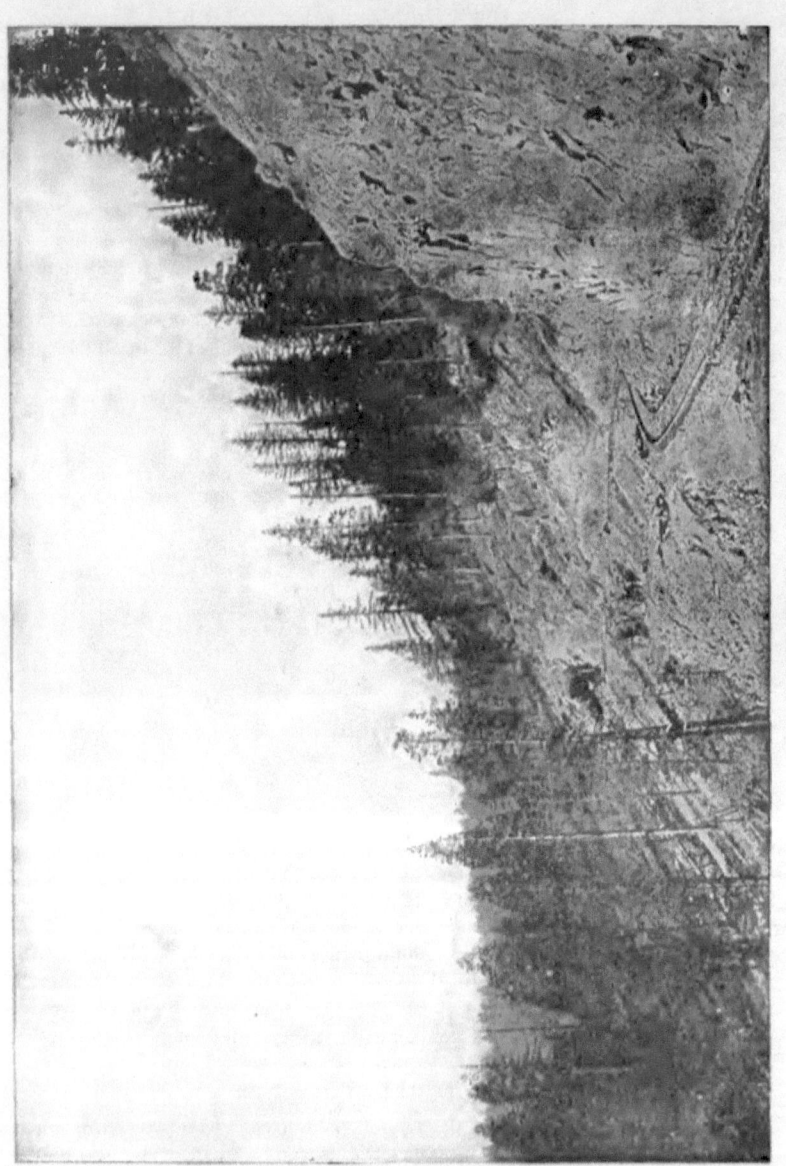

SACRAMENTO CAÑON, CALIFORNIA.

138

Yesterday morning was spent in studying the magnificent apartments of several of the palaces of millionaires on California street, and last night was largely occupied by me in the opium dens and narrow alleys of "Chinatown," where 25,000 of these sons of the "Celestial Kingdom" swarm in filth and degradation. Two such localities, so near together, cannot be found perhaps on the globe.

Sutro Heights, overlooking the Seal rocks, where thousands of these queer animals perform their fantastic capers and fill the air with their ceaseless barking; the Golden Gate Park, where the grounds and flora remind one of the tales of fairy-

SAN FRANCISCO AND THE GOLDEN GATE.

land, and the delightful drives, stretching along the waters where the bay rolls through the Golden Gates into the great Pacific—these are a few of the features that give fame to this city.

If San Francisco does not become one of the great cities of the world, the cause will be found in her failure to take advantage of the many natural blessings that Providence has lain at her door. The word winter cannot well apply to any of her twelve months; in front of her is a land-locked sheet of water some fifty miles long and of varying width opening to the sea, while she nestles in the central edge of a rich agricultural province; and at the doorstep is the terminal point of the great trans-continental routes. On the beautiful bay may be seen crafts of every kind from the tiny rowboat to the monster ocean steamer; and fringing the entire water front is a forest of masts.

The magnificent steamer, China, was trembling in her moorings, as we crossed the gangway on a beautiful October morning; and a few hours later we passed through the Golden Gate, due West. Our steamer contained a world in itself. The hundreds of passengers represented every class in society, from the charming, aristocratic bride to the wretched, sickly-looking Chinese steerage passenger on his way home to die. In the stern of the ship, we noticed queer-shaped boxes in great piles; and it was learned that these were Chinese coffins, containing the bones and dust of members of the Celestial Kingdom, whose last resting-place must be their loved land.

The days were full of sunshine, the nights full of stars, and the ocean quite pacific, during the first week of our journey; and on the eighth day we caught a glimpse of the Hawaiian Islands; soon the white houses of Honolulu were in sight; and in the twilight of the evening we were anchored in the handsome harbor facing the Paradise of the Pacific.

The Hawaiian group consists of five principal islands: Hawaii, Maui, Oahu, Molokai and Ranai, located about 2000 miles from San Francisco in the Northern Pacific Ocean, between the nineteenth and twenty-third parallels of latitude. As our steamer approaches Honolulu, on the island of Oahu, the seat of the Hawaiian government, the picturesque Diamond Head is seen outlined against the sky. This headland is an extinct volcano, whose fires in years past lit the sea far in the distance, acting as nature's lighthouse to warn the passing mariner. Passing this verdureless dome as we move toward the harbor, groves of cocoanut trees, stately palms, graceful ferns and every variety of tropical plants greet the eye; and looking upon this "Paradise of the Pacific," you can excuse Mr. Samuel L. Clemens for his enthusiastic reminiscence: "I can see its garlanded crags, its leaping cascades, its plumy palms drowsing by the shore, its remote summits floating like islands about the cloud racks. I can feel the spirit of its woodland solitudes; I can hear the gurgle of its brooks; and in my nostrils still lives the breath of flowers that perished twenty years ago." My friend of years, Mr. Willis, the distinguished United States minister to the islands, gave us an old-fashioned Kentucky welcome, and through his courtesy our visit was made most instructive and delightful.

A Charming Panorama.

From Punchbowl Hill, an extinct crater, rising in the rear of the capital city, a very fine view is taken of the surrounding land and water. The old

THE ROYAL PALACE, HONOLULU, HAWAIIAN ISLANDS.

Iolani Palace, the government buildings, the statue of Kamehameha I. in full war costume of a Hawaiian chief, the Hawaiian opera house, the barracks, the royal palm avenue leading to the Queen's hospital, the winding Pearl River, the wide-spreading rice and sugar plantations and the sloping beach, glistening under the tropical sun, attract attention and present a charming panorama. One of the most attractive drives around Honolulu takes us up a gradual ascent from the sea to a height of 1200 feet and brings us to the noted Pali. Here we visit the royal mausoleum, the last resting place of the Hawaiian royalty. The spot upon which we stand is historically very interesting.

Historical Scenes.

Here Kalamikupouli, the chief of the island, made his last stand against Kamehameha I., who conquered and consolidated the islands during the last century. The decisive battle was waged in May, 1795, and at the bottom of a great precipice the guide insists that there can be found the skulls and bones of many of the warriors who were driven to death in their struggle for independence. At Kaawaloa, on the island of Hawaii (the largest of the group), is the place where the brave Captain Cook fell. A plain obelisk of concrete, standing in a small enclosure surrounded by chains and old cannon, has been erected to his memory. The following is the inscription:

"In memory of the great circumnavigator, Captain James Cook, R. N., who discovered these Islands on the 18th of January, A. D. 1778, and fell near this spot on the 14th of February, A. D. 1779. this monument was erected by some of his fellow-countrymen."

Volcanic Forces.

Even a casual study of Hawaii causes you to realize its igneous origin. Every part of the island bears the Plutonic mark, and it is readily seen that it has been raised ridge by ridge and mountain by mountain up to Alpine heights by volcanic forces that are still in operation. Here is found Kilauea, the largest active volcano in the world, and the Hale-man-man, or House of Everlasting Fire of the Hawaiian mythology, is one of the marvels of the universe. As its brink is approached one can easily sympathize with the emotional description of a noted writer: "I think we all screamed, I know we all wept, but we were speechless, for a new glory and terror had been added to the earth. It is the most unutterable of wonderful things. The words of common speech are quite useless. Here was the real 'bottomless pit,' the 'fire which is not quenched.' the fiery sea whose waves are never weary. There were groanings, rumblings and detonations, rushings, hissings and splashings, and the crushing sound of breakers on the coast, but it was the surging of fiery waves upon a fiery shore."

The pit is nine miles in circumference: its lowest area covers six square miles, and the depth of the crater varies from eight hundred to eleven hundred feet, according as the molten sea is at flood or ebb.

The Leper Colony.

The neighboring island of Molokai is noted chiefly as the place of the leper settlement. We did not insist upon visiting this home of the living dead, but from the distance the village presented a pretty appearance, with its pure white cottages dotting the green plain, and the spires of several churches and the more imposing public buildings gave the impression of a peaceful, happy community. The place selected for the centralization of this dread disease is a plain of 20,000 acres, hemmed in by the sea and walls of rock, varying from 1000 to 2500 feet in height. The lepers are confined within the boundaries of the island, but those whose condition allows them to live outside of the hospital mingle freely among themselves, and de-

HAWAIIAN GIRLS IN FLORAL GARLANDS.

spite their dreadful and incurable malady, seem, I am told, to get some sweetness out of their bitter cup of life.

It was in the year 1865 that the Hawaiian Legislature established this leper settlement on the island of Molokai. When the official announcement was made that the isolation of lepers must take place the natives hid their leprous relatives, and friends under mats, in forests and caves, and as late as 1873 it was estimated that over four hundred of these unfortunates, with glazed eyes, bloated faces and decayed limbs, were still living among the people of the islands. No one can dwell upon this home of hideous disease and slow coming death without being thrilled by the self-forgetful devotion of Father Damiens, the heroic Belgian priest, who, following the example of his divine Master, laid down his life for the suffering and has received the everlasting crown worn by the noble army of martyrs.

The Hawaiian Tongue.

I was quite fortunate in forming the acquaintance of an intelligent New Yorker whose long residence on the islands and whose active mercantile life enabled him to give me information on numerous subjects of interest. From what he tells me I imagine that the language is not very difficult to master. Although there are only twelve letters, some of these are made to perform double duty, as K is also T, and L is also R. Each word, and indeed each syllable, ends with a vowel, and you hear nothing of the harsh explosive and sibilant consonants. These vowels as they glide from the Hawaiian tongue call to mind the soft Italian pronunciation, and the effect is most harmonious and delightful. The names of places are frequently compounded with *wai*, water, and are quite musical. Wailuku, "water of destruction;" Waioli, "singing water;" Waipio, "vanquished water." The natives have no surnames, and a man may have one name and his wife and children may be called by anything else.

Commerce and Industries.

Finding that my new-made friend was inclined to be communicative, I ventured to ask him three leading questions, namely: What is the commercial outlook of the islands? What is the political outlook of the islands? What about the decrease of the native Hawaiians? He insists that every day the business prospect of the islands is brightening and no time since his residence among the Hawaiians has he witnessed such a general but gradual revival in mercantile life. Added to the sugar and rice staples, there is, just now, a decided inclination toward the growth of coffee, and he thinks in the near future a certain portion of the islands will be as famous in the raising of this product as it has been in the culture of sugar and rice.

Political Situation.

At the reception given by President Dole, who by the way is the son of an American missionary, we were enabled to form a conception of the personnel of the present administration of the Hawaiian Islands. The president and his assistants

HONOLULU PINEAPPLE GROVE.

are substantial, conservative gentlemen; and while they must know that the existing government is only temporary, they are attempting practical and permanent
improvements. It does not take a prophet or the son of a prophet to foresee that
ere long the Stars and Stripes will be floating over these islands. Indeed, formal
steps have been taken by our government looking to this end. In transmitting the
Treaty of Annexation to the Senate President McKinley uses these words: "The
incorporation of the Hawaiian Islands into the body politic of the United States is

A HAWAIIAN GRASS HUT AND ITS OCCUPANTS.

the necessary and fitting sequel to the chain of events which from a very early period
of our history has controlled the intercourse and prescribed the association of the
United States and the Hawaiian Islands." The Treaty presented to the Senate
is a remarkable document. The Republic of Hawaii cedes absolutely to the
United States all rights of sovereignty over the Hawaiian Islands and their
dependencies, including all lands, ports, harbors, buildings, military equipments;
it provides that special land laws relative to Hawaii are to be enacted by the
American Congress; revenue from the sale of Hawaiian lands, excepting that

which is to be used for governmental purposes, is to be expended for educational purposes in Hawaii; complete civil, judicial and military control shall be exercised by the United States; the public debt of Hawaii, which is not to exceed $4,000,000, is to be assumed by the United States; and the President is to appoint five commissioners, two being native Hawaiians, to consider and recommend to Congress necessary legislation for the new territory. The Japanese Minister at Washington, representing his government, filed a formal protest against annexation, on the ground that this measure would work injustice to Japanese interests and claims on these islands; and England has shown some interest in the matter; but it is thought that any international complications arising from the ownership of these lovely islands by the United States will be adjusted satisfactorily.

Aboriginal Population.

The decrease of the Hawaiians is as pathetic as it is inevitable. For years the native stock has been dying out, and to-day, while there are nearly one hundred thousand persons on the islands, there are not more than forty thousand pure descendants of the aborigines. The intermarrying of the whites and the half-whites and the Chinese and natives is constantly going on, and the complexion and general characteristics of those whom you meet on the streets tell the tale of this amalgamation.

Our noble steamer, after taking on board five hundred more Chinese steerage passengers at Honolulu, turns her bow toward the Land of the Rising Sun; and as she glides through the placid blue waters of the Pacific, the flower and fruit-covered plains are lost to our view, and from far out at sea the peaks of Oahu can be seen through our marine glass, pointing their spires toward a sky that bends brightly over this gem of the ocean.

CHAPTER II.

LAND OF THE SUNRISE.

A S we sailed due West over the Pacific one hour was lost in each thousand miles of progress, and when we reached the half-way point around the world from Greenwich (180°) a day was dropped in mid-ocean. In passing from November 2 to November 4, or from Saturday to Monday, was quite a new experience. An officer on board tells me that he spent two Christmases last year while coming from Japan to San Francisco, and a fellow-passenger had the unique experience of having two birthdays during his voyage in the same direction. In coming my direction one stands the chance of having no Christmas and no birthday.

Yeddo Bay and Yokohama.

Early on the morning of November 10 I looked from my port window upon the beautiful Yeddo Bay, and as we crept slowly into the harbor of Yokohama a welcome sight greeted our eyes after nearly three weeks at sea. Hundreds of Japanese sloops and sampans darted in and out among the American, English, French, Russian and Japanese ships; men-of-war belonging to the five leading nations of the world were anchored near at hand; the low-roofed houses of Yokohama lay to our left, and before us loomed up the snow-capped and sunlit Fuji-yama. Our steamer anchored half a mile off shore and from a small steam tug we soon stepped on the Land of the Sunrise.

In the year 1854, when Commodore Perry reached Yokohama with his little fleet of men-of-war, it was only a small fishing village, but now it has a population of 170,000. The native and business part of the city is backed by a half moon of well-wooded hills, where the foreign concession is located and where handsome houses, in European style, are built on what is known as the Bluff.

Strange Street Scenes.

As we dash through the city in a jinrikasha new scenes open before us at every turn of the narrow streets. Men drawing vehicles like horses between the shafts; the half-nude coolies carrying heavy loads of merchandise, swung from their shoulders upon stout bamboo poles; the simple architecture of the dwelling-houses; the extremely deliberate and solemn salutations between the common people who meet on the streets; fantastic trading-booths and the brilliant display of toys and trinkets that fill them; the happy children flying kites, in the shape of hideous faces; the absence of beggars on the streets (quite a contrast to European and many American cities), and the general appearance of thrift, cleanliness and contentment that presented itself, made impressions rather pleasing than

otherwise. The women carry their children lashed to their backs like the American Indians, and the exposure of the tender eyes to the sunlight may account, partly, for the numerous cases of sore eyes and blindness in Japan.

A Tokio Chrysanthemum Show.

The winter sleep of the flowers is very short, and although we are writing in November I can walk in a garden ten yards from my room and gather a bouquet of flowers that would astonish any florist in Florida or California.

During this month the chrysanthemum is in all of its glory. I spent several hours at the chrysanthemum show in Tokio; and, doubtless, in all the world it would be impossible to witness another such exhibition of this particular flower. Dramatic and comical performances, war scenes, historical epochs and landscapes are set forth by these flowers, woven

LABORER OF THE COOLEY CLASS.

into designs, and the effect is remarkably fine. As might have been expected, the victorious battles in the China-Japanese war were favorite subjects, and in every instance a single Japanese was putting to flight a half a dozen members of the Celestial Empire. In one blood-thirsty scene the sweet flower was made to

4

depict a Japanese warrior holding a Chinaman's pigtail in one hand, while with the other he was about to behead him. In the Yokohama nursery I visited packing-rooms containing forty thousand cases of bulbs of different plants to be shipped to Europe and America.

In Fairyland.

A ride in a jinrikasha through the country gives one a great pleasure. Everything seems delicate, diminutive and fairy-like. The small rice and teafields.

GAMBLING IN JAPAN.

the tiny plots of ground around the low-thatched houses and the groves of dwarfed trees seem to correspond fittingly with the little people of this "Land of the Sunrise." As just now they are attracting the attention of the civilized world and as they are destined to become a potent factor in the future history of the Orient, it may be well to give a brief synopsis of their history and a glimpse into their social life.

The history of Japan naturally falls into four great periods. The first three comprise the history of Old Japan and the last one that of New Japan. Four

great waves of foreign influence have swept over the country. The first two
oriental, the last two occidental in character. During the first period (660 B. C.–
700 A. D.) emperors held supreme political and spiritual power.

Introduction of Buddhism.

Two important events mark this period. In the year 286 A. D. Chinese
literature, art and science and Confucius philosophy were introduced. In the
year 558 A. D. Buddhism was first proclaimed. It required a thousand years for

BUDDHIST TEMPLE, NIKKO, JAPAN.

this system to become firmly established, but its victory was finally complete. It
had transformed the nation. In the words of Professor Chamberlain, "Buddhism introduced art, science, medicine, moulded the folk lore, created dramatic
poetry and greatly influenced every department of social and intellectual life.
In a word, Buddhism was the tutor under whose instruction the Japanese
grew up."

It reached its golden age in the thirteenth and fourteenth centuries, when it
embraced the mass of the people and the land was filled with splendid temples
and monasteries.

The second period (700 A. D.–1100 A. D.) is marked by the rise of the Fujiwara family. This was a literary family, which had gradually gained supreme power over the nation. From this time one family after another held political power, and the Emperor was merely the nominal head of the nation until the restoration of 1867.

Rise of the Military Power.

During the third period (1100 A. D.–1853), in 1141, Yoritomo Minamoto consolidated the feudal system and became the first Shogun or Tycoon. The life of this great man marks a brilliant period in Japanese history.

INTERIOR BUDDHIST TEMPLE, JAPAN.

In the year 1549 Catholic mission work was introduced by Francis Xavier, bringing in the first wave of influence from the Occident. In the latter part of the sixteenth century three influential characters arose, each by his lifework to leave a lasting impression upon the history of the nation. Ota Nobunaga laid plans for the consolidation of the whole of Japan under one ruler, for up to this time the conquest of Japan had only been partial, but just on the eve of the accomplishment of his purposes he was slain. Hideyosh, a great warrior and statesman, carried to completion the work so well begun, but a greater than he was to enjoy the full fruit of his labors. Tokugawa Iyeyasu, the greatest man in Japanese history, was the first to rule over the entire empire. He founded the City of Tokio, making it the capital of the Shogunate, framed many wise laws and fostered art, science and literature. Under him the feudal system reached the zenith of its glory and power. The one blot upon his fame was the persecution of Catholics, the expulsion of foreigners and the closing of the country to

MUSIC IN THE HOME, JAPAN.

the outside world. His death, in 1616, closed this important period as far as any great event of any national importance is concerned.

The fourth period of Japan's history (1858-1895) is contemporaneous with the force wave of foreign influence. It is marked by the coming of Perry, the destruction of the feudal system, the restoration of the Emperor and the ascension to the throne of the present Emperor, Mitsuhito, in 1867. Protestant missions began in 1859 and the first church was formed in 1872. The transformation of the country is remarkable and every year witnesses new evidences of progressive life.

Japanese Social Life.

One of the first lessons that is taught a Japanese girl is that she is inferior to a boy, and this early lesson is impressed ceaselessly upon her during her life.

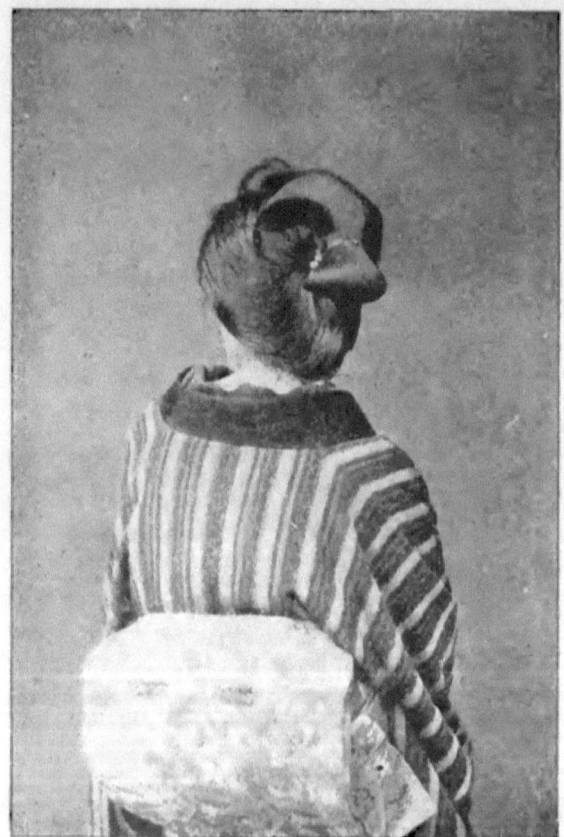

HAIR ARRANGED BY UNMARRIED WOMAN, JAPAN.

The boy calls his sister by her name, but she must call him "Ani San" (dear brother), being a less familiar term than his name. Quite commonly the brother eats with the father, and after waiting on them she eats with her mother. It is commonly understood that it is not the proper thing for a girl to play even with her brother after she is ten years old, and thus a wall separates the sexes in the same family.

Courting is an unknown science in Japan. The "Nakodo," or go-between, is not only a match maker, but arranges all the preliminary details to the hour of marriage. A father comes to the conclusion that it is time that his daughter should marry. Without speaking with her on the subject, he consults a friend, and arrangements are made to find a suitable life partner for her. Now the "go-between" takes the whole matter in hand, and, as he expects to be well paid for his trouble finally, he becomes a very busy person indeed. This official, with the consent of the fathers of the intended groom and bride, may arrange for a miyai (look-at-each-other meeting) before the marriage, but frequently the young people never see each other until the moment of marriage. But after the union

this important character, whose services we have explained, has not ceased his duties. If, unfortunately, there should occur such an uncommon thing as a family quarrel the go-between is called in and brings about a final settlement by putting them on good terms or arranges for a permanent separation.

When a woman is married two solemn duties immediately are laid upon her. In certain parts of Japan she must shave off her eyebrows and blacken her teeth. By these beautiful performances she brands herself with the information, "I am a married woman. Take care not to fall in love with me." The arrangement of the hair also indicates whether a woman is married or unmarried. It is the

FOUR JAPANESE LADIES.

duty of the mother to give parting instructions to her daughter as she enters into this slavery of marriage. This is done by impressing upon her the following rules of conduct: (1) When you marry you are legally my daughter no longer, so give the same perfect obedience to your father-in-law and mother-in-law that you have given to your father and mother. (2) When you are married you have no other lord than your husband. Be humble, be polite. Perfect obedience to

the husband is a noble virtue for the wife. (3) Be kind always to your mother-in-law and sister-in-law. (4) Don't be jealous. That is not the way to win your husband's affections. (5) Even where there is injustice on the husband's part do not be angry. Be patient, and when he is quiet, then advise with him. (6) Don't talk much. Don't tell another person mischief. Don't in any case tell a lie. (7) Get up early, stay up late at night and do not take a nap in the daytime. Don't drink much wine, and do not go into a crowd until you are fifty-one years old. (8) Do not ask a fortune-teller what your future destiny will be. (9) Be a good housekeeper; be economical in everything. (10) Though

JAPANESE BELLES.

you are married young, do not associate with young men, even if they are relatives. (11) Don't wear a gay dress; be clean always. (12) Don't be proud of your father's prosperity or position; do not boast of them before your husband's relatives. (13) Be careful how you treat the men-servants or maid-servants. The bride vows that she will keep all of these rules, and if she fails to do so, she has become false to her marriage vows. The wedding ceremony takes place in the home of the bridegroom, where the largest room is decorated for the occasion. The bride, in her long-sleeved and elaborately made furisode, and the groom, with his silk kamishimo, accompanied by a small bridal party, take their seats in the bridal room. A table is placed in front of the bride, and upon it are three-sized cups filled with "sake" or Japanese wine. The bride takes three sips

WEDDING PROCESSION, JAPAN.

from each, and at her invitation the groom does the same. This indicates that they will share each other's joys and sorrows, and after the announcement of the marriage by the "go-between" to the parents the ceremony is completed.

As a rule the completion of this form is the beginning of a life for the poor little woman that has for her very few rays of sunshine. She is the mistress rather than the queen of the home, and her chief care is to look after the comfort and pleasure of the man, who too often is cruel and overbearing.

Causes for Divorce.

There are seven recognized causes for divorce in Japan: (1) Disobedience; (2) no child; (3) adultery; (4) jealousy; (5) loathsome disease; (6) talking too much; (7) stealing. Indeed, the husband for the most trivial cause can secure a separation from his wife. No court is needed. The ever-ready "go-between" is told of his desires, and, with more speed than he arranged the union, this all-important personage brings about the disunion. The first boy is often called "Ichiro," meaning "first one;" the next "Niro," "second one;" the third

"Saburo," and so on, according to their numbers. The girls are generally given fanciful names, such as "Flower," "Glory" and the like. If their lives were as bright and beautiful as their names, the Japanese home life would be a charm instead of a curse, as too often it is.

Japanese Society.

Japanese society is divided into three classes—the nobility, gentry and common people. The latter class constitute ninety-five per cent of the entire population. We find nothing like the "caste" feeling that exists in India dominant in Japan, and although divisions are recognized they are more flexible indeed than in England.

JAPANESE GIRLS CARRYING BABIES.

Nothing has developed more quickly than the educational life of this people. During the middle ages education was entirely in the hands of Buddhist priests and the temples were the schools for the people. When the Tokugawa family came into power and for over two hundred and fifty years (A. D. 1603-1867) the educated classes came under the influence of Confucianism, and the "four books" and "five canons," composing the Confucian classics, became the literary and educational basis of the people. These were studied as thoroughly as in China itself.

Education.

Since the revolution of 1868 an entirely new state of affairs has existed, and the reform has been carried on largely under American influences. It would

AT SCHOOL, JAPAN.

surprise one who has not kept abreast of the educational progress of Japan to visit the Imperial University at Tokio and note its complete appointments. There are six distinct faculties, namely, law, literature, science, engineering, medicine and agriculture; and more than one thousand students were at the university, according to the last catalogue that is before me. The normal schools, commercial school, technical school, nobles' school, naval and military academies, musical academy, fine art school, blind and dumb school and five higher middle schools were founded and are supported by the government.

The desire is quite manifest in all of these educational improvements to assimilate the national thought to that of Western nations. It was my pleasure to address, through an interpreter, a school of young men in Tokio this week on

JAPANESE ACTRESS.

the "Need of Educated Men in Japan," and during the address it was gratifying to mark the intelligent attention given to the words spoken and the seemingly hearty approval of certain American methods of education that were urged for adoption. The Japanese as a student is differential, industrious, and especially quick to absorb new ideas. He is naturally self-confident, and consequently self-conceited; but this, let it be hoped, will pass away when more progress has been made by him. His artistic perceptions are remarkable.

National Art.

In the fifteenth century Italian painting was at its zenith and Japanese art entered upon its most glorious period, but we have no facts to prove that there was any influence of the one on the other. The founder of the first school of Japanese art was a Buddhist priest, and not seldom since have these representatives of the popular religion been found fostering

A JAPANESE ACTRESS

JAPANESE ACTOR

and encouraging, in many ways, the artistic in different directions. The bold
dash that is observed in all Japanese paintings is due probably to the national
habit of writing and drawing from the elbow, not from the wrist. The laws of
perspective and of light and shadow are disregarded to an alarming extent,
although the main study in the picture may be exact and faultless in detail. The
Japanese artist will give you a tree which is excellent in every detail, but he
will accompany it by certain atmospheric and topographical peculiarities which
defy the wildest and most eccentric imagination. He does not believe that

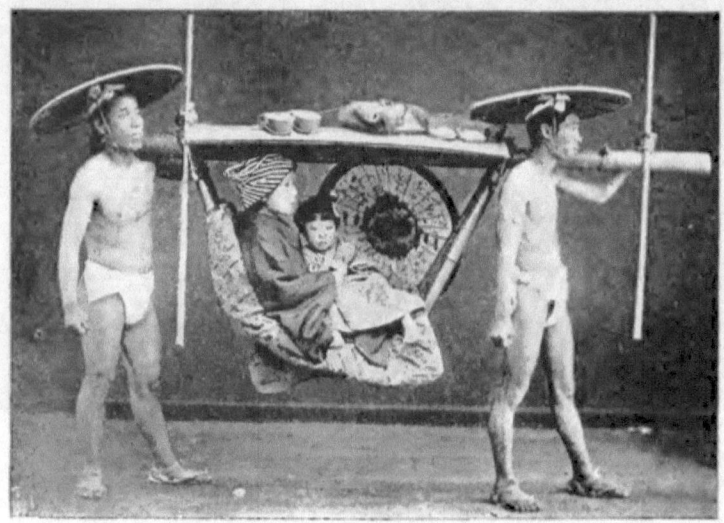

JAPANESE CARRIAGE.

mechanical symmetry makes for beauty, and, to some extent, he has revolution-
ized art by teaching the artistic world the charm of irregularity.

Its Eccentricities.

In the decorative art the Japanese may be said to lead the world in certain
respects, but in this special work their art breaks every rule of the recognized
schools. Who would look on that teapot for perspective art? Yet all of your
fine masters cannot produce such a fine work as that. What many of the European artists laughed at, not long since, they are trying in vain now to imitate.

The art of Cloisonne is seen to perfection in Japan. A thin network of copper or brass is soldered to a foundation of solid metal, and the cells of the network

—the cloisons, as they are called—are filled in with enamel paste of various colors. By baking, rubbing and polishing the surface becomes perfectly hard and smooth.

Means of Transport.

The jinrikisha (meaning "man-power vehicle") is an institution of the land, and, literally, it is the pull-man-car of Japan. The story goes that an American missionary by the name of Goble, desiring with his good wife to accomplish cer-

JINRIKISHA.

tain missionary work, and finding it hard to find conveyances through the rural districts, fell upon the invention of this two-wheel vehicle, to be drawn by a single man. The invention immediately became popular, and in 1891 there were thirty-eight thousand jinrikishas in use alone in Tokio. The ports of China and Malay have the craze, and the thousands of coolies find employment, while the residents, with more coins, are made comfortable by them. As the total cost of the outfit of a jinrikishaman, coat, tight pants, hat and lantern, is only $4.00, and he gets ten or fifteen cents for a pull of two miles, it can be made quite a paying business by a stout oriental.

The Press.

One who has had an American paper placed on his breakfast table for years is somewhat amused when he picks up a Japan daily. But considering the fact that Mr. John Black founded Japanese journalism in 1872, commendable progress has been made. Four years ago there were six hundred and fifty-eight

IN THE HOME, JAPAN.

newspapers, magazines, journals of different kinds published in the empire. Newspapers, like books, are written in the "written language," which is quite different in grammar and vocabulary from the colloquial language.

The press laws in Japan are very rigorous. Article XIX of the newspaper regulations reads thus: "When a newspaper has printed matter which is considered prejudicial to public order or subversive of public morality, the minister of state for the interior is empowered to suspend its publication, either totally or temporarily." During the month following the proclamation of the constitution the brethren of the press expressed themselves rather freely, and newspapers were suspended at the rate of two a week. What a blessing to a long-suffering public in America if there could be a few suspensions of this kind!

Railroads.

The first railroad built in Japan was eighteen miles in length and connected Yokohama and Tokio. This was opened in 1872. On account of the mountainous character of the country and the sudden swelling of the streams, Japan is not adapted for railroad construction, but, despite these disadvantages, this improvement has steadily gone on, and now the total mileage is over two thousand. Although this enterprise was begun by the government, railroads are not exclusively owned by the power at Tokio. The railways are narrow gauge and

JAPANESE DOMESTICS.

the rates are only about one cent a mile. The telegraph wire follows the railroad everywhere through the empire, and often it stretches over the mountains where the trains of cars are not seen. Messages are written and transmitted in the vernacular, and ten "kana" characters can be sent to any part of the empire for fifteen cents. Perhaps when Japan becomes more civilized she will put her railroads and telegraph system into the hands of noble-hearted monopolies, and then the dear people will pay three cents to ride a mile and five cents to telegraph a word!

5

Funeral of a Prince.

On the day of our arrival in Tokio, the national capital, the funeral of Prince Kitashirakawa, the uncle of the Emperor, took place. The Prince, it seems, had distinguished himself in bringing under Japanese power the undisciplined and demoralized Chinese of Formosa, and because of this and his near relationship to the ruler of the land, he was honored in life and death.

The *Official Gazette* published in detail the order of the funeral cortege, of the march and of the last obsequies at the temple, and these were carried out in

ENTRANCE TO JAPANESE TEMPLE.

strict adherence to the royal program. Two hours before the procession moved ceremonies began at the residence, and then the train, headed by the First and Third Regiments of the Imperial Guard, with arms reversed and two companies on foot, moved through the gates.

The Procession.

On reaching the street the order of the cortege was as follows: The herald, mounted police, inspectors, military band, detachments of the regiment of the

Imperial Guards, ten banners carried by white-robed bearers, a Shinto priest, and ornamental box containing offerings, borne by four persons clad in white; Shinto priests, clothed in ceremonial dress; the rain coat of the prince, carried by bearers in white; mounted Shinto priests, chief priest in carriage, priestly musicians in ceremonial garb, growing Sakiki trees, presented by the imperial family, borne by special messengers from the palace; forty stands of flowers, huge in size and brilliant in color; decorations of the deceased prince, borne on cushions by officers of the prince's household; the sarcophagus of snow-white pine, borne by

ENTRANCE TO SHEBA TEMPLE, TOKIO.

sixteen wrestlers, who had followed the forces to Formosa; seventy *hakucho* in attendance, wounded military officers who had come back from Formosa with the deceased prince, the princely bodyguard of ten soldiers in the frayed and travel-stained garments worn during the campaign in Formosa, imperial bodyguards, retainers of the late prince's household leading the prince's favorite horses; the prince's foreign and Japanese swords, borne by retainers; the prince's shoes, carried by retainers; chief mourner, the prince's oldest son, dressed in coarse mourning garb, straw-sandaled, on foot, followed by his two younger brothers; chief steward of the prince, on foot; the prince's family in carriages, ministers of state, dukes and marquises, officials of the second grade, holders of the highest orders of decorations, nobles by creation, peers, members of the upper and lower houses, mounted, armed and rear guard, chief inspector and police, mounted.

A Brilliant Cortege.

The procession, as may be imagined, was brilliant and of great length, taking about two hours to pass a given point. Including soldiers, the train was supposed to be composed of not less than twelve thousand persons, and it is estimated that two hundred thousand Japanese and foreigners lined the route of

TEA DRINKING, JAPAN.

march. Government schools, national and private banks and governmental departments were closed and a general holiday was observed.

The upper stories of buildings along the line of march were deserted, it being an act of sacrilege in Japan to look down upon a procession in which there are persons of exalted rank. When the temple grounds were reached the students of the Nobles' School, the foreign consular body and the diplomatic corps were given special places, and around the sarcophagus gathered the representatives of the Emperor and Empress and persons of high rank.

The services were in accordance with the ceremonial of the Shinto sect. A short eulogy was pronounced; prayers were repeated; offerings of rice, water, saki and fruits were made before the sarcophagus, and a triple salvo of guns announced that the last royal rites were over.

Japan After Victory.

The world is congratulating Japan, and just now she is in high feather among the nations. On the other hand, the stock of the people of the pigtail is far below par, and her general condition is, at present, not very "celestial."

MOUNTAIN VILLAGE, JAPAN.

But Japan's congratulation should not be given to her so unreservedly, for there is a loss and a gain, a tare and a tret to be taken into account.

What does she gain by her victory over China? She has accomplished exploits, has developed unknown resources, has exposed the weakness and corruption of her sister empire, has brought herself forward as a military factor of first-rate importance in the East, has acquired a commanding position in the affairs of Corea, has had her treasury enriched by more than two hundred millions of taels of silver and has come into possession of the great and rich island of Formosa. Of all these acquisitions the latter is by far the most substantial, and doubtless it will add more than all others to the might and efficiency of Japan.

This change of ownership is also most fortunate for Formosa. It will be developed better, and the two provinces of China, which lie just *across the straits* and are closely connected in trade with Formosa, will be found sensitive to the evolutionary and revolutionary forces.

Japan's Army and Navy.

The Japanese soldier has shown his metal and the staff scored high honors, but at the same time the fighting qualities of the soldier or the capacity of officers have not been very severely tested. If, instead of fancy, flaunting banners and the fireworks of half-trained coolies, they had to stand before the deadly hail of shrapnel and the crash of well-ordered volleys from disciplined troops, their equals in bravery and patriotism, the result might not have been invariably one-sided.

Is Japan really better off now than before the war? What does she propose to do with her large indemnity? She has become tremendously ambitious, and now she is determined to make herself a great military and naval power and to exert a potent influence in the affairs of Asia. With the money paid her by China she is going to fortify her coast, buy more battleships and get ready for another war that may grow out of the one that is just over. All the money received from China will soon be spent in these preparations, and the costly navy and the fortifications must be kept up.

Who is to pay for all of this? Japan is not a rich commercial nation like England, with colonial possessions to draw on, and a heavy tax on her own people, essential to military effectiveness, is apt to create grievous inward disturbance.

A Costly Prominence.

In other words, her victory has placed her in a position in the East that will require her to spend large sums of money to maintain her prominence, and she must necessarily be kept in constant anxiety for fear her people may be overburdened in the maintenance of the army, navy and coast defences, and for fear that the ever-watchful Russia may swallow the chestnut after Japan has cooked it.

Russia is noted for her dogged persistency of purpose, and she intends to secure an opening to the unfrozen sea, if she has to fight for it. In order to accomplish this, she cannot afford to allow Japan to gain any more power. Soon after the fall of Port Arthur the Japanese army would have been in the capital of China had not Russia, indirectly, changed the tide of affairs. In the settlement of the Corean question Russia's fine hand was again seen, and many of the intelligent Japanese think that Japan did the fighting and Russia is reaping the fruits of the victory. A leading Japan paper last week contained this significant paragraph: "Japan can supply the men and Great Britain the naval power, which would more than balance the Russian and French preponderance over Japan."

But for Japan to become a party in European politics means more war, more cost, more sacrifice and more national uneasiness. If she had kept at home and devoted herself to the industrial development of her people, she would have no apprehensions of a foreign war, and surely she has enough to keep her busy on her own unique island. But she has taken the sword, and its blade may cut her own throat before it is sheathed.

The Situation in China.

The late enemy of Japan presents an interesting study. To-day we find in China the same elements at work which brought about in India the substitution

FRUIT MERCHANT, JAPAN.

of foreign for native rule. A tottering imperial autocracy, semi-independent vice-royalties, an official class as corrupt, ignorant and self-seeking as any Indian court could produce; great unpaid armies without leaders or discipline, such as Clive and Wellesly so easily destroyed, and a people who do not know what the word patriotism means, and who will sell themselves to the highest bidder. If history repeats itself it takes no prophet or son of a prophet to foresee the inevitable.

It is currently reported that the late financial commissioner at Canton was appointed some time since by imperial edict on a special mission to convey to St. Petersburg a secret treaty between China and Russia, which concedes to the latter the right to build railways through Manchuria and it also grants to Russia other privileges of the kind, which proves beyond doubt the tendency of China to accede to the wishes of a nation, into whose hands she seems quite willing, practically, to place herself during the misfortunes that now overshadow her. The fact that China reserves the right to purchase from Russia these railroads in twenty years only proves that her star of hope is still twinkling, however dimly, in the distant sky. All these things are hastening forward the time when the much-talked-of Chinese wall will entirely crumble before the influences from without, and when a nation of 400,000,000 population will be permeated, let us hope, by the golden light of a new national life.

Japan's New Attitude.

The remarkable progress of Japan during the last score of years, in moral and intellectual, as well as material affairs, gave rise to high hopes that the Gospel of Christ, as well as forms of Western civilization, would triumph in the Mikado's empire. But the recent turn of affairs seem, for a while at least, to check this advancement. The ascendency of the Samurai, which is the revival of the old-time feudal aristocracy, means that our Western merchant and missionary must contend against an ancient conservatism, which was a blight upon Japan for so many years. The fact that there are sixty thousand Protestant converts in the country is an evidence that Christianity has made gratifying progress; but as the Samurai, lately come to power, emphasize the divine origin of the Emperor, it can readily be seen that the advance of the Bible means the decay of this nation; hence we have here a partial explanation of the new attitude toward foreigners, and especially missionaries. Again, successes in several directions, of late, have increased the conceit of the little man of the Sunrise Kingdom; and in more than one quarter of Japan the converts to Christianity are reported as exclaiming to their fathers in the Gospel: "We have no need of you any longer. We know how to preach and teach Christianity; provide us with money and you can go back home;" and a native paper suggests the introduction of a new Christianity, founded upon conditions existing among the Japanese. In every part of the empire the missionaries of the Cross are laboring prudently and untiringly against these obstacles, and we have faith that the Truth will eventually prevail.

CHAPTER III.

THE INTERIOR OF JAPAN.

A FORTNIGHT'S study of the interior of Japan brings before us many features of life that are characteristic of this people. In the little coaches of the railroad train or behind the trotting jinrikasha man we pass thousands of acres laid off in tiny squares with all the precision and regularity of flower-garden beds.

The glory of the harvest time has come; the sheaves of rice are bound most artistically about the trunks of the trees or around great uplifted and stationary bamboo poles; the peasants, male and female, are busy gathering the last of the ripened grain; the lazy hump-back cow or ox creeps along nearly wholly covered by his great burden; the farm villages, with low roofs of thatched rice straw, appear in the distance, and from trees, housetops and poles are flying bright-colored flags, for it is the beginning of the harvest festival, when the gods are eating new rice.

An Industrious People.

There is no people more industrious than the Japanese. This is true of the man and woman, the young and the old. Whether you look into the tiny shops that open into the street, or study the moving mass of coolies along the sea or river fronts, or watch the active crowds on the streets, or visit the rural districts, you are impressed by this fact. This industry is combined with a perfection in detail of their work that is remarkable.

I know of no nation that does better work on small surfaces, that can accomplish more with raw materials, and that accomplish as much with as rough tools as the Japanese.

Farming.

It is a marvel to see what they accomplish in the line of agriculture with so many odds against them. Along the steep slopes of the mountain side, in the patches of earth between great boulders of rock, in the naturally barren plains, made fertile by a perfect system of irrigation, you find fine illustrations of the farming art. All farmers in Japan live in villages, and each village is presided over by a headman, who settles all trouble among the farmers and who is the supreme local authority.

(73)

The government land tax is 2½ per cent of the land value, to which is added the *ken* or district tax, which makes the total from 3 to 5 per cent. After bad harvests it has been found impossible for the peasants to pay this tax, and not seldom has there been great dissatisfaction among this class, bordering, some years since, on insurrection.

Rice, wheat, barley, millet, guinea corn, maize and many varieties of vegetables are abundant in good seasons, and the small orange and large persimmon are found on the breakfast and dinner table table nearly the year round.

RICE PLANTING, JAPAN.

More and more attention is being given to the cultivation of the camphor tree, and this useful drug is quite a source of revenue.

Silk Culture.

Silk culture has made Japan famous, and hundreds of thousands of her citizens are employed in preparing this article for the European market.

The silk, as is well known, originates in the cocoons, a pupa covering of a group of worms which are called spinners. The mulberry spinner is the best known and most important of all of these. They differ from one another in all their stages of development—as eggs, caterpillars, cocoons and butterflies—especially as to size and form of caterpillars and color of cocoons.

As the eggs have very fragile shells, the butterflies are made to deposit them on boards made of bast paper. These stick fast, and from them the young grubs creep out on the cardboard. After the third casting the peculiar character of the grub appears—yellow eyes, with black arches and dark sickles or half-moons on the back. Until the second or third casting they must be fed with chopped mul-

WORKING WITH SILK WEAVERS, JAPAN.

berry leaves, which must be frequently given them, while they are kept in clean, dry rooms, well ventilated.

Before the silk-worm begins to spin it loses its appetite, crawls about restlessly and becomes translucent. But the internal change is even greater. The two spinning glands become filled with transparent, thick, fluid silk stuff, which comes forth from them when the worm begins to spin through the spinning teats in its head, stiffening in two separate threads and become cemented in a double thread. After two or three days the worm changes into a chrysalis. First it makes a loose case, and then, supported by this, the body gets gradually smaller, forming the cocoon. This consists of a thread from 400 to 500 metres long and becoming thinner and weaker toward the centre.

I am told upon close examination with a magnifying glass a cross section of a cocoon wall shows five to ten layers of silk formed by the caterpillar in continuous backward turns, one on another. A week or ten days after the caterpillars

STREET SCENE IN YOKOHAMA, JAPAN.

have spun, the cocoons are taken from their resting-places and separated from the floss silk that surrounds them.

Lacquer Industry.

In the thatch-roofed huts of the peasants among the mountains beyond Nikko and in the magnificent palace of the Mikado at Kioto I saw exquisite lacquerwork. This is found everywhere. While I write there is before me an "Autumnal Landscape by Moonlight," in lacquer-work, which shows ten or twelve shades of color, and which is quite artistic in design.

The material of the industry is the sap of the lac tree, cultivated in Japan and China. The extraction of the lac is done by making a horizontal slit upon the tree during the season from April to October. The autumn product is less watery and more valuable. The scratching-sickle, a thin iron plate, bent like a fishhook, and a flat iron spoon with a short, bent-over point, are the instruments used in obtaining it. The first is used to cut the tree and the other for scraping out the channels when full of lac and lifting it into the small wooden or bamboo pail.

The raw material is purified from foreign substances by being pressed through cotton cloth and hemp linen, and afterward it passes through a process of evaporation in the sun or by means of a mild heat over a coal fire. The laying

JAPAN FAN DEALER.

on of the coatings requires the greatest care, and is gone over crosswise with the brush, first in one direction and then in another. After the groundwork is completed it is rubbed until a smooth surface of dark-gray becomes gray-black. On small and large surfaces we find a great variety of patterns in lacquer-work, and some of them are richly ornamental.

Castle by the Sea.

Through the kindly consideration of the United States Minister at Tokio we were sent passports to the Mikado's palace at Kioto, the old capital of Japan, and to the neighboring castle. The decorations in ivory, bronze, wood-carving, enamel, porcelain, wall-painting, embroidery and inlaid metal-work give proof of the highest genius in certain directions; and the throne-chair, inlaid with mother-of-pearl, is a gem in art.   I pushed aside the exquisite silk curtains of his Majesty's bed and looked upon the spot where, last fall, he rested his uneasy head while in Kioto.

From Kobe to Moji we sailed two hundred and fifty miles through the entire length of the famous Inland sea.   By many this is regarded as the most beautiful water in the world, and surely it is hard to imagine anything more enchanting.

INLAND SEA, JAPAN.

Our boat winds about island after island, passes through narrow passages of water, overshadowed by great bluffs from the headland, and during every turn of our noble steamer a new panorama of beauty opened before us.   The day was bright and the night was lit by a full moon.   The play of the moonlight on the rippling face of the silver sea and the soft glow on the hundreds of islands in the still night made me quite forget my cabin-room, and much of the night was spent on the deck.

The entrance to the sea at Moji is guarded by fortifications that line the summits of the hills, and the full supply of cannon, occupying either side of the strait, would doubtless prove to be an impressive argument to an incoming enemy.

It was just here, in the town of Bakan (Shimonoseki on foreign maps), that the Chinese Viceroy, Li Hung Chang, "the Napoleon of the East," as General Grant called him, met the representatives of the Mikado, and I saw where he was shot while riding through one of the narrow streets of the village. This murderous act of a Japanese crank cost Japan dearly, but as capital punishment is no tolerated in the land, the criminal was only sent to prison.

In a Japanese Hotel.

At Kokura we had the new and, it is to be hoped, never-to-be-repeated experience of spending the night in a Japanese hotel, pure and simple. This was done at the urgent solicitation of two friends, whom we are trying hard to forgive. On entering we left our shoes at the door and were supplied with cloth slippers.

While our Japanese supper was in process of

FAVORITE GAME WITH JAPANESE GIRLS.

preparation we sat on the floor around a *hibachi* (fire jar), where a little charcoal fire was burning beneath our teapot. The Japanese maids soon appeared with the fish, rice, eggs and certain dishes that we took on blind faith, and our performance with chop-sticks was as amusing as it was deliberate. A full bill of fare was served, and we were obliged, despite hints and jokes to the contrary, to taste

everything, from the soup (an unknown quality—not quantity, thanks!) to the
pickles, which defied analysis.   At ten o'clock, after spending hours in a sitting
posture, four *futons* or thick comforts were spread on the floor, at the head of
which were placed white brick-bats for pillows, and we rolled in, or rather on.
No wonder that Jacob dreamed under the circumstances.   I dreamed, too, but my
dreams were by no means heavenly.   Far in the night, when the novelty and
romance of the performance had long passed away, I quietly hopped over my
tossing comrades, and securing my overcoat, wrapped my brick pillow in it, and
the plane of my dreams arose to the level of the earth.

AT NIKKO, JAPAN.

They say that the Japanese sit up late.   In doing so they manifest excellent
judgment and common sense and prove that they are not fond of self-sacrifice.

Japanese Scenery.

One must not come to Japan and fail to make an excursion inland of a hundred miles from Yokohama, with Nikko as the objective point.

From the moment you leave the crowded station of the city on the sea until
you look upon the little village that nestles at the foot of the most picturesque
mountains of Japan one scene of beauty and interest after another comes into view.

Although you may have an interesting novel on your lap, very few of its pages are read, for now the steep steps to a Shinto shrine attracts your attention; now a great Buddhist temple appears in a neighboring grove; now a gaudy funeral procession passes by; now your train is dashing along the outskirts of a straw-built Japanese village; now a group of rustic men and women, wearing loose upper garments and coarse blue tights, pause in the midst of their farm work, and gaze with wide-open eyes at the moving coaches; now you are passing through a bamboo grove; now you are attracted by a group of women and girls

WORK ON TEMPLE, JAPAN.

attending to the silk-worms or spinning the silk and winding the thread; now you are watching the crude process of grinding the grain between great flat rocks, or beating the straw with rods; and thus, although your train has made only twenty miles an hour, the trip seems too short when the conductor unlocks your coach-door and cries out "Nikko."

Sacred Shrines and Legends.

Nikko is especially noted for its temples which for their architecture, size and costliness, are as remarkable as any in Japan. Millions of dollars have been spent in these buildings, and the curious ornamental work, the hideously

6

grotesque idols in bronze, the elaborate wood-carvings of vines, flowers, birds and beasts display the talent as well as the superstition of the people.

The front of one building is ornamented by the figures of three monkeys; one with his hands over his eyes, that he may see nothing bad; another covering his mouth, that he may say nothing that is wrong, and the third holding his ears, that he may hear nothing that may offend his monkeyship. At the entrance of these temples are great brass gongs, and above them hang metallic hammers with ropes attached.

When petitions are to be offered most unearthly noises are made to awake and attract the attention of the Deity! No amount of clatter, however, is sup-

HOLY HORSE BEFORE BUDDHIST TEMPLE, NIKKO, JAPAN.

posed to arrest the attention of the god until the worshiper casts into the open box within the door his contribution of money.

There is an interesting legend, reminding us of a certain classic fable, that is associated with the carvings on these temples. The story goes that this wonderful work was done by a left-handed dwarf, and while he was ornamenting the temples he fell in love with a beautiful girl of Nikko, who spurned his addresses on account of his deformity of person. She was unyielding, despite the evidences of his genius and his tender pleadings; and, at last, nearly heart-broken, he returned to his native city, Tokio, where he carved an image of his loved one, which was so perfect that the gods endowed it with life, and the artist lived with it, as his wife, all during his life in the enjoyment of the greatest happiness.

Mountains and Monkeys.

Early in the morning we engaged jinrikishas, and, with two men to each vehicle, we passed out of the village on a narrow road, with a dashing mountain stream on one side and the precipitous heights on the other. For eight miles we ascended the steep and circuitous path, stopping now and then to refresh ourselves at a tea-house or to admire the mountain panorama.

We paused for quite a while before a cataract, whose waters fell nearly a thousand feet from the bluff to the echoing chasm beneath, and watched the great volume of water until it passed into a cloudy spray in its great leap.

At one time as we looked out from a bench before a tea-house, we could see three heights of mountain peaks, rising one above the other, and down the valley gorges before us three plunging streams foamed over the great boulders of rock, turning in their excited rage into pale, quivering waterfalls as they threw themselves recklessly against the sides of the mountain into the valley below!

Suddenly one of my jinrikisha men exclaimed in English that was more euphonious than classic, "Moonkee," and there before us were six or seven of these comical little creatures as self-satisfied as any other Japanese could possibly be. Whenever I look a monkey in the face I think of the words of a certain American professor, who, while lecturing on evolution, seeing that the class was inattentive to his words, exclaimed, "Gentlemen, while I am discussing the monkey I desire you to look me right straight in the face!"

One of Japan's Five Wonders.

The object of our mountain trip was a visit to the celebrated Chuzen-ji Lake, which is one of the five wonders of Japan.

Before reaching the mountain top our path for a mile or two lay through snow several inches in depth, and as we made a sharp turn there lay before us the rippling face of this beautiful sheet of water, thousands of feet above the village we had left some hours before.

No word, no brush, can describe or paint this transparent body of water, lifted so near and reflecting so perfectly the deep-blue sky, and there seems to be no satisfactory explanation of this strange phenomenon in nature—a lake filling the empty cone of the mountain!

In Virginia and in North Carolina we find similar sheets of water, but they are not so elevated and picturesque as the Chuzen-ji.

Curious Contrasts.

I noticed on this trip, more than while I was nearer the coast, how completely the Japanese are our antipodes in many respects, and how opposite are many of their methods and manners.

The few horses they have are stalled with their heads to the passageway, and they are shod with close-braided rice-straw in the place of iron shoes. The

JAPAN LADY IN JINRIKISHA.

carpenters draw the plane toward them instead of pushing it from them, and the tailor sews from him, not toward his body, holding the thread, not with his fingers, but with his toes.

Smoke from our fireplaces escapes through the chimneys outside of the house; smoke ascends from their brasiers inside of the room, finding its way out at the doors and windows.

Leaving the train and boat in my tour southward it was a pleasant experience to travel thirty miles a day in a comfortable jinrikisha, drawn by a muscular, long-winded Japanese; and thus I was enabled personally to study the customs and characteristics of the people living in the southern part of the country.

The Two-Legged Horse and Two-Wheeled Carriage.

As the jinrikisha is an institution of Japan, I may be allowed to speak more particularly of it. It is estimated that more than one million of Japanese are employed in the transportation of persons and commodities from place to place in Japan; and one-fourth of these pull the jinrikisha. The human horses who dash along the streets of the cities and roads of the country, pulling these two-wheeled vehicles, form a profession within themselves; and as the result of severe training from early youth, they are enabled to stand a strain on their muscles that is marvelous. Ten years of this toil tell on the well-knit frame of the little man; and his once strong, active form becomes bent, ill-shapen and comparatively feeble. On one of my long journeys, the jinrikisha-man cast from him every vestige of clothing except the breech-cloth; and during the trip the brave little two-legged horse trotted along at seven miles an hour, while the perspiration dropped from his brow and face, and stood in beads on his quivering, naked back.

He lives largely upon rice, and consumes as much as a sho, or more than a quart and a half during a day of excessive toil. It is painful to see an old, nearly worn-out man with a mushroom hat, staggering along in his effort to pull a double jinrikisha in which a whole family is seated. These human pullers are generally divided into three classes: The Kakaye form the aristocracy of the profession; they are well-dressed, well-fed and well-paid; and while on a fast dash they enjoy practically the right of way. The Yadoguruma class have their regular stands and regular customers; and the Tsujiguruma men are the poorest and most miserable, corresponding to the pitiable "night hawks" of the cab profession.

The cost of a new jinrikisha is about ten dollars; but for half of this amount a good vehicle can be bought. The keeper of a stand takes 15 per cent of the money made by the men under his employ, and in addition, these toilers must pay from one and a half to two yen (seventy-five cents to one dollar) a month for the use of the carriage. The prices paid for jinrikisha rides vary according to the class of men you employ. First-class men, from eighteen to thirty years of age, who are strong and swift, are paid four cents an hour; but between the ages of thirty and fifty, they are not regarded as first-class, and are paid from one and a half to three cents for the same time. Both the men and vehicles undergo annual inspection by the police, and in 1895 about two thousand jinrikishas and fifteen hundred jinrikisha-men were rejected in the city of Tokio. Before the ride and during the ride the human horse in Japan is all smiles and bows; but when you descend from your seat then comes the tug-of—wages, it matters little how distinct has been the previous agreement.

As the tourist travels through inland Japan he is impressed by the thick settlement of the country. The rural districts are full of people; nearly every woman has a baby lashed to her back, and the numerical increase seems far greater than the increase of available wealth.

Instructive Statistics.

The government statistics show that while only between twelve and thirteen millions of acres are under cultivation, over forty millions of natives live on these islands, and a still stranger fact, there are 30,000,000 pounds of tea, 5,000,000 pounds of raw silk and 40,000,000 pounds of rice exported every year.

At the beginning of the year the population of Japan was as follows: Number of families, 7,883,369; individuals, 41,810,202; males, 21,121,398; females, 20,688,804. As compared with the previous year the figures show an increase of 24,872 families and 424,695 individuals. There were 1,208,918 births and 840,-741 deaths during the year. The number of marriages was 351,146, that of divorces being 112,362.

Considering the size and wealth of Japan and the available farm land, these statistics present an interesting problem to the student as to the future of this, in many respects, unique people. From the north we have, by means of train, boat and jinrikisha, reached the southernmost point of the most southerly island of the empire, and we are now writing in the saloon of the steamer "Malacca," looking out upon the harbor of Nagasaki, one of the most important ports in the East.

Noticing the number of persons wearing eyeglasses in Nagasaki, I made mention of this fact to a resident of the place, who dryly replied: "Oh, yes; we put green eyeglasses on goats and then feed them with shavings. They think that they are eating grass!"

As the full moon rises over the crests of the mountains that form the background to the city, shooting its silver arrows through the narrow straits, and as the rising tide lifts our leviathan of the deep, we sail past the lofty island of Pappenburg, the Tarpeian Rock of the East, from whose heights Christians are said to have been hurled during the seventeenth century, and turn our bow toward the Celestial empire.

CHAPTER IV.

THE LAND OF THE PIG-TAIL.

On leaving Japan we decided to turn from the route usually taken by the "globe trotter," and instead of sailing direct for Hong Kong, we took steamer across the Yellow Sea, reaching the largest and most important city of Central China after three days of delightful experience on the "Malacca."

Shanghai is located on the Whang-pu River, twelve miles from the Yangtzse River and thirty miles from the sea-coast. Before the coming of foreigners to the city it was quite an insignificant place, but now it has a population of about five hundred thousand, is in many respects the most prominent commercial city of the empire, and is the fifth port in the world in importance.

As we neared the wharf the bund, stretching along the river front, presented a lively appearance. Hundreds of Chinese coolies crowded as near the incoming steamer as the batons of the English and Indian police allowed, filling the air with their babble; through the wide, well-paved street before us moved a great mass of people representing nearly every nationality, some in handsome equipages, some in the dashing jinrikishas, some in the bright-colored sedan chairs, borne by two or four men, some in the square palanquin, some in the queer-looking Chinese wheelbarrows and others moving on foot at a pace that would do honor to the Chicago pedestrian, and across the wide bund were rows of business houses as large and substantial in appearance as some of the business blocks on lower Broadway, New York.

In Shanghai there are three foreign "Concessions," the English, the American and the French, all of which are outside of the old city wall, and present as striking contrast to the Chinese quarters as could well be imagined. The English and American "Concessions" are governed by the same municipality, the council is elected by rate-payers, and the police is composed of Englishmen, Chinese and Sikhs from India. The French portion of the city, extending nearly half way around the walls of the native city, is managed quite differently from the others, and, indeed, is a little French republic within the Chinese empire.

The Streets of Shanghai.

The city, inhabited only by Chinese, is surrounded by a great wall, and the four entrances are called the North, South, East and West Gates, which are closed early in the night until early in the morning and guarded all the time.

Passing through the North Gate, we spent a portion of a day threading our way through streets from four to ten feet wide, oftentimes hemmed in between the moving masses of men, women, children and dogs, all equally respectable in appearance, and all except the miserable-looking dogs making the place hideous with their rasping, grating din and clatter. Here is the professional beggar, caked in dirt and partly covered with what in their better days were rags, wallowing in the filth of the street and with trembling hands and nodding head

WOMEN PRISONERS, SHANGHAI, CHINA.

pleading for "cash;" here are the juggler and the fortune-teller, plying their trades before gaping crowds; here we enter the main business street, possibly ten feet wide, where the purchasers stand outside of the shops, which are filled with every conceivable article of merchandise in every conceivable state of confusion; here the manufacturer of idols, surrounded by grinning and frowning images, is trying to make one more hideous still to add to his stock of goods; here are a dozen men, with long iron forks, turning the fire that crackles beneath great

(89)

copper bowls filled with boiling opium; here we pass into an opium den, where scores of men are stretched upon double sofas inhaling the fatal drug, which they put into their long pipes with large needles after melting it in small flames that burn in oil lamps near by.

A Typical Tea Shop.

Here we pause in the door of a typical Chinese tea-shop, where men gather to congratulate each other, to quarrel, to talk gossip, or to attend to business.

THE GOLDEN ISLAND WITH UNFINISHED PAGODA NEAR CHIN KIANG.

Here we are quickly satisfied with a passing glimpse of a home-scene which is too repulsive to dwell upon, as it was too sickening to look upon. Here we pass the fish and fowl market, where the dealers' goods become more popular and costly if they have age added to their other doubtful virtues, and at last, with a sigh of grateful relief, we pass out of the West Gate and joyfully think of our native land.

When you consider the inexpressible filthiness of the native city of Shanghai, the wonder is that some terrible epidemic has not long since swept its citizens out of existence. The municipal council attempted to persuade the Chinese official in charge of the old city to allow them to put the filtered water from the water-works throughout the city, but he replied that he preferred the muddy water from the moat around the place because it had more body to it!

The tea-shop, mentioned above, is an important institution of China. It serves as a news depot, where the people gather to hear the news of the day; as

THE ART OF PRINTING AS SEEN IN SHANGHAI, CHINA.

a business house, where men buy and sell and discuss the commercial interests of the country; and as a place of pleasure and general resort. If two men get into a quarrel on the street, one is apt to drag the other to a tea-shop and drink tea at his expense while they settle the matter between them. The stronger does the dragging and the weaker does the treating.

The shop is a large open room located in a central and popular portion of the city, and small square tables and low, narrow benches constitute the furniture. A covered cup containing a pinch of tea leaves is placed before each tea-drinker, and it is filled and refilled with hot water as desired. A man may drink this sugarless liquid all afternoon with his companion, and on settling the bill he will find that he is only about two cents poorer.

I asked my Shanghai friend as we stood in one of these shops and listened to the discordant screams of the patrons of the institution what was the cause of this confusion. "Each man wants more hot water," was his reply, as he pitied my ignorance of the ways of polite society in these parts.

The Opium Trade.

You are not long upon the streets of a Chinese city before you detect in the bleared eye and sallow features of the people, both male and female, the opium-eating habit. The disgraceful trade, forced upon China by the English at the point of the bayonet, is increasing every year, and now forms the heaviest item of import. How a nation can long exist and consume such quantities of this active poison is a mystery. The opium is shipped from India in the form of balls, is dissolved in water and boiled to a paste preparatory to immediate consumption. Yesterday afternoon a steamer arrived at the Shanghai port, and among other things it con-

RIVER SCENE AT KAYIN, CHINA.

tained, as reported in this morning's paper, were two missionaries and three hundred and nineteen chests of opium. Poor John Chinaman!

Curious Customs.

In China, as in Japan, the customs of the people are in striking contrasts to ours. A Chinese acquaintance, meeting you on the street, shakes his own hands instead of yours as a mark of greeting. The men wear their hair as long as it will grow, and they dress in skirts, while the women bind their hair tight around their heads, and dress in pants.

A TEAPICKER.

The written language is never spoken, the spoken language is never written, and in reading a book the Chinaman begins at the end and reads backward, making his notes at the top of the page instead of at the bottom, as with us.

Surnames precede the given names, white and not black is used in mourning, a horse is mounted from the off-side and a vessel is launched sideways instead of endways.

If you follow the Chinese fashion at dinner you must commence not with the soup, but with the dessert, and in hunting a dressmaker you must look for a man, not a woman. The index of the Chinese mariner's compass is placed on the opposite end of the needle, and does not point to the north pole, but to the

FARMING OPERATIONS IN SOUTHERN CHINA—PLOWING WITH AN OX.

south. The babies look sober, the grown people grin and giggle. Our bridesmaids look beautiful in white, their bridesmaids look ugly in black.

Indeed, the matters of surprise were that these contrary creatures did not go to bed in the morning and get up at night, and come down the street backward instead of forward! The beasts and the birds seem to have caught the spirit of national contrariness. Last Thursday, while taking a twelve-mile trip along the grand canal on a donkey, in my frantic efforts to make his donkeyship cover more than two miles an hour, I made a fatal mistake. I clucked, and there was a dead halt. But, stranger still, in a flock of crows I noticed even here the Chinese tendency—some of these birds had white rings about their necks! In accomplishing the unexpected, as well as performing tricks that are vain, the heathen "Chinee" is peculiar.

Among many persons in the West there exist most erroneous impressions of the political life, the imperial government and the national militia of the Middle Kingdom. Let us glance at these. The empire known to us as China is called by the Chinese Chung-Kuo (Middle Kingdom,) or Chung-hua Kuo (Middle Flowery Kingdom). The name China is thought to be derived from Ch'in, which was the name of a State in Northwestern China before the Christian era. It is

EARL LI VISITING GENERAL GRANT'S TOMB.

recorded that Prince Cheng, ruler of Ch'in in the year 221 B. C., declared himself the "first universal emperor," and extended his dominion over the whole of the country.

The vastness of the empire may be imagined from the following facts: Its present area, exclusive of Corea, is about 4,179,550 English square miles, and its population, according to the official census taken in 1842, before the outbreak of the Tai-Ping rebellion, was 413,700,000. It will be thus seen that the Chinese empire is larger than the whole of Europe and over thirty times the size of Great Britain and Ireland.

As China's neighbor on the north is Russian territory, on the southwest British possession, on the south the country that France is coveting, and on the east is bounded by the Pacific Ocean, with two thousand five hundred miles of coast, it can easily be seen why so many nations were greatly interested in the Japan-China war, and why the "civilized" powers are watching her every movement.

Three great rivers drain the vast empire, adding immeasurably to the fertility of the soil and affording convenient highways for travel and trade.   The Yellow

THE PEKIN GATE IN THE GREAT WALL OF CHINA.

River is in the north, the West River is in the southwest, and the Yangtzse (the great river), which is in the centre, is the most important of all, and is one of the greatest rivers in the world.   It is navigable for large ocean steamers as far up as six hundred miles from the sea, and while spending several days on its bosom we were impressed by its vastness and its importance to the commercial life of China.

China proper, not including Manchuria and the Eastern Turkestan province, is divided into 19 provinces, and these again are geographically divided into 8/

circuits, 189 prefectures, 34 departments, 71 districts, 114 sub-prefectures of the Ting class, 188 sub-prefectures of the Chou class, and 1334 counties.

Pekin is the name of the Chinese imperial capital city, and here is the main residence of the Emperor and the seat of the central government.

The present Emperor, Kuang-su, came to the throne in 1875, at the age of four years, and was brought up under the care of the Empress-Dowager Regent. The Emperor is the head of the church (so to speak), as well as the state, and the government of the empire is based on the government of the family, accord-

EXTERIOR OF THE ROYAL PALACE, PEKIN, CHINA.

ing to the laws and regulations laid down in the collected laws and institutes of the present dynasty.

The Emperor worships Shang-ti, the Supreme Ruler and king of kings, offers sacrifices to father Heaven and mother Earth, to the immortal sage Confucius, as the saviour of the empire, and to Kuan-ti, the deified warrior, who is supposed to have delivered China in war and calamities during the time of the "Three Kingdoms." The present dynasty claims to be ruling in China by divine right, and the Emperor is supposed to be descended from Shang-ti, the supreme ruler, whom he regularly worships.

7

Principal Offices.

The principal offices under the Emperor at Peking are the privy council, the cabinet, the board of civil office, the board of revenue, the board of ceremonies, the board of admiralty, the board of war, the board of punishment, the board of works, supreme college of literature, court of censors, colonial office and foreign office. Perhaps it may not generally be known that the Emperor is not Chinese, but Manchou, and one-half of all the high statesmen are Manchou and the other half Chinese.

The provincial viceroys and governors are expected to watch over the interests of the empire in their respective provinces and communicate direct with the throne, should this be necessary. Frequently, of late, the Emperor has sought

A KAYIN PLOUGHMAN.

the advice of these provincial magnates, and in the case of the distinguished Li Hung Chang, who was viceroy of Chih-li, the Emperor needing his confidential advice, he was called to Peking, where he now resides as a member of the inner circle of his Majesty's advisers.

The Censorate.

Independent of the cabinet and above all the boards rises the censorate, which consists of two presidents, four vice-presidents and about fifty members, all of whom have taken their literary degrees and are associated with the Supreme College of Literature. The censors are given special privileges by which they may address memorials directly to the Emperor, and may even remonstrate with him if they think that he is pursuing a course that is dangerous to the welfare of the country.

As a nation the Chinese are not heavily taxed. The full amount of the revenue levied, according to the report that is before me, in both grain and silver, is about three hundred millions of taels when all is converted into silver currency, and of this sum, it is said, one-third is never properly accounted for, another

RECEPTION OF A FOREIGN AMBASSADOR BY THE EMPEROR OF CHINA.

third is deducted to pay the expenses of collection, and not more than half of the balance reaches Pekin.

Military Organizations.

The world just now is laughing at the military standing of China, and the once much-dreaded Tartars appear to have retrograded in martial qualities. But the undisciplined coolies who faced the Japanese in the late war give us a very inadequate idea of the military force of the empire.

The Chinese army is divided into three great forces, each of which has its own peculiar organization. The first of these is known as the Pa-Chi, or Eight Banners, consisting entirely of hereditary warriors ranged under one or other of the eight banners of the nationalities—the Manchous, the Mongol and the Chinese. The total force is about 3200 officers and 350,000 privates, the majority of whom have been taught the use of the modern breech-loading rifles and field

1. Foreign Instructor J. C. Clowe.   2. Captain Interpreter Chu Lao.

A NINE-INCH GUN, CHINESE ARTILLERY, "READY FOR ACTION."

artillery. The reserves of this banner army are the total population of Mongolia and Manchuria.

Militia and Volunteers.

The next division, or indeed separate army, is the regular Chinese army, called Ying Ping, Green Regiments, on account of their colors. This force consists entirely of Chinese and is a sort of local militia, distributed throughout the empire, numbering over 7000 officers and 300,000 privates. Three centuries ago this was the finest military force in the world, but at present its lack of organization and discipline and the presence of corruption throughout the whole system threatens its disintegration.

The third Chinese army is the volunteers or braves. About half of this force is fairly well disciplined and drilled in the use of modern artillery, and is used to guard the approaches to the imperial capital. During the Tai-Ping rebellion over four millions of Chinese were under arms, and were the reorganization of the army attended to in a scientific manner China could easily place six or seven millions of men in the field.

The organization of the Chinese navy having been entrusted to officers of different nationalities, each of whom had some peculiar reform of his own to introduce, the result, it seems, is a lamentable mixture of things which is most unsatisfactory.

I was very much interested in a visit to the arsenal at Shanghai, where the largest guns are manufactured. Foo-Chow is the only other place in the empire where an arsenal of the kind is located. The most serviceable guns are nine-inch, forty tons, using projectiles of three hundred and fifty

NATIVE FARM IN THE VICINITY OF CANTON, CHINA.

pounds and charged with one hundred and fifty pounds of powder. These have an effective range of about two miles.

On my trip of one hundred and fifty miles up the Yangtzse River I was fortunate in having as one of my companions the foreign instructor to the Tse Tien Miao battery, one of the largest batteries on the river, and through this gentleman's kindness I received some valuable information.

Fortifications.

The fortifications along the Yangtzse valley are now the strongest in China, and forces are here under German instruction, with the expectation of taking the field in the coming spring against the Mohammedan rebels of the northwest. There are thirty foreign instructors in the five forts along the river, most of these American and British.

These instructors were engaged without the sanction of their countries, and those from England received employment in violation of the British foreign enlistment act, in force during the late war, thus making themselves liable to large fines and six months' imprisonment.

The armament of these forts consists of English and German guns. Here we find twelve-inch muzzle-loading guns, carrying projectiles of eighteen hundred pounds, charged with two hundred pounds of powder, with a range of five miles; also, twelve-inch breech-loading guns of fifty-two tons, nine-inch guns of forty tons, six-inch quick-firing guns and Hotchkiss machine guns.

Corrupt Administrations.

Before these forts came under foreign instruction the greatest confusion and corruption existed, and the robbery inflicted upon the government gives proof of the lack of the least semblance of patriotism. I was given this instance of the kind of dishonesty that is going on all over the empire to-day: The commander of a camp of 500 men will receive 3000 taels—about 4500 Mexican dollars—per month, for expenses. Instead of paying his men, say 71 or 72 tael-cents to the Mexican dollar, he pays them at a different rate and keeps the balance. Again, the officer has enrolled 500 men, while actually there are present only 300. The inspecting officers give a week's notice before their arrival. Coolies are called in from the neighboring villages, put in uniform for the day of the inspection only, and they line the wall, wave flags and shout with the troops. As the requisite number is present, the commander receives pay for the five hundred; the two hundred coolies are dismissed on the departure of the inspectors with a slight compensation and the officer or officers pocket the pay for two hundred soldiers. This, I am told on good authority, is going on now all over China where natives have the organization and command of the military. Where foreign instruction prevails this kind of thing is impossible, for there is regular drill, semi-foreign uniform and systematic inspection.

On our steamer going up to Nanking was the daughter of the viceroy, Liang Kiang, with her retinue of ten servants. This viceroy is said to be the most progressive man in the empire, and in him largely centres the hope of China. He has for his foreign adviser an Englishman by the name of R. B. Moorhead, commissioner of the imperial maritime customs, who has been mainly instrumental in organizing the Yangtzse River defense that we have described. Gradually this vast empire is allowing the wall of her exclusiveness to crumble. May it soon exist only in memory and not in fact.

CHAPTER V

STRANGEST OF STRANGE CITIES.

HE third day out from Shanghai, we steamed up the magnificent Typhon Bay, and dropped anchor below Hong Kong, which rose before us on the lofty range of hills that surround the famous harbor. We had reached the most easterly possession of Great Britain, and, from the scarlet uniforms that are constantly in evidence on the streets of the city, from the strong fortifications that are in view, and from the names given to many of the prominent points of interest, you are not allowed to forget who are the masters of the island, forty miles in circumference, upon which Hong Kong is located.

By means of the incline, cog-wheel railway, you reach the summit of Victoria Peak, and, standing upon this noble eminence, you can take a bird's-eye view of the country for many miles around. About you are many beautiful bungalows, with pretty surroundings; down the slopes of the hills are hundreds of handsome residences of the foreigners; toward the base of the eminences can be seen the Chinese quarters, in striking contrast to the rest of the settlement, and below and stretching far away is the sea, dotted with crafts of every description. The population of Hong Kong is of a most conglomerate character. While the English are most strongly represented, Americans, French, Germans, East Indians, Italians, Portuguese, Spaniards, and even the Parsee, are to be seen on the streets; and, from the conduct of most of these in social and commercial life, it is not a matter of surprise that the natives are accustomed to use the epithet of doubtful compliment, "foreign devils," in speaking of them.

Although it is Christmas week, in this semi-tropical climate we notice the exuberance of the flora. Many varieties of the cactus family, the camphor tree, the aloes, the cypresses, the Cape jasmines, hydrangeas, geraniums, palms and magnolias are seen quite frequently in our walks and drives about the city, and the Chinese gardeners show great skill in the cultivation and exhibition of their flowers and plants.

China's Commercial City.

Canton, the commercial capital of China, located ninety miles up the Pearl River, was the special object of our visit to Southern China, and our trip on the steamer, which gave us an excellent opportunity to study the river, the rural districts, the dilapidated villages and the fortifications, was not in the least wearisome.   As you approach Canton, there is presented a sight that is not duplicated in the world.   You sail through a floating city of 200,000 souls !   The thousands of boats that cover the face of the river fronting Canton are built as houses, and in these boats persons are born, are married and die, never knowing any other homes.   The first one of these in which we rode, contained the father, who guided the little craft; the mother and half-grown daughter, who did the rowing, and three babies, who looked as sober as judges, cuddled up in the " hole."

ON THE RIVER, CANTON.

This rude, floating affair is literally their world.   Here they cook, eat, wash, ply their only business, in which all the members of the family are engaged who can lend a helping hand; and they seem to know nothing of, or care nothing about, the population of a million and a half on the shore.   I am writing these words on the porch of the home of Dr. Graves, and just below me, within two hundred yards of my chair, can be seen this moving city on the river, that reminds me somewhat of the busy scenes on the great canal at Venice, except the boats are not so artistic, but far more numerous.

It has been well said that Canton is the strangest of all strange cities; and it is certainly the most representative one in China. The city extends for four miles along the Pearl River, and, although it has a population of about the size of New York, there is hardly a street over eight feet in width. As the narrowness of the streets will not allow the use of the jinrikishas, and as a horse is a curiosity, you must wind your way through the throngs of people on foot, or be jostled along in a sedan chair or rocking palanquin. Gamblers are found at every turn, seated about square tables, jabbering in an excited manner; the small manufacturer plies his trade in the open thoroughfare; cooking goes on in the gutters or in the open doors, filling the air with greasy odors; the barber is engaged in his active business by your side, as you pass along; the vender of eels, rats and dog-meat proudly screams the doubtful statement that he has something peculiarly deli-

A CHINESE GENTLEMAN'S HOME.

cious; the burden-bearers, of both sexes and all ages, grunt and groan as they limp past you; the gaudily decorated bridal chair, preceded by a long line of men and boys with gay banners and followed by a uniformed retinue, bearing baskets and boxes of presents, attract your attention; and thus for hours you are interested, instructed and bewildered by the ever-changing sights of the unique city.

A Chinese Dwelling.

A family street of the better classes does not present a bad appearance. The walls lining both sides of the way are formed of bluish-gray bricks, neatly pointed in mortar, with granite foundations reaching several feet above the ground. There are no windows, and you enter through a plain, massive, double-leaved door, fastened by wooden bolts. Having entered this outer door, you find yourself under a small introductory roof, which shelters the porter's room. Before you are sets of wooden doors reaching from wall to wall, and beyond these is a small court, open to the sky, where ornamental flowers and plants are placed. The house proper is now before you, and separate apartments, under different roofs, are entered: for a Chinese residence, except among the humbler classes, is a collection of small buildings. Ceilings are very seldom seen, and the walls are neither plastered nor papered. The houses of the poor are the most wretched hovels, many of them being only mat-sheds, the frame work of which is made of bamboo and the walls and roofs of oblongs formed of bamboo leaves fastened together.

TEMPLE AT NINGPO.

Sacred Hogs.

Although for two months we had been visiting Japanese and Chinese temples until we were sickened by the degradation and superstition of which the religious instinct of humanity was capable, we could not see Canton without entering some of the hundreds of these buildings dedicated to Confucianism, Buddhism or Taouism.

The one held most sacred by the natives, perhaps, is the Temple of Honan. As you enter the grounds, you are confronted by two hideous idols of colossal size, figures half animal and half human in design, with countenances that would give the nightmare to a professional cut-throat! Passing by the rows of shrines, the groups of dwarfed trees forced to grow in the shape of various animals, the cremating ovens where the bodies of the shaven-headed priests find

BIRD'S-EYE VIEW OF CANTON, CHINA.

107)

repose, the pond where the sacred lotus is in bloom, we were more interested in an enclosure where a number of sacred hogs were wallowing in filth in a most unsacred manner. If the Parsee worships fire, the Japanese bends before foxes and snakes, the Hindu makes gods of cows and monkeys, some may ask why should not the gentleman of the pig-tail have his sacred pig.

Horrors !

In the Temple of Horrors, we looked upon vivid representations of the ten hells of Buddhism. Men floating in boiling oil; women suspended by iron hooks

THE "FLOATING CITY" ON PEARL RIVER, CANTON, CHINA.

run through their backs, and all kinds of torments are set forth in ways that are apt to make the blood of the wicked native curdle.

As my pen just now is running along the line of the horrible, I must not close this chapter without telling of a heart-rending scene I witnessed yesterday. Passing out of the East Gate of the city, after walking several miles over a lonely country path, on either side of which were thousands of Chinese graves, many of them fresh during the last year's black plague, we reached the village of lepers. As we approached this place of agony, we were surrounded by scores of these death-stricken creatures; and as we passed down the main street, the whole community seemed to be at our heels craving alms. The loathsome disease had as its victim the infant at its mother's breast and the decrepit old man—all ages, in all stages of the affliction, were before me. Some with face, hands and feet enlarged, red, smooth and glossy; some undergoing spontaneous amputation of the fingers and toes; some with limbs partially decayed—but I must draw the curtain upon this horror of horrors!

Slavery in China.

During my month's stay in Canton I had occasion, through the kindness of our missionaries and consul, to study the customs and habits of the Cantonese; and nothing that I witnessed was more heart-rending than the cruel treatment and pitiable condition of the blind girls.

In China the subject knows no such a thing as liberty, and the individual, who is but the fraction of the unit of society, which is the family, knows no rights as an individual. This being true, slavery is the necessary consequence. Human beings are bought and sold as chattels, and quite frequently a childless man buys a boy from poor parents to save his family from going out of existence.

ISLAND OF THE LITTLE ORPHAN IN THE YANGTZE.

A form of domestic slavery, in which families of means buy slave-girls, is very common here in Canton, and purchasing them in early girlhood for from ten to one hundred dollars, according to their beauty and health, they work for their owners without wages until they are of a marriageable age, when they are sold in marriage or disposed of for other purposes, according to the price offered.

Sad Lot of Blind Girls.

But there is a kind of slavery more appalling still, of which I desire specially to write, namely, the slavery of blind girls. Passing down the streets of Canton, at night, my attention was called to numbers of blind girls from fourteen to eighteen years of age dressed in brilliant outer garments, with their faces rouged and their hair ornamented with flowers. A woman, carrying a musical instrument, led several of these girls, and I have since learned that they were owned by this mistress, who conducted them, by night, to the lowest parts of the city, and by their playing, singing and in most disreputable way she secures an income through them that enables her to live in ease and comfort. I have met no class of persons, not excepting the sore-covered beggar or the decaying leper, that seemed so pitiable as these blind singing girls.

It is regarded an affliction for a girl to be born in a Chinese family, and when the girl is blind her life is one of ceaseless neglect and cruelty, and often, if the family is poor, she is sold for a small amount to one of these dealers in human bodies, who plies her nefarious business until death snatches her victim from her.

Case of Redemption.

This morning I visited five of these little blind girls who had been redeemed by a Christian woman before they were old enough to be led into lives of shame. This is the sad story of one of these little creatures: Her father belonged to a literary family and was himself an intelligent Chinese gentleman. The opium habit and gambling became the curse of his life, and in order to gratify these passions he sold all of his property and his six children, including this blind baby girl. This child was rebought from a low mistress, who was training her to be a singing girl.

One of these children has a double thumb on her right hand, and it was through this deformity that she was rescued from a wretched life. Her mistress brought her to one of the hospitals and requested that one of the thumbs be cut off. When the surgeon declined to make the operation she started off, saying: "Well, I will cut it away myself, for she can't learn the guitar with a double thumb!" The doctor reported the case to my friend, and a few dollars redeemed the child, double thumb and all! She seemed as lively as a cricket.

No one can tell what these innocent children suffer when they fall into the clutches of these old harridans, and that the government has any responsibility in the matter does not seem to occur to the Governor of Canton

Massacres and Riots.

During the last score of years there have been frequent riots in Canton, in which foreigners have been the sufferers, and as missionaries are the only foreigners who go far inland away from the treaty ports, they have mainly felt the force of these uprisings.

In 1883 there were riots here in Canton, a large part of the foreign settlement was destroyed, including mission and business property, and many narrowly escaped bodily injury. Last summer there were numerous riots in West China. Almost all of the mission property in the province of Sze Chuan was demolished, and a large number of Americans were among the sufferers.

During the terrible Tien-Tsin riot several French Catholic sisters and other foreigners lost their lives, and last year a brutal attack was made on two lady physicians in the suburb of Canton while they were trying to help a plague-

REDEEMED BLIND GIRLS UNDER MISS WHILDEN'S CARE, CANTON, CHINA.

stricken Chinaman to the hospital. The lives of these women were saved only by the timely appearance of foreign customs officers with fire-arms.

The Kucheng Atrocities.

Since my arrival in China, knowing that many contradictory stories had been sent to America about the notorious massacre at Kucheng, in the Fuh Kien province, during last August, I have tried personally to learn the facts of this affair, and I find that the reports have not exaggerated its brutality.

At this place, one hundred miles inland from the port of Foo-Chow, resided a number of English missionaries sent out by the English Mission Society and several sent out by the American Methodists. For some months a sect calling itself Vegetarians (because they eat no flesh), known to be a dangerous secret political society adhering strictly to the Buddhists, had shown ill-feeling toward native and foreign Christians, and numerous acts of robbery and persecutions had been committed.

August the first being the sixth birthday of Herbert Stewart, a child of missionaries, he and his sisters started out to the neighboring hills to gather flowers with which to decorate the home in honor of his birthday. They were met by a procession of these brutes, and after they had been beaten most unmercifully they were allowed to return, only to find everything in the greatest disorder and the Vegetarians in full possession. The father and mother were murdered; Herbert died from his wounds next day; one of the sisters was torn frightfully by a spear wound; the baby's head was gashed and his eyes torn out and he lived only a few days. The nurse and six young ladies of the mission were found dead, some of them fearfully hacked and mutilated, and the houses of the foreigners were burned.

After the riot was over and the murderers had escaped soldiers were sent to keep the peace, but they magnanimously seized the opportunity of stealing everything of value that had been left on the ground, and continued to be nuisances until they were removed.

The Leader's Confession.

Although it is currently reported that over twenty of those connected with this massacre have been beheaded, during the fall there have been repeated indications of more disturbances. After some little trouble I have been enabled to secure an exact translation of the confession of Minchiang Chek, the man who led the Vegetarians on the day of the massacre. It is as follows: " I am forty-seven years of age, and reside in the eleventh township of the Minchiang district. I am the eldest of three brothers, and am a doctor and brazier by trade. At the age of twenty-six I became a Vegetarian, and on the ninth of the twelfth moon of last year I came to Kucheng and induced eight men (names given) to join the society. According to one of the fixed rules of the order, each of them paid 1680 cash as an entrance fee, and after this the leader of the sect gave me the new name of Buo Heng. The Vegetarians are divided into nine companies, of which I belong to that known as Ling Kung.

On the eighth of the sixth moon (the massacre was on the eleventh) about thirty of us met in a monastery on Kung Sang Kuoi, and at that meeting three plans were proposed: (1) To go to the village of Dank Denk and rob the house of a rich man there. (2) To kill the foreigners at Hwa Sang. (3) To murder the foreigners and tear down their houses at Kucheng City. Being unable to decide, Dowg Gau

Gang, a fortune-teller and our leader, took three pieces of paper, on which he wrote the three plans proposed, writing one on each and rolling them into little balls. He then took three incense sticks as chop sticks, and three times in succession picked out the ball on which the words Hwa Sang were written. (The massacre took place early the next morning.)

"Over a hundred of us met that night and armed ourselves with guns and three-pronged spears. The first foreigner we saw was a young lady standing at the back door of one of the houses. I rushed at her immediately and

CHINESE GAMBLING ON THE ROOF OF A HOUSE AT CANTON, CHINA.

stabbed her in the back with my spear. She fell down and died. Having killed her, I went to a Chinese house where there was another foreign woman (Miss Hartford, of the American Methodist Mission) and tried to stab her, but unfortunately her servant struck me and took from me my spear. The other Vegetarians were at work in other houses where there were foreigners."

Those men were not rebels, but murderous wretches, bitterly hating all foreigners, and it is the general opinion that the viceroy of the province and his associates could have easily crushed them out of existence months ago if they had so desired.

The letter of the treaties should protect foreigners from such brutal attacks, but physical force influences much more the conduct of an ordinary Chinaman than the moral obligation or legal significance of a treaty.

Attempt to Take Canton.

On our arrival in Japan the papers were filled with accounts of the attempted uprising at Canton, and it was feared at one time that we would be prevented from visiting Southern China. Through the kindness of our affable consul at Canton, Mr. Charles Seymour, I have secured the facts of this trouble, which threatened to be a very serious affair.

The leaders of this rebellion planned that the attack on Canton should be made on the thirtieth of October, and looking to this, arms and ammunition were smuggled into the city. Monday morning, October 28, about four hundred men boarded the steamer at Hong Kong for Canton, and as they acted suspiciously, the authorities at Hong Kong telegraphed to the police office at Canton, and on their arrival a large number of them were put under arrest.

It was found afterward that barrels that had come through the customs marked "cement" contained arms and explosives, and that secret preparation had been going on for months before these arrests were made. Their plan, as afterward announced, was to capture the treasury, the residences of the viceroy and other officials, and to set up a government after the style of Western nations.

The badge of the leaders was a red sash thrown over the shoulder and knotted under the arm. They expected the soldiers and others to join them as soon as their work of capturing and pillage began, and it is thought that many of the restless element of the community would have joined them if they had made any headway. A number of those arrested have been beheaded and rewards are offered for the heads of others.

Socialists Suspected.

As early as the fifteenth of last July an Englishman by the name of Click, who had been expelled from Honolulu, Hawaiian Islands, because he was involved in a seditious movement, leased a house in Canton, and he, with a German social-ist by the name of Stauhhmann, lived in this place for months. Immediately after the arrests were made and the uprising was nipped in the bud, these men suddenly disappeared, and in the house in which they lived were found ammunition, dyna-mite and other evidences of the fact that they were doubtless interested in the success of the attempted rebellion.

Mr. Seymour, the United States consul, expressed to me the opinion that the affair is not entirely suppressed, and, with the aid of the many societies with socialistic tendencies throughout the province, there may at any time be a general uprising, which would elicit the sympathy and aid of thousands who are dissatisfied with the present state of the government. There are clear-sounding mutterings of the smashing of old foundations and crashing of present institutions throughout the East.

Chinese Customs.

During my rambles through the cities, villages and farm lands of Southern China I find that I have filled my note-book with brief accounts of Chinese

MRS. GRAVE'S AND MISS WHITE'S GIRLS' SCHOOL, AT CANTON, CHINA.

characteristics that have impressed me as being peculiar and which I cannot well classify; so, before sailing for other lands, I shall give, in a disjointed manner, these hurriedly made descriptions of a people who are, by far, more interesting in their native land than anywhere else.

As most of the time I have had by my side on these tours foreign gentlemen who have lived for years in the " Celestial kingdom " and who speak several of the dialects fluently, my opportunities for gaining correct information during these weeks have been very gratifying.

One of the first things that attracts special notice is the dress of a people, and John Chinaman and family command your immediate attention in this respect.

Dress and Headgear.

The two necessities in all Chinese dress are the loose pair of trousers (the foo) and the almost equally loose-fitting jacket (the sham); with these two articles the Chinese is completely dressed, and if anything else is worn it is for comfort or luxury.

The upper garment is worn long or short, plain or decorated, heavy or light, according to the condition of the wearer or weather, and the balloon trousers are carefully tucked into long stockings, neatly bound with garters below the knee, and over these a pair of leggings is placed if the owner of these legs desires to be finely dressed, or if he is afraid of catching cold in his nether parts.

A woman's trousers are similarly shaped, and instead of knickerbockers, when they are dressed up, they wear something like the divided skirt, one piece hanging in front down to the ankles and the other hanging behind the same way, and these are buttoned up at one side and open at the other, while embroidery and pleats in vertical lines adorn them. In certains parts of the empire, especially on and along the rivers in the interior, nature's garb appears to be all sufficient, and one feature, at least, of the simple innocence of our parents' lives in the Garden of Eden, is seen in its unadorned perfection.

Female Fancy.

The women of China have much more time at their disposal than our women, because they do not have to select spring, summer, fall and winter bonnets or hats. Their hair is combed and plastered with a gum; thus made up it forms a sufficient head-covering for the climate of Southern China, and in colder places a handkerchief or broad band, either plain or embroidered, is often bound across the forehead.

The men wear a skull-cap of satin for the most part, with a cord button of red or black on the top, in the winter season, but go bareheaded in summer. Large bamboo hats, about a yard in diameter, are worn to protect from the rain and the rays of the sun.

The women, in every grade of life, wear earrings, some of which are as brilliant as they are tremendous, and these ornaments seem to be more indispensable than a woman's foo or sham.

The style of dress and the mode of doing up the hair, I notice, differ in different parts of China, but the men's dress is very much the same wherever I have been. There is a severe modesty in the dress of Chinese women that is in striking contrast to the state of semi-nudity that was seen frequently in certain parts of Japan. Among women the process of binding the feet and the kind of shoe worn vary very much in different places. Ordinarily the rich bind the feet of their daughters at six or eight years, the poor at thirteen or fourteen, and seldom are the feet bound later than at fifteen.

A Barbarous Practice.

One end of a bandage, about two inches wide and ten feet long, is laid on the inside of the instep; thence it is carried over the four smaller toes, drawing them down upon the sole; then it passes under the foot, over the instep and around the heel, drawing the heel and toe nearer together, making a bulge on the instep and a deep notch in the sole underneath; thence it follows its former course until the bandage is all applied, and the last end is sewn firmly on the underlying cloth.

BOUND FOOT OF CHINESE WOMAN.

Monthly, or oftener, the feet, with the bandages upon them, are put into hot water and soaked. Then the bandages are removed, the dead skin is rubbed off, the foot is kneaded more fully into the desired shape, pulverized alum is laid on and clean bandages quickly applied.

The head physician in the Fat-Shun Hospital told me that frequently the flesh becomes putrescent during the process of binding and portions slough off from the sole. Not infrequently a toe drops off, and lately he was called in to see a woman both of whose feet had become entirely dead from the lack of blood circulation and had entirely dropped off.

While the feet are being formed they are useless; the victim sleeps on her back, lying crosswise on the bed, with her feet dangling over the side, and the sensation is said to be like that of having the joints punctured with needles.

As I write I have before me a model of a bound foot. There is a notch in the middle of the sole, deep enough to conceal a silver dollar put in edgewise across the foot. The four small toes are so twisted that their ends may be seen on the inside of the foot below the ankle, and the broken and distorted bones of the middle of the foot are pressed into a mass where the instep should be. The shape is very much like a fowl's head, the big toe representing the bill.

The limb becomes a frightful and fetid thing, and below the knee there is little beside skin and bones. The tiny ball of flesh is kept bandaged in alum powder, the bandages are shortened one-half their first length, and black ones are often put over the white ones.

Embroidered satin shoes, with brightly painted heels, are worn, and a neat pantalette covers all but the toe. As you watch her toddle along, as if she was walking on the points of needles, you cannot say with the poet:

> "Her foot so light, her step so true,
> Scarce from the harebell brushed the dew."

Woman's Status.

When I protested against this barbarous practice to an intelligent Chinaman he admitted all I said, then quietly reminded me of the tight lacing among the European and American women, and informed me that certain fashionable foreign women, charitably disposed, drew up a lengthy protest against this "outrage" some time since, and when they met in a hall to sign the paper some of them were laced so tight that they found difficulty in leaning over to put their signatures to the document! It depends largely upon our point of view whether a thing is "heathen" or not.

The Chinese woman is not shut up in a harem, as in Turkey; she is not degraded by polyandry, as in Thibet; she is not denied the possession of a soul and the religious privileges of men, as in Burma, and she is not so demoralized and humiliated as in Siam; yet she is not allowed to eat with her husband, she is forbidden to walk with him, and she has no legal right to anything whatever, apart from her male relatives. A husband may beat his wife to death and go unpunished, but if a wife strikes her husband a single blow she receives a hundred blows with a heavy bamboo, and he may be divorced from her.

An infant girl is often engaged to be married by her parents; and a lady in Canton told me that, on seeing a young man carrying a baby girl on his back, she asked him whose child it was, and he replied that it was his future wife!

A Polite People.

The system of etiquette of the Chinese is very elaborate, and the urbanity and suavity of manner with which even the lower classes address one another cannot be surpassed by any nation.

In talking to a man in a superior position the eyes must not be fixed on his, but must rest on the button on the left lapel of his coat; when a room is entered

THE BEHEADING OF PIRATES NEAR HONG KONG, CHINA.

where persons are seated it is not in good form to bow to each separately, but a grave bow must be given first to the right and then to the left; the left hand is the place of honor.

Politeness forbids you to ask a person to pay a debt, but it is quite the thing to ask him to loan you the amount he owes and then never return it. It is quite impolite to wear spectacles before a guest or superior. The Chinaman puts his hat on to receive his guest, for appearing bareheaded before a visitor is considered quite impolite.

Long finger-nails are badges of respectability. Instead of shaking hands, a Chinaman clasps his two hands together, moving them up and down a few inches in front of himself several times.

To remain seated while your superior or guest is standing is not tolerated in polite society.

Sport and Superstition.

Although John Chinaman is a hard-working and industrious personage, you need but saunter through the crowded streets of one of his cities to be convinced that he is also fond of amusements. The theatres are crowded. The various birthdays of the gods are hailed with delight. The annual regattas throughout China of the dragon-boat feast, the full-moon festivals and the New Year holiday, all are celebrated by games and great magnificence of ceremonial worship.

The Dragon Emblem.

At every turn in China you meet paintings, drawings and carvings of the dragon, which is the imperial emblem of state. The dragon, which is reserved for royal use in designs on furniture, porcelain and clothing, is depicted with five claws; that in use by the common people has only four. It is thus described in an old Chinese writing: "Its head is like a camel's, its horns like a deer's, its eyes like a hare's, its ears like a bull's, its neck like a snake's, its scales like a carp's, its claws like an eagle's, and its paws like a tiger's. Its scales number eighty-one, being nine by nine, the extreme (odd or) lucky number. Its voice resembles the beating of a gong. On each side of its mouth are whiskers, under its chin is a bright pearl, and on the top of his head is the *poh-shan*, or wooden foot-rule, without which he cannot ascend the skies."

This wonderful antediluvian creature is embalmed in the literature and memory of the Chinese, and to it are referred nearly all the blessings and calamities that come upon the people.

Markets, Food and Delicacies.

Many persons have a very erroneous notion about the food of the Chinese. While I have seen dogs', cats' and rats' flesh hung up in the market places in Canton for sale, this is not a common sight. Pork, fish and fowls are abundant in the markets, and beef is also seen. Rice and dried salt or fresh vegitables are eaten at nearly every meal.

Noticing quite frequently a gelatinous substance at the groceries and other stores, I was informed, on inquiry, that it was "bird's nest," and from it a soup is made that is regarded a great luxury in China. These edible nests are built in caves along the seashore. The birds, during the building time, assemble in large numbers upon the beach, carrying in their beaks the foam thrown up by

CHINESE EXECUTION, CANTON.

the surf, of which they construct their glutinous nests, after it has undergone some preparation from commixture with saline or other secretions in the crop of the bird. The bird is called "the foaming swallow."

They say that the finest of these nests, when taken from these caves near the sea, look like pure isinglass and bring as much as thirty dollars a pound. It is thought to be very stimulating, and it forms the first dish at all grand dinners.

Capital Punishment.

In one of my walks through the city I visited the execution place, a small plot of ground which can boast of more slain than many battlefields. The malefactors are generally borne by coolies in ordinary dust-baskets to this place of death. They kneel down in rows, bending their heads forward, with their arms tied behind them, and then, with a single blow from a skillful executioner's blade the head rolls to the ground.

A friend sent to me, among other photographs, two horrible companion pictures. One taken of eight pirates just in the act of being beheaded; the other just after the fatal blow had been given, as the heads and bodies were falling to the ground. As the instantaneous process of photography was used, the expressions are dreadfully lifelike, or rather deathlike.

Punishments inflicted for an infringement of the law are mainly flogging with the bamboo, banishment for a limited time or permanently, and death by strangling or decapitation.

The Beggars' Guild.

Beggary in China is reduced to a fine art, and in all the large cities there is an organization that is perfect in its system. The beggars are united under a head, called the "king of the beggars," who is appointed by a guild, and each day the contents of the baskets of these wretches in sackcloth is pooled. The payment of a fixed sum to the "king" by any shop will secure immunity from all visits of his subjects (the shopkeeper is given a certificate to this effect, which he hangs at his door), otherwise the shop is visited daily by these creatures, who are annoying and repulsive in the extreme.

One of the most pitiable things that I have learned is that there is not an asylum for the insane in the Empire of China.

CHAPTER VI.

LANGUAGE AND LITERATURE IN THE MIDDLE KINGDOM.

DURING the weeks spent in China, I have taken special notice of the dialects, literature and educational institutions of the empire and, perhaps, some of the results of this necessarily superficial study may be of interest to my readers. The philologist, in his classification of languages, has been accustomed to place the Chinese language in a position of its own, with no certain relationship to other speeches of mankind; but through the labors of Edkins, Schlegel and others there seems to appear some connection between Chinese and the Aryan languages, while Terrien de Lacouperie and his colaborers insist that there is a striking affinity between the languages of China and Babylon.

Position is nearly everything in the construction of Chinese sentences, and the relation of words is used by them to express what we, to a great extent, show by case, mood, tense, number and person, and in addition to this relative position of words the employment of auxiliary characters, and a general symmetry of construction in the written language aid very much in the correct development of ideas.

One who has studied the language for forty years at Canton assures me that the Chinese is one of the simplest, while at the same time one of the most difficult languages in the world. Its simplicity consists of the almost entire absence of inflexional forms; its difficulty consists of the combination of different dialects, so-called, under the one name of Chinese, as, for instance, the book language in its two or three different forms, the colloquial or spoken language, in its different vernaculars and in its tones, the stumbling-block and ruin of most of those who attempt to repeat it.

Styles of Writing.

In general, the language may be divided as follows: The ancient style, in which the classics are written, which is concise and vague; the literary style, which is more diffuse and poetical, and in which the essays of the candidates at the governmental examinations are written; the business style, which is void of ornamentation and is used for commercial purposes, legal writings and official documents, and the colloquial, the spoken language, which is divided into dialects and which is very seldom used by a writer. From a literal translation of a Chinese sentence that is before me, I agree with Marshman when he says: "A Chinese character may in general be considered as conveying an idea without reference to any part of speech, and its being used as a substantive, an adjective or a verb depends on circumstances."

We speak of the Chinese language being spoken in Canton, Shanghai, Foochow and Pekin, but it is equally true that not one of the inhabitants from any one of these places could understand those from the others any more than a Parisian could understand a New Yorker, or a citizen of Berlin could converse with one from Madrid.

Divisions of Speech.

Although there are the following main divisions of speech, commonly called dialects—the Cantonese, the Hakka, the Amoy, the Swatow, the Hainanese, the

IMMEDIATELY AFTER BEHEADING OF PIRATES NEAR HONG KONG, CHINA.

Shanghai, the Ningpo and the Mandarin—yet we find that the dialect of one district is not one homogeneous whole, and the variations are often so marked between the colloquial of persons living only a few miles from each other that you would think that they are speaking different dialects.

During my trips I have passed through little settlements that seemed almost a law to themselves as to their speech, and the variety of pronunciation, the new idioms and words used and the intonations puzzled my friend, who had been speaking several dialects for years. In certain parts of China the language is said to change every twenty miles, and an estimate has been made that there are as many dialects and sub-dialects as there are days in the year. A thorough knowledge of one of these main dialects may enable a person to be understood throughout several provinces, but only imperfectly so.

The Mandarin Tongue.

The Mandarin is the most widespread; it is supposed that three-fourths of the people have some knowledge of it. All high officials are required to speak the Mandarin, and those who are associated with the official class or aspire to office must learn it.

Over two hundred years ago the Emperor Kang Hi established schools in Canton and elsewhere throughout the empire, with the view of introducing a uniform language in place of the numerous dialects, but his efforts, which have not been repeated, had no effect in hushing this confusion of tongues. In the acquisition of any of these dialects four difficulties confront the student immediately, viz., the tones, the idiom, the classifiers and the multiplicity of verbs.

Puzzling Intonation.

The meaning of a Chinese word depends upon the tone. For example: "Ngo," in one tone, means "I myself;" in another tone, "a goose." "Chu," in one tone, means "Lord;" in another, "pig." "Tin," in one tone, means "heaven;" in another "field." "Sz," means "four," in one tone, and "dead" in another. Ku," means an "orphan," "ancient," or "wages," according to the tone given to it. Referring to the idiom some one has said: "Speak your English sentence backward, and you will have a good Chinese sentence." While this would not always prove to be correct, the order of our words is always changed. For "How old are you?" the Chinese say: "You, this year, how many years old?" For "Who did this?" they ask: "This is, what man has done!" For "How long have you been here?" this is asked: "This place you came how many years?" A classifier precedes every noun whenever it stands in relation to numerals.

Our words herd (in herd of cattle), sheet (in sheet of paper), piece (in piece of silk), correspond exactly to these classifiers. They indicate to what class of thing the noun belongs. For instance, "cheung" applies to things spread out, as a tablecover, bed, mat, etc.; "chi" applies to things round and slender, as a pencil, bamboo, etc.; "pa" is applied to things held in the hand, as an umbrella, fan, knife, etc.; "tin" is put before long and slender things, as cane, snake, string, etc. There are about eighty of these classifiers.

Multiplicity of Verbs.

The multiplicity of the Chinese verbs is very noticeable. Take our word "carry," which is used so generally. In Chinese, to carry on the head one verb would be used; to carry on the shoulder an entirely different word would be used; to carry on the back another verb would be used, and to carry under the arms another; to carry on horseback still another, and to carry a letter a different word would be employed. We say close your eyes, close your mouth, close your fist, close your book, close your door, close your window; but in Chinese a different verb must be used before each of these objects. We say to lay apart, to lay before, to lay in, to lay down, to lay on top, to lay together, to lay aside. In Chinese a new verb must be introduced in each one of these expressions.

At School

The Chinese that is spoken in everyday life is as different from the book language as a dead language is from a living one. On visiting a Chinese school I found that it could be heard long before it was seen. Each pupil learns his lesson off by heart, repeating it over and over again till fixed in the memory, in a loud singsong tone of voice, and the confused babel of sounds produced by a large school of boys which I visited cannot soon be forgotten. In the school and collegiate course, extending over years, the whole of the classics (the four books and the five classics) and commentaries upon them are mastered, but geography, mathematics and the sciences are unknown in a Chinese educational course. The effect of this system is the development of the memory and imitative faculty at the expense of everything else. No school boards exist, and schools are opened independently by teachers to gain their living or established by the gentry, and there are higher institutions of learning having the sanction and support of the government.

A LITERARY OFFICER AND HIS WIFE.

In education, as in everything else, no attention is paid to women, and while it is an exception if a man cannot sign his name, it is the great exception if a woman can sign hers.

Civil Service Examinations.

The system of civil service examinations in China is quite unique in its character, and nothing attracts the wonder and admiration of the foreigner more than this. These examinations have been in vogue for centuries, and having originally started as a means of testing the ability of those already in office, it has gradually widened its scope, till now it embraces every portion of the empire and is the test of ability which all have to undergo who desire admission into the civil service of the country. With this laudable ambition in view, pupils of all ages may be seen pursuing their studies, and grandfather, father and son may be competing at the same time for the coveted goal.

Degrees and Promotions.

Every district city has its examination hall, where the initial trials are conducted under the supervision of the imperial chancellor, a sub-chancellor being in residence. Out of every two thousand only twenty of the best receive the degree which the Chinese term " Sin-ts'ai," meaning " budding genius." An original poem and one or two essays by each candidate on the subjects assigned to them are the exercises of this examination, and during a day and a night each contestant is shut up alone in a " stall " (there are thousands of these around the examination hall), after being examined to see that he has no " help " about him, and if he becomes a member of the charmed literary circle, his hat is adorned with a gold button; and he is eligible to enter the triennial examination for the second degree, styled the " Chu-jin." or " promoted scholar."

The examiners for this second test are the imperial commissioner and ten provincial officers, and he who is successful in this can enter upon a contest for the third degree, which is taken at the capital, Pekin, and which assures to the successful student an office under the government. This mighty system, when Western science is introduced, may be used as a means for the dissemination of broader knowledge throughout this great empire.

Attempts at English.

I have noticed now and then evidences of a willingness on the part of the members of this exclusive kingdom to allow the introduction of foreign ideas, and I have been amused at their " attempts " at English. Mr. Wing Wo Hing, my laundryman at Canton (the first one I have found in China), sent me the following notice:

" We the undersign wish to inform to the friends and the public that we have opened a laundry out of North Gate, where we will have advantage to do all works by using spring water and dried with pure air For times, launderers, who have used river water and dried with city air which makes clothes unpurify and

dissatisfy to the public!"   A few days ago I was startled by the following doctors'
signs: "Doctor to leprosy, nor doctor fee discharged," and, "*Ep.* Healer. Can

HEAD OF A PIRATE HUNG UPON THE ROADSIDE AT CANTON, CHINA.

doctor to surgery line, medicine line—All kind illness dispensation" (dispensary). Nor far from where I am writing a fashionable merchant has this sign in flaming letters before his shop: "*Retail* and *Wholetail!*"

As we have seen the efforts of the Chinaman to imitate the language of the Englishman, we are interested in observing how John Bull first secured an influence over John Chinaman.

The Britisher comes as near being omnipresent as any mortal on this terrestrial ball, and his motherland comes as near having her flag floating over a piece of real estate under every star as any nation on the globe.

The oratorical curl about the sun never setting on England's possessions is not fiction.

The little island, that looks like a speck on the world's map, has managed, by one way and another, to plant her colonies in every clime; and from the homeland to far India and

China, her war and mercantile ships can touch British possessions at convenient distances, without the line being broken during all these thousands of miles.

I desire especially to speak of Hong Kong, a British island in Eastern waters. In the year 1839 the Chinese authorities took strong procedures against the foreign opium merchants; British property was destroyed, a large number of foreigners imprisoned, and every effort was made by the Chinese to put a stop to this traffic that has proven to be such a curse to the nation. Matters were brought to a crisis on the twenty-sixth of August, 1839, when foreigners were expelled from the island, war was immediately declared, and, as might have been expected, in less than two years the British flag was planted on the island, the Bogue forts at the mouth of the Canton River were silenced by English guns and the provincial authorities were forced to accede to the demands of a superior power by allowing trade to be carried on at Canton and Whampoa.

How Hong Kong Became British.

The settlement of Hong Kong was commenced in May, 1841. The following month Hong Kong was declared a free port, and before the close of the same year the population had increased to 15,000.

But John Bull did not have smooth sailing for some years. The Chinese Emperor severely censured the imperial commissioner for the cession of Hong Kong, and war broke out afresh. It was not until after the treaty of Nanking, in 1842, that it was definitely settled that the island should be a British colony and the charter bears the date of April 5, 1843.

But during the coming years the trend of affairs proved, repeatedly, that one John yielded to the other John simply because the one John was weaker than the other John. Here, as in so many other places where she has planted her foot, "the other John" acted on the principle that "might makes right"—especially has this been her motto when she has been in the heavenly business of introducing the opium trade—fit harbinger, indeed, to English Christian missions!

In October of 1856 some Chinese sailors serving on the British lorcha *Arrow* were taken from the vessel by the native authorities, which led to the bombardment and capture of the city of Canton and the cession of the peninsula of Kowloong and the payment of an indemnity of eight millions of taels by the Chinese government to England.

Although I am told by the English at Hong Kong that the colony is now firmly established, I have it from the best authority that it is viewed with hatred and suspicion on the part of the native mandarins, and the repeated riots and the wholesale attempt to poison the entire European community by means of the bread supplied by a Hong Kong baker, which occurred some years since, proves that the situation is not altogether lovely.

9

The Island's Size and Sights.

The island, lying off the coast of the Kwang-tung province, at the mouth of the Canton River and about ninety miles from the city of Canton, consists of a rugged mountain ridge, running from east to west, broken into several peaks, the largest of which attain an altitude of over one thousand eight hundred feet. Its greatest length is about eleven miles, with a breadth of from two to four miles and a circumference of about twenty-seven miles. The word Hong Kong means " fragrant streams," and long before the arrival of the English it was customary for Chinese vessels to get their water supply from the sparkling springs that abound throughout the island. As you approach the city from the harbor you are reminded of Naples. The situation is truly a magnificent one.

Most of the houses near the beach are large and handsome structures, built of granite and well calculated to withstand the force of the typhoons, which have done much damage in the past. Broad roads, lined with trees, wind up the hillside from terrace to terrace. The private residences are situated principally upon the hills, rising tier upon tier to the height of several hundred feet above the sea level, and the large gardens, covered with a wealth of tropical plants and flowers, give the landscape a charming effect from the sea.

The Public Gardens are said not to be excelled by those of any other British colony, and not only are they admirably laid out and managed, seemingly, with scientific skill, but they boast a number of rare trees and plants. The palm beds, the Australian ferns, the Norfolk Island pines, and the ornamental hedge formed of the aloe attract, at once, the attention of the visitor.

Victoria Peak.

The most enjoyable excursion on the island is a trip to Victoria Peak.

This is reached by an elevated tramway, which is a work of great engineering skill; and from its height, which is 1880 feet above the water, your vision sweeps the full circumference of the island, the hill-locked harbor, dotted with every variety of craft, from the ocean steamer and warship to the slipper boat and sampan; and far into the distance, on the mainland, can be seen numerous native villages, built down to the water's edge; and still further away, with the aid of your glass, you can count a score of islands, washed by the blue waters of the bay.

On the Chinese streets here, as elsewhere, one is bewildered by the countless number of curios; for John Chinaman has studied the whim and fancies of the ' outer barbarian," and goods are on exhibition to suit every taste.

Chinese Goods Displayed.

In a walk of two blocks you see elegant embroideries on silk and satin; delicately carved ivory fans, ornaments, chessmen, and vases; walking-sticks of

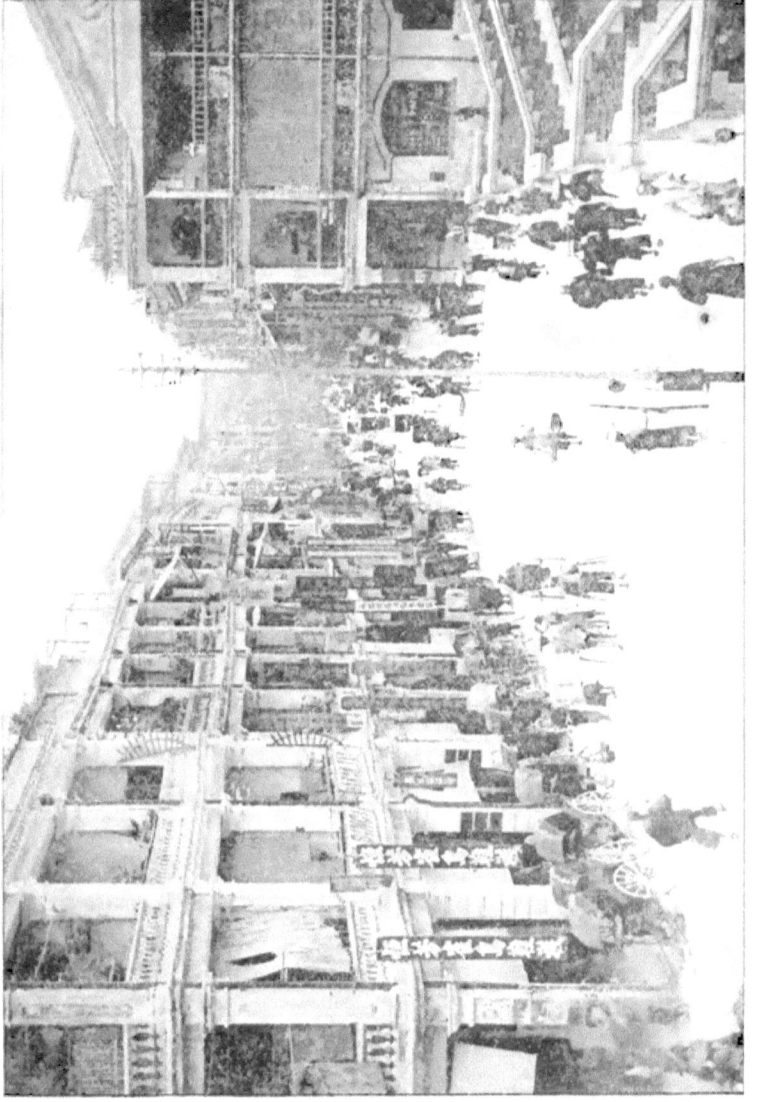

STREET SCENE, HONG KONG, CHINA

ebony, horn, ivory, and bamboo, with embossed silver knobs; fairylike bouquet holders, and any variety of filagree work; goblets, card cases, flower baskets, incense burners, and bangles, ear-rings, scarf pins and finger rings of intricate workmanship; sandal-wood boxes, carved most artistically, and curiously cut horns of the rhinoceros and water-buffalo, and inlaid ornaments made from the large bony beak of the toucan.

CREMATORY AT CANTON, USED FOR BURNING THE BODIES OF PRIESTS.

Some of the work of the Chinese in silver is exquisite. A chased and embossed salver is very attractive, as the design is often wonderfully fine and minute in detail. Every little figure has its own peculiar expression. The tiles on the roofs of the houses and tiny temples are distinguishable one from the other, and even the construction of the lilliputian bridges is plainly visible. As skilled labor is cheap in China, these fine pieces of workmanship can be obtained for amounts only very little larger than the actual cost of the silver itself.

Filagree Work.

The filagree work is made somewhat differently from that in Southern Europe. The silver frame work is first cut out, and gold leaf and mercury are mixed together until they form a paste. The frame is then warmed and the amalgam rubbed in, after which it is made quite hot to drive off the mercury, and the gilding is finished. The filagree is made of silver wire, extremely fine in texture, and designs of every description are worked out by the expert Chinamen with this silver cord.

The Chinese shops on Queen's road, here in Hong Kong, are more elaborately ornamented than most of their shops elsewhere, and although they are only twenty feet deep by ten or eleven wide, they contain great variety of goods.

In the native quarters the salesroom is a dimly lighted, unattractive place. At the back of the shop a little lamp is kept burning before some small image, surrounded by paper flowers or pots of growing plants, such as the favorite narcissus or the dwarf orange, and on the walls are frequently to be seen scrolls containing extracts from the writings of Confucius, Mensius, and others, extolling the dealings of the honest tradesman and commanding courtesy toward strangers.

CHIEF MAGISTRATE, SHANGHAI.

When you enter the shopman approaches you indifferently, disguising all eagerness to drive a bargain, salutes you with the greeting "chin-chin," and only when he sees that you hesitate in your purchasing does he seem to awaken to the occasion and exhibit his genius as a salesman.

Pidgin English.

Pidgin English, a strange mixture of English, Chinese and Portuguese, is spoken by most of the natives at Hong Kong, and it was not many days after my arrival before it was understood by me sufficiently to serve me for all practical purposes.

Its basis consists of turning the consonants "r" into "l" and "v" into "b," adding a final "ey" or "ee" to most words, and above all, the constant use of the word "pidgin," which means business in the most extended sense of the word. "Hab got good pidgin" means that the business situation is a good one. "To-day belongee number one Heaben pidgin day" is the conventional phrase for a day of Christian observance.

"That no belongee boy pidgin, belongee coolie pidgin" is the form of your servant's remonstrance if you ask him to do what he thinks ought to be done by a servant of lower rank.

Am, is, are, and the parts of the verb "to be" are generally translated by "belongee;" "hab belongee"—was; and "by m-bye belongee"—shall be.

The word "side" is used for a particular locality: "Hong Kong side hab

FARMERS AND THEIR WIVES THRESHING RICE.

got too muchee piecee Chinaman" means "there are many Chinamen in Hong Kong."

"No nan" is "impossible;" means "quickly;" "Chow-chow," "food," and "chin-chin" is "good-day" or "good-bye."

"I catchee dinner this side to-night" is the expression for "I dine here to-night."

I overheard this order and reply: " Boy, go talkee amah pay me one piecee handkerchief." " Missy, no can catchee amah; have go out."

A gentleman in Hong Kong was interrupted in his work one day by his boy, A Lin, who came into his office and gravely remarked: " Missy Smith hab got one piecee small cow chilo." This was his graceful and delicate way of announcing that Mrs. Smith had presented her husband with a daughter!

The following verses in Pidgin English are more puzzling than poetic:

Flom Fou Chou Fou I come makey walkey,
  One piecee ship, three piecee bamboo
Inside no belong, outside walkee
  My plenty good sing, all plopper can do.

CHORUS.

Hi zah-zah, chin chin chin.
Chow-chow welly good, my likee he.
Makee plenty sing song, savez by and bye.
Chinaman he plenty good, he laugh hizah.

Allee same you my face once whitey,
  Wid welly long pigtail down him back.
Sailor man he come ashore, makey plenty fightee,
  Pully welly muchy hard makee face black.

Long time plenty work sampan coolie
  Yangtzse river, way down Shanghai,
Me talkee lot pidgin, too muchee foolee,
  Allee same pletty lady no likey I.

Lady cooky welly good, she likey chow-chow,
  She lib way up topside house,
Cooky little pussy cat and little bow-wow,
  Welly good pot stew, boiley wid de mouse.

Allee same pork pig, my likee chow-chow,
  Too muchee big, no muchee small,
Topside darksky down came Chong Mow,
  He makey stealy pig and chow-chow all.

Englissy consul welly much he talkee,
  Puttee up him speecatel, makee look see,
Chop-chop policy man welly muchee walkee,
  Chong Mow runnee, no catchee he!

CHAPTER VII.

IN THE MALAY ARCHIPELAGO.

THE map of the eastern hemisphere shows a number of large and small islands between Asia and Australia, forming a continuous group distinct from these great masses of land and having very little connection with either of them.

These islands, situated upon the equator and washed by the water of the tropical seas, enjoy a more uniformly warm climate than any other part of the globe and teem with natural productions, many of which are found nowhere else.

The giant flowers of Rafflesia, the great green-winged ornithoptera, the prince among butterflies, the man-like orang-outang, and the brilliant birds of paradise are seen here.

The Malay, having no home beyond this insular tract, is seen in his crude and nude state, and as he possesses many marks of peculiarity, he presents many points of interest to the student of mankind.

Your ship sails for weeks among these islands, and their several inhabitants are often as little known to each other as are the native races of the northern and southern continents of America.

The Malay archipelago extends for more than four thousand miles in length, from east to west, and is about thirteen hundred miles in breadth, from north to south. It contains three islands larger than Great Britain, and in one of them, Borneo, all of the British isles might be set down, and they would be surrounded by a sea of forests.

The Volcanic Belt.

One of the greatest volcanic belts upon the globe passes through the archipelago, and it is said that earthquakes are of such frequent recurrence that in many of the islands the years of these great shocks form the chronological epochs of the native inhabitants, by the aid of which the ages of their children and the dates of important events are determined.

By the eruption of Papandayang, in Java, during the last century, forty villages were destroyed; in the first quarter of this century 12,000 persons perished by the lava and ashes that covered three hundred miles of sea and land, and within recent years the island of Makian, after two hundred years of perfect inaction, suddenly burst forth, destroying nearly all of the inhabitants and playing havoc for forty miles around.

Malays and Papuans.

A noted ethnologist, differing from Humboldt and others, contends that the natives of the archipelago belong to two distinct races, the Malays and Papuans, and that they differ radically in physical, mental and moral character. The Asiatic races include the Malays, all having a continental origin, while the races of Papuan type, including all to the east of the former as far as the Fiji Islands, are derived not from any existing continent, but from islands which now exist, or recently existed, in the Pacific Ocean.

It was with pleasure, after spending Christmas and the opening of the new year in Southern China, that I embarked on the P. and O. steamship "Rosetta" for these islands, and after experiencing some rough sea weather, caused by the currents from the China Sea northward, from the Malacca Straits southward and from the Pacific Ocean eastward, meeting at the entrance of the Gulf of Siam, I landed, in fine spirits, at Singapore, the southernmost point of Asia, located at the mouth of the Malacca Straits.

Singapore is an island about thirty miles in length and half as wide, containing not much more than two hundred square miles.

As we sailed up the picturesque harbor scores of Malay boys and men, nearly completely nude, in narrow "dugouts," rowed by our side, chattering and jumping up and down like monkeys, and as small coins were tossed into the transparent water from

MALAY MAN.

the moving ship they would dive for them and, without exception, the sinking money was in the hands of one of these wonderful divers when they arose to the surface of the water.

At times you could see these diving figures struggling fiercely among themselves under the clear water for the coin, and when the victor came up, holding his closed fist in the air, they all sprang in their little boats, tumbling on the waves, kicked the water out of them with one foot, exclaiming "Nay-a-yah!" "Nay-a-yah!" ("One more!" "One more!").

Passing up the streets of Singapore the products of the island were seen on every hand. Tapioca, cocoanut oil, gambia, lead, tin, indigo, coral, gutta-percha, hides, gums, camphor and many like productions were being packed for shipment on the outward steamer for the west, and the market stalls were brilliant with the greatest variety of flowers and fruit.

Near the Equator.

It is quite impossible to give a life likeness of the bright scenes that greet you in this city, located less than a degree from the equator.

NATIVES OF SINGAPORE.

Here you find perpetual summer; here the almost naked natives give full satisfaction to their pride and modesty by binding the scarlet handkerchiefs about their heads and confining one thickness of narrow cotton cloth about their bodies, with flaming sashes. The pure white, hump-backed oxen, driven singly to harness, move sedately through the streets, drawing a tremendous load, with a tar-black Malay, wearing ear-rings, perched on top.

Now you pass rows of houses built high up in the air upon stilts, to give wide berth to snakes and other reptiles that abound in this region. Yonder the wayside is bordered by the graceful rattan, the lofty cocoanut tree, ripening its fruit in clusters at the top, the waving bamboo and the brilliant hedges of the tropics. Here you see growing wild the wonderful fan-palm that springs up in the exact shape of an outspread feather fan and reaches the height of forty feet. The street peddler pleads with you to buy a dozen of his luscious pineapples for ten or fifteen cents, and if you have no money you can run into the jungle nearby and get a dinner of fruit, with no one to molest or make you afraid.

I know of no place on the globe where a person's food and clothes need cost him so little as just here, and the people do not seem to be any less happy because of this fact.

Products and People.

In the celebrated botanical gardens near the city are gathered together all possible representatives of the trees, plants, fruits and flowers of the archipelago, and these are surrounded by the most beautiful landscape gardening.

Within the limits of these gardens there thrive the bread fruit tree, palms, dates, figs, mangoes, mangosteens; the acacia flamboyante, whose top boughs are covered with scarlet flowers, with yellow centres; the stephanotis and alamanda in full bloom; the Egyptian lotus; the Victoria Regia, growing upon a lake, with leaves wide and strong enough to support a child upon the surface of the water, and acres of tropical growths in the greatest variety and abundance.

The Sultan of Johore.

A mile beyond the gardens we visited one of the palaces of the Sultan of Johore. The late Sultan died at Bailey's Hotel, London, a short time ago, and the present ruler of the small kingdom separated from Singapore by a narrow strip of water, is proving himself to be more progressive than the former Sultan.

This young man, twenty-two years of age, was educated in England, and in his European attire he looks more like an English swell than a "heathen" chief.

It would be hard to find anywhere in the world as many kinds of people gathered together in so small a space as you find in the community of Singapore. The government, the garrison and the chief merchants are English; most of the money-exchangers and mechanics are Chinamen; the boatmen, fishermen and police are native Malays; the clerks and small merchants are largely Portuguese of Malacca; the petty dealers and shopkeepers are the Klings of West India and Arabs, who are Mahometans; the grooms and washermen are all Bengalees; the money sharks are Parsees; the sailors and servants are mostly Javanese, and hundreds of traders in tin, lead, skins, shells and corals congregate here from Celebes, Bali, Borneo, Sumatra and other islands of the archipelago.

Town and Suburbs.

The harbor presents a busy scene. Men-of-war and many trading vessels of European nations, hundreds of Malay praus and Chinese junks and any number

MALAY CHILDREN.

of sampans and slipper-boats move over the quiet waters of the harbor.

The town comprises handsome public buildings and churches, Mahometan mosques, Hindu temples, Chinese joss-houses, massive European warehouses, queer old Kling and Chinese bazaars and long suburbs of Chinese and Malay cottages.

In the jungles, uncomfortably near the town, are to be found wild beasts, and during the night not seldom can you hear the roar of these unwelcome neighbors. Several miles from the hotel where I was a guest you are shown tiger-pits, carefully covered over with sticks and leaves, and so well concealed that there is danger of a person being entrapped unless he is watchful. They are shaped like an iron furnace, wider at the bottom than the top, fifteen or twenty

TRAVELER'S PALM, SINGAPORE.   (141)

feet deep and a sharp stake was stuck erect in the bottom until in recent years, when this was forbidden on account of an unfortunate traveler being killed by falling on one.

A sail of twenty-eight hours from Singapore brought us to Penang, the most

GROUP IN MALAY ARCHIPELAGO.

northerly seaport of the Malacca Straits.

This island, fourteen miles long by seven wide, is situated at the point where the straits open into the Indian Ocean, one hundred miles from the Island of Sumatra, and the town of Penang nestles near the water, with a background of thickly wooded hills that culminate in three mountain peaks.

As our steamer anchored a half a mile from shore, we were taken in a highly colored native boat to the landing-place, and soon we were on a crowded street of this interesting little city.

The lithe and graceful figures of the men and women attract attention immediately, and frequently as these nearly nude natives pose along the roadside they look like exquisite works in bronze. The women, strange to say, are very fond of ornaments, and with their ear-rings, nose-ring, arm and ankle bracelets present a most picturesque appearance, which is heightened by their brilliant single garment.

COCOA.   (143)

The Cocoanut Tree.

Here is found the areca palm, better known as the Penang tree, the source of the betel-nut; but the place is noted especially as the headquarters of the cocoanut tree. This growth is simply wonderful. We drove through a cocoanut tree grove of 2000 acres, and the view of these lofty trees, keeping an upright position, with the heavy loads in their tufted tops, is one of the most remarkable sights in the tropics. The tree gives annually several crops, without artificial cultivation; three hundred and sixty uses, it is said, can be made of its trunk, branches, leaves, fruit and juice, and there are over twenty distinct species of the fruit flourishing in and around the town. With the rapidity of a monkey, I saw a native climb over forty feet to the top of a tree, and, after twisting off a cocoanut, was on the ground again in a few seconds. After visiting the botanical gardens, the fruit market, where a basket of delicious mangosteens was bought, and after seeing a brilliant Malay

AN ORANG-OUTANG FROM PENANG.

marriage and funeral procession, I set sail for Ceylon, where the spicy breezes blow.

To the naturalist the islands of the Malay Archipelago present fields for his researches which cannot be surpassed, if equaled, in the world. Beasts, birds,

and insects of every description are found in this insular group and many of these
are peculiar to this region of the globe.

The Orang-Outang.

The interest with which I watch the gyrations of a monkey is only exceeded
by the amusement afforded me by the performances of the orang-outang. Although

my taste may be fear-
fully at fault, I am bold
to say that nothing
here in the Malay Ar-
chipelago has given
me more real pleasure,
has inspired more
hearty laughs and has
furnished more food
for reflection than my
lengthy interviews
with his majesty, the
orang-outang of Bor-
neo.

I am not quite
sure whether he un-
derstood what I said,
to him, and it is
equally probable that
I did not understand
very much that he
said to me, but I was
impressed with the
fact that he was one
of the most intelligent
inhabitants of the is-
lands, with a keen
sense of humor and a
good fund of com-
mon sense, and when
we shook hands in

AN ORANG-OUTANG FROM PENANG—THE TEMPERANCE QUESTION.

our touching farewell I, at least, felt like saying we meet to part, but may it be
that we part to meet again! Here are the native haunts of this great man-
like ape, and here you can see and study him untouched by the artificial and

detrimental influences of Mr. Barnum, Mr. Forepaugh and the other masters of
the circus ring.

The wide extent of lofty virgin forest is necessary to the untrammeled glory
of his orang-outangship, and here he is as much at home as the Indian on the
prairie or the Arab on the desert. The quiet leisure, if not the majestic dignity,
with which he makes his way through the forests affords a stinging rebuke to the
fussy, fuming, dashing citizen of this electric-car age in which we live.

He walks deliberately along some of the larger branches of the trees in the
semi-erect attitude which the great length of his arms and the shortness of his
legs cause him naturally to assume; and as he walks on his knuckles, and not on

PAPUAN CHILDREN.

the palm of the hand, the disproportion between these limbs is increased, and
while in locomotion it is not highly probable that a Grecian artist would select him
as a model of grace.

He does not jump or spring or even appear to hurry himself, and yet he
manages to make as quick speed as one who is running through the forests
beneath.

The male orang-outang, unlike his inconsiderate human brother in America,
helps his wife make up the bed. When wounded or when bedtime comes a nest,
or bed, is quickly made from the sticks and leaves of the trees, and one who has

hunted this animal a great deal tells me that a fresh one is made every night. Like the other natives of these islands, he takes life easy, not leaving his bed until the sun has well risen and has dried the dew on the leaves, feeding during the middle of the day, and never seeming to worry himself upon the grave questions of state, commerce and religion that create headaches and heartaches for the more civilized, but less contented, nations of the globe.

They are not only easily satisfied, as is well known, in the matter of clothing, but their diet is a very simple one, consisting almost exclusively of fruit, with some tender buds and shoots for occasional dessert.

Despite the jokes that we are prone to make at his expense, the orang-outang is an elevated character. He rarely descends to the ground except when the market in the trees has failed him, or when the hollows of the leaves do not contain sufficient water for his refreshment.

Although the orang-outang is peacefully inclined and desires everybody to attend to his own business, as he does, yet he is no coward, and when aroused by what he regards to be an act of injustice or persecution he is a terror. When driven by hunger to hunt shoots and roots along the water's edge the crocodile has been known to protest against this innocent mode of making his living, but he has in every case recorded in history established his rights without much ceremony.

The chief of the Balow Dyaks gives this testimony: " The orang-outang has no enemies; no animals dare attack it but the crocodile and the python. He always kills the crocodile by main strength, standing upon it, pulling open its jaws and ripping up its throat. If a python attacks the orang-outang he seizes it with his hands and then bites it, and soon kills it. There is no animal in the jungle so strong as he."

It is remarkable that an animal so peculiar and possessing such a high type of form as the orang-outang should be confined to two islands, Borneo and Java, especially as these are almost the least inhabited by the higher mammalia.

As doubtless the orang-outang, the chimpanzee and the gorilla have had their forerunners, the naturalist must look forward with interest to the time when the deposits of the tropics shall make known the history and earliest appearance of the great man-like apes, who, if they are not the "missing links," are ridiculously like some of us who make sport of them!

A Brilliant Bird.

In striking contrast to the curious and comical creature just described, allow me to present a brilliant and beautiful bird, another inhabitant of these islands, namely, the bird of paradise.

The paradiscidæ, as they are classed, are a group of birds allied somewhat in their structure and habits to starlings and the Australian honeysuckers, but they are characterized by extraordinary developments of plumage, which are unequaled in any other family of birds.

In some of the species large tufts of delicate bright-colored feathers spring from each side of the body beneath the wings, forming fans or shields, and the middle feathers of the tail are often elongated into wires, twisted into the most fantastic shapes or adorned with the most brilliant metallic colors. We find that in other species these plumes spring from the head, the back or the shoulders, and the tails are of varied shapes.

I had no idea, until I visited the Malay archipelago, that there are as many species of the bird of paradise as are to be seen on the Islands of Borneo and Java. The great bird of paradise, the lesser bird of paradise, the red bird of paradise, the king bird of paradise, the double-mantle bird of paradise, the superb bird of paradise, the six-shafted bird of paradise, the standard wing bird of paradise, and the scale-breasted paradise bird, are all marked by different colored and shaped plumage, and although they are classed under the same general name, they are quite distinct in many respects.

KANDYAN CHIEF OR HEADMAN.

It has afforded me much pleasure to gather, from one source and another, a great deal of information about this the most beautiful bird in the world, but I shall try to describe only two or three classes of the bird, which may give your readers a faint conception of their beauty and brilliancy.

The largest species known is the great bird of paradise, which is seventeen or eighteen inches from the beak to the tip of the tail. The entire top of the head and neck is a delicate straw-yellow, the feathers resembling plush or velvet; the lower part of the throat up to the eyes is clothed with scaly feathers of an emerald green color, with a rich metallic gloss, and velvety plumes of a still deeper green extend in a band across the forehead and chin as far as the eyes, which are bright yellow, and the body, wings and tail are of a rich coffee-brown, which deepens on the breast to a blackish-violet or purple-brown.

The two middle feathers of the tail have no webs at all except at the base and extreme tip, and from each side of the body beneath the wings springs a dense tuft of long and delicate plumes, sometimes two feet in length, of the intensest golden orange color and very glossy, changing toward the tips into a pale brown. The thick tuft can be elevated and spread out at pleasure so as almost to hide the body of the bird.

This brilliant plumage, strange to narrate, is entirely confined to the gentlemen, while the lady is really a very plain and ordinary-looking bird of a uniform coffee color, possessing neither the long tail wires nor a single green or yellow feather about the head. As might be expected, the male birds do most of

A KANDYAN GIRL.

the talking, and their shrill note, "wawk-wawk-wawk-wok-wok-wok," can be heard for miles, but what domestic experience occasions this alarming cry of the husband the naturalist has not yet informed us.

The mode of nidification is unknown, but the natives inform us that the nests are made of leaves, placed on ants' nests or some projecting limb of a tall tree, and each nest contains only one bird.

The birds are shot with blunt arrows, so as not to injure the plumage by a drop of blood, and they are stuffed by the natives with the greatest care.

The side plumes of the red bird of paradise, instead of being yellow, are rich crimson, and the ends are curved downward and inward and are tipped with white. The rich metallic green of the throat extends over the front half of the head beyond the eyes and a double crest of scaly feathers is formed on the forehead.

Perhaps the rarest and most brilliant of the whole group is the superb bird of paradise.

The ground color of the plumage is intense black, with beautiful bronze reflections on the neck, and the whole head covered with feathers of brilliant metallic green and blue. It supports a shield over its breast of a bluish-green color, with a satiny gloss, and back of the neck it bears another shield, much larger, of a velvety black color, glossed with bronze and purple. At first sight the plumage of the six-shafted paradise bird seems to be black, but in certain lights it glows with bronze and deep purple; its throat and breast are of a golden hue, changing to green and blue tints; the back of the head contains a curved band of feathers, resembling the sheen of emerald and topaz more than organic substance, and from the sides of the head spring the six feathers from which the bird receives its name.

But as my vocabulary of color names is about spent, I must cease the futile attempt to give a word-painting of this bird, clothed by nature with all the hues of the rainbow.

PEARL FISHERIES OF CEYLON.

CHAPTER VIII.

THE SPICY BREEZES OF CEYLON.

 OME years ago I was in the Louvre Gallery in Paris, and I was nearly as much interested in watching the performances of some of the visitors as I was in the great masterpieces. To have the pleasure of saying afterward that they had seen these miles of pictures, seemed to be the object of many who were hurrying through the galleries, and "to do" the whole thing in a few hours appeared to be a greater masterpiece to some than any work that hung on the walls.

The tourist who desires merely to trot around the globe can touch at the Japan and China treaty ports, sail through the Malay archipelago, take one sniff of the spicy breezes at Ceylon, dash through the wonders of India, from Bombay hurry on to Egypt, scratch his initials on the pyramids, take a leap, skip and a jump through Europe, and look upon the Statue of Liberty again in a few months. His friends, laboring under the delusion that this quick-step globe-trotter has seen the world, heartily congratulate him, and he is blissfully ignorant of what he has missed.

Roughing It.

As in other countries, it is quite impossible to get the faintest idea of the topography, the flora, and the fauna of Ceylon, and the customs and habits of the people, unless you, at any inconvenience, visit the villages and jungles of the interior.

The engagements of my pleasant companion from Baltimore necessitated him to leave me in Southern China, and about six weeks were spent largely by me in "roughing it" among the natives, miles from the sea coasts. As a few days were quite sufficient to see the sights of Colombo, I soon took train across the island of Ceylon, and after fours' ride the old historic city of Kandy was reached.

In Ceylon's Forests.

The talipot palm, found in Ceylon, grows to the height of seventy or eighty feet; at the age of forty years it blooms, for the first time with a loud report, and almost immediately dies.

During this railroad trip we passed cinnamon gardens, sweetly fragrant, not from the bloom or berry, but from the wounded bark while being gathered at the semi-annual harvest. Then followed widespread coffee plantations, the cultivation of which formed one of the greatest industries of Ceylon, until it was

TALIPOT PALM.

suddenly checked some years since by the leaf fungus that impoverished so many of the planters. In dense forests we had pointed out to us fine specimens of the ebony, satinwood, palms, bamboos, fragrant balsams, tree ferns, anaconda-like-rooted India-rubber trees, and the bread-fruit tree, with its deeply serrated, feathery leaves and its melon-shaped fruit, weighing from three to four pounds.

This bread-fruit is prepared for eating in many ways, a few trees supporting a large family, and, as the trees bear fruit continually for nine months of the year, it is one of the most valued trees found in these tropical forests.

DR. TUPPER AND MR. HARMON IN CEYLON.

I was very much interested in the cardamon and pepper bushes, loaded with fruit, and what is known as the kitool palm, yielding its harvest of sugar, toddy and sago.

My companion in the coach, who is an enthusiastic and lifelong student of birds, explained the peculiar nest of the tailor bird, which sews leaves together and constructs a pretty nest inside of them; the weaver bird's nest, with entrance tubes over two feet in length, and the pendant nests, built by a kind of wasp, in the high trees.

TALIPOT PALM.

On the Mountains.

Fifty miles out from Colombo we entered the grand mountain plateau and ranges of the interior, where lies the territory comprised within the Kandyan Kingdom, which maintained its independence all through the Dutch and Portuguese eras, until the British conquered it in the year in which Waterloo was fought.

As the train slowly climbed into the mountains, the terraced rice fields, in vivid green, looked like giant stairways up the mountain side, covered with their

TWO-WHEEL BULLOCK CART.

verdant carpets, and presented a striking contrast with the darker coloring of the plantations and jungles. While we were passing around "Sensation Rock," to the left, only a narrow path was visible, and the coaches seemed to tremble on the edge of the abyss. A thousand feet below, the irrigated valleys stretched far in the distance, and towering above the other peaks, with no background save the flushed evening sky, was the "Bible Rock," as if waiting silently for the finger of the Creator to write upon it a new commandment.

SCRAPING CINNAMON.

The City of Kandy.

As we pursued our serpentine way the city of Kandy could be seen miles away, perched in a basin of the mountains, 200 feet above the level of the sea. My window in the Queen's Hotel looks out upon a lake three miles in circumference, built by the last Kandyan king, and around its clear waters has been laid out a beautiful drive, which is alive every afternoon with every variety of vehicle, from the two-wheel bullock cart of the Singhalese to the four-in-hand coach of the European, who has his short yearly residence in this picturesque spot.

CART IN CENTRAL CEYLON,

Quite contrary to my usual custom, I arose early the first morning of my stay in Kandy and, during a walk of several miles in the neighboring jungles, I gathered fifteen varieties of wild flowers, many of which I had not seen in my rambles nearer the seacoast. During this walk I became interested in many things beside the abundance of the flora. Noticing a coarse cloth bag hung from the limb of a tree, which was being swung by a stout native man, American-like, I made an examination and found that the thoughtful husband was rocking the new-born baby to sleep, while the wife was cracking rocks on the roadside. The father looked very much bored, but the mother appeared quite contented. As long as

CEYLONESE WOMEN AND GIRLS ON TEA ESTATE.

the baby was in the bag asleep I should think that he would be as willing to take
care of it as to crack rocks.

Women and girls were met carrying children astraddled their hips, instead of
on their backs, as elsewhere in the East, and whole families were seen taking their
morning baths at the street pump.   Men, I noticed, were honest enough to reveal,
rather than conceal, their natural vanity by wearing brilliant nose- and ear-rings,
while the women, true to nature, were more modest in this respect. Washermen and
washerwomen were gathered by scores along the banks of a mountain stream,
washing the clothes of Europeans by rubbing them in the water and beating them
with rods, while they were stretched out afterward on great, flat rocks.   The early
fruit-seller was on the streets with his basket of cocoanuts for a few pennies and
his bunch of fifty bananas for ten cents.

A short drive from the hotel brought us to the celebrated botanical gardens,
which are said to contain 25,000 species of plants, and after spending hours
driving over miles of avenues that are bordered and overhung by tropical growth,
I was prepared to believe the statement of the Ceylonese, that here is found the
finest collection of plants in the world.

The name of Kandy is associated with the ancient temple of Maligawa, or
the Temple of the Tooth, where the sacred tooth of Buddha has been preserved,
it is said, for more than fifteen hundred years.   Because of this precious relic, the
king and priests of Burmah and Siam continue to send valuable gifts to the temple
annually; and the sacred bo tree, near by, is reported to be the oldest historical
tree in the world, its record having been kept since three hundred years before the
Christian era.

The reputed tooth of the great Buddha is about the size of the tusk of a large
boar, and is enclosed in an immense casket, decked with costly gems.   What a
terror this grinder would be to modern dentists, and how we shudder to think
that perhaps the founder of Buddhism woke up one night with an ache in this
identical monster of a tooth.

An enjoyable day was spent in driving through the tea plantations near the
city, and visiting a tea factory, where I was shown the "stages" of the tea from
the time that it comes fresh from the field until it is ready for the foreign market.
Tea grows vigorously in Ceylon from the southwest coast districts up to plantations 6500 feet above sea level, and the higher the altitude the more delicate are
the teas produced, but less the crop per acre.

Ceylon Tea Cultivation.

The Ceylon tea cultivation is different from that found in Japan and China,
and it is claimed that the purest article on the market is shipped from this island.
The tea bushes are planted in lines at regular distances over large tracts of land,

carefully drained, which is weeded every month. Once a year the bushes are pruned down to a height of about two feet, and two months after the pruning the first "flush" of young shoots is ready to be plucked, and during the height of the season the flushes reoccur every ten days. Natives, mostly women and girls, with small baskets attached to their girdles, go round and pluck the bud and a couple of the tender, half-developed leaves. Twice a day the gathered leaves are weighed and taken into the factory, where they are spread thinly on trays or shelves to wither.

The withered leaf is now placed in the rolling-machine, driven by water or steam, the rolling lasting for half an hour, and from the moist mass of twisted and bruised leaves there freely comes the juice, technically called "the roll." The roll is placed in trays to ferment or oxidize, and during this process it changes from a green to a copper color. After fermentation, upon which depends the subsequent strength and flavor of the tea, the roll is thinly spread on trays and placed either over charcoal stoves or in large iron drying-machines, and in less time than an hour it is thoroughly crisp and dried.

The tea is now sorted or sized by being passed through sieves of different meshes, giving the varieties of Pekoe, broken Pekoe, Souchong, Congou and dust. Then comes the final processes of weighing, packing and shipping. In Ceylon much more attention is given just now to the production of tea than of coffee and spices, and while in 1873 the exports of tea from the island were only twenty-three pounds, in 1895 they were 40,000,000 pounds, and 150,000 acres are under cultivation, with 700 European planters and 165,000 Indian and Singhalese laborers engaged on the tea plantations of Ceylon.

The Marriage Ceremony.

Late on Sunday night I received a "chit" from a friend telling me of a swell Singhalese wedding that was to occur next morning, and suggesting that I get my tea and toast by six o'clock and be ready for the carriage that would be at my door at 6.30, as the marriage festivities would last all day.

The early morning drive of ten miles along the beach, with the blue Indian Ocean to my right, and the green-tufted cocoanut trees to my left, was refreshing and delightful, and just as the music on the tom-tom at the bridegroom's house was well begun we passed through the throng of people on the street and the crowd of relatives of the groom in the front room. We were ushered into a compartment which was decorated most elaborately with pictures of Buddha, the royal family of England, actresses and celebrated brands of American tobacco. In the centre of the room was a huge flower-covered cake, to be presented at the proper time by the groom to the bride. The cousin of the bridegroom took us in charge, and as he spoke English very well, his explanations during the day threw

HOEING TEA.

light upon many of the mysteries of this marriage, according to the complicated rites of the Buddhist religion.

It is the custom for the relatives only of the groom to gather before the marriage at his father's house, and as these numbered several hundred, we were entertained by watching these Singhalese men, women and children, some in native, and others in half-European costumes, gathering in the rooms preparatory to taking up the march for the house of the bride's father.

Six married women, nearest related to the groom (with the exception of his mother, who was not seen during the performances), were ushered in with great pomp, and I am quite sure that Barnum's agent never caught anything alive so wonderful as these painted, brilliantly costumed, powdered creatures! My self-appointed informer whispered to me that it was the first time that these women had tried to dress like Europeans and Americans, and when I quietly said "remarkable," he seemed quite satisfied with the effect produced.

The flower girls from the groom's house were dressed in bright bodices, white skirts, flaming red stockings, and, as it was a dry, hot day, several of them were shod with brand new, shining rubbers! But some of the party were sensible enough not to try to imitate Western dress, and these looked attractive and graceful in their hatte, cambaya and kabakumththu.

When the groom appeared in the handsome Singhalese dress worn by the upper classes, everyone rose, shook hands with him, and the march was begun for the bride's home. Our carriage was placed next to the one containing the happy young man, and with him we equally divided the attention of the groups on the corners, who were expecting to see only the relatives of the groom and Singhalese followers of Buddha.

For four miles along the beach of the Indian Ocean, through cocoanut and palm groves, and along the cinnamon gardens, we moved slowly until suddenly there burst upon our ears the noise of many voices and the clatter of the tom-tom, and our carriages were surrounded by the relatives of the bride, who gave evidence of their joy by the indescribable movements of their bodies and heads and the clapping of their hands.

A white cloth was stretched over several hundred yards from the door of the house, white canopies were held aloft by gayly dressed young women; the father, uncles, brothers and other male relatives of the bride came forward in stately procession; several tom-toms, each surrounded by five vigorous persons, gave forth the most excruciating music; the female relations of the bride from near and far, dressed, if possible, more remarkably than the females of the other house, gathered in the front rooms, and after the bride had been adorned in a lace jacket brought her by the bridegroom, which was placed over her other bridal attire, she was led in, and for more than an hour she sat upon an elevated seat,

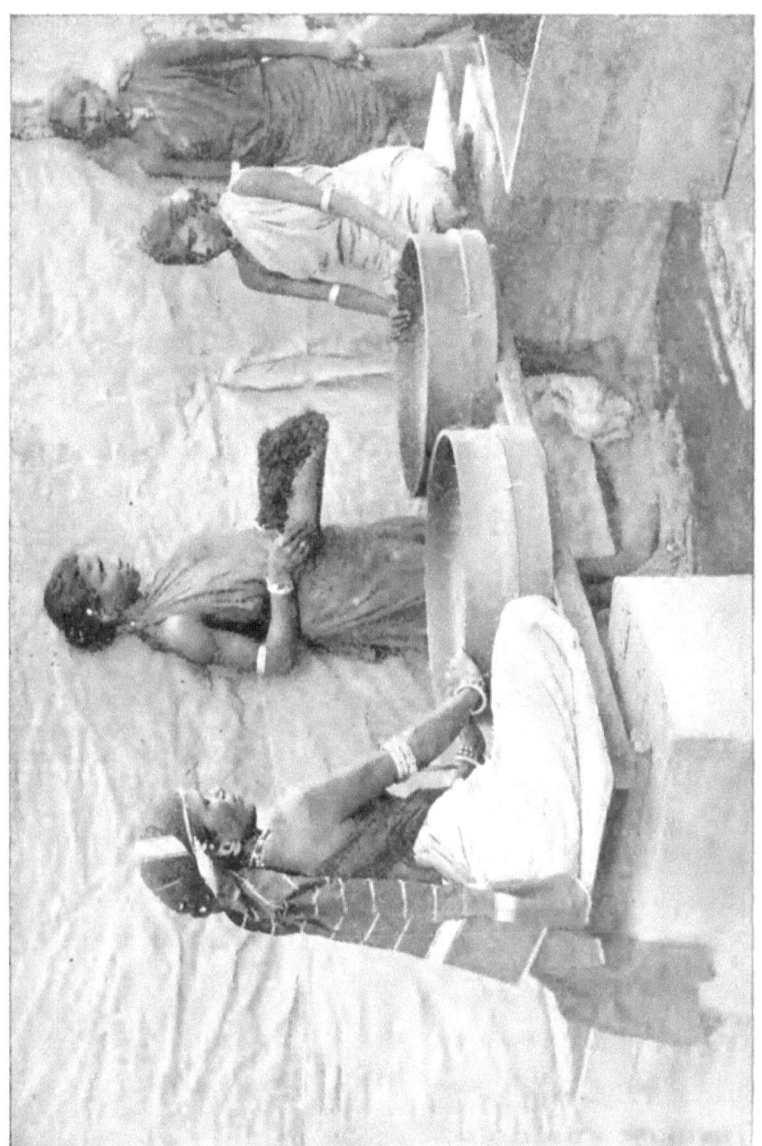

WOMEN SIFTING TEA.

made for the purpose, in the centre of the room —the bashful, if not blushing, object of the cruel scrutiny of curious eyes.

The girl bride had just passed her fourteenth year; her white satin costume fitted not much better than the clothes of English women; her poor cramped feet looked little at ease in the white slippers, and her long bridal veil, with the price tag still on it, was fastened to her jet-black hair with silver pins and white, red and pink flowers, and hung gracefully over her hazel-brown face.

After the scrutinizing process was over, and all the members of the two houses had examined her from every point of view, the bride was helped from her chair by the married women of the groom's house, and she was soon standing with her lover on a raised mat, covered with white cloth, in the large middle room, in the immediate presence of their maternal uncles.

TAMILS, CEYLON.

The marriage ceremony, according to the religion of Buddha, was commenced by the senior uncle; parts of it were repeated by the younger uncles; the thumbs of the couple were tied together with white cord, over which was poured cold water; the cords were untied, and the groom placed two rings on the bride's finger and she put two rings on his. The gray-haired father of the groom then waved over the pair a tray containing lighted tapers, and the Buddhist ceremony was closed with words of advice to the new-made husband and wife and with the announcement that presents were in order. The young husband presented his wife with a satin dress and jacket, which were put on her publicly by two women, who looked like they had been kissing the inside of a flour-barrel. The bride's father gave to his

TEA PACKING AND WEIGHING.

son-in-law a pile of rupees (a rupee is about twenty-seven cents of our money), which were counted and the amount—six hundred and five—was announced, and a tract of land as a dower, and then smaller presents followed.

After a general hand-shaking, which was the only mode of congratulation, the procession moved off toward the office of the registrar, where the record of the marriage was made according to English laws. The proposition that I made, through my interpreter, to have a photograph taken of the bridal party, was agreed to most heartily by the young couple, and at the groom's house, in the afternoon, an obliging photographer secured excellent views of the merry crowd. As I was bidding farewell to them a cousin of the bridegroom, to whom

LOW CASTE TAMIL GIRL.

I had been speaking of certain customs in America, said to me in broken English: "I have fixed it for you, if you like, to give kiss to the bride. Would you like?" I shall not give to the public my reply.

The Wild Men of Ceylon.

Far back in the central and eastern provinces of Ceylon, away from all civilizing influences, is found a class of human beings that live very much like the beasts of the forest, and from their appearance, customs and language the conclusion has been reached that they are the aborigines of the country.

They live on the game they kill, the fish they catch, the roots and seeds of certain aquatic plants and jungle plants and creepers. The wild forests in which they live abound in elk, deer, hogs, monkeys, porcupines, iguanas, peacocks and jungle fowls, all of which they kill with their bows and arrows except the iguana, which they run down with their dogs. The steaks from the larger animals they dry in the sun, and these are eaten raw, with salt. The rotten wood of a tree called bala is beaten to powder, kneaded into a paste with honey and baked into cakes, which serve them as bread. It is said when all other means of sustenance fail them they boil the leaves of the kora or tora trees, which grow abundantly everywhere in the jungle. They never use firearms, but the bows and arrows are used with great skill, with which they kill the bear, the panther and other formidable animals.

MT. LAVINIA HOTEL, COLOMBO, CEYLON.

These wild men never smoke, they know nothing of intoxicating drinks and drink nothing but water. Some of them live in trees, and if they have huts they are constructed in the rudest manner, composed of a mere roof of three or four sloping poles, one end of which is placed in the ground and the other end is supported by a cross-stick placed on two perpendicular ones. The huts are covered with bark of trees or dried grass. As they seldom stay more than two or three months in one place these stick and grass houses can easily be removed.

The men wear a string round their middle, with a narrow piece of cloth attached; the women wear a cloth something like an apron; the hair of both sexes is never cut, their bodies are never washed except by the rain, and they never have been known to laugh.

The Devil Dances.

The use of medicine is not known among them, and in case of sickness the demon priest is sent for, who leads what is known as the devil dances around the sick person, chanting certain incantations, which are supposed to propitiate the demon who is causing the illness. No respect is paid to the dead; the body is

COLOMBO HIGH CASTE.

thrown into the jungles to be devoured by the wild beasts, and, as far as it has been ascertained, they have no notion at all of a future state.

The class known as the hill Veddas is of a savage and ferocious disposition. They dress only in a small apron of plaited leaves; the women are scarcely ever seen, and they dwell in the deepest recesses of the woods or among the rocks in the hill country, living entirely on what nature affords them, especially roots, leaves and bugs.

Trade with Outsiders.

I am told that they obtain the iron heads for their arrows in the following manner: They carry a quantity of dried flesh and honey to a place near the residence of a Singhalese blacksmith and hang it up on a tree out of the reach of dogs and jackals, together with a leaf cut in the shape of the iron article they want. If the blacksmith does not make the exchange speedily, he will hear from the wild man in a more vigorous manner.

The language of these sons of the forests and mountains defies all analysis, and no one has been found who can interpret their mutterings. When the Prince of Wales visited Colombo, some years ago, several of these creatures were captured and brought into the circle of civilization for him to see, but when at liberty again they fled back to the freedom of the forests, where each, as a prince of nature, enjoyed the royal right, unlike the English prince, of doing as he pleased.

With Arabi Pasha.

Through the kindly consideration of a gentleman from Scotland, who has a large tea estate in the interior of Ceylon, I was enabled to have an interview of several hours with Arabi Pasha, the famous Egyptian, who is a prisoner of state and an exile from his native land by the authority of the English government.

This man, whose exploits in the year 1882 attracted the attention of the world, lives in an humble bungalow on the outskirts of the old city of Kandy, and with a pension of fifty pounds a month, sent him by the government at Cairo, supports a family of twenty-five persons.

On my arrival at his residence he met me at the door in quite a democratic manner, and after a hearty grasp of the hand and a few expressions of salutation he was soon, without the least hesitation, discussing his varied and thrilling experiences.

He is a magnificent specimen of an Egyptian, being six feet and two inches in height and weighing about two hundred and sixty pounds, and when he became aroused, while describing his efforts to give freedom and independence to his people, he stood erect, threw back his great head and looked every inch a hero.

The Pasha's Account.

His English is somewhat broken, but it was, without difficulty, that I followed his eloquent words, which at times stirred me thoroughly and elicited my sympathy.

SINGHALESE MAN.

" I am a prisoner of state," he said, " and I cannot discuss current politics, but as matters have changed in Egypt and as the reformation that I attempted to bring about is gradually taking place, I am willing to give to you and to the American press an account of my life and the motives that prompted my actions in 1882. I confess that I wanted to see my country free, and for this freedom and for the deliverance of my people from internal and external corruption I staked my life and my all. I think now, as I thought then, that the God above has given to different peoples different lands, and the inhabitants of those lands should be left to control them if they are willing to have law and order.

"I wanted to do for my country what Washington did for his, and if I had been successful, to-day I would be loved and honored in my own country, instead of being an exile from my home on this island. It is not for me, in my position, to say anything against the great power of England that conquered me, but all the facts are becoming known and perhaps during my lifetime I shall be put right before the world.

"If I am allowed to return to my native land, I promise never again to take part in public affairs unless my people call me to lead them, and as the movements

AN ELEPHANT MARCH.

that I started are largely being carried out by others, and as my ideas are being adopted practically in Egypt, my presence there could not possibly do harm. I do not want to die an exile from home."

The Rebellion of 1882.

These are nearly the exact words of Arabi Pasha, but as some of your readers may not recall the facts of the rebellion that he led, I shall briefly give them. In the latter months of 1881 Arabi, an Egyptian peasant, but a man of great courage and genius, who had risen to one of the highest positions in the service of the Khedive, became enraged by the absolute and grossly abused power of the Turkish ruling caste, and through his leadership the Khedive, himself a Turk, was forced to grant his subjects a parliament and constitution on Western models.

Under the new order Arabi was appointed minister of war and immediately addressed himself to certain reforms that were greatly needed in the country. The new constitutional ministers were recognized by all the European powers, including England, and at that time Arabi and his followers were greeted as reformers. But the foreign creditors of Egypt thinking that their financial interests were endangered under a government so democratic, took alarm, and such pressure was brought to bear upon the English government that, largely through the influence of Lord

ARABI PASHA, AN EXILE IN CEYLON.

Granville, vigorous steps were taken to restore the Turkish Khedive's despotic rule. As it will be remembered, English ships were sent to Alexandria to intimidate the new ministers and Parliament, but Arabi and certain trusted associates refused to betray the heroically won liberties and declined to yield to the English admiral's threats.

An attempt was now made to get rid of Arabi in a more indirect way. A commissioner was secured by Lord Granville from the Sultan to entrap the minister of war in a conference and there shoot or arrest him, but through timely warning from certain foreign friends Arabi escaped the trap set for him, and all seemed smooth sailing for a short time.

But the end was not yet. After the fashion of the fable of the wolf and the lamb, a quarrel was picked with these patriotic Egyptians and the city of Alexandria was bombarded on the plea that the feeble fleet of England was in danger!

As a last step in this unworthy performance Lord Wolseley was sent to Egypt with sixty thousand English troops. Arabi and Mahmud Sami, with thousands of others, were made prisoners of war at Cairo. A mock trial was instituted against the leaders of the national movement. Arabi Pasha ("Pasha" corresponds to our general), the minister of war, Mahmud Sami, the prime minister, Yakub Sami, the governor of Cairo, and four military officers were condemned to death, and only through the pressure of an outraged public opinion in Europe did Lord Granville at last unwillingly consent to a commutation of their death penalty to one of exile to a British colony.

The Egyptian liberal party and Parliament were disbanded, the patriotic ministers and five pashas were

SINGHALESE GIRL.

"deported" to Ceylon and an Englishman, Sir Evelyn Baring, was installed in Egypt, with the cowardly, cringing Turkish Khedive to do his bidding, or rather the bidding of the British government.

British Rule and Reforms.

After eight or ten years' rule in Egypt under English influence Sir Evelyn Baring published a report in which he claims for the British government the success of certain internal reforms by which the finances have been set in order

MALAY GYPSIES.

and check has been put on the abuses of power by the Turkish privileged class and certain European colonists. But Arabi Pasha, in his earnest declaration to me, insisted that these very reforms owe their initiative and vitality to the national movement that he headed, and to prove this he produces the program published by him in December, 1881.

An intelligent Englishman makes this public statement: "Although we have been for years in Egypt, we have introduced no reform there upon any permanent basis. The popular institutions won by Arabi, and which gave so much promise of a new life to Egypt, and through Egypt to other Mohammedan countries, have been ruthlessly uprooted. No vestige of political liberty has been left, and in spite of every effort the English representative in Egypt has nothing better to recommend than an indefinite prolongation of our military occupation and our English tutelage. What England has accomplished in Egypt has been along the lines of Arabi's program, and to allow the originator of these reforms to die in exile, an English prisoner of war, would be a monstrous shame."

I am aware that the question whether Arabi Pasha is a patriot or a criminal is an unsettled one in the minds of many, but the trend of events in Egypt since he was banished, the intelligent discussion of the rise and fall of the national movement and the conduct of Arabi during his long exile have elicited for him and his cause much sympathy in Europe and America.

Of course, Lord Salisbury's administration is inflexibly against the return of the old man to his loved land, and I suppose that there is not a Tory in her Majesty's service who would dare to differ, publicly, with the premier on this or on any other question of state; but if many others are not greatly mistaken, the verdict of history will be given in favor of this man, who thought and fought for the independence of his country, and who tried to rid his land of rulers who had proved themselves utterly incapable to govern; who had pawned the produce of their country twice over to the money-grabbers of Paris, Amsterdam and London; who had taxed every acre of Egypt far beyond its value, and who had ground down to desperation the historic docility of that laborious and loyal people, in order that a small class and caste might revel in luxury.

Letter to Lady Blunt.

Arabi Pasha handed me a copy of a letter that he addressed to Lady Anne Blunt, of England, who had shown sympathy for the Egyptian patriot and his fellow-exiles. This pathetic appeal was written some years since:

"*To the Lady Blunt:* May God preserve you. Amen. We have forwarded to the Marquess of Salisbury the petition signed by me and by the rest of the exiles here with me. I sent it, with medical certificates, on the thirtieth of last month, by the same steamer which conveyed the late governor, Sir Arthur Gordon. Sir William Gregory, who is a friend of both parties, knows the substance of the petition, and will inform you of it when you see him. We have been now seven years and a half in Ceylon, while those very reforms which we wanted to make in Egypt are being carried out by the British government, and we confidently trust in the humanity of the English nation for our return to our country for the days that are left us of life, and to enjoy the benefits of such reforms as it has obtained. Surely now the people in England must understand that to seek such reforms was our duty—one both of patriotism and humanity. Peace be with you and with all who are your friends.

"[Signed]   AHMED ARABI, *the Egyptian.*"

"Colombo, June 15, 1890."

Although five years and a half have been added to this man's banishment since this letter was penned by him, and although earnest speeches have been made by the Earl De La Warr, Mr. Wilfrid Blunt and others, in and out of Parliament, in behalf of his release, he is still an English prisoner of war, thousands of miles from his home, and his patriotic heart will doubtless beat its last pulsation in his bungalow, near the jungles of Ceylon.

CHAPTER IX.

FIRST IMPRESSIONS OF INDIA.

 URING the latter part of my stay in Ceylon I enjoyed the privilege of visiting several of the educational institutions of Colombo, and through the kindness of Professor S. G. Lee, the principal of the City College, I addressed the faculty and students of this excellent foundation. Before meeting them in the large hall of the college the boys and young men were seen in the separate classes, and in some of these class-rooms there were as many as eight nationalities represented.

The curriculum corresponds somewhat to that found in our higher academies, and a certificate from this school enables the graduate without difficulty to enter Jaffna College, in Northern Ceylon, or one of the higher institutions of India. Several hundred pupils, from the palest to the darkest complexion, gathered in the hall, and my talk on "Self-Heroism" was punctuated by youthful exclamations and hurrahs that did not add to the fluency of the speaker.

Elephants on His Hands.

As a result of the visit he found next day that he had several elephants on his hands. Six packages of Ceylon curios were sent, including two heavy ebony elephants, "with the compliments of the City College of Colombo." As the steamer trunk had been shipped on to Bombay, with the expectation that a valise was to be his sole companion through the cities, jungles and mountains of India, what was the grateful recipient to do? His embarrassment was not lessened by the message that some of the faculty and students would be at the *Nubia* when she sailed to wish the American *bon voyage*, which information seemed to forbid the propriety of leaving behind some of his burdensome wealth.

Necessity is often the mother of invention, and a pleasant farewell has been waved to the kind-hearted friends, who were only guilty of being too kind.

The City of Madras.

On approaching India you are first greeted by the noble lighthouse at Madras, over a hundred feet in height, which can be seen for twenty miles over the restless waters of the Bay of Bengal. Situated on the open bay and exposed to the fury of the northeast monsoons, Madras was one of the most unprotected spots on the Coromandel coast until the stone breakwater was built, which is composed of a

STREET OF MADRAS.

conglomerate of small stones and cement in the form of large cubes, after the plan adopted by De Lesseps in the construction at Port Said, which forms the Mediterranean entrance of the Suez Canal.

It is interesting to notice the peculiar structure of the shore boats that are used by the natives of different lands. For miles from the coast of India, in the Bay of Bengal, the waters are alive with fishermen's boats that are different from any I have seen. They are built of three pieces of timber, ten or twelve feet long, tied securely together with cocoanut fibre, the centre one being longer than the others and curved upward at each end.

CATAMARAN FISHING BOATS, MADRAS.

As our steamer was obliged to anchor some distance off shore, a boat was used to take the passengers to the wharf, which is peculiar in construction. It is made of teak, a wood peculiar to India and excellent for ship-building; the thin planks are sewed together with hide thongs, caulked with cocoanut fibre; no nails are used, which could not take the place of the yielding thongs, and eight to ten rowers propel the boat with oars shaped like spoons, being strong elastic poles with flat rounded ends securely lashed to them by hide thongs.

You soon find yourself facing an esplanade, located between the two roots of the breakwaters and facing the harbor, which is an irregular terrace of large business premises, behind which is Blacktown, the native city, which is distinguished from Whitetown, the European quarter, surrounding the fort near the suburbs. Great shade trees add beauty to most of the streets where the foreign residences and shops are located, and the marine promenade, about two miles long, is crowded toward sunset with handsome equipages and well-dressed pedestrians.

In and around Madras there are many extensive lakes and tanks, some of which are very noted. At one of the suburbs called Triplicane there is an ancient

NATIVE PASSENGER CART, MADRAS.

and sacred tank, said by its Brahmans to be more holy than the Ganges, and one bath in its waters is equal to ten thousand dips in that river.

The city, with its half million of people, and covering an area of about thirty miles, is full of interest to the sight-seer.

Sight-Seeing.

The People's Park, with its eleven pretty lakes, its well-maintained menagerie and aviaries, and its miles of shady walks; the Robinson Park, where a large fernery is placed on an island reached by a graceful iron bridge of fifty feet span; the St. Thomas Mount, sacred to many as the spot where St. Thomas the Apostle is said to have been martyred in 68 A. D. by Brahmans, who stirred up the people against him; the old palace of the Nawabs of the Karnatic, now used as a government building, and the museum, containing a collection of natural history, among which is the great skeleton of a whale fifty feet long, found dead on the Mangalore shore, said to be the most perfect specimen in existence, and departments of botany, economics, mineralogy, geology and industrial arts that are well chosen and excellently kept up. All of these places can be visited in a single day, and with

GROUP OF TODDYMEN, MADRAS.

an intelligent guide you may be sure that your note-book will be crowded by night.

The proportion of Christians is higher in Madras than anywhere else in British India, and I learned that the Church of Scotland, the Wesleyans, the London Missionary Society, the Free Church of England, the Society for the Propagation of the Gospel, the German Lutherans, the Roman Catholics, the American Baptists and others are hard at work, and I can easily imagine how the poor native who wanted to become a Christian would be utterly at a loss to know which way to turn and through what door to pass.

There is in the city a large number of schools, among which the most important are the Madras Christian College of the Free Church of Scotland, with nearly two thousand pupils, one of the most famous educational institutions in India; the City Medical College, and the Presidency Government College, all of which prepare students for the Madras University.

As in every other place in this part of the world, the shops and bazaars of Madras form a prominent and important feature of the city life. The pierced and hammered silver work is exquisite in design and workmanship, and the work known as swami, decorated with figures of the Puranic gods in high relief—sometimes repousse, sometimes soldered on the surface—was strikingly unique.

The blackwood furniture, the carvings in sandal-wood and ivory, the models of Dravidian temples made of the pith of the sola, and the artistic coconada rugs, woven in out-of-the-way villages on the Coromandel coast by the Mussulman descendants of Persian settlers, tempt you to linger in the native shops, and you are apt to come forth from them with fewer rupees than when you entered.

In the native settlement, groups of dancing girls are frequently met. These are nearly always connected with the temple services, and, for a consideration, which is supposed to be appropriated by the priests, these young women give performances of their art. Their dances are supposed to represent stories of different character, and love, hatred, jealousy and

DEVIL DANCERS OF MADRAS.

passions of different kinds are set forth by the postures, contortions and facial expressions of these dancers, whose ankles are encircled by little silver bells, the music from which is supposed to be in harmony with the instrument that is furnishing the dance music.

When these girls are unengaged by the temples, they are frequently engaged by private citizens, and, as in the East, people seldom do their own dancing, these professional toe-tippers are brought in, and afford amusement during the evening for a few rupees. It may be according to the fitness of things that these people hire both their mourners and their dancers.

The Seven Pagodas.

Thirty miles south of Madras is located Mahabalipur (or the Seven Pagodas), which is one of the most interesting places in India to the archæologist, presenting a series of architectural wonders from the early Christian centuries down to recent times, their remoteness on a sea-washed island having contributed to their remarkable preservation. The cave temples, monolithic figures, carvings and sculpture, probably of the sixth century, and the more modern temples of Vishnu and Siva are of thrilling historic interest. The whole of one ridge is

DOUBLE BULLOCK RAIKLA, MADRAS.

pitted with caves and temples, and there is seen the recumbent figure of a man, which measures 1500 feet, with its hands in the attitude of prayer. Here we find, in architecture, sculptures, and in inscriptions a religious history of Southern India carved in the imperishable rock.

The Bay of Bengal.

From Madras to Calcutta, during the month of February, the Bay of Bengal is as placid as a sleeping lake. The cyclones, which seem most at home in these waters during the rest of the year, are unknown in this month, and from the

A THOROUGHFARE IN CALCUTTA.   1854

moment that our steamer lifted anchor within the breakwater at Madras until we passed through the mouth of the Hooghly River for Calcutta our voyage was the perfection of tranquillity, the unbroken sapphire of the bay being disturbed for

A MADRAS BELLE.

days only by the little flying fish making a chain of ripples on the sparkling mirror of the deep, or by a lazy, rolling whale, bent on proving that there was something alive in the sea, spouting his fountain into the serene air.

Evening after evening as we watch the sun sinking over the Coromandel coast, turning the smooth face of the waters into a floor of ruby and purple, we can understand why Homer speaks of it as "wine-colored," and when the queen of night takes the place of the king of day the picture in water colors changes, and, assisted by the lesser lights, this generous empress of the evening scatters her jewels broadcast over the laughing waters.

The author of "The Light of Asia" grows poetically eloquent in his ecstasy over this beautiful bay:

" For, even these days of subtler air and finer delight,
    When lovelier looks the darkness and diviner the light,
    The gift they give of all these golden hours whose urn
    Pours forth reverberate rays or shadowing showers in turn—
    Clouds, beams and winds that make the fair day's track seem living—
    What were they did no spirit give them back thanksgiving?"

CALCUTTA HARBOR.

Calcutta.

Calcutta (taking its name from the ancient shrine of the goddess Kali) is located about ninety miles from the mouth of the Hooghly River, and as the navigation of this stream is attended with many dangers, expert pilots, who are at the head of their profession and who draw large stipends, are employed to guide all steamers up and down the river.

The chief peril is known as "James and Mary" (from the name of a ship that was wrecked at this point some years ago), and the shoal thrown up by two tidal currents meeting the broad stream of the Ganges causes, at low water, a frightful "rip," which has often torn the steering-gear of a ship to pieces and flung her broadside on the sand. Even the best pilots do not dare to pass this place at night time, and must seek to cross it as nearly as possible at high water.

MADRAS COOLIE.

Nearer the mouth of the river is Saugor Island, where the Ganges runs to sea out of the great delta formed by her own flood and that of the Brahmapootra, and I am told that the forests of this lonely place abound with tigers of a large and ferocious kind. But, unhurt by tide or tiger, in due time we reach the political capital of India.

It has been a little over two hundred years since the East India Company first established its factory at Calcutta, and on the twenty-fourth of August, 1690, the English flag was hoisted by the noted Job Charnock. Twenty years afterward its population was only twelve thousand and now it is not very far from a million.

The Calcutta of our day is modern in all of its improvements, and the famous Black Hole, the Maratha Ditch and other historic spots that we associate with the names of Charnock, Hamilton, Clive and Warren Hastings have lost their identity and the ground that witnessed scenes that thrilled the world is covered by magnificent public buildings.

The Government House, a noble palace, situated in a park of six or seven acres, with a central building, contains handsome suites of reception and enter-

AVENUE OF PALMS, BOTANICAL GARDEN, CALCUTTA.

(189)

taining rooms, connected by galleries with four outlying blocks, in which are the private apartments of the viceroy and his household; the town hall, the legislative council chamber, the high court, the treasury and the currency office, located near together: the imperial museum, the zoological gardens, the horticultural gardens

HINDU SACRIFICE, KALI GHAT, CALCUTTA.

and the Fort William are all evidences of British influence, which has shaped the appearance as well as the government of Calcutta according to the notion of John Bull.

A Noted Antiquity.

The most noted antiquity in the city, perhaps, is the Kali Ghat, where Kali or "The Black One," who is supposed to be a furious goddess, hideous in features,

GREAT BANYAN TREE, CALCUTTA.

dripping with blood, with a necklace of human skulls, has held her shrine and greeted her worshipers for ages past. She is thought to send pestilence and famine, and, as she is only appeased by blood, during the fearful famine in 1866 human heads decked with flowers were found before her altar.

This is the only place of public worship for Hindus in Calcutta, and on religious festivals thousands of natives repair to the shrine of Kali, sacrifice goes on continually and ghats and tanks are crowded with bathers.

RIVER FRONT, CALCUTTA.

In this connection allow me to speak of the burning ghat on the banks of the Hooghly, where the Hindus cremate their dead.

Cremation of the Dead.

The pyre is laid in dry wood, mingled sometimes with sandal-wood for the sake of its fragrance. The corpse is placed at full length on the pile and covered over with more wood, the head and feet only being visible. Passages from the sacred books are read by the officiating priest. The eldest son or nearest relative,

BOTANICAL GARDENS, CALCUTTA.

having walked three times round the pyre, kindles it, and in two or three hours the body is reduced to ashes, which are cast into the river.

As we watched the smoke noiselessly ascending from several pyres, while the relatives of the dead solemnly and quietly, with bowed heads, stood near by, the thought occurred to us that this was a far more impressive funeral than many we had seen in a more civilized land, where false notions, based upon unacknowledged superstition, made such services most repulsive. But I turn to pleasanter scenes.

The Banyan Tree.

In my walks I visited a noble specimen of the banyan tree. It sends down aerial roots, striking into the ground and forming new trunks, and these again make fresh branches and rootlets until a colonnade of living pillars is formed, canopied with a roof of green.

The name of this tree is *aswattha*, and an old writing says that he who knows the *aswattha* knows human life, for the tree is an emblem of the life of man, who, growing to maturity in the air and sunlight of the sense-world, throws forth ever and ever new roots to bind himself more and more to the earth and its allurements.

These wonderful, outspreading banyan trees adorn many of the private grounds in and around Calcutta, and in its refreshing shade the family can be seen during the pleasant days gathered about the lunch table.

The botanical gardens, which are situated beyond the village of Seebpur, on the bank of the Ganges, contain, perhaps, the finest banyan tree in the world.

Nearly every American and English school child is familiar with the picture of this superb tree, and it is regarded the greatest glory of these famous gardens. Although it is only one hundred years old, its trunk is more than fifty feet in circumference, and over two hundred air roots have descended to the earth from its mighty limbs. Its outside measurement is more than eight hundred feet in circumference.

The Indian Museum.

Those who are interested in archæology will visit, with interest, the valuable contents of the Indian Imperial Museum, which was founded by the Asiatic Society, whose journals are the source from which almost every authority on Indian antiquities, philology, literature and natural history has come.

The archæological galleries contain a gateway and railing of the great Buddhist Stupa of Bharhut, which is nearly two thousand years old, and which is richly sculptured with representations of the various births of Buddha, giving pictures of the dress, tools, weapons, furniture, buildings and domestic life of the people who lived one and two hundred years before the Christian era.

On the opposite side of the river an imposing building is pointed out, which reminds the student of history of an act of injustice on the part of England, the

BATHING GHAT, CALCUTTA.

like of which has not been infrequent in her foreign policy. This structure was the palace of King Oude, who was dethroned while he was the ruler of one of the richest provinces of India, and under some specious pretence his private property was seized, including his valuable jewels, and sold to enrich the treasure of the Queen of England. Even the British press acknowledged at the time that the English had no more right to that private property and to those precious stones than they had to the crown diamonds of Russia.

If might makes right then our Anglo-Saxon cousins have had a supremely righteous career. It was with peculiar interest that I visited Serampur, a few miles from Calcutta, and looked upon the places made immortal by the heroic efforts of Carey, Marshman and Ward, those pioneers of missionary enterprise in India.

CHAPTER X.

IN THE HIMALAYAS.

 FTER spending some days sight-seeing about Calcutta, and after witnessing a fine display of the Indian tactics at a brilliant military tournament, it was with pleasure that we boarded a coach on the East Bengal Railway, and, crossing the Ganges at Damookdea, resumed our journey by the North Bengal State Railway until we reached Siliguri, where the Himalayan Railway was taken, which has a gauge of only two feet, and which is the most wonderful piece of engineering in the world, not excepting the railway up the Pilatus, near Luzerne, Switzerland, or the one running up Mount Washington, in New Hampshire. The locomotives are sturdy little engines weighing ten tons. Each open carriage holds six in comfortable arm chairs, and the railway is a light tram, the rail weighing about forty pounds a yard. The four-wheeled bogies wind in and out along the hillsides, running at times excitingly near the edge of tremendous gorges and precipices, assuming the shape of the letter S for two-thirds of the journey. At one place the train crosses a bridge, which a moment afterward it runs under, and rising again the line makes a complete figure eight.

Scenery and Vegetation.

On this toy railway you are now passing through dense primeval forests, now you look out upon dark green tea gardens, that spread for miles along the slopes of the mountains. A moment afterward you are looking thousands of feet below you upon the vast fertile plain of Bengal, the meandering rivers rolling through it, flashing like molten silver in the sunlight, and further on, as the train commences to make the steeper ascent, you are carried through jungles of cane fifty or sixty feet high, grasses that shoot their blades fifteen feet and seed-stalks twenty-five feet from the ground, with great feathery tops.

As the ascent is made it is interesting to notice how the vegetation changes. For the first three thousand feet oaks, banyans, mimosas, acacias, fig, india-rubber and the giant bamboo, sixty feet high, with stalks as thick as a man's thigh, are seen in every bend of the serpentine road. About four thousand feet above the plain the spreading chestnut and the blooming almond and mango trees come in sight, and now you come into a wilderness of graceful Himalayan tree ferns from fifteen to twenty-five feet high.

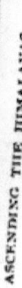

ASCENDING THE HIMALAYAS.

(198)

The Mountaineers.

The attention is now divided between the natural scenery, which is becoming transcendently grand, and the new types of people that gaze from the doors of their dirt shanties or lie about smoking iron pots hanging over the fire on tripods, quite in gipsy style, partaking of their midday meal. By the dress, physiognomy and figure three nationalities could be easily distinguished—the people from Thibet, Nepal and Cashmere—which countries are separated from this part of Northern India by the Himalayan mountains.

The men were all armed with long sword-like knives, carried in their belts which support their single garments. The women, with their brilliant costume and more brilliant ear, nose and toe rings, are more attractive-looking than their southern sisters, and the children wear no artificial adornment except rings about their ears, noses and ankles.

The wild country through which we passed abounds in ferocious animals, and our talkative conductor has just given us a description of a great Bengal tiger that was seen lying near the railroad track, and as the train approached him he leisurely arose, quietly gave a parting glance at the noisy engine and disappeared in the thick jungles.

A LEPCHA MAN.

Approaching Darjeeling.

When the ascension is very steep and the curves are sharp we can see from our coach, near the rear, two natives sitting on the cow-catcher sprinkling sand on the rails to prevent the busy little wheels from slipping, and while passing over the many horseshoe turns about the cliffs we frequently find ourselves exactly opposite the scarlet-turbaned man at the throttle of the engine.

We wind in and out, around and about, up and down, and as our snake-twisting train passes the white board that marks seven thousand feet above the sea level, the puffing little machine at the front, which has fought bravely and can claim a noble victory, sends forth a shout of triumph. Sweeping around a sudden

DARJEELING RAILWAY.

turn, we see the hundreds of white houses of Darjeeling perched upon the sides of the Himalayas as if they had been dumped from the floating sheets of clouds above, and, lifted far over tier after tier of moving sky vapors, which hide from view over twenty thousand feet of the range, the sunlit, snow-crowned Kinchinjunga stands forth like the pearl-white palace of the king of kings in the heaven of heavens. Words seem quite inadequate to describe the stupendous magnificence of the view as we entered Darjeeling, which signifies "up in the clouds."

The "Halls of Snow."

It is located at the end of a long wooded spur of Sinchul, a mountain about nine thousand feet high, and from the peak near my hotel the eye sweeps over a perfect amphitheatre, resting in turn upon the snow summits of Janu, twenty-five thousand and three hundred feet above Calcutta; Kabur, twenty-four thousand; Pandim, twenty-two thousand; Chomiamo, twenty-four thousand and six hundred, and then a succession of unnamed mountains, which lead on to Donkhia, twenty-six thousand, and towering above all of them, whose irregular snow roofs can alone be seen, is the Kinchinjunga, which is more than twenty-eight thousand feet in height.

In the valleys of these mountains, which stretch in a chain of over two hundred miles in extent, are unbroken successions of snow fields and glaciers, and in the centre

A LEPCHA WOMAN.

of the whole range rises the hoary monarch just spoken of, whose dazzling crown is lifted more than five miles over the plain of Bengal.

In the early morning I was disappointed to find Kinchinjunga buried under a thick mass of cloud, but my disappointment lasted only for a short time. As the rising sun gathered strength, arrows of light pierced the vapory nightrobe of the sleeping giant: a glow of glory rested upon the snows, changing into mingled gold, ruby and purple, and as the king of day kissed the white-turbaned peaks good morning a bright smile spread from summit to summit, and, leaping down the stairway of snow, the early morning light spread a veil of gold upon the dewy lap of the valleys.

THE CITY IN THE CLOUDS, DARJEELING, INDIA.

Mount Everest.

To see Mount Everest, the highest mountain in the world, is the supreme desire of every one who visits Darjeeling, and in order to have this pleasure one must take an early morning ride to Tiger Hill, a distance of eight miles, and frequently after taking the ride the desired object is not attained.

Accompanied by two gentlemen and one lady I took the trip about daybreak, and we all agreed that this delightful ride up the Himalayas (which means, in Sanskrit, " Halls of Snow ") amply repaid us for the inconvenience of rising so early on a cold morning, although we might not see the king of mountains.

A RUSTIC SCENE IN INDIA—BUFFALO PLOWING

Our path, at times, led about the mountain ranges, with only a few feet between the perpendicular granite walls and the gorges of thousands of feet in depth; but our sure-footed little ponies, with the exception of one slight accident did their work well, and in due time we were standing on Tiger Hill, two thousand feet above Darjeeling. A deep mist enveloped us, and after straining our eyes in vain to get a glimpse of the part of our globe that reaches nearest to the skies we were about to descend, when our lady companion, whose intuitions are worthy of her superior sex, insisted upon a delay, declaring that there would be a break in the misty clouds, and we would be rewarded shortly. Of course she was right, and of course we were wise in following the lady's advice.

Far out and up in the direction where our guide said Mount Everest was located a brightness appeared, then a patch of blue, and as speechlessly we watched

DARJEELING BAZAAR TYPES.

for the appearance the pure dome of Mount Everest, 29,000 feet above the sea, stood against the deep blue sky, unsupported, apparently, by any base; and a moment afterward it was wrapped again in the clouds. The picture is as impossible to forget as it is impossible to paint.

Himalayan Tea.

Accepting the invitation of an English gentleman, I visited his tea plantation and factory, and from his gardens, covering about two hundred acres, I was informed he ships over fifty thousand pounds of tea leaves every year. This tea, in the Himalayas, has a distinct flavor of its own, and with the exception of that tasted in Ceylon, I have found none so delicious as this.

The peoples that are found in these mountains are of peculiar interest. The Lepchas, of the Sikkim race, who have no religious rites; the Limboos, whose out-door temples are seen on the hill-tops; the Moormis, of large stature and originally from Thibet; the Nepaulese and Cashmere people, with short, stout frames, and the long-haired, unnamed men of the hills, present types and habits of mankind that cannot but elicit attention and interest.

A Native Bazaar.

The native bazaar here in Darjeeling is one of the sights of the place, and at noon the noise of the peddlers and more important tradesmen can be heard for squares away.

The old saying that " it takes two to make a bargain " does not apply here, for before a trade is closed scores of merry women and children gather about you, shouting, pushing and gesticulating like so many lunatics.

The open market-place is crowded with traders, many of whom have come from Thibet, Cashmere and further distances, and heterogeneous assortments of goods, consisting of brass Buddhas, ironmongery, pottery, skins, flashing jewelry, coins, curios of every description, besides tamed snakes, birds and monkeys, are offered for remarkably low prices. To stand on an eminence overlooking this bazaar, and watch the brilliantly colored costumes and excited manners of the people as they mingle in a great labyrinth of noisy confusion, is a wonderfully interesting study.

The most attractive person in all the throng is the Bhutia woman, with a great circlet round her head formed of large beads of coral and turquoise, four necklaces of amber, agate, coral and moonstones; enormous ear-rings, pulling down the lobes of the ears, and a massive silver girdle about her loosely worn garment, with hanging ornaments like a chatelaine. After all, is not the most charming creature in every land a – woman ?

On an Indian Railway.

A sleeping-car on an oriental railway is death to aristocratic airs. The early morning (the tourist joyfully rises with the sun) finds his meekness only exceeded by his shabbiness, and during the long, long night how often does he wish that he

THE DARJEELING BAZAAR.

was sleeping amidst the jungles through which he is passing, instead of tossing up and down, round and round, over and over, in this wabbling, rattling, snorting, creaking thing that is carrying him ten or fifteen miles an hour.

I am sure that the Indian sleeping-car possesses a patent of its own, and that it has never been duplicated is a blessing to that part of humanity that does not enjoy the nightmare while taking nocturnal trips through this country.

The car itself is a wonder in inconvenient workmanship. When it remains still long enough to be measured, you find that it measures about ten by six feet, contains four indescribable affairs called beds—two stationary and two hanging in a threatening manner from above by leather-covered ropes; is lit by a single flickering light that is too dim to read by and too bright to sleep by, and is entered by the tourist through a side door, which is often too narrow for the bundle of bedclothes that the railroad kindly allows him to furnish.

In an Indian Sleeping Car,

Having as my companion during the first night out on my way to the mountains of India a bright, congenial fellow from the "City of Brotherly Love," the trip was crowded with incidents, some of which were very laughable several days after they happened.

Far in the dark night it turned suddenly very chilly, and we were aroused to find everything in a stiff gale, and fearing that the monkeys in the jungles would have the joy of appearing next day in some of our garments, we arose to seize them in the midst of their wild career as they danced in the whirlwind, and to our surprise we found that our door was swinging wide open, and from the mountains the cold air was sweeping through the car from door to window and window to door.

These sleeping-cars encourage domestic economy, in that they require you to carry about with you all the bedclothing that you use, and make up your own bed when you desire to use it! As my good-natured friend possessed a passion for such art, and as it is my creed that every one should be encouraged in developing his talent in any given direction, I allowed him to practice on my bed; but when the time came to blow up my newly patented air-pillow, then came the tug-of-war! We blew into that perversely empty pillow by turns until our heads grew dizzy and we seemed to be blowing our brains out; but as we held it up after every windstorm, it resembled in diameter a pancake rather than a pillow.

At last, my companion, thinking, perhaps, that it was not worth while to put on airs while trying to put in air, assumed an attitude of strength rather than of grace, and turning himself into a veritable bellows, inflated the pillow to an enormous size and uncomfortable tightness, which he now handed to me with an air of triumph.

Crossing the Mountains.

In the morning we expected a scene of desolation to greet us, as we would be in the mountains, but, as we looked through the windows, everything was green. Not only the trees and grass, but our eyes could not rest upon anything that was not green—green birds, green cows, green pigs, green goats, green ducks, green skies, and, stranger still (a sight which we look for in vain in our country), green men and women!

What kind of country is this, anyhow? In mute wonder we gazed upon the green panorama, fearing to speak lest we exposed our greenness.

In a few moments the window pane was dropped, and the verdant delusion came to an end. The windows were of green-colored glass, and the greenness, alas, was not outside, but inside of the car!

Deliberateness to a painful degree is the dominant characteristic of these trains, especially in Northern India.

While riding horseback with a party near Darjeeling, the cars were seen approaching us, and the steed of one of the young men became unmanageable, and succeeded in getting away from the rider, who had dismounted. The engineer stopped his train and the brakeman caught the horse, which had run some distance away!

Slow Progress.

While on a railroad near the boundary line of India and Assam, the conductor was asked why there were not more collisions, as there was only a single track. "The reason is very simple," he replied; "we have only one engine."

To pass away the time during a tedious delay of the train in the wilds of Assam, my friend from Philadelphia and I tossed small coins in the grass, and the violent scramble that followed on the part of the natives was a remarkable sight. I counted sixty-seven grown men struggling in a heap over a coin valued at about one-half of our cent.

When the amusement became a little monotonous, I exclaimed, "Is it not time for us to be going, or what causes the long delay?" A gentleman near me said, "Yonder is the engineer scrambling with those other men for the coin just thrown out," and sure enough, there he was, with his firemen, in the midst of the melee.

In order to test the speed of these fast-running Assamese, I placed a man with a few coins in his hand about two hundred yards from a group of fifty or sixty men, and told them that the first who reached the holder of the money could have it. At the drop of the handkerchief they all started, but what was my surprise when I saw the man to whom had been given the coins to hold, just before the swiftest runner reached him, turn about and run off with the bag.

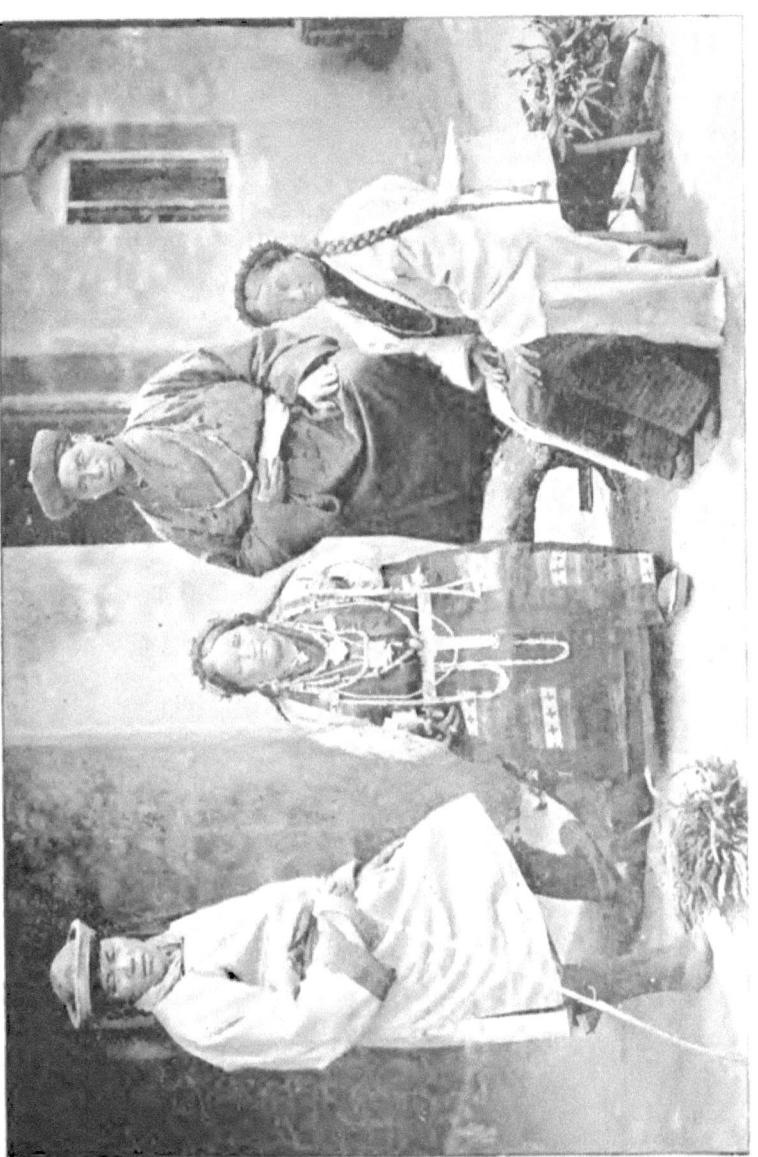

GROUP OF BHOTEAS, DARJEELING.

(219)

On a Sacred River.

Our trip up the sacred Brahmapootra ("Son of Brahma") River on our way into Assam was most delightful in every respect. It is impossible to bridge this river, as it changes its course so often, and the most expert native pilots are employed to guide the steamers through the treacherous channels.

Wild animals of nearly every description abound in the thick jungles on either side of the stream, and alligators, storks, cranes and quantities of many-colored birds are seen as we near Dhubri.

One of the most noted rajahs in the country has his magnificent palace in this neighborhood, and as he keeps 150 elephants solely for hunting purposes, he is very popular with English huntsmen. A hunting party is being formed this week, and one of the sportsmen told me that if they were as successful as when they last went out, a number of tiger skins would be carried home by the party.

DANDY, DARJEELING, INDIA.

In a Dak Bungalow.

My nights in Assam are spent in what is known as a dak bungalow, which is built and owned by the government, and as these bungalows are located in places out of the usual route of travel, they are great conveniencestogovernment officials who must traverse the land from one end to the other, and to tourists who desire to get a glimpse of the places and peoples untouched by civilization.

These one-floor buildings are in charge of natives, who present to each guest a book, in which he enters the time of arrival and departure, and on the opposite place is a blank space for "remarks."

The column of "remarks" shows the varied characters of the persons who have rested under the low roof of this forest hotel. A certain Delia Symonds, shocked at the frivolity of the dak bungalow library, which consisted of a few broken-backed novels and a pile of dry magazines and weekly papers, delivered herself, too many novels for the good morals of the public." This could not be left unnoticed.

The next person who made his remarks was evidently of a different frame of mind from Miss Delia, and his entry proves that he was much more of a wag than a poet:

" If fair Delia here would stay
   Our faulty morals to better,
I'm sure we all should say
   That we'd gladly be her debtor.
Bad books no more we'd peruse,
   Enchained by her charms so entrancing,
The bad boy, poor chap, he would lose,
   While we to glory should be dancing.'

A new deputy commissioner writes under this: " Travelers are reminded that the remark column is not designed with the view of affording them an opportunity of firing off brilliant flashes of wit or recording mawkish expressions of cant."

Fearing that I might break one or the other of these governmental prohibitions, I refrained from making a " remark."

In these parts it is impossible from the clocks in use to tell the time of day or night unless you perform mental gymnastics equal to working a problem in calculus. I was awakened last night by the unearthly sound of a clock striking twenty-seven, and next morning when I asked for an explanation and expressed a desire to know how I could tell the time by this erratic timepiece, the solution given me called to mind a certain clock that served a purpose, if you remembered that when the long hand was at quarter after twelve and the short hand half-past eight it was going on to ten o'clock.

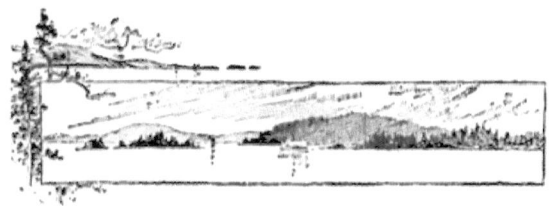

CART FOR THE HIGH CASTE, INDIA.

CHAPTER XI.

BENARES ON THE GANGES.

 HESE words are written in a city that is supposed by many historians to be the oldest known habitation of man on earth. Five and twenty centuries ago, when Rome was not yet on the records of the world, and when Athens was in its infant splendor, Benares, on the noble Ganges, exerted a mighty power and her fame was established among men. Here the great Buddha proclaimed his doctrines first, sending forth missionaries from this centre to Ceylon, China, Japan, Burmah and Thibet, bringing, in time, nearly half the race of man under the influence of his teachings. But centuries afterward, during a powerful religious and political upheaval, Buddhism succumbed to Brahmanism, leaving behind only the ruins of its topes and temples. And to-day, what Mecca is to the Mohammedan, Jerusalem to the Christian, Benares is to the Hindu.

The city is located along the crest of a hill over one hundred feet above the sacred Ganges. For three miles on the sloping west bank, palaces, temples and mosques, surmounted by domes, pinnacles and minarets, rear their irregular tops. Giant flights of stone stairs, interrupted by wide platforms, on which are built shrines of every description, reach to the water, and on the edges of the bank are bathing ghats, which are crowded with pilgrims from every part of India and from other countries, in every stage of dress and undress, whose supreme desire is to plunge into these holy waters before death overtakes them.

Hindu Pilgrims.

These pilgrims are not all from the lower or middle classes, but include every rank of Indian society, from the elaborately dressed rajahs, followed by long retinues of attendants, to the unsightly looking ashes-covered fakir and the miserable deformed beggar, and from the little boys and girls to the aged grandfathers, lifted by bearers to the stream, all bent upon dipping in the mother Ganges for the remission of their sins.

The private boat of a rich rajah was anchored at one of the ghats, and a covered canopy, which extended to the bank, hid him and his wife from view as they went through their religious ablutions.

I noticed that many of the women and girls carried wreaths of white and yellow flowers into the river, and as they most devoutly turned their faces toward the rising sun and inaudibly whispered their prayers, the garlands were broken in pieces and scattered upon the river.

Hundreds of these devotees were seen with brass jars and other vessels, in which they carry away to their distant homes some of the holy water, and employes of the temples, from Central and Southern India, were there with their leather water-bags, which were to be filled and borne on the backs of the pedestrians for scores and scores of miles to their houses of worship.

The thoughtful man, it matters not what may be his religious predilections, has no disposition to sneer at these worshipers, who freely and quietly give their time and money to what they sincerely believe to be true; which fact presents a striking contrast to the loud professions and selfish, covetous lives of not a few church-goers in Christian lands.

Along the river bank there are not less than fifty of these ghats, which have for their background magnificent flights of steps leading up to imposing castles and palaces, great white mosques and soaring minarets.

The Pauchganga ghat, where five rivers are supposed to meet underground, leads to the noble mosque which the iconoclast, Aurangzeb, built on the site of the noted Krishna temple which he destroyed.

This is the finest mosque in Benares, the foundations of which rise from the bed of the river in huge stone breastworks, which support the four walls and domes of the mosque, and springing lightly in the air are two graceful minarets, lifting the whole structure three hundred feet above the swarm of bathers at the water's edge.

In sailing up the river I passed the ghat where Vishnu dug his famous well, where Brahma made his celebrated sacrifice of ten horses, the Golden Temple, and many other spots that have made the city known the world over.

The Burning Ghat.

In the midst of these places of worship is located the Burning Ghat, where bodies are brought from all over India to be bathed in the Ganges, and then cremated on its banks.

Smoke from four pyres was seen as we approached the ghat, and several corpses, wrapped in white cloth, and lashed between two stout sticks, were being washed in the sacred stream, while the relatives of the dead were preparing the wood, near by, for the cremation.

Bedecked with flowers, and sometimes wearing jewelry, the bodies are lain between layers of wood, the ashes are cast into the water, and we saw a number of men at work who make a regular business of searching the shore and filtering the water through baskets in search of jewels or money that perchance might have dropped from the dead.

BURNING GOAT, BENARES.

What a comment on humanity—the religious devotee, the fakir, the beggar, the mourner, the stiff corpse and the money-grabber (who is always and everywhere on hand), mingled together in the holy city on the sacred river.

A Monkey Temple.

One of the most curious places visited was the Durga, or Monkey Temple. Durga is thought to delight in all kinds of bloodshed and destruction, and while I watched the worshipers, a man approached the blood-bedabbled altar in front of the shrine, and, having placed a number of coins in the hands of the officiating priest, was given the privilege of having a little kid that he held under his arm beheaded, and after the sharp blade had descended, he made an offering of the head and carried the body away to his home.

A MOUNTAIN MUSICIAN, INDIA.

In the yards and trees about the temple are hosts of monkeys, who spring into your pathway, peer round the walls, snatch at your clothes and make the most comical grimaces at you on the least provocation, but it is a crime to molest them, for they are gods and goddesses, held in the highest veneration.

I could hardly suppress an irreligious laugh as I watched one of these goddesses, holding a baby god under her left arm, while she held a nut in her right hand, on which she was nibbling in the most human fashion, and during the performance she was making the most unholy faces at me because of my inferiority.

What the monkey is to Vishnu the cow and bull are to Siva. To slaughter these animals is a horrible crime, and in every part of India can be found temples dedicated to their honor, where they are kept with the greatest care.

The "Holy Man."

One of the curiosities of humanity is the "holy man of Benares," whom I visited last evening. His long-continued acts of penance have worn his body to

BUDDHIST FESTIVAL.

skin and bones. He is thought by many to be above all passion and sin; he declines to receive anything from visitors, and his bright eyes, sweet expression

HOLY MAN.

and soft voice seem to indicate that he possesses a serenity in life that is enjoyed by few. On leaving him he presented me with a book containing his favorite studies. As I have not yet finished pronouncing the author's name on the first page, I am not prepared to pass an opinion on the merits of the work. It is written by Matparamahansaparinrajakacharyaswamibhaskaranandasaraswati! I am doubtful whether penance or pronunciation caused the thinness of the "holy man of Benares," for after my frantic efforts to pronounce the name of this distinguished author I feel that I weigh less! Perhaps the celebrated anti-fat preparation is an extract from this tiresome name, whose owner died of exhaustion, and whose owner's disciple is growing thinner and thinner every day.

In the Bazaars.

To those who enjoy examining curios and artistic manufactures the bazaars of Benares will prove to be especially attractive. The city is famous for its beautifully engraved brasswork. and trays, water vessels, bowls, lotus dishes, candle-sticks,

PALACE, AGRA, INDIA.

(219)

lamps, fancy boxes, bells, spoons and scores of other utensils, engraved most exquisitely, can be purchased for remarkably cheap prices.

Rich brocades wrought with figures of animals in gold and variegated colors, the oldest survival of ancient loomwork extant and the finest of its kind in the world, are found in the tiny shops in the bazaars, and this beautiful work is done by experts who receive about three or four dollars a week.

When a piece is finished it is "worth its weight in gold," but the poor fellow whose genius created the masterpiece lives and dies in poverty, while some merchant in Europe or America gets the "weight in gold."

Some of these brilliantly figured brocades bring to mind the description of Ulysses' dress, as given in the nineteenth book of the Odyssey:

> "In ample mode
> A robe of military purple flowed
> O'er all his frame, illustrious on his breast
> The double-clasping gold the king confest.
> In the rich woof a hound, mosaic drawn,
> Bore on full stretch and seized a dappled fawn;
> Deep in his neck his fangs indent their hold,
> They pant and struggle in the moving gold.
> Fine as a filmy web beneath it shone
> A vest that dazzled like a cloudless sun."

An Elegy in Marble.

In nearing Agra and Delhi we were soon to look upon the most superb monument ever reared to woman and the most magnificent palace in the world. From every elevated point of view in and around Agra, this city of castles and palaces, can be seen the shining domes and minarets of the Taj Mahal, the most beautiful tomb and one of the most renowned buildings in the world. It was erected during the first half of the seventeenth century by Shah Jehan for the body of his wife, Arjamand Banu, and history tells us that it required twenty thousand workmen to labor twenty-two years and necessitated an expenditure of four million pounds sterling before it was completed. It was the ambition of the great Mogul Emperor to erect the most superb monument ever reared to commemorate a woman's name, and the verdict of the ages is not only that his purpose was fulfilled, but that in this effort to translate his loyal and royal love into marble, Mohammedan architecture reached its climax and the world was enriched by the most perfect poem in stone.

Passing over a road amidst the ruins of many ancient palaces, you stand before a gateway of red sandstone, inlaid with floral designs and passages from the Koran in white marble. Through this splendid entrance, which is 140 feet high and 110 feet wide, you enter a garden filled with palms, peepuls, thuja and

TAJ MAHAL, AGRA, INDIA.

pomegranate, in the centre of which is a long tank of pure marble, reaching away for three or four hundred feet, containing a score of fountains, and the lovely vista closes at the base of the snow-white platform on which the Taj rests.

Arjamand's Mausoleum.

The building itself, 186 feet square and 220 feet high to the top of the dome, is raised upon a plinth 313 feet square, 18 feet above the level of the garden. At each corner of this platform stand four tapering minarets 137 feet high, and at each side of the Taj, 400 feet back across a great court flagged with marble, are imposing mosques of red stone, richly decorated with mosaics of marble, topped with three white domes, which are among the finest in India.

The milk-whiteness of this great mass of marble is broken only by the carving and inlaid flowers done in precious stones, combined in wreaths, scrolls and frets, which greet the eye as you enter through the wonderful door.

The inner walls of this burial place of the loved Arjamand are found to be as much a marvel of subtle shadow and chastened light, decked with exquisite jewelry, as the exterior is noble and sublime, and, as you study panel by panel, column by column, trellis-work after trellis-work, inlaid most gracefully and elaborately in jasper, coral, bloodstone, nacre, onyx, turquoise, sardonyx and the most precious gems, you are willing to agree that the Moguls designed like giants and finished like jewelers.

Memory of Undying Love.

Beneath the glorious dome, in the centre of the edifice, are two sarcophagi covering the spots in the vault below where the ashes of the one for whom the tomb was built and the builder of the tomb rest. At the threshold are inscribed the words: "To the memory of an undying love," and the Emperor has immortalized, if he could not preserve alive for one brief day, the one whom he named "Exalted one of the palace."

My first view of the Taj was when its pure dome was dazzling under the bright sunshine of midday, and I was sure that nothing could exceed its splendor and brilliancy. My next view was more enchanting, and the impression made upon my mind by this ghostly hall of death is fadeless.

The silver moon, set in a cloudless sky, cast a soft glow over the scene as I passed into the garden scented by roses and jasmine; the quiet shrubs and trees were reflected in lakes of clearest water, and as I quietly sat on the extreme end of the snowy platform overlooking the sacred Jumna and studied this masterpiece of love, my admiration and astonishment gave birth to the overpowering thought that seldom, if ever, in human history has man's affections struggled so ardently,

TAJ MAHAL, AGRA, INDIA.

passionately and triumphantly against the oblivion of death as in this mass of marble that is unmarked by the relentless tooth of time.

The marble of the structure came from Rajpootana, the diamonds and jasper from Punjab, the carnelians and agates from Thibet, the corals from Arabia, the sapphires and other precious stones from Ceylon, and the genius that turned this stone into "frozen music" was the gift of Heaven to Austin, of Bordeaux, who, driven by a strange fate from his European home, was employed by Shah Jehan in the erection of more than one architectural monument by which his name, as the "greatest of builders," has passed down the ages.

Reign of the Moguls.

Here in Agra, as in many other places in India, have I tried to study the stupendous ruins that mark the places where the great Mogul dynasty, under its different famous rulers, held absolute sway over millions of souls, and by this *debris* of the ages can you trace its history from its crowning period, in the time of Babar the Lion, down to the siege of Delhi.

The Mogul Humayun, whose brilliant court was known the world over, was succeeded by his son Akbar the Great, who did more than any other to establish the imperial system, during whose reign several magnificent palaces and strong forts were built, and who caused the gates of Chittor to be set up at Agra.

His son, Jehangir, did not greatly distinguish himself, but his grandson, Shah Jehan, who was proclaimed Emperor at Agra in 1628, gave a new impetus to architectural works, and during his reign the Pearl Mosque, the Great Mosque and the famous Khas Mahal were built, and the erection of the Taj and other tombs by him associate his name with some of the most remarkable and unique structures in the land.

Palace at Delhi.

The imperial palace, erected by this prince of builders at Delhi, is regarded by many as the most splendid palace in the world. The area within the massive and lofty red sandstone walls is more than a thousand yards long by five hundred yards wide, and is entered by a gate which is one hundred and forty feet high, its interior being a vaulted hall three hundred and seventy-five feet long, resembling very much a gigantic gothic cathedral.

Within the inclosure the first building you reach is the Diwan-i-am or public hall or audience, a beautiful colonnaded structure of red sandstone and inlaid marble. In the centre of the back wall is the royal throne and canopy of white marble, decorated with bits of precious stones representing flowers, fruits and birds.

The Dewan-i-Khas, or private hall of audience, is a building of white marble, ornamented without and within by inlaid work, and the ceiling is decorated richly with gold. In the centre of this hall stands a pure marble dais, on which rested

TAJ MAHAL AND JUMNA RIVER, INDIA.

the noted peacock throne, a seat between two peacocks, whose spread tails were decked with sapphires, diamonds, rubies, emeralds and other stones in imitation of the natural colors, and perched above all was a parrot, said to have been carved from a single emerald. It seems in design, proportions and decorations to be perfect, and one can easily appreciate the feeling that prompted the Persian inscription that is written over the north and south arches of the hall: "If there be a Paradise on earth, it is this, it is this, it is this."

The Jama Musjid.

Not far away rises the great dome of the Jama Musjid, which is without rival among mosques. Six years Shah Jehan was engaged in building it. There are three stately gates, approached by great flights of steps; the courtyard is 450 feet square, paved with granite, inlaid with marble; the mosque is 260 feet long and 120 feet wide, and the building is crowned by three domes of snow-white marble, with two lofty minarets of marble and sandstone in alternate stripes.

The floor is paved with slabs of white marble, with a border of black; each slab is three feet long by one and a half broad, and forms "a pew" for one person on Friday, when devout Mohammedans throng the place.

Delhi's Ruins and Monkeys.

For centuries Delhi was the proudest capital of the Mogul empire, and I spent a week visiting and studying the ruins of seven distinct ancient cities within a circle of twenty miles about the present city, each of which was, in its time, a place of oriental splendor, but all that can be found of them now are broken streets, crumbling forts, decaying pillars, leaning towers and tottering walls of grand old castles and palaces, and where the mighty Moguls reigned in glory the jackals and wolves awake the echoes, by night, with their hideous cries.

The monkey seems to be the present Mogul of Delhi. Hundreds of these comical creatures are seen on the pavements, fences, trees and housetops of the city, and although they are up to all kinds of pranks, you dare not injure one of them unless you are willing to pay a fine of fifty rupees in court.

A school teacher told me that she rented a large building for her classes for a very small amount of money because the monkeys were so troublesome in the neighborhood. Several times they entered the building most unceremoniously, scuffling and fighting as they dashed through the door or windows, and, of course, during the edifying performances her classes suspended operations. A child asked her, one day, whether she would be excused while she went on the roof for her shoe. A monkey had quietly slipped into the room, snatched up the child's shoe, which had been left near the door, and there it was on the flat roof trying to make an external application of the pupil's understanding!

ENTRANCE TO PALACE, DELHI, INDIA.

A veteran missionary told me that a workman of his acquaintance placed his lunch, wrapped up in a cloth, on the limb of a tree, while he was working near by. A monkey carried the bundle to the top of the tree, sedately unrolled it, ate the contents and politely took the cloth back and hung it in its proper place. The next day the workman placed a snake in the cloth; his monkeyship repeated his theft, but when the snake sprang out, after blinking his eyes for an instant to help him take in the situation, the monkey rubbed the snake's head off against the limb, threw the limp thing at the man, and hung the lunch cloth on the highest twig of the tree. Doubtless you will think I commenced with the sublime and closed with the ridiculous.

An Indian Wolf-Man.

While in Japan a friend, who spent several years in India, spoke to me of the wolf-boy who was caught some years ago in one of the northwest provinces of the country, and urged me on my arrival in Agra to call at the Secundra Orphanage, near the city, and see this human curiosity. As this strange creature has never, as far as I am aware, been mentioned by tourists, and as I have secured reliable information about him from Dr. C. S. Valentine, principal of the Agra Medical Missionary Training Institute, I desire to give these fact to my readers.

In the Spring of 1867 a number of natives in search of game in the unfrequented jungles of Bulandshahr, situated in Northwestern India, surprised a stray wolf, which they followed to a hillock, out of which rose a rock, and on this rock, apparently sunning itself, sat a dark, curious-looking object which, to their great astonishment, turned out to be a human being, who, on seeing the hunters, sprang from the rock, and, running on all fours, entered a cave with the pursued wolf.

The frightened natives returned immediately to Bulandshahr, and, having related what they saw to the magistrate of the place, they were advised to kindle a fire at the mouth of the cave and smoke the thing from its den. This was done. The strange creature rushed out, and after a struggle, during which several of the natives were bitten, it was overpowered and captured.

The Wolf-Boy.

Here, in the wild jungles, running on all-fours, covered with filth and vermin, his face partially hidden by long, matted hair, and having no companion but the wolf, was a boy, who at the time when he was found could not have been more than seven or eight years of age. As one listens to Dr. Valentine telling the story he is tempted to believe in the ancient fable of Romulus and Remus.

A few weeks after he was caught the wolf-boy was sent by the magistrate to the Secundra Orphanage, and as he entered the institution on Saturday he was

THE KUTUB MINAR, DELHI.

named Sanichar. For a long time after he came to the orphanage it was impossible to get him to act as a human being. He persisted in eating his food from the ground, picking up vegetables with his lips and gnawing flesh from bones with his teeth, like a carniverous animal, and the clothes with which he was supplied he tore into shreds and cast them away as encumbrances. By degrees he grew more docile, and, although he has never spoken a word, he gradually conformed somewhat to his surroundings, but he insists upon eating with his fingers.

It is thought that he is now about thirty-six or thirty-seven years old, although he looks much older.

His Appearance and Training.

His head is small, his brow uncommonly low and contracted, while his eyes are of a grayish color, restless and squinting. He has a small, thin, wrinkled face, on which are two large cicatrices, marks, doubtless, of severe bites that were received by him. On other parts of his body are found scars and other signs of rough treatment to which he was subjected no doubt while living in the cave with his wild companions. When he stands erect he is five feet and two inches in height ; in walking he lifts his feet as if he were wading through wet grass, and when he moves along all the muscles of his body seem to be undergoing a series of jerks, while his arms are thrown about in such a manner as to convey the impression that they must greatly assist him in his progress.

His head is continually in motion, turning from side to side with great rapidity, while his eyes, which at all times have a hungry appearance, glare as if he expected an attack from some unseen enemy. When viewed from behind as he walks, or when he stands in front of you with his head hanging on one side, flashing his sharp eyes and beating his stomach to show that he is hungry, while he utters inarticulate sounds, he presents a strange appearance indeed. He has evidently been totally deaf and dumb since his capture, and although all attempts to teach him to speak have failed, by signs those who care for him can get him to sit, stand, and run.

If poor Sanichar, the wolf-boy, had received the same care that was bestowed upon the afflicted Laura Bridgeman, it is possible that his faculties might have been sufficiently developed to enable him to impart at least something concerning the first years of his life, which must now always remain an unsolved mystery.

Invasions of India.

India has suffered from nine great invasions during its checkered history. The first was the Aryan invasion, which took place many years before the Christian era; the second was headed by Alexander the Great, when the Bactran empire was established in the second century B. C.; then followed the Scythian

AURUNGZEB'S MOSQUE, BENARES.

invasion, first century, A. D.: the Mahmondef Ghazins' conquest, when a Turk established rule and Mohammedan religion; the invasion of Tamerlane the Great, 1398; the Mogul empire, founded by Baber, 1524; the Persian conquest of Mohammedanism and the setting up of the Hindu reaction in 1739; the Ahmed Shah Abdalis invasion in 1761, in which the Mahratta power was crushed and more than 700,000 men were killed, and, lastly, the English invasion.

To-day nearly all of India is ruled absolutely by Great Britain, while by sufferance there are certain States supposed to be "independent," ruled over by Maharajahs. In these are placed English "residents," or rather English spies, and the home government at London knows exactly what is going on and the "policy" of these native rulers is decided for them by the little island across the seas.

A Native Ruler.

The beautiful city of Jeypore is the capital of the territory belonging to Maharajah Mardozing, whose province is about the size of Massachusetts, and as the ruler is a cultivated, progressive gentleman, quite democratic in his manner of dealing with foreigners, no difficulty was encountered in visiting his palaces and seeing something of him personally.

His travels in Europe have made their impressions upon him, and the well-paved streets, the public mint, the museum, the observatory, the hospitals and the excellent school buildings all go to prove that he is much more Western than Eastern in his ideas. Indeed the general appearance of the small dominion of this native prince exhibits a favorable contrast to India generally, over which the authority of England extends.

The Maharajah's stables contain nine hundred horses, seven hundred camels and eighty-five elephants; and five hundred servants wait upon his wives and keep the magnificent palaces and gardens in order. By the kindness of his honor four elephants were placed at the service of our party of sixteen; each elephant was attended by two servants from the palace, in livery; and each swaying elephant back carrying four jolly Americans we proceeded to the royal summer palace, several miles from the city walls.

A Ride on Elephant-Back.

These great creatures are easily controlled by their drivers, who sit just back of their ears and frequently use the sharp iron-pointed rod to guide them; but when the shuffling, flat-footed tread became monotonous, and at my urgent request the beast was made to trot, we could imagine that we were again on a rolling ocean steamer, and the performance was soon brought to a close.

Passing through the old city of Ambar, which is now in ruins, the elephants wind slowly up the steep slopes which lead to the entrance of the palace, which is

PALACE OF MAHARAJA OF INDORE, BENARES.

defended by a narrow approach with three massive gateways, the last of which opens on a great square, where the elephants at the command of the drivers drop on their knees and, with the aid of short ladders, the riders alight. Through brass doorways and alcoves of embroidered marble we pass into the second court-yard, and about us are the "Court of Honor," the "Men's Abode," which is said to contain the finest portal in the world, the "Hall of Victory," adorned by panels of alabaster, inlaid with birds, flowers and arabesques in various colors, the roof glittering with the mirrored and spangled work for which Jeypore art is renowned, and beyond these is the "Alcove of Light," which glows with tender colors and exquisite inlaid work and looks through arches of carved ala-baster and laced marble work upon the placid lake and silent mountains. In

AN INDIAN RUSTIC.

the independent State of Baroda, ac-companied by my host, Captain Lynn, I visited the palace which contains the famous regalia of Baroda, among which is seen the gorgeous collar of five hundred diamonds, the pendant of which is the famous "Star of the Deccan," and a carpet ten feet by six woven entirely of strings of pure pearls, with central and corner circles of diamonds. Near this palace are two gold cannon, weighing two hun-dred and eighty pounds each, with two companions of silver, the wagons, bullock harness and ramrods being all of silver. It is the ambition of each Maharajah to outshine his predecessor.

Indian Customs.

The country is inhabited by people of various colors, customs and lan-guages, although it is generally sup-posed that the different tongues can be traced to the mother Sanskrit, and the people to a great extent find a common origin in the Indo-Caucasian stock.

The Bengalee, which is very much like the Sanskrit, is spoken in Bengal; the Orria in the Orissa; the Tamul in Madras, by the Moharaslitros; and the Hindoosthanee, in all its different forms, is spoken in the northwestern provinces.

The Brahmans, in their religious services and frequently in conversation, use the Sanskrit, but the other castes generally adopt the Bengalee.

THE MAHARAJAHS OF NAGPUR GHAT, BENARES.

The Bengalees, in bodily structure, are delicate, and in disposition are mild and peaceable; on the other hand, the peoples of Upper India are brave, haughty and warlike, and physically they are robust and muscular.

Use of Tobacco.

In the use of tobacco these people are much more careful than more "civilized" nations. The tobacco leaves, with other ingredients, are chopped up,

LLAMA WITH PRAYING WHEEL.

put in the earth for several days, and the smoker does not draw the smoke directly into his mouth, but it passes through a long pipe, comes into the bottom of the hooka, which is full of cold water, and making its way through another pipe at last reaches the mouth. The *taric*, or the juice of the palm or date tree, is used by the low caste people generally; it can be easily pressed from the stalks of the plant and it quickly intoxicates.

I noticed that the Hindus frequently appealed to the heavenly bodies. On the temple walls you find the signs of the zodiac, and by the motion of the stars and the eclipses they base their prophecies of good or evil.

Sacred Time.

Three months in the year are regarded by the Hindus as sacred, viz., Bois-Ak (April), Kartic (October), and Magh (January). The first, commencing the new year, is the holiest of all. The stores and homes are fancifully decorated, the scales and weights are washed and worshiped, the first page of account books is ornamented at the top with two round figures marked with red and yellow powders. Every day the book begins by a deposit of a small amount of money to the credit of a favorite deity, and when the year draws to a close the money is accurately collected and used for purposes of worship.

On New Year's Day (first of April) all orthodox Hindus are expected to dedicate pitchers to the gods and deceased ancestors. As these are supposed to be thirsty at this hot season earthen, brazen or silver pitchers (according to the circumstances of the dedicator) are placed in a row, with trays full of fruit on their tops. The first is offered to the gods, the second to the gooroo, or priest, the third to the father of the dead, the fourth to the grandfather, etc. Each day of this month is marked by some feast or ceremony, and full thirty days are spent in the most reckless forms of dissipation and idolatrous superstition.

A Marriage Procession.

The visitor to India cannot well miss a marriage procession, for it is of daily occurrence in the large

DANCING GIRL, OF JEYPORE, INDIA.

cities, and, as the whole affair is of the most fantastic character, accompanied by the most fearful strains of music, he cannot but be attracted by it.

In the ranks are generally to be seen white horses, painted sky-blue or bright yellow; sacred bullocks, caparisoned in the most brilliant style, drawing covered

carts, with peep-holes, in which the women of the harem ride. In the midst of
the crowd are painted and powdered men carrying banners, on which are ludicrous
figures, and near the band of musicians is seen the boy bridegroom, perhaps
conspicuously perched
on an elephant, unac-
companied by his
bride, who does not
appear in public.

This is usually
known as a marriage
procession, but it is
really a betrothal, for
years may elapse be-
fore the youthful
groom of ten and the
baby bride of six
summers have any
communication at all
with each other, al-
though nothing but
death can interrupt
the union after the
ceremony is over.

Women's Ornaments.

The brilliant or-
naments worn by girls
and women in every
part of India attract
more attention than
admiration. This
morning I took a men-
tal photograph of a
swarthy female, flash-
ing and tinkling

INDIAN ACTRESS.

with bangles on her wrists, ankles, arms, ears and nose. The heavy rings
dragged her ears quite out of shape; her perforated nostrils were ornamented
with trinkets that extended nearly to her chin; her brown limbs and arms were
decked with great rings of silver and gilt, and part of her bosom was tattooed
with blue and red ink. She was a poor fruitseller in the market-place, but her

AN ORNAMENTED WOMAN OF INDIA.

poverty could not gain the victory over her vanity, which, to some extent, seems to be a trait of character among all nations and of both sexes.

There is a class of women called Nautch dancers who are sometimes seen on the streets, but those whose performances are regarded as most artistic are monopolized by the rajahs and maharajahs, who allow them to dance in public during royal receptions and festivities. At the "audience" given by the maharajah at Jeypore, sixty-five of these toe artists entertained the ruler, about a thousand natives and a small party of Americans, and I suppose the ridiculous shuffling gave a fair idea of the typical Oriental dance.

One who is much more gifted in describing a woman's attire than I, furnishes me with the description of one of these professional and royal dancers, which I append.

Royal Dancers.

The leading dancer was dressed in a close-fitting garment, with long sleeves and a very full skirt, much plaited in at the waist, made of the finest transparent muslin of a light violet color, trimmed nearly to her waist with rows of broad gold brocade lace, as also about her shoulders and bust with the same. This dress was confined slightly at her waist by a scarf of bright green muslin spotted with gold, whose ends of gold brocade fell on her left side, and had the effect of raising the skirt a little so as to show her trousers of the richest cloth of gold. With one end tucked into her waistband, a splendid Benares scarf of filmy amber muslin-gauze, profusely flowered with gold, having borders and ends of the same, passed over her left arm and head and fell over her right shoulder.

The gold ornaments on her head and arms were all handsome and in great profusion, and her gold anklets, whose tiny bells jingled as she moved, had a row of large brilliant stones on their bands, which flashed as she danced, and gave, so some of the Americans thought, a charming effect to the tiny, graceful feet on which they rested.

The Indian Mutiny.

There is no bloodier chapter in the history of this century than that recording the heartrending scenes of the Indian mutiny of 1857. As I visited the places in Cawnpore, Delhi and Lucknow, which have been made historic by the bold uprising of the natives of India, by the fearful suffering and slaughter of English women and children, and by the heroic bravery of British soldiery, I experienced mingled feelings of horror, sadness and approbation.

While making these studies, I have had by my side most of the time an old soldier who was wounded three times during the mutiny, who followed Havelock and Outram in their noble charges and sieges, and whose eloquent recital of these thrilling events added no little to the interest elicited by these localities.

OUDH EXHIBITION AND SURROUNDINGS, LUCKNOW.

16

After much controversy on the subject the weight of testimony seems to support the opinion that the origin of the outbreak can be found in both political and religious tendencies that had been growing in power for years before it actually burst forth.

Long before 1857 it was known that the Mohammedans were dissatisfied with their subordinate position, and their increasing idleness and immoral conduct rendered them insolent and fractious. This restless feeling was fanned into a flame when the royal family was dismissed from their residence in the fortress at Delhi by the English government, and especially when, through the influence of Lord Hastings, the kingdom of Oude was annexed to the British possessions. But the Mohammedans, on account of their numerical inferiority, could do nothing as long as the Hindu soldiers remained true to England. The wily Mohammedans, aided by a concatenation of circumstances, were enabled to overcome this difficulty. It was sedulously reported that the British government had determined to force all of its subjects to embrace Christianity, and, in order to accomplish this end, a plan had been devised by which the whole of the Hindu sepoys would become defiled and break their caste.

As it was well known that no Hindu could remain clean and touch with his lips the grease of animals, the Mohammedan emissaries declared that the government had adopted the device of issuing cartridges greased with pigs' and bullocks' fat for the Enfield rifles, the end of which must be bitten off before they could be used. When a Hindu touched the unclean thing with his lips and teeth of course he would become an outcast, and there could be no other resource for him except to join the religion of his masters.

The leaders of the two great classes of natives were soon united in their purposes; regiment after regiment rebelled; fort after fort was besieged; and the spirit of the insurgents spread rapidly throughout northern India. The King of Delhi was proclaimed sovereign of the whole country; the stores of firearms and ammunition were seized; English officers were shot down by the native soldiers while at drill; the residences of foreigners were broken into and plundered as quickly as they could be reached; neither age nor sex was spared, and within twenty-four hours from the time when the first gun was fired a frightful massacre was being perpetrated in fifteen or twenty villages and cities.

Nana Sahib's Perfidy.

My old friend, Captain Lee, who received a terrible sabre gash while fighting on the streets of Cawnpore, pointed out the scenes of the struggle at this place and vividly described the disaster that befell the British arms early in the combat.

Sir Hugh Wheeler intrenched himself in the barracks with a force of about three hundred soldiers, who were protecting five hundred women and children,

THE HOOSEINABAD EMAMBARA, LUCKNOW

the families of officers and civilians. The insurgents were commanded by Nana Sahib, who nurtured a deadly hatred against the government for declining to recognize in him the successor of a late ruler to whom he was connected by adoption, and, wearied by the desperate resistance of the men in the barracks, he offered to give to all a safe passage to Allahabad if a surrender was made.

The terms of the perfidious enemy were accepted. Unarmed men, with hundreds of helpless women and children, marched to the river bank, and just as they were about to embark a masked battery opened fire on them, the murderous shots killing six hundred and fifty out of the eight hundred. This apparent success seemed only to inflame the demon Nana. The one hundred and fifty prisoners were brought into his presence. The men were tortured and slowly put to death, and the others, after undergoing the most horrible ordeal, were butchered by savages and their bodies cast into a well.

Marochetti's beautiful monument raised over this well is a pure white marble figure of an angel, with folded wings and palm-laden hands, with its eyes sadly cast downward toward the spot where the dead and dying were hurled.

The Defence of Lucknow.

Although the mutiny broke out in the early summer, Havelock and Outram did not succeed in forcing their way into Lucknow until the twenty-fifth of September, when they came to the relief of the British residency. During these months a handful of men held the place against thousands of native soldiers. Many within the walls died from wounds and exhaustion, while several officers, among them Sir Henry Lawrence, fell before the shot of the enemy. Women, as is always the case under similar circumstances, acted with transcendent heroism, and when at last succor came, tears of men, women and children mingled in thanksgiving.

As I walked through the hushed chambers of the Residency, Tennyson's "Defence of Lucknow" came to mind, and in leaving, as I looked back upon its broken and shot-scarred walls, I recalled the words of the angelic chorus over the birth of one greater than Tennyson.

England may well shudder as she notices the indications of another Indian mutiny. While victory has crowned English arms of late, in Northern India, and the warlike tribes have been driven from their strongholds in the mountains, the end is not yet. There is danger now, as there always has been, of a Mohammedan uprising. The Mohammedan does not make a clear distinction between the English and other European nations. The reports have been spread among them that the Sultan's army has defeated the Greeks; this means to them that the Crescent has been victorious over the Cross; and their hatred against the Christian

SPECIMENS OF LOW CASTE.

never was more intense than now. It is thought by some that the mutinous rumbling will grow louder; the bloody scenes of 1857 will be repeated; and the map of the East may be changed.

Caste and Outcasts.

The caste system, which is so closely connected with the origin of the mutiny, exists in India as nowhere else in the world. Among the primitive Hindus there

HIGH CASTE INDIAN WOMAN.

were only four castes, viz., the Brahman, the highest, which embraced the priesthood; the Kais-th, which included the trading classes; the Khetryas, the governing and soldier caste, and the Soodras, embracing the laboring population.

The members of these primary castes, notwithstanding they had a common language and religion, socially were separated by insurmountable walls.

In course of time the four divisions grew into many more castes, and at the present day every line of activity is formed into a kind of close corporation, and each is absolutely exclusive of the others. For instance, there is a

weaver caste, and a weaver's son can marry only a weaver's daughter, and a weaver's daughter cannot marry any one except a weaver's son; members of the

MAHARAJAH'S PALACE, JEYPORE.

shoemaking caste cannot intermarry with any other caste; and so with the blacksmith caste, the goldsmith caste, the washer caste, the farmer caste, the barber caste, and so on. With the exception of the Soodra caste, the members of which are virtually outcasts, no one can come into any of the castes except by birth.

In other countries, by opulence, learning, application, etc., a person of obscure birth can exalt himself in the social scale, but not so in India. An orthodox Hindu will tell you that a person's position at birth is a dispensation of nature, and as it is impossible to transform a dog into an ox, a deer into a camel, a horse into an elephant, so you cannot make a barber out of a weaver, a physician out of a cobbler, or a priest out of a farmer.

One of the greatest calamities that can befall a Hindu is to have his caste broken, for then he is known as an "outcast," and he and his family are disgraced forever. If a member of one caste eats anything or drinks anything that has been touched by any one not belonging to his caste, or if he eats with, drinks with or sleeps with any such person, he loses caste immediately, and the restoration of his loss is an impossibility.

Unintentionally I came very near bringing a calamity upon a man's business and getting myself into a serious complication. In the market-place of Agra I paused before a stand containing Indian sweetmeats, and desiring to sample the dark-colored sugar I touched a small lump to my mouth, and was about to replace the sugar, when three men sprang forward, and such a fuss I have not heard for many a day. An old gentleman, who has lived fifty-six years in India, told me that if the lump that had been placed to my mouth had fallen among the sweetmeats the Hindu would have been obliged to close out his business, and any court in India would have given him damages to the value of his stock.

Generally it is dangerous for a man to put his mouth into another man's business. In this instance, I came near making the fatal mistake of putting another man's business into my mouth! Since studying this question I learned of the enemy of a certain high caste Brahman who secretly kneaded the flour in the Brahman's kitchen. The Brahman and his family ate the bread, and they irretrievably lost their caste and social standing.

If a man of one caste should intentionally or accidentally run his finger into the mouth of a man of a different caste, immediately the latter becomes an outcast. Not an external, but an internal, touch does the business. If a pin should drop from the mouth of a low Soodra, and a high and mighty Brahman (they all go barefooted) should step on it, he would not only jump high, but he would fall low, for he would lose caste forever.

The names of thirty-four distinct castes, the outgrowth of the original four, have been given me, and, doubtless, there are many more recognized by the

STREET SCENE, CALCUTTA.

Hindus of India. Every caste has its panchayat, or governing committee, and these committees have absolute power in all social questions. If a young man desires, or, rather, if his parents desire him, to marry a woman (of course, of his caste,) the panchayat committee is called together, and they arrange all details; but the committee sometimes disagrees, a division takes place and the formation of another caste is the result. A man cannot marry a girl of a higher caste than the one to which he belongs, for such protection is thrown around her that he can have no communication with her, but by becoming an outcast he can marry a damsel belonging to a lower caste.

The visitor to India is immediately attracted by the brilliant marks on the foreheads of the Hindus. At Calcutta I was informed that these are caste marks, but this is a mistake. There are two great religious sects—the Shaivs, worshipers of Mahader, and the Vishnavi, worshipers of the incarnations of Vishnu. The horizontal mark indicates the former and the perpendicular mark the latter.

The corrupted Mohammedanism of India, in imitation of the Hindus, recognizes four divisions—the Sheikh, the Mogul, the Bathan and the Saiyad—but these resemble family tribes more than they do the inflexible caste of the Hindu.

CHAPTER XII.

THE QUEEN OF THE EAST.

ALCUTTA is the political capital and Bombay is the commercial metropolis of India, and the two are located on opposite sides of the country, the one looking toward the Bay of Bengal, the other washed by the sea of Arabia.

Nowhere in Asia have I seen such a variety of peoples moving through the streets, dressed in every conceivable oriental garb and representing so completely every degree of Asiatic life as here in Bombay. Probably nowhere else in the world, not even in Alexandria, can be found a population so motley and conglomerate, and where such striking varieties of race, nationality and religion are seen as on these wonderfully busy streets.

While visiting the bazaars, accompanied by an intelligent guide, I passed Banians of Guzerat, Mahrattas from the Deccan, Mussulmans, Afghans, Persians, Bedouin Arabs, Turks, Malays, Chinese, Japanese, Abyssinians, Indo-Portuguese, Jews, Armenians, Europeans, and, of course, the omnipresent Yankee.

Religious Divisions.

But I desire to speak especially of certain sects that thrive in Bombay, and whose antagonistic opinions on social and religious questions have given rise to many riots and much bloodshed.

The Jains, together with the Brahmins, Lingaets and Bhattias, comprise the castes which scrupulously abstain from eating meat.

They form about one-eighth of the population. In religious tenets they resemble closely the Buddhists and they are a wealthy sect, accumulating much money in the different trades.

The Brahminical, or orthodox Hindus, form three-fifths of the entire population of Bombay, and they are separated into two divisions of worshipers, the one class paying homage to Vishnu, the preserver, and the other bowing before Shiva, the destroyer, the second and third persons of the Hindu trinity.

The Banians.

The most important class among the Hindus, and the best known outside of India, are the Banians. They have the commercial instinct remarkably developed and largely control the foreign commerce of India with the countries bordering on the Persian gulf and the Indian ocean. To-day the trade of the whole east coast of Africa and Southern and Eastern Arabia, I am told, is mainly managed by the great Banian merchants of Bombay.

BOMBAY HARBOR.

Many of them are Jains, and they have the utmost veneration for animal life. You can see them carefully laying grains of sugar along the walls by the roadside for the ants to eat or picking up worms and caterpillars and placing them where they will not be trampled upon; and they have temples dedicated to animal life, in which the lowest and most repulsive forms of vermin are religiously preserved. In some of these miserable men are reported to receive a small recompense for allowing insects to feed upon their bodies while they sleep.

The Mahrattas, who are loyal and enthusiastic Hindus, have no commercial instinct and few of them are merchants of any note. They were originally

SILENT TOWER, BOMBAY.

warriors, politicians and farmers, and to-day most of them hold inferior places in the community.

The Mohammedans, forming one-fifth of the population, are divided into the Soonees, who only accept the historical succession of Caliphs after Mohammed, and the Sheeahs, who are followers of Ali, the fourth Caliph. The Turks and Arabs are the chief Soonee nation, while the Persians are mainly Sheeahs.

The Parsees.

The Parsees, followers of Zoroaster, and commonly known as "fire-worshipers," do not comprise a large proportion of the citizens of Bombay, but owing to their energy, commercial genius, freedom, to a great extent, from caste prejudices and the readiness with which they have adopted European ideas and learned the English language, have made themselves the most influential and wealthiest class in the city.

More than eight centuries ago the Parsees, expelled from Persia, sought an asylum in this part of the world. Their temples contain no images; in some of them burn still the sacred fire brought to these shores by their fathers, and

A HINDU SACRIFICE.

the flame at the altar and the sun in the heavens are worshiped as symbolic of God, who is declared to be the source of all illumination.

The hat worn by the Parsee is quite characteristic and marks him out in any crowd. It is in the shape of a cow's hoof, and tradition has it that on their arrival in India, as a token of subjection, they were compelled to adopt this style of head-gear by the Hindus, who regard the cow as the most sacred of animals.

The manner in which the Parsees dispose of their dead is characteristic of this people alone, and it impresses the visitor to Bombay as strangely repulsive. I drove to Malabar Hill, an elevated piece of ground in the outskirts

MOHAMMEDANS AT A RELIGIOUS FESTIVAL.

of the city, on the top of which are located the five noted "Towers of Silence," constituting the cemetery of the Parsees.

The Towers of Silence.

These towers are approached through beautifully kept gardens, and the scenery in the neighborhood is made as attractive as possible.

When a Parsee dies the body is brought up long flights of steps, which are only touched by the feet of this race. Taken to a temple, where the sacred fire has been burning uninterruptedly for hundreds of years and funeral services are held, the corpse is carried on a stretcher into one of these towers and placed, completely exposed, upon a grating; and, after the bearers and mourners retire, hundreds or vultures, which are always waiting on the cornices of the towers and on the tree-tops, swoop down to their human meal, and in less than thirty minutes nothing is left but the bones, which fall into a large open space below, where they are decomposed by time and the elements.

DR. TUPPER IN CENTRAL INDIA.

As fire, earth and water are all held by the Parsee to be sacred, a body must not be burned, for this would defile the fire; it must not be buried, for this would defile the earth; it must not be cast into the river, for this would defile the water; but it may be taken into the life of the birds without violating any tenet as to defilement.

I was informed of one strange fancy and superstition of these Parsees. A dog always accompanies the funeral procession, and when the white cloth is lifted from the body, before it is left alone with the vultures, if the dog approaches the corpse and notices it in any way, the dead is believed to be in a

THE INNER VAHAL FROM GARDEN, JEYPORE.

state of happiness: on the contrary, if the pup slights the body the friends are left without hope!

At a distance of a quarter of a mile from the "Towers of Silence" I noticed these baldheaded vultures, larger than our buzzards, lining the fences and tower-tops, eagerly looking out for a procession. As our party passed through the gates, among the birds there was great excitement, but this joyful anticipation was changed into solemn disappointment when, with vigorous step, we all passed out again.

Filth and Holiness.

The thought of this disposition of the dead was not so repulsive to me as the manner in which a band of Hindu priests or fakirs are living not far from this

DR. TUPPER AMONG BUDDHIST ASCETICS, BOMBAY.

Parsee cemetery. It is a peculiar trait of the Hindu religion that its filthiest men are often reckoned among its holiest. I witnessed an illustration of this.

Around the crumbling steps of an ancient temple were gathered a score of nude fakirs on piles of ashes who are supposed to have passed into a state of sinlessness. Their hair, faces and bodies—unwashed for years—

were covered with dust and dirt, and some of these deluded creatures had remained seated in one position for so long a time that their limbs had become enormously swollen and were rendered entirely useless.

I was told that one of these men took an oath twenty-five years ago that he would not drop his arm from a lifted position during his life—and there he is. The member is perfectly dead, and now it is impossible for him to break his oath should he desire. Another fakir is pointed out who thirty-eight years ago pledged the gods that he would neither sit down nor lie down as long as he lived, and during all these weary years he has found physical rest only by leaning over the

HINDU FAKIR WHOSE ARMS HAVE BEEN UP FOR MANY YEARS AND CANNOT
TAKE THEM DOWN.

(259)

rope of a swing or by supporting himself against a wall. By these frightful penances they expect to win happiness in the life to come.

Brilliant Scenes.

Along the Elphinstone Circle and the Esplanade, Bombay presents one of the most brilliant street scenes in the world. Some of the improvements compare favorably with those in Vienna, Berlin, Paris or London, and the beautiful gardens, handsome statuary and ornamental fountains add no little to the general effect. Many of the broad roads are lined with oleanders, magnolias, laburnums,

jasmines, orange and lemon trees, and the white, scarlet and yellow honeysuckles and other bright creepers often completely cover the walls and fences.

A delightful sail of ten miles from the city brought me to the Island of Elephanta, six miles in circumference, where are found the celebrated rock caves, for so many centuries the holy temples of worship. The entrance and walls of the main Cave of Elephanta are sup-

DR. TUPPER AT JEYPORE, INDIA.

ported by elaborately carved pillars, hewn out of the native rock, and the sombre chambers are decorated by numerous idols that give proof of the sensual superstition, as well as the unique art of these religionists of ages gone, whose faithful successors are here to-day.

An Asylum for Animals.

The members of the Society for the Prevention of Cruelty to Animals would enjoy a visit to the Asylum for Aged and Decrepit Animals at Bombay, where birds and beasts are as carefully nursed as are human beings in well-appointed hospitals. The establishment was founded by a wealthy native, and here bullocks, cows, horses, dogs, cats and birds, otherwise homeless, find excellent care, food and shelter.

These animals are never killed, and it matters not how aged or badly injured they are, an experienced doctor and nurse give them every attention until nature ends their lives. The kind consideration shown all animals through the East, especially in India, is marked, indeed, and this fact accounts for the tameness of these creatures on the streets of all the large cities. In a hotel at Allahabad I made my toilet in the morning while two bright-plumaged birds were hopping on my floor, and on several occasions I have dined while rooks were perched in the open windows of the dining-room, looking at me with their heads turned to one side, as if to say, "Hurry up, there; my turn next!" If I was an American cat, rat or jaybird and possessed my present knowledge of the world, I would hie to the land of the Hindu and defend his religion with all my teeth and claws.

Famine in India.

Human life has received far less attention in India than brute life. The horrors of famine have overshadowed the land, and if it were

BUDDHIST PRIESTESS.

not for the information given to the world by Americans there would be great ignorance on the subject, and if it were not for the aid rendered by Americans the list of those who have died of starvation would be much longer. As in the famine or 1877–78 millions of these miserable beings starve to death without the knowledge of the government.

Twenty years ago Lord Lytton, then viceroy, declared in a public address that only three or four persons in all India had died for lack of food, while, it was proved afterward, that in the district where he spoke sixty thousand persons were starving at the very time of his optimistic deliverance. That famine was not so widespread as the one that has lately afflicted this unfortunate people. It raged eighteen months; two-thirds of the entire country was affected by the terrible scourge, and the number of victims, according to Reuter's agent in India, exceed eight million! Boarding a train at Bombay, within a few hours' ride beyond the Ghats, or mountain-range, north of the metropolis, you enter upon a parched desert of yellow-brown soil which is the home of millions of human souls, and which extends for thousands of square miles, its hard and grassless surface relieved now and then by the mango tree and collection of mud huts, with thatched roofs, about which are huddled groups of emaciated human beings. A few miles away from the railroad you are attracted here and there by the gruesome sight of skeletons of men, women and children, glistening and bleaching in the sun, and no one knows and no one cares who they were. No, this cannot be true; for far across the Pacific have come to famine-stricken India tokens of a universal love and sympathy. In the pulpit, on the platform, and through the press earnest appeals have been made throughout America for India's starving millions; and no efforts in this line have been more prompt, more eloquent and more successful than those that have been made through the columns of the *Christian Herald*. Dr. Klopsch, the proprietor of this journal, with his characteristic energy and foresight, early took in the dreadful situation, and by means of his widely-circulated paper he has raised in corn and money nearly $300,000, which has been distributed by over sixty missionaries in the famine district. Free shipment of corn was allowed by Congressional action; the " City of Everett," loaded with provisions, sailed from the Pacific coast, and through the *Christian Herald* Commissioner and the Inter-denominational Relief Committee (of which Bishop Thoburn was chairman) the distribution of money and provisions was ably managed.

CHAPTER XIII

FAREWELL TO INDIA, GREETING TO EGYPT.

 OR a number of days our steamer plowed through the waters of the Arabian and Red seas from Bombay to Suez, and the monotony of the long trip was relieved quite delightfully by the companionship of agreeable Americans, Englishmen and Frenchmen, by the entertaining program arranged through the genius of the "amusement committee" day by day, by the appearance now and then of the great fish and strange birds of these seas and by our short stay at Aden, where I enjoyed a ten-mile drive through two Arabian villages and saw the Arab for the first time on his native heath.

I am now looking upon the narrow waters of the Suez Canal, and, although the cutting of this canal and the repeated struggles and disappointments of the noted M. de Lesseps are old stories, I shall venture to give some facts that are of fresh interest to me and may be also to my readers. It is popularly supposed that the union of the Red and the Mediterranean seas were not effected until the famous French engineer came upon the scene, but this is a mistake.

Planned by the Pharaohs.

The Isthmus of Suez, a neck of land which joins Asia to Africa, is a little over ninety miles wide, and modern investigations have proved that as far back as Rameses II., one of the oppressors of the Israelites, a canal was cut partly through the isthmus. This work was continued by Nekan (B. C. 610), Darius and Ptolemy Philadelphus, and, still later, the completed canal joined the two seas.

During the middle ages several unsuccessful attempts were made to cut a new canal, but no serious effort was made until the year 1798, when Napoleon Bonaparte directed M. Lepere to survey the route across the neck of land, but after great waste of time and money the report was sent to the French Emperor that, as the difference between the levels of the Red Sea and the Mediterranean was thirty-three feet, it would be impossible to build a canal that would prove to be of permanent benefit.

The New Canal.

Not until the year 1846 was it found that the level of the two seas is practically the same, and in the year 1854 M. de Lesseps laid his plans for a canal before Said Pasha; two years afterward they were sanctioned, and two years later the work began. The canal leads into several lakes. The filling of the Bitter Lakes with sea-water from the Mediterranean was begun on the eighteenth of March, 1869, and the whole canal was opened for traffic on November 16 of the same year. An enthusiastic engineer, in whose company I spent some time, gave me some interesting details on the subject of the construction of this important commercial highway.

The channel which leads into the canal at the Suez end is three hundred yards across in the widest part, the average width of the dredged canal is about ninety feet, and the average depth is about twenty-eight feet.

On a mound nearly half-way between Suez and Shaluf are granite blocks

bearing traces of cuneiform and hieroglyphic inscriptions recording the name of Darius, and these are evidently the remains of one of a series of buildings erected along the line of the old canal, which was restored and probably completed by Darius.

Records of Persian Work.

While digging the canal M. de Lesseps and his work-men found the ruins of sev-eral buildings which have

DR. TUPPER AND FRIENDS SAILING UP THE RED SEA.

thrown light upon the subject of ancient architecture, and some of the granite slabs excavated by him and his associates, inscribed with the names of Darius and other distinguished characters of history, are held as precious relics.

The track of the canal through the Bitter Lakes is marked by a double row of buoys. The distance between each buoy is about three hundred and thirty yards, and the space between the two rows is thirty feet. After passing out of the lake channel into the canal proper you enter what is known as the plain of El-Gisr, or the "bridge," which is fifty-five feet above the level of the sea, and through this a channel eighty feet deep had to be cut.

A few miles further a more remarkable formation is seen. It is a height between the lakes of Bahah and Menzaleh, and as it forms a natural bridge it is supposed that over this passed the invading armies that entered Egypt, which supposition gave rise to the name, "The Bridge of Nations."

The town at the Mediterranean entrance is called Port Said, in honor of Said Pasha. Its harbor and two breakwaters are wonderful pieces of workmanship.

The breakwater on the east is over a mile, and the one on the west is still longer, and the latter is lengthened yearly to protect the harbor from the mud-carrying current which always flows from the west and would block up the canal but for the breakwater.

The Great French Engineer.

We are convinced that the completion of the canal is due, perhaps, less to originality of conception than to the intensity of conviction and invincible perseverance of the great engineer, whose faith in his enterprise seemed to remove mountains, and whose magnetic personality appealed successfully at last to those who were at first his most persistent antagonists. The British government was resolutely hostile to the scheme; the Ottoman Porte, the real suzerain of Egypt, partly influenced by the attitude of England, and partly by its dislike to anything tending to possible complication within the bounds of its own dominions, did everything in its power to discourage the affair; the leading engineers in Europe declared against the practicability of the enterprise, and their adverse verdict did much toward sealing the coffers of European capitalists, and, worst of all, as so often is the case in important matters with us all, those to whom he confided, and upon whom he absolutely depended, failed him at the critical moment.

But M. de Lesseps seemed never daunted by the political and financial difficulties which lay in his path, and with that power of persuasion that in his latter years led him to make some fatal mistakes, he convinced the Viceroy of Egypt that his reign would be made glorious by granting the powers for the construction of the canal; he persuaded the French people to embark their savings in a foreign and romantic undertaking; he inspired with his hopeful enthusiasm his engineers, contractors and every member of his staff, and, indeed, his magnetic influence extended from the throne to the trowel; from the Arab sheiks to the humblest laborer.

I am told that up to the moment the canal was opened it was thought by some who posed as experts that the largest steamers would be unable to navigate its waters, and at best it would only become a channel through which barges might be towed with goods in competition with the Egyptian Railway.

New Era in Commerce.

The opening of the canal marked a new era in the commercial life of Europe. Heretofore the long and expensive route by the way of the Cape of Good Hope was taken by steamers from London to the ports in India, China and Japan, but now scores of days and thousands of miles can be saved by this narrow highway of less than a hundred miles in length. The distance from London to Bombay via the Cape of Good Hope is 10,719 miles, the distance from London to Bombay via the Suez Canal is only 6274.

At the opening of the canal, and for several years subsequently, the dues were levied at the rate of ten francs ($2.00) on the registered or net tonnage of steamers, but in 1872 the company determined to levy the same toll, not on the net, but on the gross tonnage of all vessels. But as ships had been built and capital invested largely on the strength of the canal charges levied on the principle of ten francs on net tonnage, there arose serious complaints. Strong appeals were made to the English government to protect British interests; the Message-

THE PORT OF ISMAILIA, ON THE SUEZ CANAL.

ries Maritimes of France and other foreign companies protested against the change; an international commission was appointed by the Ottoman Porte to determine the basis on which dues should be levied, and, after some delay, a compromise was effected, which seemed to satisfy the interested parties.

Cost of the Canal.

The amount of £16,000,000 is often quoted as the entire cost of the construction of the canal, but this is not correct. To this enormous sum must be added the amount of the indemnity paid by the Egyptian government, according to the award of the Emperor of France in 1864, for the retrocession of territory and other privileges, and, as this indemnity amounted to nearly £4,000,000, the total for constructing the canal aggregated £20,000,000, or about $100,000,000.

On account of the narrowness of the canal, every five miles a siding is provided to enable ships to be moored out of the main channel, so that other vessels may pass, and other expensive improvements have been made in recent years. But, apart from these practical considerations, the Suez Canal is of thrilling interest.

To open the way for the world's commerce, the pickaxe and shovel of modern enterprise have cut through a region enriched by the memory of the greatest events of history. On either side of the canal stretches the plain where Abraham, four thousand years ago, wandered from far-away Ur, of the Chaldees; not far from this spot are the ruins of ancient Zoan, where Moses performed his miracles; nearby is where the host of Pharaoh perished through the sudden rising of a southwest gale, and thus this narrow ribbon of water links together the great past and the greater present, pointing, let us hope, to a still greater future.

Three Egypts.

Three Egypts attract the attention and elicit the interest of the traveler—the Egypt of the ancients, the Egypt of the "Arabian Nights," and the Egypt of modern enterprise.

The first is seen in excavated cities, in pyramids, temples and tombs; the second is witnessed in the strange scenes of the narrow streets of portions of Cairo and in the queer towns of the country districts, and the last displays itself along the Suez Canal and in the commercial din of modernized Alexandria. You recall the words of the Jewish physician in the story of "The Hump-back:" "He who has not seen Cairo has not seen the world. Its soil is gold, its Nile is a wonder, its women are like the black-eyed virgins of Paradise." While we may differ from the opinion thus expressed, we must agree that as we visit the labyrinth of narrow lanes which intersect the mediaeval city, sights appear in this Mohammedan capital that cannot be duplicated in all the world.

In Narrow Streets.

Passing down the winding alleys, where a tiny patch of sky marks the narrow space between the lattice windows of the over-hanging upper stories, crowded and jostled by a swarming mass of human beings, camels, asses and donkeys, we can readily imagine ourselves in the gateway of Ali of Cairo. We can nearly hear the Three Kalenderis entertaining the portress and her fair sisters with the history of their lives, and if we come this way by night, we would not be much

(272)　　　　　STREET IN MODERN CAIRO.

surprised to see the good Harun-al-Rashid himself, coming stealthily on his midnight rambles, with Jaafer at his heels and black Mesrur clearing the way. The histories of the Thousand and One Nights are enacted every day upon these streets, and the truth of to-day is stranger than the fiction of yesterday.

Bazaars and Public Buildings.

I have just returned from a five-mile walk up the street called "Muski" and through the native bazaars. Here is the Norman-looking eleventh century gate of the old Fatimi city; yonder is the Mosque of El-Hakim, the mad founder of the Druse superstition; there is the exquisite tomb of Kalaun. Now the Azhar University is passed, where 2000 students from all parts of Asia and Africa, even from distant Sierra Leone, are taught gratuitously by professors learned in the erudition of the Egyptians. Here the massive gate Zawila is passed, where the people still offer mysterious trophies of hair and teeth to the famous saint who is believed to hide behind the door, and where, in 1517, the Turkish conqueror of Egypt, Selim the Grim, hung the last of the Mamluke Sultans by his neck until he breathed his last; and just beyond is the Sultan Hasan's mosque, the largest in Cairo, with its splendid arches and spire-like minarets.

Picturesque Costumes.

In picturesqueness of costume the peoples you meet on the Esbekyeh or Broadway of Cairo lead the world. Instead of the abominable trousers and buttoned coats of the Europeans you are greeted by the graceful turban and flowing robes that remind you of the classic antique.

Before the walk is over you have passed and repassed representatives of nearly every nation under the skies, and your mind is confused with images of green-turbaned *sherifs*, or descendants of the Prophet Mohammed, blue-turbaned Copts, red-fezzed, frock-coated officials, extremely naked children, sedate professors with snowy coils of muslin round their shorn skulls, tradesmen in striped *kaftans*, squatting cross-legged in their little boxes of shops, solemnly puffing at their *chibuks* or *narghilas*, and the endless number of donkeys, carrying upon their tiny backs and pipe-stem legs enormous loads, big, lazy men, or a balloon of black silk, which nearly extinguishes the little trotting creature, and which, from the pair of lustrous black eyes shining above a white face veil, you speculate to be a Turkish lady.

Now and then a "clear-the-way" cry is heard, and here comes dashing along a handsome equipage, preceded by runners gorgeously dressed and carrying long white wands in their hands.

AN ARAB FAMILY.

Among the Shops.

But the candle and rose bazaars have greater attractions for us. In these famous alleys the old Turk, with flowing caftan and pure white turban, from his dark dingy shop dispenses delicious odors, mysterious pastes and essences, with

LOWER CLASS WOMAN, CAIRO.

kohl for the eyes and henna for the fingers; the roaming peddlers patronizingly offer you sandal-wood fans, beads, trinkets, gaudy Syrian crapes, Egyptian sweetmeats, fruit in baskets balanced on their heads, colored slippers of kid and satin, elaborately wrought in gold, silver and gilt, turned up at the toes, and wonder-

A MORNING RIDE.

ful pipes of every description, with graceful stems of carved amber. From this scene we pass into another quite different.

Saracenic Architecture.

Before you loom up the stately line of mosques, which present the most beautiful and continuous series of Saracenic monuments in the world. They show

DANCE GIRL, CAIRO.

us the chaste and restrained stage of Art between the over-elaboration of the Alhambra and the heaviness of the Mohammedan architecture of India.

18

The study of the cloistered mosques requires several days at least. Separated not far apart, you find the ruined but beautiful Ibn-Tulun (ninth century), the spacious Azhar and El-Hakim (tenth century), and among transept or cruciform mosques Kalaun (thirteenth century), Sultan Hasan and Kait Bey (fourteenth century), which are found eastward out of the city among that wilderness of tawney domes and minarets, miscalled the "Tombs of the Khalifs." In every mosque here is an inlaid, carved or painted niche in the wall, indicating the kibla or direction of Mecca. Round this niche centres the best decorations—mosaics of marble and porphyry of ivory and mother-of-pearl, wood and plaster carving, stained glass set in cunningly, shaded borders and Kufic inscriptions, and near by is the pulpit, frequently a splendid piece of carved and inlaid paneling, arranged in complicated geometrical patterns, and in front stands the lectern or platform, where the Koran is recited.

Mohammedan Homes and Women.

While many of the columns of the cloisters are Roman in style, the domes and minarets were first used in Egypt before they were known in Europe. A glimpse of the interior of a good Mohammedan residence reveals the skillful use of paneling and tiles, the rich effects of facets of stained glass, and the mazy inter-twinings of the latticed *meshrebuja*, but very few visitors are allowed to go beyond the inner court, round which the house is always built, where the windows are thickly webbed with carved and turned lattice-work, through which, now and then, you can detect female eyes, fringed with *kohl*, peering at the intruder. How wretched must be these Mohammedan women!

They have no mental resort; education is unknown among them; they are entirely shut out from all society; it is a disgrace for them to show their faces; they know no such thing as conjugal love, and, perhaps, the worst cross of all to them, they can only see what is going on in the outside world through the medium of stolen glances!

At the Citadel.

We now stand on the great parapet of the magnificent Citadel of Cairo, where Saladin stood when he had built the fortress. The sweep of vision takes in all of the "Mother of the World;" miles away can be seen the mighty pyramids, standing against the deep-blue sky, and far in the distance you can trace the historic Nile until it is lost in the sands o the Arabian Desert. Just below you is the narrow passage where Mohammed Ali massacred the Mamlukes; yonder is the gate through which a handful of dragoons rode on September 14, 1882, in the face of eight thousand of Arabi's followers, and spread beneath us is a labyrinth of crumbling flat-roofed houses and green shady courts, overtopped by hundreds of chiseled domes and tapering minarets, whence the evening call to prayer may now be heard resounding from the muezzin's throat: "*Allahu Akbar.*" There is no

A DERVISH.

god but God. Mohammed is the Apostle of God. Come to prayer. Come to salvation. *Allahu Akbar Lailaha illa-llah.*

With the Dervishes.

On Friday, at 1 o'clock, a sacred day and hour, we beheld the ridiculous performances of the whirling and howling dervishes. Mingled feelings of pity, amusement and disgust possess one as these senseless antics are watched. Upon a raised platform a ring is made of mats upon which thirty or forty of these long-haired, half-nude howlers sit, with wagging heads, until the monotonous notes of a fife and a sort of Chinese tom-tom break the silence, and now led by the patriarch

DANCE OF THE DERVISHES.

in the centre, both lungs and each particular muscle of every man are put into vigorous exercise.

The first motion is that of throwing the head and upper portion of the body forward and bringing it back with a sudden jerk, which would ordinarily break a man's neck, but which seems to make these creatures more lively, and, encouraged by the success of this first feat, they enter upon a series of vocal and gymnastic exhibitions that are only terminated when their brains seem to be addled and physically they are completely exhausted. But before these afflictions befell me I quietly departed. A short and pleasant excursion was made to the Island of Roda, where we were shown the identical spot (!) where Moses was rescued by the King's daughter, and the nilometer, which marks the rise and fall of the Nile, but a donkey ride of eight miles to the famous ostrich farm afforded greater pleasure. Fourteen hundred and fifty of these immense African fowls are kept in walled yards, and they can be seen at every age, from the awkward little creature that has just broken the immense egg to the giant black-plumaged male ostrich twenty-five years of age.

TEMPLE AT ABYDOS.

CHAPTER XIV

THE HISTORIC NILE AND THE EXCAVATOR'S PICKAXE.

OR weeks I have been looking upon walls that are books. From their elaborate picture-writings we learn the daily life, the religion and the superstitions of the people who were buried from four to five thousand years ago.

It is my purpose, in this chapter, to give a partial account of my brief investigations of these excavated cities and temples of Egypt that are throwing so much light just now upon the past records of this wonderland of history.

About five miles northeast of Cairo is a little village built upon part of the site of the ancient town of Heliopolis, called "On" in Genesis, the "House of the Sun" in Jeremiah, and here may be seen the sycamore tree, usually called the "Virgin's Tree," under which, tradition says, the Virgin Mary sat and rested with the young child during her flight to Egypt. Near by stands an obelisk, sixty-five feet high, set up by Userten I., about B. C. 2433.

Heliopolis.

This ancient city, whose ruins cover an area of three miles square, played an important part in history. The greatest and oldest Egyptian college for the education of the priesthood and the laity stood here. During the twentieth dynasty the Temple of Heliopolis, with its staff of thousands, was one of the wealthiest in all Egypt. It was here that Joseph married the daughter of Potiphar, a priest of On (or Heliopolis), near the Goshen of the Bible. At this place the Mnevis bull was worshiped, and here it was that the Phœnix, or palm bird, brought its ashes, after having raised itself to life at the end of each period of five hundred years, and it was round about Heliopolis that Alexander the Great camped on his way from Pelusium to Memphis.

Memphis.

The ruins of Memphis and the antiquities of Sakkarah are even of greater interest. On the ground lying for miles about these two villages once stood the glorious city of Memphis, which Herodotus tells us, was built by Menes, the first ruler of Egypt.

The original city was located upon a fertile and well-wooded tract of land. Diodorus speaks of its green meadows, intersected with canals, and of their pavement of lotus flowers. Pliny talks of trees there of such girth that three men with extended arms could not span them, and Martial praises the roses and wine brought from thence to Rome.

About 4000 B. C. the city reached a height of splendor which was probably never excelled. When Rameses II. returned from his wars in the East, he set up

WATER-WHEEL ON THE NILE.

a statue of himself, which can now be seen. Cambyses, the Persian, conquered the city and established his garrison there, and until the founding of Alexandria, its power and glory were unexcelled.

The colossal statue of Rameses II. was discovered in 1820. The name of Rameses is inscribed on the belt of the statue. On the end of the roll which the

King carries in his hand are the words, "Rameses, Beloved of Amen," and by the side of the King are figures of his daughter and son

Antiquities of Sakkarah.

The tract of land at Sakkarah, near the present Memphis, which formed the great burial ground of the ancient Egyptians at all periods, is about one and a half miles long and one mile wide, and the most important antiquities to be found there are the "Step Pyramid," oblong in shape, with an extreme length of 396 feet and a height of 197 feet, supposed to be older than the great pyramids of Gizeh; the pyramids of the kings of the fifth and sixth dynasties, on which have been found some valuable inscriptions, and from which have been taken fragments of the royal mummies. The tomb of Phi, which represents this confidant of the king superintending all the various operations connected with the management of of his large agricultural estates, with illustrations of hunting and fishing expeditions, and the Apis mausoleum, which contained the vaults where all the Apis bulls that lived in Memphis were buried.

According to Herodotus, " Apis is the calf of a cow incapable of conceiving another offspring, and the Egyptians say that lightning descends upon the cow from heaven, and that from thence it brings forth Apis. The calf is black, has a square spot of white on the forehead; on the back the imprint of an eagle; in the tail double hairs, and on the tongue a beetle."

Above each tomb of an Apis a chapel was built, and on the tombs writings have been found that give accurate chronological data for the history of Egypt.

On the Banks of the Nile.

But we must turn toward the banks of the historic Nile, where the most important and interesting antiquities have been found. On the east bank of the river, 150 miles south of Cairo, is the lonely Convent of the Virgin on the Bird Mountain (Gebelet-Tayr), where the monks swing themselves down the steep rock which overhangs the water, priding themselves, despite the discomforts of their lives, on the fact that they belong to the sleepy old Coptic Church, which has remained crusted in its simplicity for 1500 years, since the council of Chalcedon.

Sailing down, or rather up the Nile, to which nature has given her own unspeakable loveliness and art and history have added their own inspiring associations, we pause only a short while to see the tombs where the mummied "serpent of the Nile" was reverently laid to rest by the crocodile worshipers, and we take only a lingering glance at Asyut, the capital of Upper Egypt, nestled in the glowing Libyan hills, for we are bound for the great temples of Egypt and we are not tempted to tarry.

PROGRESS OF ANCIENT AND MODERN IRRIGATION ON THE NILE.

We first reach beautiful Abydos—embraced by hills, veiled in palm groves, surrounded by waving fields of ripening grain—with its noble ruins carved all over with delicate reliefs, wherein King Seti stands forth, offering to Osiris, and where the Tables of Kings is set forth, with all their names, to the joy of modern scholars.

Abydos and the Memnonium.

Abydos, Thebes and Heliopolis represented the homes of religious thought and learning in Egypt, and Abydos, especially, was the centre of the great Osiris, the type of the conflict between good and evil, life and death, resurrection and immortality to every pious Egyptian of old. This sacred city is mentioned by Plutarch, Athenæus, Ptolemy and Pliny, and Strabo tells us that at one time it was second only to Thebes. There are two magnificent monuments here.

The Temple of Seti, or the Memnonium, is built of fine white calcareous stone, the pillars are inscribed with religious scenes and figures of the king and the god Osiris. On the south wall is an inscription in which Rameses II., relates all that he has done for the honor of his father's memory, how he erected statues of him at Thebes and Memphis. The second hall is supported by thirty-six columns, elaborately sculptured, arranged in three rows.

The scenes on several of the walls set forth, with remarkable artistic power, royal ceremonies, and in one of the corridors is the famous tablet of Abydos, which gives the names of seventy-six kings of Egypt, beginning with Menes and ending with Seti I.

The Temple of Osiris.

A little to the north of the building of which we have spoken is the Temple of Rameses II., dedicated by this king to the god Osiris, and it was thought by many distinguished scholars to be the famous shrine which all Egypt adored, but the excavations of M. Mariette proved that it was not.

The fragment of a tablet containing the names of Egyptian kings, now in the British Museum, came from this temple, and the inscriptions and ornamentations on the walls are of value.

Our next stopping place is over five hundred miles up the Nile, where the wonderfully preserved Temple of Denderah calls forth exclamations of pleasure. Although it is thought not to be older than the later Ptolemies, it is the most majestic monument that has so far been visited by us.

The names of several of the Roman emperors appear on various parts of the temple ; the well-known portraits of Cleopatra and Cæsarion, her son, are on the end wall of the exterior; a dromos of about two hundred and fifty feet leads into a portico, supported by twenty-four, Hathor-headed columns. Several chambers show beautiful decorations, and on the highest ceiling is the famous " Zodiac," which was thought to have been made in ancient Egypt, but which is disproved by the inscription A. D. 35, written in the twenty-first year of Tiberius.

All through this marvelous structure we meet a happy blending of Egyptian seriousness with Grecian grace, which lends enchantment to every part of it. We now turn our faces again up the river, and with thrilling anticipations of the

INTERIOR OF TEMPLE OF ABYDOS.

fulfillment of many dreams, we approach the site of ancient Thebes, "the city of a hundred gates" of Homer's verse.

Wondrous Thebes.

Beautiful for situation was the ancient city of Thebes.

The mountains on the east and west side of the river sweep away from this historic spot and leave a broad plain on each bank of several square miles in extent. In this wide space, where modern Paris could stand, was located the renowned city which Homer sings about in his ninth Iliad, and which Diodorus, who visited it about B. C. 57, tells us was not only the most beautiful and stateliest city of Egypt, but could not be excelled in all the world.

Within her hundred gates were kept 20,000 chariots of war. The succeeding kings from time to time adorned this pride of their kingdom with monuments of gold, silver, ivory, alabaster and granite. Multitudes of colossi and obelisks were reared in her streets. Wonderful sepulchres of the ancient kings, forty-

OUR NILE BOAT.

seven in number, excelling in grandeur, according to Strabo (B. C. 24), everything of the kind in the world, were built in her neighborhood; and as little by little the local god, Amen-Ra, became the great god of all Egypt, his dwelling-place, Thebes, gained in importance and splendor, reaching its highest point of glory during the rule of the eighteenth and nineteenth dynasties.

Up and Down the Nile.

The two great divisions of Egypt into Upper and Lower, made from time immemorial, and the expressions of "up" and "down" the Nile are somewhat puzzling to the tourist when he first travels through this land of historic interest.

CLEOPATRA PORTRAIT AT DENDERAH ON THE NILE.

Toward the Mediterranean Sea is known as Lower Egypt, way out toward Nubia is Upper Egypt, and around Cairo and Alexandria we are down the Nile, while way down here at Assouan, between seven and eight hundred miles south of the sea, we are far up the Nile. Everything is decided by the course of the great river, the river and country toward its mouth is " down;" toward its source it is " up."

Although vast preparations are being made by the British and Egyptian military powers for the war in the Soudan, and nearly all the boats on the Nile

THE NILE'S DELTA.

are being chartered by the government for the transportation of troops, after negotiating for some days, a party of five Americans (including the writer) and one Scotchman was formed, and securing a steam launch, manned by an Egyptian engineer and fireman, a Libyan pilot, a Greek cook and steward, a Nubian waiter and a Soudanese dragoman, we steamed up the river, passing numbers of boats crowded with bright uniformed and fierce-looking militia, and after nearly two weeks of life on the water of a stream that has supported by its annual overflow countless millions during the last sixty centuries, we are at the extreme southern

ALONG THE NILE.

boundary of Egypt, surrounded by the evidences of a civilization that existed four thousand years before the commencement of the Christian era.

Centre of Ancient Culture.

It must not be thought that the real Egypt is the vast country outlined on our maps, reaching to the Indian Ocean, the Red Sea, and embracing equatorial regions. It is and was, even far back in the days of the Pharaohs and Ptolomies, the valley of the Nile, from the first cataract, where I am now writing, to the Mediterranean Sea, shut in by the Libyan and Arabian deserts.

In this district, less than a thousand miles in length, were centred much of the art, science and philosophy of the ancient world, and here were reared those time-defying monuments which after a burial of thousands of years are being resurrected by modern enterprise, and to-day are the wonder of an age that until lately supposed that these ancients were uncivilized barbarians who could add nothing to our boasted omniscience.

The Orientals compare the long, narrow valley of the Nile and its broad, triangular-shaped embouchure or delta to a long-stemmed fan, and the city of Cairo is called the "brightest gem in the handle of the green Egyptian fan." Just before it reaches the sea the river parts into several streams, and, during flood time, it pours 700,000,000 cubic metres of water daily into the Mediterranean through its different mouths.

Once clear of the belt of salt lagoons that fringes the sand hills behind Alexandria, the Delta spreads before us the richest soil of Egypt. The alluvial deposit washed down annually by the flooded Nile from its gigantic reservoirs in the Abyssinian mountains nourishes magnificent crops, and the spreading arms of the river, the intersecting network of canals and multitudes of *sakiyas* or water-wheels regulate the distribution of the water to perfection.

Wheat, maize, barley, rice, millet, beans, cotton and indigo are grown here in luxuriance, and a succession of three crops in the year is not unusual with skillful farmers.

The mud villages, with their little white mosque and minaret, their pigeon towers and the sparse cluster of palms or tamarisks by the well, where women and girls are filling the great earthen pitchers, which they afterward balance with a stately grace upon their heads, make a characteristic picture, but in the Delta there is nothing, perhaps, that need detain the traveler save the wonderful excavations and discoveries of the "Egypt Exploration Fund" at the Bible cities of Pithom and Zoan (Tanis) in the land of Goshen and the famous Greek port of Naucratis.

At Pithom you may see the ancient sun-dried bricks which Pharaoh's taskmasters set the children of Israel to make without straw. In this part of the

SCENE ON THE ARABIAN DESERT.

country the only town worth a visit is Tanta during the great periodical festivals of the Saint El-Bedawi, when revels take place which are the modern representatives of the Bubastian orgies of which Herodotus writes.

Scenes of the Voyage.

A Nile voyage, with a small, congenial party, in a well-appointed and well-furnished boat, under our own control, is one of the most perfect forms of human

THE VOCAL MEMNON.

enjoyment. The charm is something quite peculiar. In all the world, perhaps, no river shows such varying moods as the Nile, despite its smoothness; and the exquisite tints of the scenery, presenting a vivid contrast between the brown, Nile-mud villages, fringed with palm groves and crowned with white minarets, and the waving fields of pale-green corn or sweet-scented bean and purple lupin blossom, are indescribable.

THE SAKIEH.

During the day the book that you bought in Cairo to while away the weary hours of the long journey is frequently forgotten as you watch a strange-looking craft exactly after the pattern of those used five thousand years ago, or a long line of fifty or a hundred camels, followed by Bedouins of the desert, attract your attention, or you interestingly follow the movements of the nude Nubians as they work the shadufs, lifting the leathern buckets, filled with water from the Nile over three or four terraces and dash the fertilizing liquid into the furrows of the fields; and you lay aside your book altogether toward the hour of sunset, when the color which was lost in the quivering white heat of noon returns to clothe the land with hues of unspeakable beauty and the evening breeze begins to rustle in the palms, whose long, thin shadows now steal toward the stream, and a deep, violet haze begins to creep along the clefts and hollows of the rose-red range of the Lybian hills, flushing the whole sky with the tender tints of the after-glow till the twilight deepens under the palm groves and the rippling river glides silently by under the twinkling stars, as, one by one, they dot the growing darkness of the sky, bright harbingers of the brighter morn that now shows her beaming face over the trackless Arabian Desert.

A Co-operative System.

I find that there is a co-operation of labor adopted by the people of this Nile Valley that has been in existence for ages, and which goes far toward the solution of certain vexed questions that are now giving Western nations no little trouble.

Besides small specified wages the workers at the shadufs and water-wheels get a certain percentage of the crop; those who do service on the boats share the profits of the business, and into every form of labor this just principle seems to enter. The possession of land passes from father to son. The tax rates (which, by the way, have caused nearly all the trouble in Egypt for so many years) are now decided by the tax commission under British appointment, and there is an air of contentment and prosperity among the docile, simple-hearted children of the Valley of the Nile that does not create wrinkles on their glossy black skin.

The Ruins of Thebes.

For centuries these monuments of human skill and pride were swallowed in the sand of the desert, but during these latter years they have one by one been unearthed, and to-day we can look upon their magnificent ruins and imagine what they were.

After a long dusty donkey ride I climbed the Libyan hills, which here trend away and leave a beautiful amphitheatre, girdled with peaked ramparts of yellow cliff and smiling with golden harvest fields of ripening grain in the face of the

THE NILE WATER CARRIERS.

burning sun, and there about me the greatness of old Thebes stood partly revealed.

There below us on the mountain's side in the terraced temple of Deyr-el-bakri, which Hashop, first of the great queens of history, built as the vestibule of her tomb. Lower down, on the sandy carpet of the level plain, is the grand

KARNAK IN RUINS.

colonnade which tells us what a structure the Rameseum, or " Tomb of Ozymandias," must have been.

Statue of Rameses the Great.

Near by are the battered blocks of what was once the most gigantic figure ever carved out of a single granite rock, the statue of Rameses the Great.

> " Half sunk, a shattered visage lies, whose frown
> And wrinkled lip, and sneer of cold command,
> Tell that its sculptor well those passions real
> Which yet survive, stamped on these lifeless things,
> The hand that mocked them, and the heart that fed.
> And on the pedestal these words appear :
> ' My name is Ozymandias, king of kings,
> Look on my works, ye mighty, and despair.' "

The Vocal Memnon.

Out in the grain fields, not far from the Nile in lonely majesty and turning their solemn gaze toward the east, sit side by side those twin colossi one of

STATUE OF RAMESES.

whom by a strange confusion with the son of Tithonus and Eos, the valiant ally of the Trojans, has become famous forever as the "Vocal Memnon." For, according to tradition and the ancient poets, as the rays of the rising sun smote upon the stone a sweet sound, as of a human voice, came forth, and pilgrims came from afar to Egypt to hear Memnon softly chant his orisen to his mother the rosy-fingered Morn:

> " Beneath the Libyan hills
> Where spreading Nile parts hundred-gated Thebes."

The whole statue is covered with the names of the pilgrims, from Sabina, the consort of the Emperor Hadrian, to one Gemellos, " who came here with his well-beloved wife, Rufilla, and his children."

ISLAND OF PHILÆ.

This vocal statue of Memnon is composed of two parts. The lower and older consists of a single block of sandstone conglomerate; the upper part was broken off by an earthquake in the year 27 B. C., and was not restored until the reign of Septimius Severus, a number of years afterward.

INTERIOR OF TEMPLE EDFOU, NILE.

(297)

Tombs of the Kings.

In the steep hollows of the hills, a mile or so away, are those marvelous "tombs of the kings," discovered by Belzoni, which are hewn out of the living

ODELISK AT LUXOR.

rock mountains. These tombs consist of long inclined plains, with a number of chambers receding into the mountain, sometimes to a distance of 500 feet.

Here lay the mummied bodies of Seti I. and a number of the Rameses, who exerted such mighty influence on the history of Egypt, and other rulers, whose dried, pinched faces may be seen in the Gizeh Museum, in Cairo.

Away yonder across the Nile (for ancient Thebes extended along both sides of the river) we can see the ruins of the Temple of Luxor, in the midst of which stands forth the obelisk of Rameses II., its fellow being in the Place de la Concorde, Paris.

From the Temple of Luxor there was an avenue of about 6500 feet long and eighty feet wide, on each side of which was arranged a row of sphinxes leading to the superb Temple or Temples of Karnak, now a wilderness of broken walls and obelisks, fallen columns, mutilated statues, with here and there a noble propylon, a stately column, or a wonderful wall painting, which tells, like the sculptured epic of Pentaour, the poet, how the king smote his enemies and drove them before his chariot.

The Temples of Karnak.

The ruins of Karnak are a priceless library, upon whose carved pages we children of these last years can read of the ancient majesty of the house of Amen-Ra.

Under the brilliant Egyptian moon and at the hour when the shadows were lengthening and the western sky was crimsoned by the setting sun, I quietly studied these eleven shattered Temples of Karnak. Passing through the second and greater pylon, we enter the famous "Hall of Columns." The twelve columns forming the double row in the middle are sixty feet high, and the other columns, 122 in number, are about forty feet high. The court is 275 feet deep and 338 feet wide and covers an area of 9755 yards.

The columns that support the roof of this hypostyle hall are adorned by calyx capitals of gigantic proportions, and upon them are sculptured a record of the names and deeds of the princes of the times and the customs and superstitions of the people.

"It is impossible," says Lepsius, "to describe the impression experienced by every one who enters this forest of columns for the first time and passes from row to row, amidst the lofty figures of gods and kings, projecting, some in full relief, some in half relief, from the columns on which they are represented."

The Hall of Columns.

Some of the columns are prostrate, others lean as though on the verge of falling, and architrave and roof slabs seem on the point of tumbling, but this ruinous condition of everything adds a picturesque charm to the general impression. The outside of both the north and south walls of the Hall of Columns are ornamented with scenes of the great warriors moving against the peoples who lived to the northeast of Syria and in Mesopotamia.

The inscriptions found at Karnak show that from about B. C. 2433 until the time of Alexander IV., B. C. 312, the religious centre of Upper Egypt was Thebes,

(310)   INTERIOR OF TEMPLE OF KARNAK.

and that the most powerful of the kings of Egypt who reigned during this period spared neither pains nor expense in building, adding to and beautifying the temples of this place of power.

While there is a wealth of monuments heaped together at Thebes and Memphis that cannot be equaled, yet at Edfou is perhaps the most perfect single temple in all Egypt, looking as though its priests still offered sacrifice to Horus, as they did in the days of Ptolemy Philopator. Except the cornice, the immense pylon is entire, and the building itself is as perfect nearly as when the architects left it—thousands of years ago.

Two hundred and forty steps of a square staircase lead up to the summit of each of its twin towers; the walls of the temple are covered not with epics of battle, as at Karnak, but with the rites of religion, geographical lists, astronomical tables, inventories of temples and their lands, their priests and precentors, and here we find that the chisel, rather than the pen, has handed down to coming ages an Egyptian encyclopedia

The Island of Philæ.

Most tourists return toward Cairo after seeing the wonders of Thebes, but having chartered our launch for nearly three weeks, we continued to the extreme southern limit of Egypt, a little below the first cataract of the Nile.

At Assuan exiled Juvenal avenged himself in remorseless satire. Here we visited the quarries whence came the material of all the statues, obelisks, shrines and facings of tombs, temples and pyramids at Thebes, Memphis and Heliopolis, and here, after riding past old Kufic tombstones and ruined mosques scattered over miles of yellow desert, we meet the river again, and see before us the pylon of the Temple of Isis and the imposing columns of "Pharaoh's Bed" rising out of the dark green palm groves of the Island of Philæ.

As we walked through and around this Nile-girt island we recalled that to millions for many centuries it was a holy place, whither devout pilgrimages were made to pay homage to the beloved Osiris. We turn from these scenes, where fifty centuries strew their records at our feet, astonished at the revelations of the most ancient, and in some respects, the most wonderful civilization of the world.

Explorations of Professor Petrie and "Sayings of Christ."

While visiting the excavated cities on the Nile, it was my pleasure to see Professor Flinders Petrie, the noted Egyptologist, at work in the rubbish of one of his excavations; and it was at this time that the Professor brought to light an important tablet, the first which has been found giving a description of the wars between the Pharaohs and the ancient Jews. More recently this gentleman, together with Drs. Grenfell and Hunt, and others, have made noted discoveries, all of which throw light upon the customs and habits of the ancient Egyptians, and some of them confirm Bible history. While at work on the banks of the Nile about fifty miles south of Cairo, Professor Petrie found a cluster of tombs, dating

HALL OF COLUMNS, KARNAK.

over five thousand years ago. The peculiarity of these tombs is that they do not contain any of the mummies which are usually found in Egyptian tombs; but instead boxes containing only bones, wrapped carefully in cloth. These tombs

THE TEMPLE OF PHILÆ, NILE.

belong to the fifth dynasty of Egyptian kings; and here are found the bones of Nenkheftka, a prince and royal priest, and those of his wife Nefersen and their son; and as there are statues found in these tombs, it is thus known that at a period earlier than that assigned Abraham, sculpture was a well-known art. While exploring under the auspices of the Egyptian Exploration Fund, Bernard P. Grenfell, M. A., and Arthur S. Hunt, M. A., discovered on the site of the ancient African city, Oxyrhynchus, about one hundred and twenty miles south of Cairo, a precious leaf containing the "Sayings of Christ." The date of these "sayings" is supposed to be about A. D. 200. The page is written on both sides, and is evidently torn from a book, as there is a folio number on it; it contains forty-three lines, each line consisting of about four words; and of the eight sayings, two cannot be deciphered at all. Three of the remaining six "sayings" are similar to passages found in the Gospels of Matthew and Luke; and the remaining read thus: "Jesus saith, I stood in the midst of the world, and in the flesh was I seen of them, and I found all men drunken, and none found I athirst among them; and my soul grieveth over the sons of men because they are blind in their heart;" "Jesus saith, Except ye fast to the world, ye shall in no wise find the kingdom of God, and except ye keep the Sabbath ye shall not see the Father;" "Jesus saith, Wherever there are . . . . and there is one . . . . alone, I am with him. Raise the stone, and there thou shalt find me. Cleave the wood, and there am I." As this page is apparently a part of a volume, other parts may be found which will, doubtless, add interest and importance to the discovery of this fragment. We hail with joy every stroke of the excavator's pickaxe in Bible lands; for as light falls upon the buried memorials of the past, the pages of both secular and sacred history will be illumined.

CHAPTER XV

THE PYRAMIDS OF EGYPT AND THE ANCIENT EGYPTIANS.

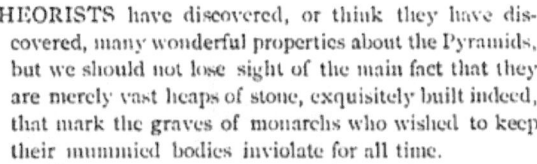

THEORISTS have discovered, or think they have discovered, many wonderful properties about the Pyramids, but we should not lose sight of the main fact that they are merely vast heaps of stone, exquisitely built indeed, that mark the graves of monarchs who wished to keep their mummied bodies inviolate for all time.

The Egyptians built their houses for the living of perishable brick; they built their houses for the dead of immortal granite. There was a reason for this, founded upon their theory of human life and death.

They regarded man as composed of several entities, each having its separate life and functions. First, was the body; then the *ka*, or double, which was an ethereal duplicate, feature for feature, of the corporeal form; then was the soul, which was popularly represented as a human-headed bird, and after the soul came the "luminous," a spark from the divine fire.

By process of embalmment they could suspend for ages the decomposition of the body, and by means of prayer and offerings the other component parts were saved from the second death, thus causing prolongation of existence.

Egyptian Psychology.

The "double" never left the body, but the soul and the "luminous" went forth to follow the gods, returning, now and then, to the resting place of the body. Thus, the tomb was called the "eternal house" of the dead, compared with which the houses of the living were but wayside inns, and, therefore, if possible, these eternal houses were built as durable as all time.

The tomb must contain a private room for the soul, which was closed at the time of burial, not to be opened under any circumstances. It must also contain a wide passage or reception-room, where priests and friends made offerings for the dead. Indeed, the tomb was looked upon as a permanent dwelling, and it was built to promote the well-being and insure the preservation of the dead.

The construction of the Pyramids and other imposing tombs illustrate this idea, and the success with which these ancient Egyptians preserved the mortal remains of their royal dead is seen in the mummies that retain their facial expressions after these thousands of years.

(306)

ROAD FROM CAIRO TO THE PYRAMIDS.

The Pyramid of Lights.

The great Pyramid of Cheops, at Gizeh, the most prodigious of all human constructions, covers thirteen acres at the base and weighs about seven million tons. Originally it was four hundred and eighty feet high, and it is estimated that the materials that were used for its construction would build over twenty thousand eight-roomed cottages and house a population of one hundred and fifty thousand.

Like most of its fellows, it stands exactly square to the four points of the compass. The great limestone blocks, some of them five feet broad and high and thirty feet long, were brought from distant quarries, and propelled, doubtless, on rollers from the river along a well-laid causeway to their present site. Mechanical appliances, as well as the art of cutting and polishing the hardest stone, were familiar to these Egyptians of five thousand years ago.

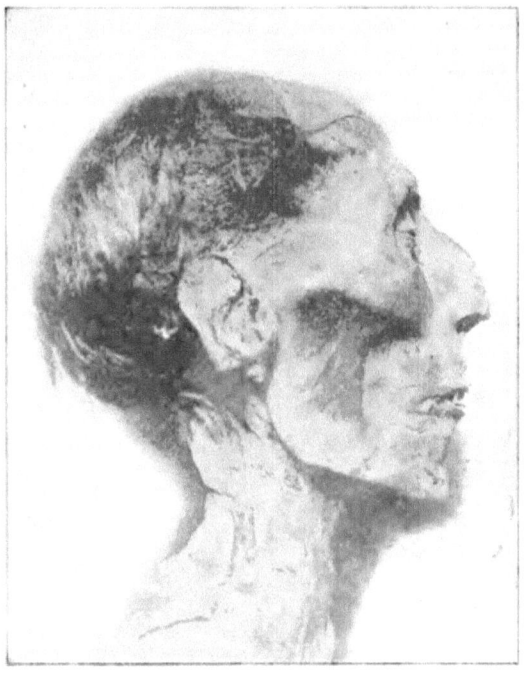

RAMESES II.

Its Colossal Dimensions.

Twenty years, Herodotus tells us, the great Pyramid was building, and, when it was completed, instead of presenting the rough series of steps it does now the whole edifice was cased with shining red syenite, brought from the first cataract, five hundred miles away, which caused it to glisten so brightly that it was known as the "Pyramid of Lights." Until the Arab conquest it preserved this stone casing, so wonderfully joined as to appear like one block from base to summit.

In the inside everything was arranged so as to hide the exact place of the sarcophagus and thus baffle all would-be spoilers of the royal tomb. It was necessary first to discover the entrance under the casing, which masked it. This was found to be nearly in the middle of the north face, at the level of the eighteenth course, about forty-five feet from the ground.

PYRAMID OF CHEOPS.

When at last the casing was torn off and the block of stone was displaced which covered the entrance, an inclined passage 41.2 inches wide and 47.6

inches high was revealed, the lower part of which was cut in the stone. This descended for three hundred and seventeen feet, passed through an unfinished chamber and ended sixty feet further in a blind passage.

The Interior and Contents.

Although the spoilers were disappointed here, by careful examination in the roof, sixty-two feet distant from the door, a block of granite was found which shut from view another passage. Having passed this obstacle, they came to an ascending passage which divides into two branches—one running into a limestone chamber in the centre of the Pyramid; the other, continuing upward, becomes a gallery one hundred and forty-eight feet long and twenty-eight feet high, built of Mokattam stone, so polished and finely wrought that we are told it was difficult to put a needle or even a hair into the joints.

A NILE BELLE.

Another difficulty must now be surmounted. The final passage leading to the chamber of the sarcophagus was closed by a slab of granite, and further on was a small vestibule divided in equal spaces by four partitions of granite which must be broken. When at last it was reached, the royal sepulchre was found to be a granite chamber nineteen feet high, thirty-four feet long and seventeen feet wide.

Thus we may see how painstaking these old Egyptians were to guard the safety of the body of the great one among them, and in this and other cases they kept it untouched by human hands and unseen by human eyes for ages and ages. The mummy of the founder has long since been removed, but his stone coffin is on exhibition.

Queen Nitocris.

The second pyramid of Gizeh, built by the brother of the builder of the first (according to Herodotus), retains some of its original casing at the top, and round the third, the red pyramid of Menkara, where it is supposed once lay the body of

S. HINX.

the beautiful Queen Nitocris, a Loreley legend has grown up; the queen's blushing face caused her to be confounded with the rosy-cheeked Rhodopis, the Greek favorite of King Amasis, and superstition imagines that a fair but treacherous woman haunts the Red pyramid and bewitches travelers:

" Fair Rhodope, as story tells,
    The bright unearthly nymph who dwells
    'Mid sunless gold and jewels hid,
    The Lady of the Pyramid !"

A short walk from the great Pyramid brings us face to face with a statue, the most ancient known, that is more of a mystery, if not more of a wonder, than the royal tomb—the Great Sphinx of Gizeh.

An Old Monument.

We have historic proof that it was already in existence in the time of the builder of the great Pyramid, but its real age is unknown. It is hewn in the living rock; its battered body presents but the general form of the lion, the paws, and the breast, restored by the Ptolemies and the Cæsars, retain but a part of the stone facing with which they were originally clothed. The lower part of the head-dress has fallen and the neck is badly broken: the nose and the beard have been cut away and the red hue which enlivened the features is almost wholly gone.

But notwithstanding the ravages of time

DAME SOUDALL.

and fanatics, it has an expression of strength and greatness. The eyes gaze out upon the waste of desert sand with intense thoughtfulness, the mouth wears a smile, and the whole countenance possesses power and repose.

The body is about one hundred and fifty feet long, the head is thirty feet

CLEOPATRA AT DENDERAH

long, the face is four-teen feet wide, and from the top of the head to the base of the monument the distance is about seventy feet. The condition in which it now appears is due to the barbarous destruction of its features by the Mohammedan rulers of Egypt, some of whom caused it to be used for a target.

We turn from these masterpieces of ancient skill with the unanswered and unanswerable question in our mind: How long did it take to arrive at this degree of maturity and perfection?

The Ancient Egyptians.

During the three weeks I have been studying the sculptures and monuments of Upper and Lower Egypt, the query, whence came the original Egyptians, has been of increasing interest. There can be but little doubt that they belonged to the Caucasian race; that their first home was Asia, and that they made their way across Mesopotamia, Arabia and the Isthmus of Suez into Egypt.

Historians do not fix for us a period when these new-comers from the East came west of the Red Sea, but the strongest evidence points to the remote age of B. C. 5000.

From carvings and inscriptions excavated recently we have proof that these people from the East found in Egypt a race following agricultural pursuits, navigating the Nile with their rude crafts, dressing scantily and having dark skin.

CARVING AT SAKKARAL.

This aboriginal race called the country Kamt, which means "black," and the name may have originated either from the complexion of the people or, more probably, from the dark, rich color of the cultivated land of Egypt.

Bible Lore and Picture Record.

The Bible gives the name of "Ham" to this country. The children of Ham are said to be Cush, Mizraim, Put and Canaan, and we find that the second of these, Mizraim, is the name given to Egypt by the Hebrews.

The descendants of Cush are represented on the monuments by the inhabitants of Nubia and the negro tribes which live to the south of that country. The children of Put, the third son of Ham, appear to have dwelt on both sides of the Red Sea, to the south of Egypt, carrying on a large trade with the Egyptians as far back as 2500 B. C., and the descendants of Mizraim are supposed to have been related to the aboriginal inhabitants of Phœnicia, called in the Bible Canaanites.

Without a single exception every representation of the ancient Egyptian depicts him as having a slender form, rather broad shoulders, long hands and feet, sinewy legs and arms, high forehead, square chin, short and rounded nose, jaws slightly protruding and hair fine and smooth.

The skulls and bones of mummies which anthropologists have examined and measured quite recently, support and confirm the pictures on the tombs, over-throwing utterly the theory that the Egyptian is, from what we understand by the expression, of negro origin.

WATER CARRIER, CAIRO.

Ancient and Modern Type.

Several times I have noticed that the nose of one of the later Egyptians, as seen in the carvings, is slightly aquiline; but this is explained by the intermarriage of the Egyptians with people of Semitic origin.

I have been greatly impressed with the fact that the Egyptian of to-day is an exact reproduction of his ancestors who lived fifty centuries ago. Yesterday I was accompanied during the day's ramble amidst the ruins of an ancient temple by a pure Egyptian, and in his dress, attitudes, form and face he was the living picture of a figure that was repeated over and over again on the crumbling walls which were decorated twenty centuries before the Christian era.

The invasions of the Babylonians, Ethiopians, Assyrians, Persians, Greeks, Romans, Arabs and Turks seem to have had no permanent effect either on their physical or mental characteristics, and the type of the Egyptian fellah which we meet to-day is just what it was in the earliest dynasties.

The Fellahin.

These Fellahin compose four-fifths of the entire population of Egypt, and are chiefly employed in agricultural pursuits—indeed, the whole of the cultivation of Egypt is practically in their hands. The Egyptians represented on the earliest monuments to which we can assign a date were already highly civilized and possessed an alphabetic system of writing, a grammar, a government and a religion. Perhaps there are no people in the world whose wonderful history is so accurately traceable in their laws, customs, costumes and religion as the Egyptians, and much of this pictorial record on stone, after having been buried from the eye of man for thousands of years, is an unsealed volume to the children of the closing years of the nineteenth century of the Christian era.

Other Nationalities.

Besides the Fellahin, of whom we have spoken, about one-fifth of the population of Egypt is composed of Copts, Bedouins, Jews, Turks, Negroes, Nubians, Abyssinians, Armenians and Europeans, all the inhabitants of the land not exceeding much more than seven millions. It is estimated that there are about three hundred and fifty thousand Copts in Egypt to-day.

YOUNG NEGRESS IN SOUDAN.

They are descendants from the ancient Egyptians and live mostly in the cities of Upper Egypt, are engaged in the different trades, and physically they are of a finer type than the Fellahin. As is well known, they are famous in ecclesiastical history for having embraced with remarkable zeal and rapidity the doctrines of Christianity as preached, it is supposed, by St. Mark at Alexandria, and before the close of the third century many thousands of these Copts had cast away the

weird religion of their fathers and embraced with enthusiasm the gospel of the
Nazarene.   Because they held persistently to the doctrine that Christ had but one
composite nature and denied that He was both human and divine, they were called
Monophysites, but to-day, like many other so-called Christians, they are too much
occupied in watching the main chance to trouble themselves on theological ques-

TYPE OF THE NEGRESS.

tions.   Generally speak-
ing, the knowledge of the
Coptic language is extinct,
and the Arabic seems to
be spoken by them en-
tirely.

The Bedouins.

The Bedawins (or Bed-
ouins) comprise the diff-
erent Arabic-speaking and
Mohammedan tribes who
live in the deserts along
the river Nile, and
although it is impossible
for me to secure correct
statistics on the subject,
it is supposed that they
number perhaps two hun-
dred and fifty thousand.
During my trip of six
hundred miles up the Nile,
I rode for miles over a
barren desert, and a sight
of these independent men,

living far away from city or village, confirmed the opinion already formed that
they are possessed of brave and heroic characteristics.   But I have no special
desire to meet them after dark, as I hinted to my guide.   The Nubians (from
"nub," meaning "gold,") live nearly altogether in Nubia, extreme Upper
Egypt, which was a gold-producing country, and they speak a language that is
allied to some of the North African tongues.   The negroes, forming a large part
of the non-native population of Egypt, are held practically as slaves by the
natives, and the Turks, although comparatively few in number, hold many civil
and military appointments and possess keen business instincts.   The European

SYRIAN BEDOUINS.

population in Egypt consists of Greeks, about sixty-five thousand ; Italians, thirty thousand; French, fourteen thousand; English, nine thousand, and Germans, Austrians and Russians, perhaps ten thousand.

Greek Merchants.

In Alexandria the most prosperous business men are the Greek merchants, and although it is said that these citizens contribute most largely to the crime of the country, no one can deny that their commercial genius has made Alexandria

NEGRO (SOUDANESE).

the great city that it is. Yes, it is "great," as measured by the narrow tape-line of modern materialistic greatness, but its ancient pomp, power and prowess have vanished forever. The shades of Alexander the Great! Where is the city that was founded by the world's mighty conqueror in 332 B. C. ? Where is the Serapeum, the wonderful museum, the library with its million volumes and the magnificent palaces and temples? Where are the twin obelisks which Cleopatra stole from the Temple of the Sun at Heliopolis? One stands in the fog of London, the other in the flash of Central Park, New York. British guns and European commerce have blotted out all that told of the glory of the great Alexandria, by Alexander the Great, and the

ENGLISH CAMEL CORPS GOING UP THE NILE.

deeds of the Ptolemies, the heroic past of Antony's "Royal Egypt," of Hypatia and Cyril, are naught but the fading memories of bygone history, that are nearly hushed and crushed by the din, dust and dirt of our boasted modern progress.

Soudan Expedition.

Fifteen years ago England abandoned the Soudan, after the unfortunate death of General Gordon; and since that time it has been controlled by the Khalifa, the

NUBIAN ON THE NILE.

Mohammedan fanatic, who succeeded the Mahdi. During these years England has not been idle. There has been a reorganization of the English government in Egypt; the Egyptian army has been drilled, newly equipped and officered by Englishmen; and since the spring of 1896 progressive means have been adopted to reclaim this blighted region. Fighting on the Nile entails many dangers. To avoid the peril of having communications cut off and the advanced post of the army surrounded by the enemy, every position as it is occupied is strongly fortified and connected by railroad and telegraph, so that news can be quickly received and troops can be readily moved to the field of action. After hard fighting, Abu Hamid, only one hundred and thirty miles from the equator, was captured; and this is regarded as an important event in the Anglo-Egyptian expediton. As the oppression of the Khalifa became unendurable, the natives of this region hailed with joy the victory of the Egyptian and British army; and now that the flotilla of steamers built for the navigation of the upper Nile is doing effective service it is

THE FIRST CATARACT.

hoped that the expedition will press its way into the heart of the Soudan, and bring liberty and hope to an enslaved and despairing people.

All Europe, as well as Egypt, is greatly excited over the war in the Soudan, and thousands of Egyptian and hundreds of English soldiers crowd the Nile boats, hurrying on to the seat of war. I have arrived at the extreme southernmost point to which tourists are allowed to go by the command of the Egyptian government, and as I write three boats, filled with native infantry, two packed with boys of the "Union Jack" and one appropriated by the camel corps, are passing up the Nile.

To make clear the present status of affairs in this country allow me to refer to certain historical matters.

I have given an interview I held with Arabi Pasha, in Ceylon, which gave an account of the uprising of the fellahin under Arabi, in 1882,

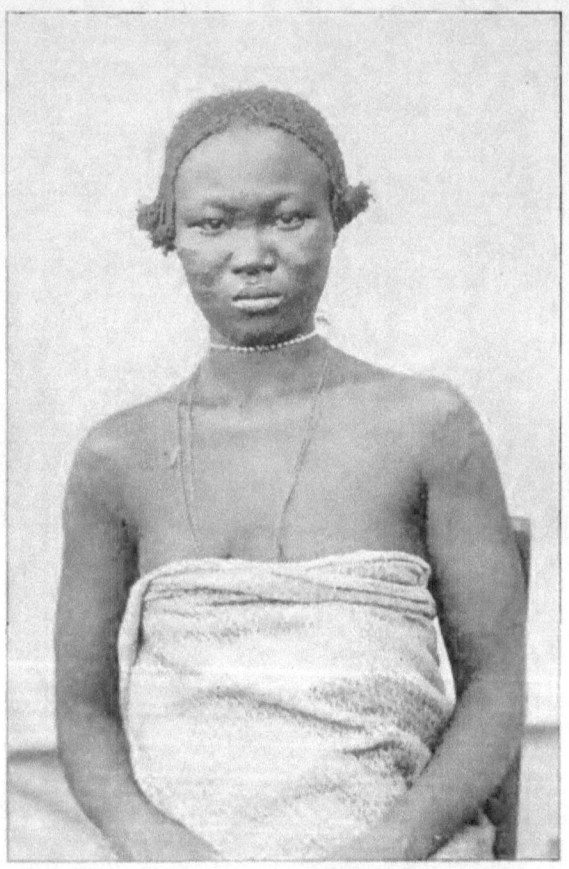

FEMME ABARAMBOU DE MAMBETOU (EQUATEUR).

and of their defeat by British arms. In this same year came the news from Khartoum from the Governor-General of the Soudan that his troops sent against the Mahdi had been entirely destroyed.

The Mahdi's Career.

This " Mahdi," or Mohammed Ahmed, is the son of a carpenter, and his rise
to power is, perhaps, the most remarkable event in the history of the Soudan. He
was a religious fanatic, and while yet a young man he, surrounded by a number
of devoted disciples, went to live on the Island of Abba, in the White Nile, and,
having hollowed out a cave in the mud-bank, lived in comparative seclusion,

NILE WATER CARRIERS.

fasting and praying for days at a time. His renown soon spread throughout the
whole country and he was recognized as the Mahdi el Muntazer, the expected
guide, the messenger of God.

Now the Mahdi came forth, and under his leadership the flame of active
rebellion was kindled and burned with intensity throughout all of the Soudan at
the time of English conquest of Egypt. In November, 1883, the Mahdi defeated
Colonel Hicks, who had been appointed chief of staff in the Soudan, and now he

held the country from the Nile to the Red Sea and far on toward the Great Lakes. Victory followed his arms until the regular English army partly checked his course.

SOUDANESE (NEGRESS).

General Gordon's Fate.

The sad story of Gordon is doubtless familiar to my readers. In April, 1884, he telegraphed to England: " I shall hold out here as long as I can, and if

I can suppress the rebellion I shall do so. If I cannot, I shall retire to the equator and leave you the indelible disgrace of abandoning this garrison." The

EGYPTIAN DANCE GIRL.

British government criminally neglected Gordon's pleas for aid, and after months of untold torture of mind he sent another telegram in answer to one ordering him

to retreat: " Retreat impossible. You ask me to state cause and intention of
staying at Khartoum. I stay because the Arabs have shut us up and will not let
us out." After a long delay in London and in Cairo an expedition was started

TYPICAL ORIENTAL DRAGOMAN.

for the rescue of the most heroic Englishman of the century. Although in the
early spring he had sent message after message begging for reinforcements, which
were unheeded, he sent a final one in December: " I have done all in my power

EGYPTIAN ARMY IN CAMP.

to hold out; the position extremely critical." The expedition reached Khartoum forty-eight hours after poor, noble Gordon had been cut to pieces by the Mahdi and his fellow-fanatics.

Smarting under this disastrous failure to save Gordon, the British government, under pressure, decided upon another expedition "to lay the Suakin-

FELLAH WOMAN.

Berber Railway," but after losing five hundred and fifty men in a twenty minutes' battle with the Mahdists this enterprise was abandoned.

British Plan of Revenge.

Since this time the followers of the Mahdi, especially his right-hand man, Osman Digna, have been giving continual trouble, and from the decisive action taken by the English and Egyptian forces, it is supposed that with them patience has ceased to be a virtue, and that now it is determined to clear out the troublesome dervishes and open up the Soudan once for all.

It is rumored (and rumors are nearly as plentiful as flies and fleas in Egypt just now) that there is an understanding between England and Italy, and that the Soudan campaign is for the purpose of assisting the Italians in their sore straits in Erythrea.

Essentially it is an Egyptian question that is involved. For some time past the dervishes have been concentrating in menacing numbers at Dongola, and there has been some reason to fear that an attack upon the Egyptian frontier would be made. The defeat of the Italians at Adowa undoubtedly made the situation more critical. It exposed Kassala to attack, and it sent a thrill of reviving fanaticism throughout the Soudan.

Under the circumstances Lord Wolseley thought that military operations were necessary, and the Egyptian war office was obliged to act accordingly. It cannot be denied that the success of the dervishes had greatly encouraged them, and as the inhabitants of this part of Africa make no definite distinction between European nationalities, this victory means to them a triumph of the blackskins over the whiteskins, which, it is feared, may lead them to be more pugnacious and progressive than ever, involving the interests of several European powers in the country.

Egypt and the Dervishes.

During the month that I have been in Egypt I have on several occasions seen representatives of these dervishes, and I can easily imagine that the descriptions that come to us of their recklessness in times of war are not at all exaggerated. They are said to be absolutely fearless of death, and, inspired by a deathless love for their religion, which they think is endangered by the presence of Europeans in Africa, their fanaticism knows no bounds.

Egypt is, and has always been, a land of mystery, and all those who live any time in its atmosphere—whether native or alien—partake of this spirit. After all that has been said, the English as well as the Egyptians are acting most mysteriously in this campaign. Two reasons are given out publicly for this rush of troops up the Nile: first, for the protection of the frontier of Egypt, and, second, for the indirect benefit of Italy by attracting the forces of the dervishes away from her defeated army. If the former is true, why should not the Egyptian and English soldiers stop here at Assouan, the frontier town of Egypt, and build their fortifications at this place of entrance instead of taking the offensive and pushing on toward Dongola? If the second reason has foundation, why go toward Dongola, which is six hundred miles from Kassala, where the Italian army is in distress? The facts justify a different conclusion.

The " affairs " in Europe necessitate England having an active policy in this country, which has been under her protectorate for more than ten years. She would prove to France, Russia and other powers that the time for her to evacuate Egypt is not at hand, and that her process of trying to whiten the black hearts, if not the black skins, of these children of the desert must be continued by the flash of the sword and the crack of the rifle ! This may exterminate the der-

SCENE IN THE VALLEY OF THE NILE.

vishes, but it will not terminate the restless rumbling that is rolling through the heart of the Dark Continent.

From Egypt to Syria.

After a month's study of the wonders of ancient and modern Egypt, most regretfully we took leave of the Shepheard's, the most comfortable and best equipped hotel, not only in Cairo, but in the East, and within a few hours we

were passing through the fertile fields of Goshen on our way toward the land of
the Sultan. On these plains, made historic by biblical events and as the battlefield of contending armies in olden times, the frightened forces of Arabi Pasha
gathered after the bombardment and fall of Alexandria, and it was here that the
last stroke was given to his cause by English arms.

Before taking ship at Port Said we spent a short while at Ismailia, located
exactly midway on the Suez Canal, between the Mediterranean and Red seas, at

SCENE BETWEEN JAFFA AND JERUSALEM.

the Bitter Lakes, through which the canal runs. In this pretty little city, where
flowers and fruit trees seem to be in great abundance, the representatives of the
civilized nations of the world met on the occasion of the inauguration ceremony
at the time of the completion of De Lessep's grand canal, and here it was that
certain international friendships were created that gave a new impulse to commerce
between Europe and the East. At Port Said, in a sandy plain, and which receives
its importance alone from the fact that it is connected with the trans-shipment of
vessels to and from the Red Sea by way of Suez, we embarked for Jaffa, Palestine.

The City of Jaffa.

In the early morning, after a rough night on the Mediterranean, we caught our first glimpse of the mountains of Judea; then the yellow shore came in view, and in the distance we could see the red-tiled houses of Jaffa rising in terraces on the slope of a beautiful hill.

This city on the sea—one of the oldest cities in the world—is where Hiram, King of Tyre, undertook to send to Solomon wood from Lebanon for the building of the Temple; here it was, according to ancient myth, that Andromeda, the daughter of Cepheus and Joppa, is said to have been chained to the rocks in order that she might be destroyed by a huge sea monster, but was released by Perseus, and it was from this port that Jonah embarked just before his remarkable experience with the big fish. This latter reference prompts us to remark that Jonah, not Samson, was the strongest man that ever lived, for even a whale could not hold him down.

The present city is uninteresting except for a few biblical events that are associated with it. We visit the reputed home of Simon, the tanner, and have pointed out to us the place on the flat roof where the Apostle Peter had the vision that is recorded in Acts, which put a new interpretation on the gospel that he preached, and a short walk away brings us to the place where the same great apostle is said to have raised Tabitha and given her back to her distressed friends.

On the Road to Jerusalem.

The forty miles from Jaffa to Jerusalem can be made in a short time in a train of cars, pulled by a puffing, snorting steam engine. But as this mode of journey seemed to violate a deep-seated sentiment, and would not afford an opportunity to study the places of interest en route, we secured a carriage with the privilege of taking all day for the trip. For miles out of Jaffa we drive through orange, lemon, pomegranate and apricot gardens, and on every hand there are evidences of the greatest fertility.

About thirty years ago a German colony secured a thousand acres from the Sultan, and large fortunes have been made by these thrifty men and women in horticulture. I am told that £80,000 worth of oranges and shiploads of other fruit annually are exported by the colony and what was a barren plain has been converted into gardens of the richest beauty.

The Rothschilds and other wealthy Hebrews have established and supported a Jewish agricultural school near by, but this has not been a success, for these sons of Abraham are so intuitively biased toward commercial life that when a few pounds have been accumulated at the school, they bid good-bye to the hoe and plow and go forth as traders.

Approaching the Holy City.

In less than two hours from Ramleh we passed into the beautiful Valley of Ajalon, where in Joshua (x. 12) we have it recorded that Joshua commanded the moon to stand still. Through this valley and over the adjacent hills I walked ten miles, and having as my companion an enthusiastic botanist and a good Syrian scholar, this walk was much more enjoyable than the carriage drive. Within a space of not more than three hundred yards I gathered twenty-two kinds of flowers. The fields and hill slopes looked as if they were covered by many colored carpets; the single-handed plow, used from time immemorial, was seen moving through the rich soil, drawn by an ox and an ass, and driven by the bearded Syrian; peeps were made into wells that were like those used by Father Jacob; Latron, the reputed home of the penitent thief, was passed (which is now said to be full of thieves, none of whom are penitent); the meadow is reached where some insist that David let fly the stone from his sling that buried itself in the forehead of the great giant; and having resumed our carriage we soon came to Kuloniah, thought to be the Emmaus of Luke xxiv. 13, where Christ appeared on the day of His resurrection. Just as the crimson light from the setting sun lit the western sky over the Judean hills, casting a rosy glow on meadow and vale, we passed through the gate into the city of the Great King.

CHAPTER XVI.

PILGRIMS IN PALESTINE.

IT is estimated that fifteen thousand visitors land upon the shores of Palestine annually, the large majority of whom come on religious pilgrimages. The Holy Sepulchre is visited every year by nearly twelve thousand "pilgrims"—six thousand of these are Russian peasants, four thousand are Greeks from the various countries that fringe the Levant, or Armenians; nearly a thousand are French and Latin, about two hundred are Copts from Upper Egypt, and the rest are native Christians.

The Russian Visitors.

I have been greatly impressed by the quiet, earnest, serious manner of the Russian peasants, men and women, as they come in from the great Russian convent and barrack that dominate the city on the north, and with bared head and taper in hand make the round of the sacred places; or as they trudge along the road from Jerusalem to Jericho, with great bundles on their backs, bound for the Jordan River. Most of these are past middle age; all are carrying out at last the intention of a lifetime, over the consummation of which they have long brooded and prayed and many of them have walked on foot one or even two thousand miles from their native village in the interior of Russia before they arrive at the port of embarkation on the shores of the Black Sea, and have voluntarily undergone much inevitable suffering and hardship on the way. Each peasant pays for his own passage and all expenses of the long journey out of the earnings carefully stored up from year to year with this intent, and the Russian government requires, before granting permission to any of them to leave Russia at all, a specific pledge and contract that they will return, and demands also that each one shall deposit in the hands of the authorities enough to defray his return fare. Besides this each has to contribute his toll and fee to the local fund of the Eastern Church, and it is this money that furnishes the means for the many renovations of older buildings and for the erection of new chapels and shrines that are springing up here and there and everywhere in Southern Syria under the ægis of the Eastern Church.

JORDAN RIVER.

French Catholics.

Most of the pilgrims who belong to the Latin communion are French. There exists in France a benevolent society for helping poor French Catholics to make this pilgrimage, and this fund allows about one thousand of these pilgrims to visit the Holy Sepulchre every year. There are not so many Moslem pilgrims, and the Jews are coming in large numbers, not as travelers, but as colonists. The number of tourists who spend from two to six weeks in Palestine is increasing

THE ANCIENT GATEWAY OF SAMARCAND, IN TURKESTAN.

every year, but I have been unable to secure reliable statistics on this point. Three-quarters of these attempt no more than a sight of Jerusalem and its environs, perhaps go to Bethlehem, five miles to the south, and to the Jordan, eighteen miles to the east, and then sail from Beirut, after having run up to Damascus. These do not, apparently, take any real or abiding interest in the associations of the land, and seem not desirous of enlarging or giving reality to the impressions they had derived by study at home. It is quite impossible to take but a most superficial glance of the country under a month's time, but during this time the visitor, by a well-conceived and well-executed plan, can proceed from the extreme south to the extreme north (about one hundred and twenty-seven miles), and from the Mediterranean to the Jordan, studying somewhat carefully the localities associated with the Old and New Testament.

Doing Jerusalem.

Many who attempt "to do" Jerusalem on schedule time and dash from one place of interest to another seem not to realize that the modern city is but the topmost stratum of several former cities; that beneath its outward aspect lie entombed the remnants of those who have played their part in what every one must acknowledge to have been the most remarkable drama of history, and where the ruins of the work of at least three distinct Jewish periods, as well as those of the Herodian, the Roman, the Byzantine, the Crusader and the Moslem lie piled together. In our study of this wonderful city, if we do not go beneath the dust of its present streets and alleys, we are naught but slaves to a bald external materialism. The excavator's pickaxe is yet to unearth stones that have tongues, beneath the spots where the knees of devout pilgrims now touch, and a new historic revelation shall be brought to light.

The Valley of the Jordan.

Those who are interested in the "Palestine exploration fund" are addressing themselves earnestly to this noble work, and I am assured by the honored secretary that the association is greatly encouraged in its work. The tourist, it matters not how quickly he must depart after entering the Holy Land, cannot afford to miss the wondrous ravine of the Jordan, unlike anything else on the face of the globe. Here he passes the threefold interesting site of the prehistoric, the Jewish and the Herodian Jericho, haunted by the martial memories of Joshua's raid, with the vanguard of the Ben-Israel, and by those of many romantic and picturesque episodes belonging to the schools of the prophets, by memories of the Egyptian Cleopatra, of Herod's funeral that here wound its way, of the last journey of Jesus, of the Essenes and early Christians and many other events of sacred and secular history of thrilling interest.

Magnificent Landscape.

The topography of Palestine is an agreeable surprise to me. In my trip around the world, with but one exception, I have seen no view that surpasses in grandeur the one to be had from one of the heights in the Jordan Valley, near the traditional spot where the prophet sweetened the bitter waters. The panorama of

22

all Central Palestine lies outspread as a map before your gaze, and from the deep blue, rippleless waves of the Dead Sea, to the south, to the dazzling snow fields of Mount Hermon, on the north, a distance of a hundred miles, the magnificent landscape extends, dimpled by numberless vales and domed by many hillocks, flanked on the east by the grand mountains of Moab and Gilead, from which spring the heroic Nebo and Pisgah, watch-towers of the Land of Promise.

An Old Highway.

This view, so multiplied and beautiful, must have been the very prospect which presented itself to the eye first of Abraham and then of Jacob as they came in from Mesopotamia, and is substantially the same to-day as it was when unfolded before the eyes of Balaam and Moses. Looking toward Jerusalem, you can see Mount Olivet, and winding through the hill country you can trace the white road that was pressed by the feet of the Christ and His disciples as they came over the road from Jerusalem to Jericho, a part of which you have passed, and must repass before you enter the Holy City again. Along this old highway, through your field-glass, you can distinguish long caravans of Russian and French pilgrims solemnly moving toward the Jordan, that flashes in the sunlight below you.

The Holy City.

It is well, before studying a great city in detail, to ascend to an elevated place and take a bird's-eye view of the city and its surroundings as a whole. This was done the day after our arrival in Jerusalem. From a tower two hundred feet high, erected on the Mount of Olives, looking toward the west, you have the Garden of Gethsemane and the Valley of Jehoshaphat below you; beyond spreads out the Holy City, and behind, nestling in the hills, is the town of Bethany, while twenty miles away is Jericho, not far from the waters of the Jordan and the Dead Sea, which are distinctly visible. The four hills upon which Jerusalem stands were once separated by deep valleys, which are now filled by the debris of successive destructions of the city. On the southwest rises Zion, the most celebrated of these, which is three hundred feet above the Valley of Hinnom and five hundred feet above the Kidron. It was the old citadel of the Jebusites and "the City of David." Mount Moriah, which was the site of the ancient temple and is now crowned by the Mosque of Omar, is on the southeast, separated from Zion by the Tyropœon Valley and from Olivet by the deep gorge of the Kidron. On the northeast is Mount Bezetha, which was enclosed within the walls, after the time of Christ, by Herod Agrippa, and Mount Akra, which is the highest point of the city, is on the northwest. Thus it will be seen that the city slopes down from the northwest to the northeast, and standing on the northwest angle of the wall, you are at the highest point and see Moriah far below on the southeast, with the Tyropœon

Valley on the west of it, running down between it and Zion to the junction of the Kidron with the Hinnom.

The city covers an area of more than two hundred and nine acres, has a circumference of nearly two and a quarter miles, is enclosed by walls averaging about thirty-five feet in height; around the walls are thirty-four towers, and in the walls are eight gates, six open and two closed. The population is variously estimated

JERUSALEM MERCHANTS.

from 75,000 to 100,000, and the Jews, who have been coming in large numbers in recent years, largely outnumber all others.

The Holy Sepulchre.

The Church of the Holy Sepulchre first attracted our attention. As to the genuine site of the holy sepulchre there has been no end of controversy, but it is quite certain that there is no historical evidence that the question was at all settled until the third century, when it appears from Eusebius that over the sepulchre

THE CENTRE OF THE EARTH, CHURCH OF THE HOLY SEPULCHRE, JERUSALEM.

(340)

had been erected a temple to Venus. In the present building there are thirty-seven stations, at which the Roman Catholics, Greeks, Armenians and Copts hold services. The following are some of these: The stone of unction on which they say Christ was laid and anointed when taken from the cross; the spot where Mary stood to see what would be done with the body of her son and Lord; the sepulchre itself and the stone which closed the door; the place where Mary met the risen Lord,

ENTRANCE TO THE CHURCH OF THE HOLY SEPULCHRE.

supposing Him to be the gardener; a hole through the marble pavement where the cross is said to have stood, and what may well surprise us, we are shown at last the tomb of Melchizedec and the tomb of Adam.

The holy sepulchre stands in the centre of the rotunda. The slab is cracked through the centre, is much worn by adoring pilgrims, and the little chapel that encloses it is lit by forty-three lamps, always burning. The church is the joint property of the Greeks, the Latins (Catholics), Armenians and Copts, and each take their turn in making processions to the holy places and worshiping at the sacred shrines.

The Mosque of Omar.

Upon Mt. Moriah, where once stood the great temple designed by David and built by Solomon, is now the Mosque of Omar, and tradition declares that it covers the spot where Ornan had his threshing floor, where Abraham offered up Isaac and where David interceded for the plague-stricken people. Standing in this magnificent building, one's thoughts rush back to the past, when psalmists wrote and patriots sung of the temple's glory. Hither the tribes came up; here shone forth the light of the Shekinah; here was the centre of the religious, the poetical and the political life of God's chosen people, and to this spot still devout Jews in every land turn with tearful eyes and prayerful lips, longing for the restoration of their loved land. The Christian thinks of the little Child presented here by His mother, of the divine Youth asking and answering questions, and of the man-God "teaching and preaching the things concerning Himself."

The Sacred Rock.

The spacious area known as the Haram esh-Sherif, upon which the mosque stands, is surrounded by a wall 1601 feet long on the west, 1530 on the east, 1024 on the north and 922 on the south, and is entered by eight gates on the west. In the building there are many things to attract attention, but the greatest interest centres upon the Sacred Rock, immediately beneath the dome, about sixty feet long and forty-five feet wide. Numberless legends cluster about this rock, Jewish, Christian and Moslem. Here, it is claimed, Melchizedec offered sacrifice, Abraham brought young Isaac as an offering, the ark of the covenant stood, and through the circular hole is said to have passed the blood of the sacrifices, which was carried by way of the brook Kidron outside of the city. In the cave below are shown the praying places of Abraham, Elijah, David, Solomon and Mohammed.

The next building of importance in the enclosure is the Mosque-et-Aksa, which contains the tombs of the sons of Aaron, the praying place of Moses, and other places of traditional interest. From the Haram a fine view can be had of the Valley of Jehoshaphat, where devout Jews long to be buried, for to this place will the Messiah come when the prophecy of Joel is fulfilled: " I will gather all nations and will bring them down into the Valley of Jehoshaphat, and will plead with them there for my people, whom they have scattered among the nations, and parted my land."

The Via Dolorosa.

The Via Dolorosa is a narrow but remarkably picturesque street leading from a point near St. Stephen's gate to the Church of the Holy Sepulchre, and, remem-

THE "WAILING PLACE," IN JERUSALEM.

bering that it is sacred with the tears of many generations of pilgrims who strove to walk in the footsteps of the agonizing Christ, we cannot step upon its rough pavement with indifference as we visit Pilate's Judgment Hall, the place where the cross is said to have been put on Christ's shoulder, and the different " Stations of the Cross " until Calvary is reached. I have visited no spot in Jerusalem more pathetic than the Jews' Wailing Place.

Jews' Wailing Place.

Every Friday afternoon the old wall of the temple, composed of enormous blocks of marble, is lined with Hebrews of every age and station in life, who spend hours reading their psalter and prophets, while they weep over the ruins of the Holy City. Jerome makes an affecting allusion to the remnant of mourners in his day who paid the Roman soldiers for the privilege of leaning against this wall while they bemoaned their fate; and as I watched these children of ancient Israel, holding their sacred books, their bodies waving to and fro, their lips muttering and wailing out lamentation after lamentation, while tears rolled down their faces, I could not for a moment doubt their sincerity, and a thrill ran through me as I recalled their past history and their present condition in the city of their fathers.

The subterranean quarries which run under nearly the length and breadth of the city give the probable explanation of the place where the mighty stones of the temple were secured. As you pass through a vast succession of mighty aisles and mammoth chambers you see the marks of chiselings left centuries ago, you pass niches for the lamps of the quarrymen, and now and then you stumble against huge blocks partly cut from the rocks, and pillars partially shaped and left unfinished.

In the Holy City.

The exact localities of Calvary, where the Christ was crucified, and the tomb in which He lay, have greatly interested the hosts of pilgrims who have visited Jerusalem for many centuries.

The Empress Helena, mother of Constantine, visited the Holy City in A. D. 326, with the purpose of identifying these spots, and tradition tells us that it was by means of a dream that her desires were fulfilled. Her son erected a magnificent basilica over the place where the tomb was supposed to have been, and although this original edifice has long since disappeared the present Church of the Holy Sepulchre is located where the dream of the devout Empress led her to suppose were the tomb of the Lord and the place of the crucifixion.

In this church we are surrounded by everything that human invention and modern art could devise, but we turn away sickened at heart to think that such folly and superstition should be associated with the most sacred events of the world's history.

Here we are shown where the Empress sat and threw pieces of gold into the rubbish to encourage the workmen in their search for the cross; there we are shown a slab of limestone where, it is said, the Lord's body was anointed when taken from the cross, and scores of other evidences of the baldest superstition are marked and labeled in the most artificial manner.

GOLGOTHA.

It is surpassingly strange that this place was selected, if the biblical record was consulted at all. It occupies a position, not on a solid rock, but above the ground, in space. The chamber of the tomb is lined with marble, and has not the least resemblance to a cave cut in the rock, and it is located inside the city walls, as they existed in Christ's time, while all admit that the true Calvary must have occupied a place outside of these walls.

Major Conder's Discovery.

We are indebted to Major Conder, who labored in connection with the Palestine Exploration Fund, for ably pointing out in 1878 that in all probability the place where the crucifixion took place is a rocky knoll outside the Damascus Gate, and known as "Jeremiah's Grotto." This knoll presents a striking resemblance to a

THE "ECCO HOMO" ARCH, JERUSALEM.

human skull, which corresponds to the words in the New Version, "the place which is called the skull."

The following points of evidence in favor of this being the actual scene of the crucifixion are striking: It was certainly outside the walls of the city in the time of Christ; it was at the junction of the two main roads, from S. to N. and from W. to E., and consequently there would be many passers-by (Matt. xxvii. 39, Mark xv. 29). This hill is called by the Jews to-day, as it has always been called, the "Hill of Execution;" it is held as an accursed spot, and Jews even now, when they pass it, spit and throw stones in its direction, uttering this imprecation: "Cursed be He who destroyed our nation by aspiring to be king thereof."

The Writer's Impressions.

For ten days I studied this and other localities, and I confess I was deeply impressed by the place and its surroundings.

On this skull-shaped mound outside of the gate of Damascus the whole transaction could have been seen by the vast multitudes that thronged the public

CHURCH OF NATIVITY.

thoroughfares at that season, and the priests could have witnessed the terrible tragedy from the wall of the city or from the tower of Antonia.

If this little hill is established as the Golgotha of the New Testament, it necessarily follows that the sepulchre in which our Lord was laid must have been situated somewhere in the immediate vicinity.

Biblical Testimony.

In John we read: "Now, in the place where He was crucified there was a garden, and in the garden a new sepulchre, wherein was never man yet laid.

There laid they Jesus, therefore, because of the Jews' preparation day, for the sepulchre was nigh at hand." The garden containing the tomb was, therefore, quite close to the spot where the cross stood.

A tomb that seems to correspond remarkably with the biblical account has lately been excavated, and while as yet there has been little published about it, a company of English Christians have bought the spot and the garden near by, and doubtless we shall hear much of it in the near future.

The Probable Tomb.

It is located 230 feet from the summit of the knoll supposed to be Golgotha; it is hewn out of the solid rock, and evidently was the tomb of a rich man—Joseph of Arimathea. It is located in a garden, and the whole structure of the tomb shows how the disciple could have stooped down and looked in without entering.

It consists of a chamber cut in the rock, seven feet six inches in height, fourteen feet six inches long and eleven feet two inches wide, having a low partition dividing the tomb into two parts. In these are three receptacles for human bodies, but only one of these appears to have been actually completed, and portions of the "scale," which was loose at the bottom of the receptacle that was evidently used, was taken to the British Museum, where the authorities declared that "no body has ever decomposed in the tomb, if this is from the bottom of it."

There are strong evidences that the Crusaders knew of this tomb. At the east end two crosses are inscribed on the wall in red paint, with the letters Alpha and Omega at the corners, and it has been ascertained that an arched building once existed in front of the tomb, supposed to have been erected about the twelfth century.

There are the faint outlines of an inscription which, if ever deciphered, may tell us how those who, centuries ago, looked upon this sepulchre regarded it.

From what has been written certain inferences may fairly be drawn, namely, that the traditional Holy Sepulchre cannot possibly be the true site of the tomb of Christ, as it lies within the walls of the ancient city; that the skull-shaped hill is in all probability the true Calvary, and that the rock-cut sepulchre in the immediate vicinity of the hill answers all the conditions of the tomb in which the body of the Christ lay.

I have penned these words in a room cut into the rock, just below the Skull Hill, where lives the old Christian man who watches over the new-found tomb, who insists that he stays in the house occupied by the gardener whom Mary thought she saw when she looked upon the resurrected Lord.

Christ's Birthplace.

Mounted upon a fine horse, it was with anticipations of great pleasure that I passed through the Jaffa Gate, and leaving Jerusalem to the north, passed into the Valley of Gihon, on the way to the birthplace of the King of kings.

THE TRADITIONAL STONE OF ELIJAH, NEAR BETHLEHEM.

Every new view of the historic valleys, meadows and hillocks recalls events that are and shall always be of stupendous importance and thrilling interest to the world.

We are now in the plain which marks the boundary line between Judah and Benjamin, where the Philistines were defeated by David; presently there is pointed out a well where tradition tells us that the wise men from the east on their way to the manger of the child Jesus, stooping to draw water, saw the star reflected in the water.

Here is the spot where it is said the prophet Elijah rested on his flight from the fiery Jezebel, and less than a mile farther we approach the tomb of Rachel, which brings to mind the touching story of the death of Jacob's loved wife, as given in the thirty-fifth chapter of Genesis, just before she reached her journey's end.

After a short six-mile ride on an elongated hill, well cultivated in terraces round the sides and with fertile grain fields in the valley below, we look upon Bethlehem.

The groups of women in white robes standing yonder on a terrace just under the town, gesticulating to one another in vigorous conversation, remind one of the group that surrounded Naomi, the sorrow-stricken widow returning to this, her native home, with exclamations of surprise at her haggard face.

The men and women in yonder field cutting the golden grain give you a vivid picture of Ruth gleaning after the reapers, when Boaz saw her in these very fields about Bethlehem, loved her for her love, and in process of time she became the grandmother of David the king and the ancestress of Christ.

It was upon one of these hills that David, the ruddy youth, kept his father's sheep, as the young boy is doing on the green slope before you, and it was in the sunshine and shadow of these vales and hillocks that God created within him those treasures of music and poetry that have enriched all the centuries.

The Scripture allusions to Bethlehem, which we now enter, are very numerous. Here it was that Samuel anointed David to be king of Israel, and in the adjacent hill country the shepherd boy encountered wild beasts, and composed his earliest Psalms. From here he was sent to minister to the diseased mind of Saul by his melodious harpings. Hence he went forth to see his brethren with the army and slay the giant champion of Philistia.

This little city was one of the strongholds fortified by Rehoboam after the division of the kingdom, and it figured conspicuously in the political life of the ancient Hebrews; but, above all, it was the prophecy of Micah and its wonderful fulfillment which make Bethlehem a household word wherever Christianity is professed, and cause millions all over the world to turn their thoughts toward this Judean village as Christmastide comes round. "And, thou, Bethlehem, Ephratah, though thou be little among the thousands of Judah, yet out of thee shall He come forth unto me that is to be ruler in Israel, whose goings forth have been from of old, from everlasting."

The angelic announcement made to the shepherds as they kept their sheep by night nearby, and the wondrous events recorded in detail by the Evangelists Matthew and Luke, and summed up by St. John in the statement that "the Word was made flesh and dwelt among us," have made this place known in all civilized lands.

A BETHLEHEM MERCHANT.

(351)

At the eastern extremity of the village we find a confused fortress, like a pile of buildings, which comprises the Church of the Nativity, and the three contiguous convents belong respectively to the Latin, Greek and Armenian Churches.

Church of the Nativity.

The nave of the church, which is the common property of all Christians, is supposed to be the oldest monument of Christian architecture in the world.

In the chapel of St. Helena (named for the mother of Constantine) there are forty-four marble columns, taken from Mount Moriah, supposed to have been originally in the porches of the great temple.

Descending a spiral staircase we enter the Grotto of the Nativity, which is a cave in the rock, over and around which the church and convent buildings are reared. The vault is 33 feet by 11 feet, encased with Italian marble and decorated with numerous lamps, figures of saints, embroidery and other ornaments.

A silver star on the floor of the grotto indicates the traditional spot where the Saviour was born; above it sixteen silver lamps are perpetually burning, and around the star are the words: *Hic de virgine Maria Jesus Christus natus est.*

That caves in the hillside adjacent to the inn were utilized as stables for the cattle, especially when the inn was crowded, and that in such a cave the Redeemer was born, is a tradition commonly accepted as early as the time of Justin Martyr, about a hundred years after the facts occurred. This, therefore, may be the actual place of Christ's birth.

St. Jerome's Grotto.

St. Jerome, who ardently believed in this grotto as his Saviour's birthplace, spent the greater part of his life just here. Here he fasted, prayed, dreamed and studied; here he gathered round him his devoted followers in the small communities which formed the beginnings of conventual life in Palestine; here his fiery spirit vented itself in the treatises, letters and commentaries which he sent forth from his retirement to terrify and enlighten the western world; here he made the famous translation of the Scriptures which is still the *"Biblia Vulgata"* of the Latin Church; and here took place his pathetic death, which Domenichino has so vividly portrayed in his world-renowned picture.

Near the outskirts of the town is seen the well of Bethlehem, or David's Well, which is referred to in 2 Samuel xxiii. 13-17, and 1 Chronicles xi. 15-19.

When David and his men were in the cave of Adullam (which is still pointed out), and Bethlehem was garrisoned by the Philistines, David expressed the desire, "Oh, that one would give me to drink of the water of the well of Bethlehem, that is at the gate." Three brave men heard the wish of their leader, rushed through the hosts of the enemy and brought him the cooling drink he longed for, but David would not drink of the water because the lives of his men had been hazarded.

The Shepherds' Field.

From an elevated and most picturesque spot near the walls of the old city can be seen the Shepherds' Field, which stretches for miles over the green meadows and hill slopes.

As we looked out upon the charming landscape, yonder in the distance could be seen a group of shepherds, with long crooks in their hands, watching over the flocks as they quietly fed in the vales. My guide informs me that all during the spring months, in these fields the shepherds watch their sheep by night. "And there were in the same country shepherds abiding in the fields, keeping watch over their flock by night. And lo! the angel of the Lord came upon them, and the glory of the Lord shone round about them; and they were sore afraid. And the angel said, Fear not; for behold I bring you good tidings of great joy, which shall be to all people. For unto you is born this day in the City of David a Saviour, which is Christ the Lord. And this shall be a sign unto you: Ye shall find the babe wrapped in swaddling clothes, lying in a manger. And suddenly there was with the angel a multitude of the heavenly hosts praising God, and saying, Glory to God in the highest, and on earth peace, good will toward men."

The Pools of Solomon.

The immense basins, a few miles south of Jerusalem, known as Solomon's Pools, are in such an admirable state of preservation that you can hardly realize that they are more than a century old, but it is probable that they date from Solomon's time, although we know that they were restored by Pontius Pilate.

At present water is conveyed from these pools only as far as Bethlehem, although the course of the aqueduct can be traced to the old court of the temple, a distance of nearly fourteen miles, and it is reported that the Turkish government has on hand funds for the restoration of these pools to their original state of usefulness.

There is near the upper pool a huge building with castellated walls, obviously of Saracenic origin.

The Sealed Fountain.

A short distance to the right of this castle is the sealed fountain of Solomon (Song of Sol. iv. 12), which regulated and secured the constant supply of water for the Holy City.

The pools consist of three enormous cisterns of marble masonry, and their measurements are as follows: The lower pool is in length 582 feet; breadth, east

23

end, 207 feet; west, 148 feet; depth at east end, 50 feet.   Dr. Thomson says that "when full it would float the largest man-of-war that ever plowed the ocean."

The middle pool is located 248 feet above the lower pool and is 423 feet in

GIBEON, THE SCENE OF SOLOMON'S SACRIFICE.

length, 250 feet in breadth at the east end and 160 feet at the west end and is 39 feet in depth at the east end.

The upper pool is 160 feet above the middle pool and in length is 380 feet, in breadth at the east end 236 feet, at the west end 229 feet, and has a depth of 25 feet.

For more than three hours from these pools we passed over a rough road southward. Valleys and spurs of hills are crossed and olive groves, vineyards and fig gardens are seen on either side during much of the way. Merchantmen, with their long camel trains, are frequently met; and husbandmen are seen following their one-handled plows, drawn by donkeys and oxen.

The House of Abraham.

Soon we reached a spot where the Jews declare that their Father Abraham pitched his tent, which is still known as the House of Abraham.

A crowd of thoughts rushed through our minds as we passed over the old road to Hebron, probably the oldest road in the world. Over it Abraham passed on that journey of faith to sacrifice his son of promise on Mount Moriah; over it David led his faithful host to conquer the stronghold of the Jebusites, on Zion; here, doubtless, Isaac, Jacob and Solomon walked, thinking of the destiny of that nation which promised to be the centre of universal empire, and along this way, perhaps, the child Jesus was borne in His mother's arms on the flight to Egypt.

The Town of Hebron.

We were somewhat wearied when we passed through the gate of the old city of Hebron, one of the most ancient cities in the world. We know that it was built seven years before Zoan (Numbers xiii. 22), that is, Tanis in Egypt, and when Josephus wrote it was 2300 years old. It was a walled city in the time of Abraham (Gen. xxiii. 10), and we also learn from Genesis that Damascus was a city at the same time, but which can claim seniority is not known.

Here lived the father of his people and the "friend of God;" from this place Joseph went forth to seek his brethren in Shechem, where his strange fate befell him; here it was that Joshua waged fierce struggles; this was selected as one of the cities of refuge, unto which the pursued man-slayer might flee; it was here that David had his residence for over seven years, when he reigned over Judah alone. Here Absalom was born and led his wild, faithless life; and in this place was Abner treacherously murdered by Joab.

Hebron is situated in the narrow Valley of Eschol, still abounding in vineyards; the streets are dark and dirty and the houses are mostly built of stone and covered over with cupolas or small domes, which give a curious and interesting effect.

Of the 12,000 people who live in this unique old town about 600 are Jews, who attract attention by their pale faces and long ringlets. The Moslems, who compose the rest of the population, are noted for their rank fanaticism and superstition, which fact makes it dangerous for Christians to visit the place unguarded.

At the entrance to the city we were met by a Turkish official, who, armed to the teeth, went before us in all of our walks and drives through the streets.

Only recently an Englishman was set upon by a crowd of these roughs and only escaped with his life.

The Cave of Machpelah.

The Cave of Machpelah is the object of the greatest interest in Hebron. It recalls some of the most touching of the Old Testament scenes.

When Sarah, the wife of the patriarch, died, we read that "Abraham stood up from before his dead and spake unto the sons of Heth, saying: 'I am a stranger and a sojourner with you; give me a possession of a burying place with you, that I may bury my dead out of my sight.'" The contract was made in the gate of the city, and the field, the cave, the trees in the field, all were "made sure to Abraham for a possession, and Abraham buried Sarah, his wife, in the cave of the field of Machpelah." (Gen. 23.)

Patriarchs' Burial Place.

As old Jacob lay a-dying he tenderly spoke of this Cave of Machpelah, and said: "There they buried Abraham and Sarah, his wife; there they buried Isaac and Rebekah, his wife, and there I buried Leah." He gave explicit directions that his body should rest there with his fathers.

Perhaps there was never a grander funeral than that of Jacob, when Joseph, "with all the servants of Pharaoh, the elders of his house, and all the elders of the land of Egypt, and all the house of Joseph, and his brethren and his father's house, and chariots and horsemen" carried the embalmed body from Egypt into the land of Canaan to the Cave of Machpelah.

Closed to Jew and Gentile.

It seems strange that the brutal Turkish government should be allowed to close the doors to this cave, that is of such great interest to the Christian world and to all who are concerned about ancient Israel. The only Christian visitors who have ever crossed the threshold of the building that covers the cave are the Prince of Wales, the Marquis of Bute, the Crown Prince of Prussia, General Lew Wallace, Princes Albert Victor and George of Wales.

I was shown cracks and rents along the walls where devout Jews are accustomed to place written prayers addressed to their Father Abraham. I have before me an exact copy of one of these prayerful epistles, and the Jewish mother who wrote it and attempted to put it into the cave where the bodies of her distinguished ancestors rest appeals most pathetically for individual, domestic and national blessings.

The Oak of Abraham.

This is believed to be the only spot on earth which attracts to it all who possess the one creed, "I believe in God." The Holy Sepulchre in Jerusalem separates Moslem, Jew and Christian, but here they meet with a reverence equally affectionate. Not far away from the cave the Oak of Abraham is visited, where it is supposed that the Lord appeared to the patriarch as he sat in his tent door and gave him the account of the coming destruction of Sodom and Gomorrah. It is certain that in this neighborhood this wonderful conference took place, but that this oak, old as it seems, was then standing is as probable as that the grave of Adam has been identified.

SYRIAN PEASANT MOTHER AND DAUGHTER.

CHAPTER XVII.

PEOPLES AND PLACES OF THE SOUTH AND NORTH.

 URING the course of a month I have ridden on horseback more than four hundred miles through Palestine and Syria on my way to Asia Minor.

On this long tour, with the aid of an excellent dragoman, I have not only been enabled to visit the principal cities and towns of these historically interesting countries, of which I have written, but I have had occasion to study the habits and customs of the wild Bedouin tribes that live their unsettled lives in these valleys and along these mountain slopes.

On the western side of the Jordan river there are many of these roving bodies of men, women and children, divided into different family tribes, but on the eastern side of the river there are only a few tribes much larger than the others and very much wilder. Each tribe has a sheik or prince, who is final authority on all questions, and often has the power of life and death. This office is hereditary, as a rule. When an election is necessary it is done by vocal declaration, must in all cases be unanimous, and must be endorsed by the government at Constantinople.

The head of each tribe is legally required to pay to the Sultan one Turkish pound (nearly five dollars), for each man who is able to go to war, which amount, paid yearly, rids these men from military duty under the government. Certain districts of country are allowed these tribes where their tents and herds are usually found, but frequently they roam in other parts of the land, carrying on their independent raids until they are driven into their own regions by Turkish guns.

Their tents are generally made of the hair of goats, ingeniously woven, and their food consists nearly altogether of bread made into thin wafers, looking very much like sheets of sandpaper, butter made from the goat and buffalo cow and fish, which abound in all the streams.

The Bedouins are natural born robbers, and it is always unsafe for any one to pass through their country unguarded.

Some time ago a party was visiting the Jordan and Dead Sea with the usual guard; but four of the number separated from the others, and in less than two hours they were seized, and robbed of their horses, money and clothing. A most pitiable set they were, I am told, when they reached their tents after night.

An American Guide's Story.

Mr. Rolla Floyd, who is the only American dragoman in Palestine and Syria, entertained me for several days by a recital of some of his experiences during a thirty years' stay in the country.

Not long since, while accompanying a number of ladies and gentlemen through the desert, in the neighborhood of ancient Shechem, a noise was heard in the hills near by; and, on turning, he found they were being surrounded by forty or fifty Bedouins, headed by their sheik. Of course there was great terror among the party, and for a while Mr. Floyd was stricken with fear. But a fortunate thought occurred to the dragoman. It is a custom among these wild tribes to befriend any one who is in trouble, if he reaches the sheik and, seizing his belt, exclaims: "I am your guest."

While demands were being made upon Mr. Floyd and those under his protection, and the robbers were in the act of carrying out their desires, he rushed forward and, taking a strong grip upon the belt of the sheik, exclaimed, in Arabic, "These are all your guests." This acted like magic. The robbery was ordered off; the sheik drew his sword and in a most pompous manner announced to his men that the party was under his protection and guidance, and, leading the way, he guided them for hours through the desert.

When I was suddenly approached by a band of these barbarians at ten o'clock at night, in the wild country east of the Jordan, by the moonlight I saw that there was no belt to seize. As all of them were clothed in single and unadorned garments, I resorted to another device, which proved just as effective, though not so dignified, and which put me quite a distance from them in a very short time.

A Missionary's Adventure.

Mr. Carey, whose life-long residence in Palestine and Syria furnishes him with a fund of information on this subject that is possessed by few, gave me an account of a personal episode with the Bedouins which illustrates their exceeding kind-heartedness after they have robbed you of everything that they can lay their hands on.

Mr. Carey left his home in Nablous on a missionary tour among the mountains once owned by the tribe of Reuben, east of the Jordan river. After crossing the stream he had not gone many miles when he was surrounded by a score of these men, who, lifting him off his beast, stripped him of his clothing and, while he sat on a cool rock near by and watched the performance, they examined carefully all of the garments, ripping open the linings of his coat, and after they had taken everything, even his pocket-knife, they tossed him his clothing and politely informed him that he could go his way.

As it was now late in the evening, he told them that he could not continue his journey after dark without losing his way, and requested that they would take care of him until the next morning. They immediately and gladly agreed to do this, helped him on his donkey, led the way through the valley to the place of

PALESTINE MAT WEAVERS.

their encampment, cooked him food, listened most attentively while he told them Bible stories, tucked him in bed and started him on his journey next day with everything that he had when he met them except his money and other things in his traveling-bag that they could possibly use.

It seems that the belt trick is not known among the inhabitants of Reuben's ancient province. I had occasion to visit one of their encampments, but it is impossible for me to picture adequately their mode of living.

THE TOMB OF JOSEPH NEAR SHECHEM.

Each family in the general family tribe occupies a small tent of one room, which is the sleeping, cooking and working apartment. The floor is the bare ground, which in a few cases may be partly covered by bits of dirty goat-hair cloth.

The eating is done in front of the tents, where the family sits in a semicircle, using their palms as plates and fingers as forks. A peculiarly distasteful butter, churned from the milk of the goat and buffalo cow, is their chief means of support, and, as a rule, they reside in one locality not more than two months.

They claim a direct descent from Abraham, who was, they insist, a wealthy sheik of a large tribe.

Home of Eli and Samuel.

It was in the city of Shiloh that Joshua divided the land among the tribes, and here the tabernacle was reared; here dwelt old man Eli and the boy Samuel, whose strange experiences are recorded in the first book of Samuel.

As we ride northward the fields abound in heavy-headed grain, the fig and olive groves stretch for miles before us, and to the right Mount Ebal and to the left Mount Gerizim loom up.

At Jacob's Well.

In the valley dividing them we reach the famous Jacob's Well, where Christ held His memorable conversation with a Samaritan woman.

The authenticity of this place has never been doubted. Doubtless here the Saviour sat, and over to the right is the parcel of ground that Jacob gave to his son Joseph.

The well is not a spring of water bubbling up from the earth, nor is it reached by an excavation, but it is a shaft cut in the living rock about nine feet in diameter, and now more than seventy feet deep. The mouth is funnel-shaped, and its sides are formed by the rubbish of a church building that was once erected over it.

Passing between the mountains of Gerizim, where blessings were pronounced upon the people, and Ebal, where curses were poured out upon them, we encamped for the night at ancient Shechem.

Somewhere about here Joseph was seized by his brethren and sold to the Ishmaelites, and his bones were brought from Egypt and buried here.

On these plains all Israel assembled in the time of Joshua. After the death of Solomon this city was made the seat of government under Jeroboam. After the return from the captivity it became the centre of Samaritan worship.

After His talk with the Samaritan woman Christ tarried here two days and many believed in Him.

The Samaritans.

There is, and always has been, a bitter animosity between the Jews and the Samaritans, and it became a sin on either side to extend the rights of hospitality.

The greatest curiosity to be seen in the old synagogue is the celebrated Samaritan Codex of the Pentateuch, which is affirmed to have been written by a grandson of Aaron, but which is certainly not older than the Christian era

On Mount Gerizim.

The view from the summit of Mount Gerizim is exquisite. In the far west are the waters of the Mediterranean; in the north the snowy top of Hermon, partly intercepted by Mount Ebal; below, to the east, is the fertile plain that was the arena of so many important events in sacred history, and beyond are the mountains of Gilead.

There is only a small number of them left who exclusively follow their old customs and inhabit what is known as the Samaritan quarter of the city. They believe in one God, the resurrection of the body, the advent of the Messiah, the Mosaic system of feasts, and they acknowledge only the authority of the Pentateuch in the Old Testament writings.

The journey from Shechem (now called Nabulus) to Samaria is through the beautiful valley, where every variety of vegetation is seen, and where I counted in one large field thirty-two plowmen at work.

The City of Samaria.

Entering the city of Samaria, as one looks upon the desolate scene, the burden of prophecy comes to mind (Hosea xiii. 16), and the story of the siege of Samaria, as given in 2 Kings vi. 24-33, lend a peculiar interest to a place that once exerted such

WEAVING.

a mighty influence, but is now largely a pile of magnificent ruins.

From this desolation we turn toward the romantic plain of Esdraelon, which stretches from the Mediterranean on the west across Central Palestine, with an average width of ten or twelve miles, to the river Jordan, on the east. These fertile meadows, which now smile in their gay dresses of wild flowers and ripening grain, have for centuries been the scene of plunder and war.

CHAPTER XVIII

IN SADDLE AND TENT.

TO spend thirty days in saddle and tent is not the most restful experience, but this must be accomplished if one would cover the length and breadth of Palestine and visit all the places of sacred and secular history that have made this wonderful land so famous.

In former chapters I have written of the country between Jaffa and Jerusalem, of the Holy City, of the region about the Jordan and Dead Sea, of the country south of Jerusalem, and of the city of the Samaritans.

Accompanied by an intelligent conductor and a native dragoman, who furnished horses, servants, tents and provisions for several weeks' trip, a congenial party of ten Anglo-Saxons, forming quite a caravan, moved out of Jerusalem northward.

From the beautiful hill Scopus a last view is taken of the Holy City, which leaves an indelible impression on the mind.

The town of Nob is soon passed, where David came for Goliath's sword, where he ate the shewbread which Christ commended and where the tabernacle and ark were stationed in the time of Saul. A mile or two further the site of Gibeah, the native place of the first king of Israel, is pointed out, where seven descendants of Saul were hanged by the Amorites, and which was the scene of one of the most touching stories of motherly love on record, as given in 2 Samuel xxi chapter.

To the left we now have Mizpah, where Saul was chosen king, and to the north is Gibeon, the place where Solomon offered a thousand burnt offerings and the Lord appeared to him in a dream.

We pause for a short while at the spot where tradition tells us Mary missed the young boy Jesus and returning to Jerusalem found Him in the temple asking and answering questions, and an hour later we reach Bethel.

Records of Bethel.

Here Abraham reared an altar, and from this place he went into Egypt and fell into temptation, dishonoring God before the heathen king, who dismissed him from the country; here Jacob, weary with his forty miles' journey, lay his head upon a pillow of stone and had that wondrous dream of angels ascending and descending the mystic ladder which made him exclaim: "This is none other than the house of God and this is the gate of heaven," and he called the name of that place Bethel. At this place Jeroboam set up a golden calf and tried to wean the people from the service of God, and hereabouts the bears tore forty-two children, who cried to Elisha: "Go up, thou bald head."

After passing over a barren, rocky hill, we enter the vineyards and orchards of the land of Ephraim, which is as fertile and picturesque as any part of Palestine. But Shiloh must not be passed unnoticed. Its large heap of ruins seem to be a singularly graphic fulfillment of the terrible prophecy of Jeremiah.

Following the Footsteps of the Christ.

The fourth day out from Jerusalem in our northward journey we camped on the Plain of Esdraelon, with the mountains of Gilboa on our right.

The following day, as we entered the Valley of Jezreel, associations crowded upon us.

Here is where Ahab coveted the vineyard of Naboth; in this neighborhood is where the painted Jezebel proceeded with her wicked machinations, and where the prophet Elijah came down upon her with messages of wrath. It was along this way that Jehu came "driving furiously" and put Jehoram to death; and it was in this valley that Gideon gained his famous victory over the Midianites.

The Valley of Jezreel.

On this very ground Saul pitched his camp, while the Philistines encamped over there at Shunem and here it was that he was alarmed when he saw the host of the Philistines, and under cover of darkness visited the witch of Endor.

During the next two hours' ride we pass Gideon's Fountain, where his 300 men lapped water, putting the hand to the mouth. Next comes Shunem, where the woman lived who entertained Elisha and whose son he raised from the dead. Beyond lies the village of Nain, where Christ raised the widow's son (Luke vii. 11–16), and a short ride across the plain brings us to the foot of Mount Tabor, from whose altitude of 2017 feet, the traditional scene of the transfiguration, the eye can range from the vicinity of Dan on the north to Beersheba on the south.

Mount Tabor.

Standing almost alone in the plain, Mount Tabor presents a most striking appearance. It is somewhat in the shape of a sugar-loaf, flattened at the top. On the southern side it is rough and rugged, with nothing but barren limestone visible; northward it is covered with thick foliage, oak, terebinth and syringa ornamenting it from base to summit; elsewhere it presents the appearance of a series of well-planted terraces.

The summit of the mountain is a broad plateau, covered with the ruins of buildings of all ages; there are the thick, beveled stones of a wall, very ancient, undoubtedly, and there are the remains of towers, houses, cisterns and vaults, probably belonging to the age of the Crusaders.

As we approach the high hill on which Nazareth stands a sharp, precipitous spur of the mountain, called the Mount of Precipitation, is pointed out, which name arose from the worthless tradition that alleges that it was from here that the people of Nazareth sought to cast the Saviour down headlong. It is about two miles from the town and about as improbable a site as could have been selected.

Nazareth.

After climbing a sharp ascent through glens and gullies and over steep and rugged places, where the well-trained Syrian horses pick their way with marvelous sagacity, we at length enter Nazareth, where the Christ spent thirty years of His life.

FARMING IN VALLEY OF JEZREEL.

The town, as seen from the enclosing hill, is very picturesque, backed by high cliffs and approached from under the shade of spreading oaks, with substantial looking houses of stone, the massive walls of a large church and monastery and the graceful minarets of two mosques, overtopped by the tall, spiral forms of the dark green cypress tree. Nazareth was the residence of Joseph and Mary, the scene of the annunciation, the place whence Joseph went to Bethlehem "to be taxed with Mary, his espoused wife," and the home of our Lord until He entered upon His public ministry. Afterward He visited the place of His boyhood and young manhood, when His townsmen attempted to cast Him from the brow of the hill and kill Him.

Tradition has marked many spots in the town, associating them with the life of Christ, but nothing positive can be asserted about these localities.

It was with some degree of satisfaction that I visited a carpenter's shop, and as it is quite certain that for centuries and centuries these shopmen have been

BIRD'S-EYE VIEW OF NAZARETH.

doing the same kind of work, I imagined that the man and boy whom I watched at work were engaged in the same kind of activity as were Joseph and the boy Jesus nearly nineteen hundred years ago.

The Virgin's Fountain.

At the Fountain of the Virgin, a plentiful spring of water issuing from three mouths, the village women in their white robes and bright head-dresses assemble, and gracefully bear away their well-filled pitchers on their heads; and as the same fountain has been in use ever since the town was inhabited, doubtless she who was "blessed among women" would often come here, perhaps carrying the infant Saviour in just the same fashion as that young mother yonder, who moves away from the sparkling stream, with her pitcher poised on her head and her babe in her arm.

Among the remarkable things in the modern history of Nazareth are the circumstances that Napoleon supped here on the night of the battle of Tabor, and that a plot was laid here by Pasha Jezzar to murder all the Christians in his dominions as soon as the French had evacuated. His

A PALESTINE BEDOUIN.

bloodthirsty scheme, however, was thwarted by Sir Sydney Smith, the English admiral.

Cana and Mount of Beatitudes.

As we ride toward the Sea of Galilee we soon approach the village of Cana, where Christ performed His first miracle at the marriage feast, when "the conscious water saw its Lord and blushed," where He healed the nobleman's son who lay sick at Capernaum, and where Nathaniel, "the disciple in whom there was no guile," was born.

THE TOWER OF JEZREEL, PALESTINE, AS IT NOW APPEARS.

Resuming our journey, we have now on our left, rising up out of the fertile plain, a curiously shaped hill, having on its summit two peaks or horns, from which it derives its name of Horns of Hatton.

This is known as the Mount of Beatitudes, where it is supposed our Lord preached the Sermon on the Mount.

Another tradition makes this also to be the scene of the feeding of the five thousand, as recorded in the fourteenth chapter of Matthew.

The plain before us was the last battlefield of the Crusaders. Here, in July, 1187, Saladin defeated them.

The Crusaders' Battlefield.

As faithfully chronicled by Michaud we read that at nightfall they gathered together by the Horns of Hatton, Guy of Lusignau, with Raynald of Chatillon, the grand master of the Knights Templar, and the Bishop of Lydda, bearing the holy cross.

But a great triumph awaited the Moslem, and the power of the Crusaders was broken forever in the Holy Land. King Guy was taken prisoner; Chatillon, whom Saladin hated with a peculiar hatred, was killed, and all the army of the noble knights were slain or taken prisoner.

The more one sees of the Moslem rule the stronger is his wish that ere long some power may rise and sweep from this land of blessed memory a nation of brutes, whose barbarous cruelty is only exceeded by their religious hypocrisy.

On the Sea of Galilee.

A magnificent view of the Sea of Galilee can be obtained several miles before its waters are reached.

The whole of the lake, from below Tiberias on the right to Capernaum on the left, is distinctly seen, lying in a basin more than a thousand feet below the steeply-sloping and well-clothed hills upon which you approach it.

Across the lake rise the irregular hills, bare and barren in foliage, but rich and varied in tone and tint; behind are the mountains of Galilee, and way to the north snow-capped Hermon stands in its spotless purity against the clear azure sky.

The natural beauty is only exceeded by the divine associations.

The City of Jesus.

Cast out from Nazareth, Jesus made Capernaum on the lake His city. Along these shores He spent the principal part of His public ministry, and to record the mighty works performed within sight of these blue waters would be to transcribe a very large part of the four gospels.

A PALESTINE BURDEN BEARER. (371)

From the banks of the lake He called Peter, James and John, the inner circle, of His chosen band.   From Simon's boat He taught the people on the shore, following His talk by the miracle of the draught of fishes, and using a ship as His pulpit He delivered that marvelous discourse on the kingdom of Heaven.   Here it was that He gave those striking parables of the sower, the wheat and the tares, the grain of mustard seed, the leaven and the net cast into the sea.   It was on these waters that a great tempest arose, when He rebuked the winds and the sea and there was a great calm.

Divine Associations.

It was on the slope of the hill over yonder that He cast the devils out of the men from the tombs, causing the destruction of the herd of swine; near there He fed the five thousand and afterward walked on the crystal pavement of the sea toward His disciples, rowing in the storm.

From these waters He caused to be caught the fish, in whose mouth was found the piece of money with which He paid tribute, and after His resurrection in the gray dawn of the morning He suddenly appeared to His disciples, after they had toiled all night, and caught nothing.   There on the shore He kindled the mysterious fire of coals, spread the farewell meal, and there the impulsive disciple, who, three times warned, had thrice denied his Lord, by threefold confession, was restored and reinstated in the apostolic office.

Camping Near Capernaum.

On the site of Capernaum we camped, and from my tent door the views were very striking.

The hills, except where there are cliffs, recede gradually from the lake; they are of no great elevation, but everywhere from the shore the snow fields of Hermon are visible.

The shore-line, for the most part regular, is broken on the north into a series of little bays of exquisite beauty, especially at Gennesaret, where the beaches, pearly white with myriads of minute shells, are on one side bathed by the clear waters of the lake, and on the other shut in by a fringe of oleanders, rich at this time of the year with their blossoms, red and bright.

Lake Gennesaret and the Jordan.

The lake is pear-shaped, the broad end being toward the north.   The greatest width is six and three-quarter miles, and the extreme length is twelve and a quarter miles.

The Jordan river enters at the north, coloring the lake for a mile from its mouth, and passes out pure and bright at the south.

On the northwestern shore is a plain nearly three miles broad, known as Gennesaret; on the west there is a recess in the hills containing the town of Tiberias; on the east are small tracts of level ground before the hill country is reached, and on the south the open valley of the Jordan stretches out toward the Dead Sea, covered near the lake with luxuriant vegetation.

The lake is from 600 to 700 feet below the Mediterranean Sea. It is still

GROUP SHOWING COSTUMES OF PALESTINE AT PRESENT DAY.

subject to sudden and violent storms, as in the time when Christ and His disciples rode upon its bosom.

In the lake there are a number of warm springs, and violent earthquakes are not infrequent, as in 1837, when half of the inhabitants of Tiberias perished.

A Prophecy Fulfilled.

Capernaum, Bethsaida, Chorazin—mounds of rubbish, tangles of thistles, heaps of ruins—recall those pathetic words of our Lord: "Then began He to upbraid the cities wherein most of His mighty works were done because they repented not:

"Woe unto thee, Chorazin! Woe unto thee, Bethsaida! For if the mighty works which were done in you had been done in Tyre and Sidon, they would have repented long ago in sackcloth and ashes. But I say unto you, it shall be more tolerable for Tyre and Sidon at the day of judgment than for you.

"And thou, Capernaum, which art exalted unto heaven, shall be brought down to hell! For if the mighty works which were done in thee had been done in Sodom, it would have remained until this day. But I say unto you that it shall be more tolerable for the land of Sodom in the day of judgment than for thee."

A Moonlight Sail.

Accompanied by a single friend and four boatmen I can never forget the eight hours spent on the Lake of Galilee.

During the afternoon a whistling wind dotted the water with white caps, but as the sun was setting behind the crimson curtains in the western sky, and as the full moon calmly looked into the depths of the lake, a voice seemed to speak, "Peace, be still," for suddenly there was a great calm.

The white houses of Tiberias were distinctly visible in the glowing moonlight. The sombre ruins of the cursed cities lay like black heaps upon the shores. The hill platforms upon which the multitudes were miraculously fed and taught were outlined in the distance.

The mighty hills on the eastern shore stood like giant sentinels against the sky, and the placid moon-kissed Galilee seemed a fit pavement for the feet of the Prince of Peace.

Far in the night we passed into the Jordan at the extreme northern point of the lake, crossed to the eastern side, and after quite a thrilling experience with a band of Bedouin robbers, which somewhat disturbed the placidity of the occasion, we turned our boat toward the tents on the western shore, some miles away.

CHAPTER XIX

THE EYE OF THE EAST.

WHILE the ancient cities along the Nile are known only by the magnificence of their ruined temples, while Baalbec and Palmyra have long since passed away, while Babylon is a heap in the desert and Tyre a ruin on the shore, Damascus, which Josephus declares was standing before Abraham's time, and which is called in the prophecies of Isaiah "the head of Syria," is to-day, as it has been for thousands of years, a mighty city, influencing the customs and trade of a region of hundreds of miles around it.

Its importance in the flourishing period of the Jewish monarchy we know, from the garrisons which David placed here and from the opposition it presented to Solomon. How close its relations continued to be with this people we infer from the chronicles of Jeroboam and Ahaz and the prophecies of Isaiah and Amos. Its mercantile greatness is indicated by Ezekiel in the remarkable words addressed to Tyre: "Damascus was thy merchant in the multitude of the wares of thy making for the multitude of all riches, in the wine of Helbon and white wool."

Alexander the Great saw its greatness and sent Parmenio to take it while he was engaged in marching from Tarsus and Tyre. Julian, the apostate, describes it as "the eye of the East." Recognized at one time as the metropolis of the Mohammedan world, its fame is mingled with the exploits of Saladin and Tamerlane.

The tradition that the murder of Abel took place here is alluded to by Shakespeare (I King Henry VI., i. 3).

> *Winchester.*—Nay, stand thou back, I will not budge a foot;
> This be Damascus; be thou cursed Cain
> To slay thy brother Abel if thou wilt.

The Streams of Lebanon.

The cause of its importance as a city in all the ages is easily seen as you approach it from the south.

Miles before you see the mosques of the modern city the fountains of a copious and perennial stream spring from among the rocks and brushwood at the base of the Anti Lebanon, creating a wide area about them, rich with prolific vegetation. These are the "streams of Lebanon," which are poetically spoken of in the Songs of Solomon, and the "rivers of Damascus," which Naaman, not unnaturally, preferred to all the "waters of Israel." This stream, with its many branches, is the inestimable treasure of Damascus.

While the desert is a fortification round Damascus, the river, where the habitations of men must always have been gathered, as along the Nile, is its life.

Modern Damascus.

The city, which is situated in a wilderness of gardens of flowers and fruits, has rushing through its streets the limpid and refreshing current; nearly every dwelling has its fountain, and at night the lights are seen flashing on the waters that dash along from their mountain home.

As you first view the city from one of the overhanging ridges you are prepared to excuse the Mohammedans for calling it the earthly paradise.

Around the marble minarets, the glittering domes and the white buildings, shining with ivory softness, a maze of bloom and fruitage, where olive and pomegranate, orange and apricot, plum and walnut mingle their varied tints of green, is presented to the sight, in striking contrast to the miles of barren desert over which you have just ridden.

Damascus remains the same true type of an oriental city. Caravans come and go from Bagdad and Mecca, as of old; merchants sit and smoke over their costly bales in dim bazaars; drowsy groups sip their coffee in kiosks overhanging the river; the bread boy cries aloud, "O Allah ! who sustainest us, send trade;" the drink-seller as he rattles his brass cups exclaims, "Drink and cheer thine heart," and all the brilliant costumes of the East mingle in the streets.

Its Bazaars and Streets.

Although Cairo contains a much larger population than Damascus, its bazaars are by no means as extensive or imposing. These bazaars are in long avenues, roofed over, and each is devoted to some special trade. There we find the silk, the saddler's, the tobacco, the coppersmith's, the bookseller's, the shoe and many other bazaars, and now and then we come across an "antique Damascus blade" which was made last year in Germany.

While passing through the city on Friday, the great market day, I was attracted by Persians in gorgeous silks, Nubians in black and white, Greeks in their national costumes, Jews with long ringlets, Bedouins, Druses, Kurds and Armenians mingling together, and lines of pilgrims on their way to Mecca—a marvelous medley of humanity, not to be seen, perhaps, elsewhere on the globe. The great mosque (there are over two hundred smaller ones) exhibits three

DAMASCUS.

distinct styles of architecture, marking three epochs in the history of the place, and proclaiming the three dynasties that have successively possessed it. In the transept is a chapel said to contain the head of John the Baptist, which was found in the crypt of the church.

The "street called Straight," which is interesting to all New Testament readers, is about a mile in length and runs across the city from west to east.

In round numbers the population is about one hundred and fifty thousand, one hundred thousand of which are Moslems. These are notorious for their fanaticism, which has a terrible proof in the massacre of July, 1860, when six thousand Christians were slaughtered in the streets and nine thousand more in the district about the city.

In this butchery we have a true picture of the "unspeakable" Turk when he is aroused.

The churches and convents, which had been filled with the terror-stricken Christians, presented piles of corpses, and the thoroughfares were choked with the slain.

WOMAN GRINDING FLOUR AT DAMASCUS.

Through the influence brought to bear upon the Turkish government the governor and three city officers were shot, fifty-six of the citizens were hanged, one hundred and seventeen others received the death penalty, four hundred were condemned to imprisonment and exile and the city was made to pay the sum of one million dollars.

The Unspeakable Turk.

Some refused at first to believe that the Turks were responsible for the massacre, but it has been shown beyond a doubt that they connived at it, they instigated it, they ordered it, they shared in it. Their conduct north of Damascus at present is a repetition of the same thing.

Besides the biblical allusions that have been made to Damascus it will be remembered that Paul was converted on his way here, and that when the governor sought to apprehend him he was let down in a basket through a window and made good his escape, and that during his residence here "he preached Christ in the synagogue, that He is the Son of God, and confounded the Jews which dwelt at Damascus, proving that this is the very Christ." We are tempted to think that it would take more than the eloquent voice of a Paul to disturb the consummate indifference of the average pipe-smoking, coffee-drinking, sleepy-eyed citizen of modern Damascus.

The Ruins of Baalbec.

Standing among the ruins of this inglorious city you look upon the remains of two distinct but blended civilizations. The popular natural religions, which for centuries held Asia captive, mingle the wrecks of their colossal architecture with the exquisite forms that the artistic genius of Greece created.

Camels, sheep and goats graze on the grass which grows over the fallen, crumbling columns and capitals, and the opening spring casts fresh, green garlands over these relics of the dead past.

Great columns lean heavily against tottering walls, as if determined to postpone their fall to the last moment, and over the scene of desolation the white chain of the Lebanon, capped by perpetual snow, gives a chilling look.

Sun Worship and Temples.

Here is the ancient Heliopolis of the Greeks and Romans, celebrated for its sun worship in the temple which was one of the wonders of the world. Here you may witness how the pride and pomp of paganism arrayed itself before its death; here you see the ruin of an entire city, full of disorder, poetry, grandeur, and as you study some of this enormous debris in detail you find that nowhere is the Corinthian acanthus carved with more delicacy than on these gigantic blocks.

The temples of Baalbec, dating at least from the reign of Antoninus Pius, were erected on the Acropolis of the city, which was placed on an eminence, surrounded with gigantic walls, the stones of which belonged to that Phœnician architecture which has earned the name of Cyclopean.

First, there was the Great Temple of Jupiter, which has preserved a large part of its portico, its ornate architrave, its fluted columns and a rich profusion of decoration; then there was the Temple of the Sun, the ruins of which clearly indicate its past grandeur, and the last was what was known as the Circular Temple, the only remains of which are a few highly decorated chapels.

Courts and Porticoes.

Passing through a long passageway we enter a court, seventy yards long by about eighty-five wide, which is in the form of a hexagon, with here and there rectangular recesses in the wall, each with columns in front.

From this hexagon originally a handsome portal led into the great court, about a hundred and fifty yards long by a hundred and twenty-five wide, in the centre of which stood the basilica, while around were rectangular recesses, called by the Romans exedrae.

In front of this great court the principal temple of Baalbec stood. This temple had columns running round it, only six of which are now standing. These are sixty feet in height, with Corinthian capitals and bordered with a frieze.

Sacred to Jupiter.

When the temple was in its glory there were seventeen columns on either side of the temple and ten at either end, fifty-four in all, the building enclosed by them being two hundred and ninety feet long by one hundred and sixty broad.

The masses of broken columns and falling walls indicate not only the work of the "tooth of time," but the ruthless ravages of the Arabs, who have destroyed priceless treasures in art in order that they might secure the iron clamps in the columns.

In the grand portico of the temple there is an inscription, which may be translated as follows: "To the great gods of Heliopolis. For the safety of the Lord Ant. Pius Aug. and of Julia Aug., the mother of our Lord of the Castra (here it is quite indistinct) Senate. A devoted (subject) of the sovereigns (caused) the capitals of the columns of Antoninus, while in the air, (to be,) embossed with gold at her own expense."

Sun's Trilithon.

The second temple, or Temple of the Sun, stands on a platform lower than that of the Great Temple; nineteen out of the forty-six columns, each sixty-five feet high, remain, and the capitals and entablatures of the columns and the friezes round them are as exquisitely executed as anything in Baalbec.

The portal of the temple claims one's special attention. The door-posts are monoliths, most richly ornamented with foliage and genii; the architrave is of three stones, on the lower side of which is the figure of an eagle, the emblem of the sun, and the basement, which is one hundred by seventy feet, is ornamented most profusely.

Built into the outer wall are three stones, the largest ever used in architecture. The temple was, at one time, called Trilithon, or three-stoned, probably from these stupendous blocks. One stone measures sixty-four feet long, another sixty-three feet eight inches, and a third sixty-three. Each is thirteen feet high and thirteen feet thick, and placed in the wall at a height of twenty feet above ground.

It is still an unsolved problem how they were ever raised to their present position.

The Quarries of Lebanon.

At the quarries in the Lebanon mountains, where doubtless these stones came from, I examined an unfinished block which is seventy-one feet long and nearly eighteen feet in thickness. The Circular Temple, which is located near to the modern village, is surrounded by Corinthian columns, is richly adorned by a frieze of flowers and the entablature is heavily laden with elaborate decoration.

As I sat upon an ornately sculptured parapet and, quietly and alone, studied this wilderness of magnificent ruins, where were displayed Phœnician glory and power, the poetry of Grecian art and the pomp of Roman pride, the transitory character of even the most permanent and glorious of the material was pictured before me as never before.

ORPHANS IN CAMP ON A TRIP TO THE JORDAN IN 1897.

CHAPTER XX.

IN ASIA MINOR.

N the Levant, which is chiefly in Asia Minor and belongs to Turkey, there are two cities which are of special interest to the tourist. The first is Smyrna, the capital of Anatolia, the second city of Turkey and the great port of Asia Minor and the Levant trade. As you enter the bay, a noble inlet, forty-five by twenty-two miles, the city presents a most striking appearance, with its two harbors, covering seventy acres; its fine breakwater, 1125 yards long; its splendidly built quay, over two miles in length, which cost $1,500,000, and the Governor's palace, the barracks, the imposing Vizier Khan, the numerous mosques, the large warehouses and the well-built residences, holding a population of 270,000, the bright picture having as its background the green slopes of the hills.

Smyrna is the centre of the caravan trade in Asia Minor; it is the great market place for the whole Levant, and the merchants and traders who are found on her streets represent every nation in the Orient.

Smyrna's Busy Scenes.

From my hotel window, that overlooks the busy scenes on the quay, by their costumes I distinguished representatives of seventeen different nationalities. Their facial expressions and features, their modes of salutation, their manner of talking, walking, laughing and quarreling, and their peculiar ways of attracting and convincing customers, were indeed a rich study which was greatly enjoyed.

The fruit-seller, the fish-cryer, the trinket peddler, the vegetable cartman, the man with cooling drinks, the flower and match girls, the curio vender of the Orient and the pug-nosed, bow-legged dogs rub up against one another with a degree of intimacy that is more than touching.

After all, what is more interesting and instructive than a quiet study of a mass of human beings, with a few dogs thrown in, provided you are out of reach?

There are five or six Smyrnas, one over the other, and some of the excavations that have been made while digging the foundations of houses and cultivating the neighboring fields go to prove that this city, so admirably located, was in the far past, a place of great commercial and political importance.

It claims to be the birthplace of Homer, and here the distinguished Bishop Polycarp was martyred in the year A. D. 169, whose tomb is pointed out.

The Byzantine Castle is on the site of the Acropolis, on Mons Pagus, and has in it many remains. Its corner nearest the city is Cyclopean, and the further walls were built by Lysander.

The way to it leads past a cliff marked by three streaks of shells like flints, and the road brings you past parts of aqueducts that were evidently built by the Romans.

The antiquities of Smyrna are scattered, for the most part, two or three miles apart on the site of the old Ionian town, where Homer is supposed to have been born, up to Meles, in view of Mount Tmolus.

It was rebuilt in 627, B. C., and half ruined by Tamerlane A. D. 1402.

The whole district is very rich in archaic remains. From Smyrna, one of the famous Seven Churches, five others are accessible by rail.

My chief concern in coming to Smyrna was to take a trip from here inland to see the country and people of this part of Asia Minor and visit the ruins of the ancient city of Ephesus, which are found about one mile from the modern village of Ayasoluk, at the foot of Mount Prion.

The Ruins of Ephesus.

Ephesus was the old capital of Ionia or Lydia, birthplace of Diana, a sacred city of both Pagans and Christians and a capital of the Saracenic Sultans.

It was located in a fine plain at the head of Port Panormus, on a surface raised by deposits of the Caystrus or Cayster, was founded B. C. 1040, half swallowed up by an earthquake about A. D. 17, and has been mostly in ruins since the year 527.

To the Christians at this place St. Paul addressed his " Epistle to the Ephesians," and the old fort is shown where it is said he was imprisoned.

The ruins, consisting chiefly of broken columns, crumbling walls and fragments of pavements, are spread over a wide district, and after visiting them one is prepared to give credence to the supposition that before the Christian era more than a million people inhabited the place.

Pagan and Christian Records.

You are possessed by strange feelings when you attempt to realize that you are at the Cyclopean city of the Amazons, the refuge of Latona, the home of Apollo and Diana, the place of the metamorphosis of Syrinx into a reed, the lurking place of Pan, the asylum of Apollo on Mount Soimissus, the deathplace of Orion, the panionium under Mount Mycale, the great gymnasium, the odeum, the aqueduct, the magnificent Ephesus Theatre, 600 feet in length, and the marvelous temple of Diana " of the Ephesians "—one of the seven wonders of the world, built 552-352 B. C.

AN ENCAMPMENT OF KURDS IN THE MOUNTAINS OF ASIA MINOR.

Some of the columns from the temple are now in the mosque of St. Sophia, at Constantinople.

An English excavator in 1876 found the remains twelve to twenty feet below the surface to correspond with Pliny's account, the dimensions being 418 feet by 240 feet, with one hundred columns, 56 feet high and an elaborate cedar roof.

Other names connected with Ephesus are Bacchus, Homer, Crœsus, Artemisia, Queen of Caria; Julian, the Emperor, and Tamerlane.

The famous Council of Ephesus was held here in 431 A. D.

To the Bible student the most interesting fact is that the Apostle Paul spent three years here and taught in the school of Tyranus, the supposed ruins of which are pointed out.

Turkish Tyranny.

It is impossible for the citizens of free America, who have never visited the Ottoman empire, to imagine the corruption of the Turkish government. From the most subordinate officer to the Sultan himself this official rottenness is traceable; and how the thing has held together so long is a wonder of wonders.

As this terrible state of affairs is supposed to be kept in secrecy from the outside world, and a man's head is at stake if he is caught speaking or writing on the subject while in these regions, I have found no little difficulty, although I have had the aid of a discreet native interpreter, to reach the reliable facts that are now in my possession.

In the shop, on the farm and within the humble family circle, through my assistant, I have interviewed a number of the inhabitants of this cursed land, and everywhere the same sad story of governmental injustice, dishonesty and oppression is heard.

Official Rottenness.

Here the seed of patriotism is crushed, if it ever exists at all; here the young Turk, it matters not how noble may be his ambition in commercial, civic or military life, has no opportunity for its expansion; here the farmer is yearly and systematically robbed by the merciless agents of the government at Constantinople, and here an official premium is put on any and every vice from which the Sultan can possibly receive a revenue.

In the light of these facts it is not a matter of surprise that every influence from without that has a tendency to reveal or improve the condition of the country is indignantly opposed by the government, and that the basest deception is perpetrated to mislead the nations of the civilized world.

Book and Press Censorship.

No publication is allowed in the country that is not first carefully examined by agents of the Sultan. If a book is written, it matters not of what subject

25

it treats, the original manuscript must be sent to Constantinople, and is closely
read by a committee created for the purpose. Every word that is at all objection-
able is expunged. The revised manuscript is sent back after a copy is taken. At
the author's expense an edition of only two copies of the book is first published,
one of which is sent on to be compared with the copy which is retained, and if
there is the least variation the volume is not allowed to see the light of day.

A TURKISH PASHA.

Nothing can be published
which gives the people information about the true government of the land, and no
word is printed about the do-
ings of other nations which
would have a tendency to give
rise to a comparison between
the way of doing things in the
Ottoman empire and else-
where.

When the president of the
French republic was assassinated the order went out from
the Sultan that no such words
as corresponded to "assassi-
nate" or "murder" should
be used in the report of the
event, but it should be circu-
lated that the president died
of a lingering disease.

I was in a Syrian village
last week when the news of
the murder of the Shah of
Persia reached the place. A
Mohammedan at the head of
a printing establishment told
me that the same deception
would be perpetrated by the press of the country. The Sultan, knowing his own
unpopularity, is not willing that his people should be educated in the art of easily
getting rid of a hated ruler.

Administrative System.

The large cities are ruled by pashas; the towns have over them governors,
and the villages have sheiks.

A man receives and holds his appointment only because he pays for it more money than any one else is willing or able to pay. The idea of efficiency does not enter into the question at all.

A few weeks ago a man living near Damascus found out through a spy what the governor of the place was paying to hold his office. He consulted with his friends as to how much he could make out of the office, sent a higher offer to the Sultan than the acting governor had made and was immediately installed.

This principle, or rather lack of principle, holds in reference to every office under the government. Everything is for revenue only.

Oppressive Taxation.

The tax collecting system is one of the most wretchedly unjust in the world. The whole thing is farmed out to the highest bidder.

The one who gets the position of tax collector for a district must necessarily pay the government an exorbitant price for the privilege; the money is, in nearly every case, borrowed to send in advance to Constantinople, and now, in order to reimburse himself and make money, the collector goes to work on the long-suffering citizens, and with the soldiers that are placed at his disposal the most cruel extortion is enacted.

According to the written law (which is a snare and delusion) he is allowed to collect one-tenth of the produce of a farm. On three farms I was shown how eighty per cent of the whole crop went into the pockets of the collectors.

An old man, who owns an olive orchard, told me that he gave in a true report of the yield of his place as ten barrels of oil. The legal tax would have been one barrel of the stuff, but the collector reported the yield of the orchard as eighty barrels of oil, taking one-tenth of this, leaving two barrels for the owner of the orchard.

This instance may induce certain ward politicians in America to leave their seemingly lucrative business and apply for a job under the gracious Sultan.

Justice with a Vengeance.

To illustrate how justice, so called, is administered, let me give a case in point, the truth of which is vouched for by an American, who has lived in this country for thirty-five years, and who is personally acquainted with characters involved. A wealthy man by the name of Aly made accusation against his enemy Jacob, and swore in court that he owed him 100,000 francs. For about six pence each he bribed two witnesses to testify for him.

The accused was brought before the judge, and although he did not owe a cent in the world he confessed judgment, but declared that his accuser owed him 200,000 francs, and that he was waiting patiently for a settlement.

SULTAN'S MOSQUE.

Being asked to produce his witnesses, he started out to secure them, when Aly requested the judge to send a guard along to prevent him bribing men to testify in his behalf. The chief of police was sent with him.

Jacob, after walking about for some time, slipped a Turkish pound in the chief's hand; the head of the police took him to his office, where two witnesses were bribed for a few pennies; they returned to court, and, after secret consultation with the judge and testimony of new-bought witnesses, judgment was given in favor of Jacob, who paid the 100,000 francs that he didn't owe to Aly, and collected the 200,000 francs that Aly did not owe him.

This, verily, is justice with a vengeance.

The City of the Sultan.

Constantinople, or Stambool, the city of the Sultan, is located on the western shore of the Thracian Bosphorus, in a situation equally remarkable for beauty and security.

A gently declining promontory, secured by narrow seas, at the southeast corner of Europe, stretches out to meet the continent of Asia, from which it is separated by so narrow a strait, the Bosphorus, that in fifteen minutes you can row from one continent to the other.

This channel, running for about twenty miles from the Black Sea, looks like a stately river until it sweeps by the angle of Constantinople and enters the Sea of Marmora. But just before it is lost in that sea it makes a deep elbow between the triangle of Constantinople proper and its foreign suburbs of Galata and Pera, thus forming the port of the Golden Horn.

At this corner of Thrace the Megarian leader, Byzas, planted the city of Byzantium about 660-70 B. C. It was taken by the Romans A. D. 73, and here Constantine fixed the eastern seat of the Roman empire in 328-30, calling it Constantinopolis, the city of Constantine, of which the Orientals make Stambool, from the Greek *es tan poli*, or "the city." "Room," or Rome, is also a popular name for it to this day, and the province in which it stands is Roumeli, which name appears in Roumania.

Godfrey de Bouillon was here in the first crusade—1096-97—in the reign of Alexius Commenus. It was taken by the Venetians and Franks, led by "Blind Old Dandolo," and held till 1261, during which period the Greek emperors reigned at Nicæa and Trebizond. Their rule terminated with its capture by the Turks in 1453, under Mahomet II., after fifty-three days' siege.

Stambool, like its prototype, is said to have been built on seven hills, which appear to rise above one another in beautiful succession, and was thirteen miles in circumference. It is of great interest to study the many decaying and neglected remains of Roman and mediæval times which it contains.

Life and Scenes.

The ridge of the first hill is occupied by the Seraglio, behind which a little on the reverse of the hill the imposing dome of the Santa Sophia can be seen. This was the site of the first city of Byzantium.

Four of the hills are covered with magnificent mosques, whose domes are strikingly bold and lofty.

The city proper, occupying the triangle between the Golden Horn and the Sea of Marmora, is partly surrounded by the remains of decaying walls, which are fast disappearing.

TURKISH WOMAN.

Galata, founded by the Genoese in 1216, on the north side of the Golden Horn, is joined to the main city by an iron bridge, and is the chief business quarter for European merchants, who, strangely enough, go under the general name of Franks.

A steep street leads up to Pera, which stretches two miles along a hill, and is the residence of diplomatic corps from the different nations of Europe, where each has a fine palace. The tremendous conflagration of 1870 swept away a great part of Pera, destroying 6000 houses, including the British embassy.

The Town of Scutari.

Scutari is a mile and a half across the Bosphorus from Galata, and is mostly inhabited by Turks, Greeks and Armenians. Here are located the Sultan Selim barracks, used as the English military hospital during the Crimean war, and which are specially noted as the scene of Miss Nightingale's heroic and memorable labors. In the adjacent cemetery are buried 8000 English soldiers, victims of that terrible struggle.

From the hill of Bulgaria, overlooking the column of Marochetti in the military cemetery, a splendid panorama of Constantinople is had, taking in the Black Sea, Therapia and Buyukdere on the Bosphorus, the castles of Europe and Asia, near the water, and the Golden Horn. On this hill, where ancient Chrysopolis was located, Constantine defeated his enemy and rival, Licinius, A. D. 325, and not far from this place of victory the great conqueror was conquered by his last enemy.

On entering the city the visitor is first attracted by the wilderness of mosques and minarets. Within the walls there are sixteen imperial mosques, 150 ordinary

THE SULTAN'S PALACE OF DOLMA-BAGTCHE, CONSTANTINOPLE.

ones and 200 mesjids, the last of which are only distinguished as being places of worship by having little minarets or towers contiguous to them.

The Mosque of St. Sophia.

I shall speak of only one of these mosques, which is the most wonderful building of its kind in the world. St. Sophia was dedicated A. D. 360 to Agia Sophia, "Holy Wisdom," by Constantine II., the son of Constantine the Great, and was rebuilt by Justinian, 532-48, in the shape of a Greek cross.

Among the numerous pillars brought from all parts of the empire are some from Delos and Baalbec; six of green jasper from the Temple of Diana at Ephesus, and eight of porphyry, which had been placed by Aurelian in the Temple of the Sun at Rome and were removed here by Constantine.

It is an immense marble basilica, 270 by 245 feet, with sixteen bronze gates, and a stupendous dome, 115 feet across, adorned with mosaic work.   It is illumi-

PEASANT VILLAGE GIRLS OF ROUMANIA.

nated with globes of crystal and lamps of colored glass at the Ramadan, and ornamented with ostrich eggs and flags.

On Fridays you can count the worshipers by the thousands, and from the great galleries you are allowed to watch the congregation of believers at prayers, with their faces turned toward Mecca.

Every mosque has, in general, a large area in front, surrounded by a lofty colonnade of marble, with gates of wrought brass, and in the centre a fountain of polished marble.

Curious Sepulchral Chapels.

Adjoining each is the sepulchral chapel of its founder. Some of these tombs, in which the sultans, viziers and other great personages repose, are exceedingly handsome; others in their workmanship, defy all laws of art and display a decided genius on the part of the builders for making what is supposed to be very solemn exceedingly laughable.

Looking through the grated windows you see the coffins, surmounted by shawls and turbans, and slightly elevated from the floor, with lamps continually burning and immense wax torches, which are lighted on particular occasions.

The slender and graceful minarets form one of the pleasing features in the architecture of Constantinople, and two, four or even six of these are connected with some of the mosques. Near the summit there is a little gallery, from which, at the five appointed times in the twenty-four hours, the Muezzin calls the Mohammedans to prayer.

A fountain, with its marble front, elaborate arabesque ornaments and Chinese-like roof, stands by every mosque, for before a Turk prostrates himself in prayer he must perform his ablutions. The supply for these many fountains in the city is brought from artificial lakes in the forest, about twelve miles from the city, by means of subterranean aqueducts and hydraulic pyramids, contrived so as to overcome the inequalities of surface.

The Bazaars and Their Crowds.

The bazaars, where you see the people acting naturally, are much more interesting than the mosques. The former consist of lofty cloisters or corridors, built of stone and lighted by domes, which, during the hot hours of the day, afford a pleasant retreat.

The Grand Bazaar, called Bezesteen, is a hive of small shops walled in with thirty-two gates, and here, as nowhere else in Constantinople or perhaps in the world (with the exception of Cairo), can you see displayed the brilliant, ever-changing picture of oriental life to such perfection.

A world in miniature is continually moving to and fro. In the bewildering multitude of nationalities you get a glimpse at the Albanian, with his tasseled cap, white, short skirts, flashing scarf, buckskin leggings and bright rosettes on his toes; the swaggering Turk, looking little like he was a member of a corrupt

A TURKISH SALON AT CONSTANTINOPLE.

and bankrupt nation, with his turban and flowing robes, or puffing a cigarette under a jockey red fez and over ill-fitting European vest and trousers; comical-looking women, waddling along in formless sacks for dresses, their faces hidden lest some one should be stricken by their bashful loveliness, and an army of soldiers, beggars, priests, patriarchs—each one a drop in the rushing, rolling, rumbling stream of humanity.

It matters little how interesting may be the palatial residences and busy streets of a great city, when the brain is tired reflecting upon the manners and methods of man, it is joyful and restful to hie away from these scenes, and find repose in some rural place, at the foot of a noble mountain or by the side of a leaping, laughing, limpid stream, or on the banks of a beautiful bay.

Taking a steamer across the Bosphorus (so called after Io, who swam over it in the shape of a heifer), you soon reach a pretty spot beyond a little village on the Asiatic side at the bend of the water. Here you have at once the mountain, the brooklet and the bay. From the summit of the Giant's Hill there is a striking view of the shores of several seas and the nearby united lands of two continents.

As this picturesque panorama spread before him the poetic soul of Byron went forth in the exclamation: " 'Tis a grand sight, from off the Giant's Grave, to watch the progress of those rolling seas, between the Bosphorus, as they lash and lave Europe and Asia."

ARMENIAN FUGITIVES ON THE TURKO-PERSIAN BORDER.

CHAPTER XXI.

A REIGN OF TERROR.

 despair of being able to give any adequate impression of the terrible condition of affairs in Armenia.

One must be on Turkish soil and hear for himself the heart-rending tales of torture and torment to have any just conception of the scenes that have been enacted, and the fearful ordeal through which hundreds of thousands of Armenians are now passing.

It is now openly confessed by certain Mohammedans that the systematic massacres that went on from village to village was simply the prosecution of a plan well understood by the Turks to exterminate all native Christians in Armenia, and it is generally believed that the Sultan ordered these massacres, those who led the bloodthirsty business being under his appointment.

I went as near the town of Oorfa as I was allowed to go, and from the most reliable sources I have positive proof of Ottoman persecutions more diabolical than any reports that have come to us through the American or English press.

The Massacre at Oorfa.

So far as magnitude is concerned Oorfa heads the list with fully 3500 victims in the last massacre alone. The number sacrificed in the great church, where they had fled for safety, is now ascertained to be about 4000, and in the streets and suburbs of the village nearly the same number of bodies were found cut and mangled most terribly.

It is evident that if special honorable recognition by his Majesty the Imperial Sultan is to be bestowed upon those of his loyal warriors who have carried out the task assigned them on the grandest and the most satanic scale, his Oorfa legion will come in for the highest awards.

A private letter from a missionary who is at present in Oorfa, that is before me as I write, explains what has hitherto been a mere conjecture—namely, as to how the Turkish soldiers succeeded in burning these 4000 victims in the church.

This missionary, who has made careful investigation on the spot, explains that a gallery extends around three sides of this church, and from here a great quantity of petroleum was poured upon these defenceless men, women and children, who were jammed together on the floor below.

Numbers of them had been butchered before this was done, and the fifty or sixty who escaped to the roof were overtaken and tossed into the flames.

It seems that after the petroleum had been poured down upon them from the galleries, lighted torches were thrown among them. Is it possible to conceive of anything more diabolical?

Among those who thus perished were aged men and women, mothers with babies at their breasts, ill persons just taken from their beds and hundreds of boys and girls.

The church building where this occurred, which has been used for many years as a place of worship by the Armenians, has been converted by these murderous

RECENTLY MADE ARMENIAN GRAVES IN THE SUBURB OF VAN.

Turks into a Mohammedan mosque, where prayers are now daily offered to the prophet Mahomet.

The Victims at Biredjik.

The massacre at Biredjik, only a few miles from Oorfa, is hardly less revolting. The facts below are given by a Christian citizen of the place, which were received by me last night.

The Christian population of Biredjik consisted of about two hundred houses. For some months the Christians had been kept almost wholly within their houses from fear.

One morning, about two hours after sunrise, a massacre began without any apparent cause and continued until far into the night. The Turkish soldiers and Mohammedans in the city generally participated in it.

At first the principal object seemed to be plunder, but later on the soldiers undertook the work of systematic killing, and profession of Islam or death was the alternative of all those who named the name of Christ.

Many of the victims were dragged to the river Euphrates, and with stones tied to them, were drowned. In some cases several bodies were found tied together and thus thrown into the river.

One young man was caught, a rope put around his neck, and while he was being dragged to the Euphrates he succeeded in freeing himself three times, but finally, after being tortured in a nameless manner, he was overpowered, and amid the shouts of the demons he was tossed into his watery grave.

Islam or the Sword.

Every house belonging to a Christian in the village was plundered, except two, which were saved by Moslem neighbors, who claimed them as their property.

Christian girls were eagerly sought after, and much dispute and quarreling occurred in dividing them among the captors. If they refused immediately to marry young men of the Mohammedan faith they were tortured into obedience or cast into harems.

There is not a single Christian remaining in Biredjik. Scores of men and women were brought forward, offered protection if they would embrace the Islam religion, and those who refused (and nearly all of them did refuse) were put to death after lingering persecution.

As the Turks doubted the sincerity of the new converts they arranged a new massacre, which was only averted by the new converts promising to change the Armenian churches into mosques.

They are now at work making the required alterations in the buildings. The Protestant church will be turned into a Moslem schoolhouse if the missionaries do not claim it as Armenian property.

The misery and suffering among the plundered cannot be described.

Lady Teachers Captured.

The wife (a recent graduate of the American Girls' College at Marash) and child of the Protestant preacher (who is imprisoned at Oorfa) and two young lady teachers, with some twenty other persons, hid themselves in a cave, but were discovered and seized by the Turkish mob. All the men and boys were killed and the women and children carried off to the Moslem houses.

The women were dragged by the hair and badly beaten, but being unable to compel them even in this way to go with them, the Turks carried them on their backs.

They tried to kill the babe of the pastor's wife, but she pressed it so closely

MOHAMMEDAN WOMEN.

to her bosom that at last they desisted, as they feared she would be harmed, and she was wanted for their harem. For more than three weeks every effort was made, including threats of death, to make these three women (the pastor's wife and the two lady teachers of the mission) to profess Islam, but they steadfastly refused. Wedding preparations were being made for these women, who were to be forced to marry Mohammedans, when the district governor received an order from Aleppo commanding them to be sent, under guard, to the missionaries in Aintab, which changed their fate.

Distress and Work of Relief.

The news from Marash was of the most distressing nature. Nearly ten thousand were receiving daily help from the missionaries, and there was every indication at that time this number must be greatly increased in the near future if the funds at the disposal of the missionaries permitted of it.

One who was appointed to visit the district and distribute funds, referring to the condition of affairs, exclaimed: " This region has been one vast flaming hell."

In Van between 15,000 and 20,000 are dependent upon the relief work that is carried on through the agency of the missionaries.

A letter from there, that is lying before me, says: "I am sure that all who have interested themselves in raising funds would feel abundantly repaid for their trouble and self-sacrifice if they could see the misery their money is relieving. We are at present spending at the rate of a thousand dollars per week, and I am confident that another thousand could be spent in the same way of relieving only the most distressing need, and that, too, in a meagre enough fashion.

" Hundreds of refugees are living in cold, damp places on earth floors, with absolutely no bedding, very little, in some cases, no fuel, and with nothing to eat save the dry bread we gave them.

" Since last winter the bazaars have been closed, hence everybody in the city is out of employment, while life in the villages is, for the most part, well nigh or absolutely impossible."

The Turkish officials watched carefully every effort to distribute money and provisions among these wretched victims of their cruelty, and they have been known repeatedly to force the widows and orphans of those whom they murdered to give up funds that came to them to provide against starvation.

Who Are the Armenians?

If we accept Armenian histories, the first ruler of the Armenians was Haik, the son of Togarmah, the son of Gomer, the son of Japheth, the son of Noah, and it is interesting to note that they, even to this day, call themselves Haik, their language " Haiaren " and their country " Haiasdan."

The word " Armenian " was given them by other nations because of the bravery of one of their kings, Aram, the seventh ruler from Haik.

Until A. D. 1375 they were a proud and independent nation, but since the latter quarter of the fourteenth century their country has been under the governments of Russia, Persia, and during the most of the time, under Turkey.

During the period from 600 B. C. to nearly 400 A. D., the time of their greatest advancement, they showed remarkable prowess in the wars of the Assyrians, Medes, Persians, Greeks and Romans.

From the incomplete government returns it is estimated that, at present, there are between two and a half and three millions of Armenians in Turkey, and these are everywhere surrounded by Turks and Kurds, many of whom are armed

ARMENIAN SCHOOL.

by the government, while the Armenians are forbidden to carry or possess arms under the severest penalties.

Their Religion and Clergy.

In the third century, under the influence of Gregory the Illuminator, the Armenians as a nation became Christian, and this was the first time in the history of the world that Christianity was adopted as a national religion.

By the outsiders their church was then called "Gregorian," and afterward the Gregorians and Greeks worked in a fraternal spirit in the great councils of the church until 451, but at the fourth Ecumenical Council, which met at Chalcedon that year, the Gregorian Church separated from the Greek upon the Monophysite doctrine, the former accepting and the latter rejecting it.

There are nine grades of Armenian clergy. The spiritual head is a Catholicos, but in addition to him there is a patriarch, whose duties have largely to do with the political side of the national life as related to the Ottoman government.

In the fifth century the Bible was translated into their language; but the book has largely been a sealed one so far as the people are concerned.

For more than a thousand years the Armenians have been subject to the bitterest persecutions, and during these centuries they have willingly chosen death, with terrible torture, rather than prove false to their faith.

Culture and Education.

As is pointed out by a recent writer, and generally admitted to be true, the strong tendency to disagree among themselves has greatly weakened their national character, and the wily Turks have repeatedly taken advantage of their suspicions of each other and their internal rivalries by playing one party off against another. There can be no question but that the Armenians are the most intelligent of all the people of Eastern Turkey, and in Western Turkey their only rivals are the Greeks. For more than a score of years Armenian young men have attained high scholarship in the universities of Europe and America, and the eager desire among the people for a liberal education is very marked.

It is worthy of note, especially in this part of the world, that this people give special encouragement to female education, and it was my pleasure to address a college of two hundred and fifty Armenian girls in Smyrna, where there was every indication of culture and refinement.

Traders and Farmers.

The Armenian is the trader and banker of this part of the world. The Mohammedan is no match for him, and this is where the rub lies.

An impartial judge, who is neither a Christian nor a Mohammedan, informed me in an interview yesterday that if you put five Armenian shopkeepers and ten Mohammedan shopkeepers on the same street, in a short while, provided both are granted the same privileges, the former will control the whole business from one end of the street to the other.

Although the Turkish government has imposed upon them the most unjust laws and excessive taxes, they have kept well to the front, and until these persecutions and massacres commenced some of the leading business operations of the country were in their hands.

They are also the leading artisans and farmers. I have the statement from a reliable source that twenty-five years ago in certain large sections the land was owned almost entirely by Moslems, but rented and farmed by the Armenians, but lack of industry on the part of the Mohammedans have led them to sell many of their large estates to the Armenians, many of whom became proprietor farmers.

A Turkish governor is quoted as saying that if the Armenians should suddenly emigrate or be expelled from Eastern Turkey the Moslem would necessarily follow soon, as there was not enough commercial enterprise and ability coupled with industry in the Turkish population to meet the absolute needs of the people.

TURKISH SOCIETY WOMAN.

Home and Family.

While at one time in their history they gained distinction as warriors, they seem at present to be domestic in their thought and habits, and, apparently, they are possessed with little military ambition or desire to rule.

I have had the privilege of seeing something of their home life, and seldom have I seen sweeter pictures of domestic life than were witnessed in their quiet family circles.

The home life is patriarchal, the father ruling the household as long as he lives, and at his death the eldest son takes his place at the head of the family.

Children have the highest respect for their parents, sons and daughters never become too old to seek the counsel and obey the word of fathers and mothers, and special respect is given to the aged.

An Unmixed Race.

In the eloquent words of another, here we have a race old in national history when Alexander invaded the East, and with its star of empire turning toward decline when the Cæsars were at the height of their power; a nation not mingling in marriage with men and women of another faith and blood, now as pure in its descent from the undiscovered ancestors of nearly three decades of centuries ago as the Hebrews stand unmixed with Gentile blood; with a language, a literature, a national church distinctively its own, and yet a nation without a country, without a government, without a protector or friend in all God's world.

This is not because it has sinned, but because it has been terribly sinned against; not because of its intellectual or moral or physical weakness, but because it has little to offer in return for the service which the common brotherhood of man among nations should prompt the Christian nations of the world to render.

In all of her varied history I suppose that the sky over the national life of Armenia was never as starless as it is to-day. The great powers on the European continent turn deaf ears to her cries, some of them apparently giving indirect endorsement to the rotten rule, satanic cruelty and murderous madness of the Moslem Sultan; and if substantial aid is rendered in putting bread in the mouths of these widowed, orphaned and plundered thousands, and in creating a world-wide sentiment in their favor, it must come from that country which is to-day the hope of the world and the inspiration of mankind—generous, liberty-loving America.

Armenia's Plight.

In view of the widespread sympathy that is now being manifested in both England and America for this practically enslaved and downtrodden race in the overwhelming calamities that have so recently befallen them, it may be reasonably supposed that the governments and peoples of these two countries are interested in the asking and answering of the question, "What is to become of the Armenians?"

Whether we regard this question as referring to a choice between Islam and the sword on the one hand, or to a choice between a continued struggle for existence under Moslem oppression and extortion, with the constant additional dread of torture and massacre and complete emancipation in some form or the other, it is a question which forces itself upon the Christian world to-day for solution. If we are to judge by the attitude of the great powers of Christendom toward the Armenians in their indescribable sufferings during the past months, England and America are the only two nations that choose to concern themselves with the present or ultimate fate of these people. It is for this reason that the arms of the Armenians are to-day outstretched toward Anglo-Saxon Christendom for help and deliverance.

Attitude of the Powers.

To those who know the situation as it stands here to-day in Asiatic Turkey the future holds not a single ray of hope for any permanent betterment of condition of the Armenians so long as the Ottoman empire holds together, and the apparent determination of the European powers that it shall not go to pieces so long as they can agree together to bolster it up, leaves but little prospect of relief from that source. The utter inability of these same powers to afford them any protection while they remain subjects of the Turkish government, and scattered as they are to-day in every corner of the empire, has been so painfully demonstrated during the past months that no hope of help or protection can ever be reasonably expected in the future from Christian Europe. It has also been just

A GROUP OF ARMENIAN ORPHAN BOYS OF CÆSAREA AND TABAS.

as fully demonstrated that some, at least, of the European governments are absolutely determined that no part or parcel of the empire shall be assigned to them where they would enjoy any measure of independence or opportunity to work out their own legitimate destiny. In a word, it has now become not only perfectly evident that the Sultan is to be allowed to work out his own will toward his Armenian subjects with impunity, so far, at least, as European interference is concerned, but it is also equally evident that it is the will of his Majesty to give them over to every form of cruel oppression and diabolical torture and outrage which his fanatical and inhuman followers may choose to devise and inflict upon them. This, then, is the answer to our question, "What is to become of the Armenians?" so long, at least, as they remain the subjects of his Imperial Majesty Abdul Hamid II. The history of the past is to be the history of the future. The only possible hope of even temporary amelioration is that which a change of rulers might bring. But even a change of rulers or a change to a more responsible form of government will not alter the attitude and spirit of Islam toward a subject Christian race.

"Christian Herald" Work.

The noble and extensive relief work which has been carried on with the funds sent from England and America prevented much suffering and saved many lives. Through the activity of Dr. Klopsch, proprietor of the *Christian Herald*, a great Relief Depot was established at Van under Dr. Grace Kimball, American Missionary; and there is at present in Oorfa a large number of Armenian orphans, under Miss Corinna Shattuck, supported by *Christian Herald* contributions. No less than $60,000 has been raised by Dr. Klopsch through his journal from sympathetic American readers for this persecuted people, which was distributed by American missionaries at seventeen different stations.

A Colonization Scheme.

Every instinct of true manliness and Christian sympathy rises against the thought of abandoning the Armenians to the inevitable fate that awaits them as subjects of the Turkish empire. God has other and higher purposes for them to serve as benefactors of our race, and shall we not seek to open to them the opportunities which will afford them deliverance from their present bondage and scope for enlarged activity and usefulness?

The very suggestion of colonization raises at once a number of questions of primary and essential significance, and among these: Colonize where? Do they wish to emigrate? Will the Turkish authorities permit them to leave the country? Would such a scheme be practicable? Do they possess the qualities essential to successful colonization, such as the power of adaptation to new surroundings and conditions? Are they desirable neighbors? etc., etc. In the space of the present chapter it will not be possible to discuss each of these questions separately and in detail. In answer to the question, "Where?" I answer unhesitatingly, to the United States and Canada. In view of the sympathy shown by the American and English governments and the generous response of the people of these two nations to the appeals for relief, it may be taken for granted that every facility would be offered for colonizing portions of the western territories and provinces of the

United States and Canada with these people, and that they would receive welcome to our hospitable shores.

"Do they wish to emigrate?" Let the thousands who have been imprisoned for attempting to emigrate answer this question.

Will the Sultan Allow It?

"Will the Turkish government permit them to leave the country?" Although the Turkish government has persisted in representing the Armenians as the only disturbing element to the peace and prosperity of the empire, and as being the constant objects of Turkish pity, compassion and toleration, it is a strange fact that laws have been made prohibiting them, on pain of severe penalties, from leaving the country. These laws for some years past have been rigorously enforced, though in spite of this some have escaped from this forced imprisonment by bribing port officials. Now, however, I learn the government has suddenly adopted a different policy and is readily giving passports to Armenians who wish to emigrate. This fact would much facilitate any scheme for colonization which might now be undertaken. Even should the government again attempt to prevent the emigration of the Armenians surely even those powers which are most fearful of disturbing the *status quo* of the "Eastern Question" could be trusted at least to use their authority to compel the Sultan to refrain from an attempt to prevent any scheme for the emigration and colonizing of the Armenians.

Would It Be Practicable?

Would a scheme for colonization be practicable? Of course, in the present impoverished state of a large portion of the Armenians in the interior provinces, any scheme for successful colonization would require the sanction and at least partial support of the American and British governments. The people of these two countries could also be trusted to respond promptly and generously to an appeal to carry out any such scheme of practical and permanent relief for those they are now supplying with daily bread and raiment. Government grants of land or special facilities for easy purchase would of necessity become a factor in any such scheme. A very large proportion, however, of Armenians would undertake to emigrate on their own charges and would at once form a self-dependent element in each colony or community. I have every confidence in the practicability of colonization if taken up in an earnest, determined spirit.

But it may be asked, Would the Armenians make good colonists and are they desirable neighbors? English and American missionaries and others who have lived among the Armenians and who have had the best of facilities for studying their national characteristics are accustomed to designate them the "Anglo-Saxons" or

"Yankees" of the Orient. It is unquestionable that they possess some of the characteristics which distinguish the Anglo-Saxon race. They are a hardy, energetic, intelligent and progressive people, and with the favorable environment of our free Western institutions and civilization, and under the authority of capable and responsible governments, they would unquestionably become an important and stable factor in our Western life and progress. They are a peaceful, law-abiding race, devoted to agricultural and commercial pursuits. They possess also the faculty of becoming skilled artisans, and are both capable and eager for intellectual advancement. They wish to live at peace with their neighbors and would most assuredly prove themselves not only good neighbors, but also loyal, devoted citizens of our responsible governments.

AN ARMENIAN HOME.

Going to Cyprus.

An effort is now being quietly put forward by certain influential Englishmen to transport the thousands of widows and orphans in Armenia to the Island of Cyprus, where they would be granted land and helped to at least partly support themselves. Difficulties that were expected have arisen, but these are supposed not to be insurmountable. Hundreds of men have secretly escaped the country, but the shores are all patroled; no Armenian is allowed to go from one village to another without giving a full account of his movements and without securing bond for his return in a certain number of days; every road in Armenia is guarded by brutal Turkish soldiers, who shoot down Armenians on the least pretext; and we may depend upon it that this wretched state of affairs will continue to exist until some strong national voice is raised, and, if necessary, some strong national arm is stretched forward in defence of a down-trodden race that has on its neck an iron heel and over its prostrate body the flashing sword of a heartless tyrant.

Missions in Turkey.

It is generally thought in these parts that the conduct of the Turkish government in regard to the American missionaries is an attempt to see how Europe would regard any measure taken for the expulsion of Christian missionaries generally. The result can hardly be satisfactory to the Turk.

The Roman Catholic missionaries are fully alive to the meaning of the experiment and the activity of Monsieur Cambon shows that France intends to claim the full rights of French citizens, whether clericals or not.

For many months an attempt was made to distinguish in the massacres between the Armenians of the national church and the Catholic Armenians, that is, those who are in union with Rome, but this distinction could not be observed in Armenia itself. A Moslem ruffian at Trebizond exclaimed: "Are they not all Giaours (infidels) alike?" And no satisfactory answer could be given him.

Foreign Mission Work.

This attempted distinction did not deceive the foreign Catholic missionaries, and their silence was not to be purchased by securing the safety of their own flocks. In many places they have done their best for the Christian population, whether they were in communion directly with Rome or not.

It must not be forgotten that the Christian population of Asia Minor and Syria had sunk into a condition of ignorance which is not remarkable, in view of the repeated and periodical massacres and plundering.

It is quite true that the Mekitarist congregations of Armenians in Vienna and Venice, established by men who escaped from Turkey, have accomplished a noble work, which has called forth congratulatory words from both Mr. Gladstone and Mr. Ruskin. But it has mainly been for the education of Armenian priests and did not affect the mass of the laity.

The American Board of Missions, some fifty or sixty years ago, set itself to remove this ignorance. As America could not possibly have any political ends to serve by sending missionaries into the country, there seems to have come about an understanding and arrangement with English and German missionary societies by which it was agreed that the Turkish mission field should be left almost exclusively to Americans.

American Institutions.

Whatever might be said of England, no one would believe that America coveted an inch of Turkish territory. American missionaries, as every one admits, have worked solely for philanthropic, educational and religious ends.

The American missions have colleges at Kharpoot, Marsovan, Beyrout and Aintab. They have splendid colleges for girls at Smyrna, Scutari—on the

Bosphorus—and in Stambool. They have hospitals at Aintab, Mardin and Cæsarea. They have boys' and girls' schools at such centres as Broussa, Adana, Trebizond, Sivas, Mosul, Van and other places, and until a few years ago wherever an educated Armenian was met he had in all likelihood been educated at one of these missionary schools.

Robert College.

I spent a pleasant evening at Robert College, nine miles from Constantinople, on the Bosphorus.

This college was founded thirty-three years ago by Mr. Robert, a New York

DECORATED BY THE SULTAN.

merchant, and is to-day one of the greatest powers for good in all Asia Minor.

It owns magnificent property under imperial charter; has all the equipments of a well-furnished American college; has in its classes 350 boys and young men from different portions of Turkey, Syria, Palestine, Bulgaria, Roumelia and Greece, and its distinguished American president, Dr. Washburn, and his assistants are doing much for the rising generation of this part of the world.

Some years ago a good deal of opposition was encountered by the missionaries, on the ground that their object was to establish rival churches and to obtain proselytes from the Armenian Church. Such opposition has long since been overcome by the sturdy common sense of the missionaries.

Light for Asia.

One hundred and fifty American missionaries, many of whom are highly educated, are now centers of light throughout Asia Minor and Syria; their influence would do honor to any civilized government and they are everywhere respected and trusted by the population, Turkish as well as Christian, and by the foreign consuls of every part of Asia.

Many of these are qualified medical men, and the value of their medical services meets with unbounded appreciation in districts where no doctors are to be found.

Although they take no part in politics, their instincts are, of course, against anything in the nature of rebellion, and so careful are they not to become complicated in the present political condition of affairs that Mr. Greene had to abandon all connection with the mission board before he published his volume of evidence on the Armenian wrongs.

Taking in consideration these facts it may be asked: "Why should the Turkish government wish to get rid of missionaries, Protestant and Catholic alike?"

No Conversions Possible.

There is no question of converting Mohammedans to any form of Christian faith, for the penalty of such conversion is immediate death, and neither Catholics nor Protestants make any efforts in this direction.

The reason must be sought in another direction.

The influence of the missions and missionaries have a tendency to elevate the tone of morality among the various Christian populations, and the education they have given has enabled thousands to become comparatively prosperous.

As in the case of Bulgaria, a score of years ago, the prosperity of the Christian portion of the community aroused the envy of those who belonged to the ruling class and creed, so instinctively, the Turk recognizes that the education given by these foreign "infidels" places the Christians at an advantage in trade and even in agriculture.

There are, indeed, a number of cases, both in the provinces and in the capital, where boys and girls have secretly been sent by their Moslem parents to mission schools to obtain secular education, but this is always attended by grave dangers, and just now Mohammedan authorities are more watchful than ever.

It is also felt and admitted by the agents of the Sultan's government that these missions, with their schools and colleges, their hospitals, their medical men and trained nurses, are the symbols of the advance of a civilization along western lines, and as progress in this direction is the sure death-knell to the corruption and tyranny of Mohammedanism, the thought of it is the waving of a blood-red flag before the bellowing Turkish bull.

Keeping in mind these facts we can easily trace the cause for the recent outbreak against Christian missions.

Protestant and Catholic missionaries have been largely instrumental in turning the lights upon the sad events in Armenia during these latter months. Newspaper correspondents could be forbidden to travel in the interior; the letters

of Armenians and other Turkish subjects could be ostentatiously examined and
their writers imprisoned, but these foreign missionaries could not be prevented
from telling the truth.

M. Cambon's notification to the Grand Vizier that if any French citizens at
Sivas were injured he would require the head of the Vali, shows how far France
was prepared to protect her missionaries.

A TYPICAL TURKISH DWELLING OF THE POORER CLASS.

As these and the American missionaries know more of the Armenian massacres than any other bodies of persons, and as they were active in the distribution of relief among the survivors of the massacres, there is not a very sweet
taste in the mouth of the man who sits upon the Ottoman throne.

The Massacres of the Armenians.

Certain persons in Europe and America have ascribed the dreadful massacres
which have taken place in Asia Minor to sudden and spontaneous outbreaks of
Moslem fanaticism. The truth is that these outbursts, while sudden, have taken

place according to a deliberate and preconcerted plan. According to the statements of many persons, French, English, Canadian, American and native—persons trustworthy and intelligent, who were in the places where the massacres occurred, and some of whom were witnesses of the horrible scenes—the massacres were strictly limited with regard to place, time, nationality of the victims, and generally with regard to the method of killing and pillaging. The following facts have been received from one who does not desire his name to be used:

With Regard to Place.

With only a few exceptions of consequence, the massacres have been confined to the territory of the six provinces where reforms were to be instituted. When a band of mounted Kurdish and Circassian raiders, estimated at from one to three thousand, approached the boundary line between the provinces of Sivas and Angora, they were met and turned back by the local authorities and certain influential Mussulmans of the latter province, who told the raiders that they had no authority to pass beyond the province of Sivas. The only places where outrages occurred outside of the six provinces were, first, in the flourishing seaboard city of Trebizond; secondly, in Marash, Aintab and Oorfa, and in these places Moslem fanaticism was specially stirred by the success of the Armenian mountaineers of Zeitûn in defending themselves against their oppressors, and in capturing a small Turkish garrison; and, finally in Cæsarea; and here, as in the places just mentioned, the Moslems were excited by the nearness of the scenes of massacre, and by the reports of the plunder which other Moslems were securing.

With Regard to Time.

The massacre in Trebizond occurred just before the Sultan, after months of every kind of opposition, was at last compelled by England, France and Russia to consent to the scheme of reforms, as if to warn the powers of Europe that, in case they persisted, the mine was already laid for the destruction of the Armenians. In fact, the massacre of the Armenians is Turkey's real reply to the demands of Europe. From Trebizond the wave of murder and robbery swept on through almost every city and town and village in the six provinces where relief was promised to the Armenians. When the news of the first massacre reached Constantinople, a high Turkish official remarked to one of the Ambassadors that massacre was like the small-pox—they must all have it, but they wouldn't need to have it the second time; thus quietly, if not maliciously, hinting at what was to be expected. Even the Sultan, when striving to avoid assent to the scheme of reforms, told the Ambassadors, by way of intimidation, that troubles might ensue, and the event shows that he knew whereof he spoke.

The Nationality of the Victims.

These were almost exclusively Armenians. In Trebizond there is a large Greek population, but neither there nor elsewhere, with possibly one or two exceptions, have the Greeks been molested. Special care has also been taken to avoid injury to the subjects of foreign nations, with the idea of escaping foreign

AN ANCIENT EASTERN CHURCH, NOW DESECRATED.

complications and the payment of indemnities. In Marash three school buildings belonging to the American Mission were looted and one building was burned, but the houses and the Girls' College occupied by Americans were not touched. In Karpoot the school buildings and houses belonging to the American Mission were plundered, and eight buildings were burned; but none of the Americans were hurt, though shots were fired at two of them. In this place and in Marash, had the fanatical Moslems not been restrained by special orders, they would probably have killed the Americans since they regarded the Americans in those centres of educational and religious work as the chief agents in enlightening and elevating those whom they wished to keep as their docile and unambitious subjects and serfs.

The Method of Killing and Pillaging.

With slight exceptions, the method has been to kill within a limited period the largest number of Armenians—men of business capacity and intelligence— and to beggar their families by robbing them, as far as possible, of their property. Hence, in almost every place, the massacres have been perpetrated during the business hours, when the Armenians, in whose hands in almost every plundered city at least nine-tenths of the trade was concentrated, were in their shops. In several places, where, on account of fear, the Armenians had shut their shops and stores, they were induced by the assurances and promises of the authorities to open them just before the massacres began. In almost every place the Moslems made a sudden and simultaneous attack on the market-place just after their noon-day prayer, killing the shopkeepers and their clerks in their shops, or when they attempted to flee, and then plundering the shops. In Diarbekir, not satisfied with the killing and plundering, they also burned the shops; and in Erzroom and Sivas, where the plunderers were many and the booty insufficient, they looted many houses.

In every place the perpetrators were the resident Moslem population, rein-forced in Baiboot and vicinity by the Mohammedan Lazes from the southeasterly section of Asia Minor bordering on the Black Sea; in the provinces of Erzroom, Bitlis, Diarbekir, Harpoot and Sivas the Turks were reinforced by the Kurds, and in the province of Sivas by the Kurds and Circassians; while in the city of Erzroom the chief perpetrators were the Sultan's soldiers and officers, who began the dreadful work at the sound of a bugle, and desisted, for the most part, when the bugle signaled to them to stop. In Harpoot, also, the soldiers took a promi-nent part, firing specially on the buildings of the American Mission with Martini-Henry rifles and Krupp cannon. A shell from one of the cannon burst in the house of the American missionary, Dr. Barnum. In most places the killing was by the Turks, while the Kurds and Circassians were intent on plunder, and gene-rally killed only to strike terror, or when they met with resistance. The surprised and unarmed Armenians made little or no resistance, and where some of the Armenians, as at Diarbekir and Gurun, undertook to defend themselves, they suffered the more. The killing was done with guns, revolvers, swords, clubs, pick-axes, and every conceivable weapon, and many of the dead were horribly mangled. The dead were generally stripped and dragged to the Armenian ceme-teries, where the surviving Armenians were compelled to bury them in huge trenches, as in Erzroom, where over 500, and in Sivas, where over 800 naked and mutilated bodies were covered with earth in one grave.

The plundering was perpetrated with remorseless cruelty. The shops were absolutely gutted. In the great city of Sivas, not a spool of thread or yard of cloth was left in the market-place. Even the doors of some of the plundered houses were torn off and carried away. But the refinement of cruelty was inflicted on the inhabitants of hundreds of villages, upon whom the Kurds came down like the hordes of Tamerlane, and robbed the villagers of their flocks and herds,

ARMENIANS HELD PRISONERS AFTER THE TREBIZOND MASSACRE.

stripped them of their very clothing, and carried away their bedding, cooking utensils, and even the little stores of provisions which the poor villagers had with infinite care and toil laid up for the severities of a rigorous winter. Worst of all is the bitter cry that comes from every quarter that the Turks and Kurds seized and carried off hundreds of Christian women and girls.

The number killed in the massacre in three months' time is estimated at over fifty thousand—almost entirely the well-to-do, capable, intelligent men of the

Armenian population in the six to-be-reformed provinces. The amount of property stolen from their prostrate subjects by the Moslems is estimated at £10,000,000. (The latest estimate is much larger.)

The Motive of the Turks.

This is apparent to the most superficial observer. The scheme of reforms devolved civil office, judgeships and police participation on Mohammedans and non-Mohammedans in the six provinces, according to the population of each element of the locality. This was a bitter pill to those Mohammedan Turks who had ruled the Armenians with a rod of iron for five hundred years. Hence the resolution of the Turks was soon taken. It was to diminish the number of the Armenians, first, by dealing a vital blow at those most capable of taking a part in any scheme of reconstruction; and, secondly, by leaving as many as possible to die by starvation, exposure, sickness and terror during the rigors of winter. Surely the arch fiend could not have suggested a more terrible and effectual method of crippling and ruining and terrorizing the Armenian Christians in the entire six provinces concerned.

Some may wonder how the Turkish authorities should be so blind as to destroy so large a part of their best tax-paying subjects in Asia Minor. And it is indeed a wonder. The explanation is that fanatical hatred of those whom they had held so long in cruel subjection, and who were, according to the scheme of reforms, soon to enjoy some form of equality, was stronger than self-interest. The thought of the Turk was to make sure of the country, and he could conceive of no other way than by diminishing the number of Armenians and utterly terrorizing and impoverishing the survivors.

But did not the Turks fear the intervention of Christian Europe? Not much; certainly not enough to keep them from carrying out an effective, albeit diabolical, plan of vengeance. And they were right, for did not 400,000,000 of Christians witness, last year, the slaughter in Sassoon of some thousands of Armenians by Turks and Kurds without extorting from the responsible Turkish authorities the punishment of a single man engaged in the diabolical work, or even the slightest indemnity for the utterly impoverished survivors? Nay, more, has not the Sultan laughed Europe to scorn by decorating Zekki Pasha, commander of the troops engaged in the carnage, and Bahri Pasha, the former cruel governor of Van? And have not the Kurds been again permitted to rob the survivors of the Sassoon massacre, and even to destroy the little huts put up by British charity during the past summer?

Mendacity of the Authorities.

But, while the Turkish authorities have thus deliberately aimed to extermi-nate, as far as possible, the Armenian element in the six provinces, they have

27

attempted to cover up their deeds by the most colossal lying and misrepresentation. By the publication of mendacious telegrams from provincial authorities, they have tried to make Europe and America believe that the Armenians have provoked these massacres by attacks on Moslem worshipers during their hours of prayer, and by other like acts of consummate folly. It is true that on September 30 some 400 young Armenians, contrary to the entreaties of the Armenian patriarch and the orders of the police, attempted to take a well-worded petition to the Grand Vizier in the main government building in Stamboul, and thus precipitated a conflict; it is also true that the oppressed mountaineers of Zeitun captured a small garrison of Turkish soldiers; it is likewise true that in various places small

WOMEN AND CHILDREN WAITING THE DAILY DISTRIBUTION OF FOOD.

bands of Armenians, driven to desperation by the failure of Europe to secure the fulfillment of treaty stipulations in behalf of their people, have enraged the Turks by revolutionary attempts, and the Turks have retaliated by imprisoning, torturing and killing hundreds of Armenians, many of whom were innocent of any rebellious acts. The universal testimony of impartial foreign eye-witnesses is that, with the above exceptions, the Armenians have given no provocation, and that almost, if not quite, all the telegrams of the provincial authorities accusing the Armenians of provoking the massacres are sheer fabrications of names and dates. If the Armenians made attacks, where are the Turkish dead? For while the Armenian victims are numbered by the thousand, even the authorities have mentioned but a few as slain among the Turks, and those few were killed in only one or two places, and in self-defence, as at Diarbekir. Is it probable that 7000 unarmed and defenceless Armenians—sheep among wolves—would attack 23,000 Kurds and Turks in the city of Bitlis? Yet this was the charge of the Turkish authorities—a fitting device to cover up their bloody work.

They Could Have Prevented It.

It is an utter mistake to suppose, as many Europeans have done, that the local authorities in the cities of Trebizond, Erzroom, Erzengan, Bitlis, Harpoot, Arabkir, Sivas, Amasia, Marsovan, Marash, Aintab, Oorfa and Caesarea could not have suppressed the fanatical Moslem mobs and restrained the Kurds. The fact is that the authorities generally looked on while the slaughter and pillage were going on without raising a hand to stop it, save in one or two places; and everywhere the authorities did intervene and stop the slaughter when the limited period during which the Moslems were allowed to kill and rob had expired. At Marsovan the limit of time was four hours. Here, as in almost every city, the adult male Mussulmans performed their noon-day prayer in their mosques, asking God to help them in their bloody work, and then rushed upon the Christians. Within less than four hours the merciful Governor of Marsovan interfered with soldiers and police, and stopped the horrid work, but meanwhile 120 of the leading Armenian traders and business men had been killed and their goods stolen. In several places the slaughter and pillage continued from noon till sundown or later. At Sivas they continued for a whole day, and even afterwards, for several days, some twenty-five Armenians a day were killed. In every place, however, the carnage was stopped as soon as the authorities made an earnest effort to do so. Had it not been for the intervention of the authorities after the set time of one, two or three days, the entire Christian population would have been exterminated. And the bloody work was stopped, not because the Moslems did not desire to make a clean sweep of the Christians and pillage all their goods, but because those who inspired the slaughter thought that one or two or three days of killing was about as much as Europe would stand at one time.

The Reason for the Massacres.

Nor let it be supposed that the Turks as such hate the Armenians as such. The Armenians have been for centuries the most submissive and profitable subjects, and they would still be most loyal if, instead of the increasingly oppressive policy of Sultan Abdul Hamid, their lives and honor and property had been even tolerably protected. All this many Turks know very well, and regret the cruel and utterly impolitic course of the present sovereign. The Turk as a man has many excellent qualities; it is his religion which, at certain times, makes a devil of him. It is the very essence of Mohammedanism that the Giaour has no right to live save in subjection. While assured of their power, the Turks treated the Armenians and their other Christian subjects, not with equality, but with a measure of toleration. It is Europe insisting on reforms for the Armenians that has enraged the Turks against the Armenians. The Turks know that in a fair and equal race the Armenians will outstrip them in every department of business and industry, and they see in any fair scheme of reform the handwriting on the wall for themselves. Save for this fear, the Turks would be content to tax and fleece the Armenians for an unlimited period, as they have done for the last 500 years. If the scheme of reforms had had in view the sections of the country where the Greeks predominate, the Turks would have killed and robbed the Greeks as readily as they have killed and robbed the Armenians. It is not a race fight at all; for the Mohammedan Turks cordially affiliate with the Mohammedan Slavs (formerly Christian) and with Kurds and Circassians and Lazes. It is a religious contention, and the Mohammedan Turks are resolved to keep their Christian subjects, of whatever nationality, under foot; and in case attempts of any kind are made to give the Christians real equality and participation in government, the Turks will kill them one by one, or, occasionally, in open massacre, unless the Powers who intervene for the relief of the Christians do it with armed force.

AMERICAN MISSION AT OORFA.

CHAPTER XXII.

AMIDST CLASSIC RUINS.

KNOW of no spot on earth from which I could more accurately describe the ruins of the classic city of ancient Athens than just where I am at this moment—sitting on a broken, fallen column, lying amidst the wonders of the Acropolis. The general location of Athens reminds one very much of the rugged beauty of Edinburgh, Scotland. Both are situated round a rocky fortress, which rises from the street, both possess a great hill dominating the town from a short distance, and Edinburgh has its noble castle and its Arthur's Seat, corresponding strikingly to the Acropolis and Mount Lycabettus, here at Athens.

But here the similarity ceases; in no place in all the world, perhaps, can you find gathered together in the same space so many marvels of art as in the circumference of two miles about the place where I am writing these words.

This sacred rock, first fortified and covered with buildings and votive offerings, was captured by the Persians in 480 B. C., and when the victorious Athenians returned to their loved city they found their monuments defaced and their Acropolis, the pride of the artistic reign of Pisistratus, in ruins.

For coming generations of those who admire the æsthetic and the beautiful this historic event was a fortunate one.

A greater age supervened. Athens was now richer, nobler, more gifted in her sons than she had ever been, and the brilliant victory of her arms was followed by a more brilliant age of art, a generation of unparalleled energy—a period of rapid growth in design and in the control of materials.

The Acropolis.

As one ascends toward the Acropolis the great Propylæa, or entrance portico of the architect Mnesicles, first arrests attention. While the outer row of pillars in both directions are Doric, the richer Ionic order is employed for the inner supports, which are under the marble roof.

We can readily imagine that it required no small labor to quarry and bring up to the Acropolis beams of marble twenty-two feet long and to set them over pillars twenty-five feet high.

There are stray mentions of a windlass and once of a pulley in Aristophanes and in Plato, but, having an unlimited supply of slave labor, there is evidence to show that usually the use of ropes, rollers and inclined planes was employed, which we see in pictures of Egyptian and Assyrian transportation of colossal statues.

Standing in the inner gate of the Propylæa the visitor at once is impressed by the perfect features of the ruins.

Over his head are the enormous architraves of the Propylæa, which span the gateway from pillar to pillar. To the right is the mighty Parthenon, so con-

PORT FOR ATHENS.

structed that sun and shade would play upon it at moments differing from the rest and thus produce a perpetual variety of light.

The Parthenon.

To the left, overlooking the town, is that beautifully decorated little Ionic temple, the Erechtheum, with the graceful and stately caryatids looking inward and toward the Parthenon.

In these two buildings, set opposite each other, you have the embodiment of majesty and grace, the ornaments of the Parthenon being large and massive, and those of the Erechtheum being refined and delicate.

There are three kinds of sculptured decorations on the Parthenon.

Sculptured Decorations.

The triangular pediments over the east and west fronts were each filled with a group of statues, larger than life size, the one representing the birth of Athene and the other her contest with Poseidon for the patronage of Athens.

The plaques of stone inserted into the frieze between the triglyphs and carved in relief with a single small group on each, form a second kind, and a band of reliefs, representing a great Panathenic procession, runs all around the external wall at the top of the cella, which gives evidence of the extraordinary power of grouping in the designs of Phidias.

The cella was surrounded by a peristyle with eight Doric columns on the facade and sixteen on the sides.

The building was 227 feet in length, 110 feet in width, and the surface upon which it stood was 228 feet long and 66 feet high.

The Statue of Athens.

The most imposing statue was that of the goddess Minerva, which stood erect, covered with the ægis and a long tunic, holding a lance in one hand and a shield in the other, her helmet bearing a sphinx and on either side two griffins, and on her shield Phidias represented the battle of the Amazons and the battle of the gods and giants.

The statue was about thirty-six feet in height.

The Parthenon was erected under Pericles, and it is said to have cost 2000 talents, or nearly $25,000,000.

Classic Scenes.

Sloping up against one side of the Acropolis are the two famous theatres—that of Herodus Atticus, of Hadrians' time, and the Theatre of Dionysus, where the tragedies and comedies of the great Greek masters were produced.

On the other side is the Areopagus, or Mars' Hill.

Within sight of the former are the colossal columns of the Roman-Greek Temple of Jupiter, and overlooked by the latter is that perfect gem of Doric grace—the Temple of Theseus.

The Areopagus.

It was on this Areopagus, or Mars' Hill, that the old philosophers of fashion came in contact with the burning eloquence, the profound convictions and the fiery zeal of the Apostle Paul.

It is now a bare, rocky knoll, upon which evidences of old cutting show that it was smoothed for seats and, perhaps, some wooden structure applied to make the rude stones more comfortable.

The Theatre of Dionysus.

The Theatre of Dionysus is of great interest.

As the Greek religion was essentially a religion of joy, the Athenian state thought it just to apply the public funds to give every free citizen a day's wages

VIEW OF ATHENS.

in order that he might be able to enjoy himself at the drama produced as part of the festival of the god Dionysus.

In the Attic tragic and comic dramas were combined moral improvement, political instruction and religious enjoyment, which we cannot fully appreciate unless we make a careful study of old Greek life.

This theatre, dedicated to Dionysus, was open to the weather, contained an immense orchestra, and, according to recent measurements, fifteen thousand persons could have found room at a performance.

Dramatic Art.

The masterpieces composed by Æschylus, Sophocles and Euripides in honor of the gods and for the benefit of the imperial democracy of Athens, did not set forth before the public vulgar, everyday griefs or misfortunes, as are represented on the modern stage, but dealt with legendary heroes, the triumph of virtue and greatness over cruelty and vice, and the victory of human prowess over the reign of tyranny.

One of the famous dramas of Sophocles (Œdipus Rex 863,899) contains this inspiring truth: "May it be my lot to observe strict holiness in every word and deed—holiness whose august laws are proclaimed from their birthplace far above the earth, for Heaven alone, and no mortal race of man hath begotten them, nor will oblivion ever lull them to sleep. Great is the Divine Spirit in them and of eternal youth."

Its Religious Bearing.

I suppose that every intelligent man must conclude that it was only with the rise of æstheticism that religion ever became a doctrine of sadness and fear, robbing the wine-cup of life of its sweetness and sparkling beauty.

In the fifty years between the end of the Persian and the commencement of the Peloponnesian wars Athenian genius, both political and artistic, reached its most perfect development.

'Tis true that the Hermes of Praxiteles, the gem of the Olympian excavations, is of its kind unique, and beyond compare, but, with few brilliant exceptions, the middle of the fifth century B. C. witnessed the climax in sculpture, architecture and poetry, if not in painting, instrumental music and eloquence.

The Decline of Hellas.

This supremacy excited jealousy and led to tyrannical rule, and after the fourth century B. C., which produced Plato and Demosthenes and Apelles, the chief glory departed from Athens to settle in Alexandria, Antioch, Pergamum and Rhodes.

After the days of Alexander the once glorious Athens fell under the sentimental favor of the Romans, and their touch is traceable in the ruins that are crumbling about me.

The last struggle for old Greek independence was fought before Corinth, a short distance from Athens, and the burning of that splendid city in 146 B. C. by the Roman Mummius marked a great epoch in history.

The Epistles of St. Paul to the Corinthians give us glimpses of the customs of this collection of mercantile people under the favor of Roman influences,

ATHENIAN EXCAVATIONS.

Nothing of the great Corinth remains except the noble Doric pillars of one old temple, which points to the seventh century before Christ, and which, if they had tongues, could doubtless convince us that the facts of history are more thrilling than the fictions of the wildest imagination.

About Ancient Troy.

I suppose that it will not be disputed that Dr. Schliemann, by his excavations in this part of the world, proved himself to be the most intelligent, enterprising and indefatigable explorer of modern times.

His death was a greater calamity than would have been the death of any crowned head on any throne on earth. He was taken away while in the midst of the exploration of fields that are rich in the treasures of the past, and while he left some noble followers, it is quite doubtful if any of them will equal the enthusiastic pioneer in their labors.

In coming to Athens, where is located his palatial home, I hoped to have personal interviews with members of his family and receive much information about his life work.   I have been greatly favored in these respects.

Madame Schliemann.

Through the kindness of the talented artist, Mr. Gifford Dyer, who is doing excellent work in Athens, I was presented to Madame Schliemann, and after hearing her talk of her husband's labors and listening to her lucid explanations of the " finds " in the museum of her home, one can appreciate the remark of an admirer of hers who said to me that the Doctor could never have accomplished his success had it not been for the warm sympathy of his intelligent wife.

While a widower the report is that the learned gentleman declared that he would never marry until he found a woman who could recite from memory all of Homer's poems.   The condition was met in the cultured Grecian woman who became his inspiration.

The lovers of the Iliad and the Odyssey will agree, perhaps, that Dr. Schliemann did nothing by his excavation that merits to a greater degree the gratitude of the world than his successful efforts in throwing light on the question of Homer's place in history, and his discovery of what is, beyond all reasonable doubt, the location of ancient Troy.

The Explorer's Discoveries.

Professor Gildersleeve, of Johns Hopkins University, and Professor Wheeler, of Cornell University, who are at present in Athens, visited the place of these excavations, and both regard the conclusions reached as pre-eminently satisfactory.

These excavations have undoubtedly contributed much toward clearing up a hitherto very muddy subject, and of linking the Homeric poems with the general history of the world.

Before Dr. Schliemann's explorations were rewarded with success many believed that the city which played such a thrilling part in the poems of Homer existed only in the poet's imagination; but now a real Troy, for the first time with marked notes of probability, is presented to our view.

It is interesting, if not positively conclusive, to notice the striking comparison between the testimony of the poems and the testimony given in through these excavations.

SCHLIEMANN'S EXCAVATIONS, OLD TROY.

Historic Troy.

While we cannot say, nor does any one contend, that they definitely fix for the Trojan war a place in chronology, yet the relation between the excavations and the Homeric text bears a correspondence that is so close as to be most remarkable, to say the least.

Since the death of Dr. Schliemann this work has been ably prosecuted by several distinguished gentlemen with increasingly gratifying results. The excavations bring before us the remains of a large city, which point to the days when there were great builders in prehistoric times.

HISTORIC TROY.

It will be remembered that the Homeric poems represent the walls of Troy as the mighty work of Poseidon, and thus, by means of the pickaxe of the modern excavator, we are brought in relation to a race of people which has left many traces of its work along the shores of the Mediterranean Sea.

The Excavations.

In these excavations we have presented to us the fact that the inhabitants of this old, but new-found city, used copper as the staple material of the implements, utensils and of the weapons of war, generally, when any metal was brought in service, and in this respect again we have a correspondence with certain descriptions by Homer. But there is an apparent exception to this.

Several large battle-axes have been found, and by means of chemical analysis these have been determined to be bronze. These battle-axes were found with a mass of very precious objects, and the supposition is that they were possessed by the royal family or by the wealthy.

We know that Homer speaks of tin as a metal of high value and rarity, and consequently the *kuanos*, or bronze, of which he writes, was even more costly, the use of which was confined to the wealthier classes.

A CLASSIC HEAD, ATHENS.

Homer's Testimony.

The brilliant passage in the poems which describes the twined or plaited fillet of gold which formed a part of the head-dress of Andromache, and which was torn off in agony of grief on Hector's death, is strikingly illustrated by two exquisite head-dresses or ornaments of pure gold which the excavations have brought to light.

The presumption is, and it does not seem to be unreasonable, that these are the ornaments worn by Andromache, which the Iliad testifies to have been of great significance, and which were carefully put away in an effort to save them on account of their importance.

Dr. Schliemann was congratulated on another "find," which strengthens the relation between the poems and the excavations. Six oblong plates of silver, weighing from 171 up to 190 grammes, or about five ounces each, were found among certain treasures, and experts seem to agree that these are the *talanta* of Homer, which belong to an epoch when the use of gold and silver was unknown in the smaller transactions of exchange.

The poem agrees with the conclusions thus reached, as for instance the descriptions of the foe presented to the successful judge and the fourth prize awarded in the chariot race (Iliad xviii, 507; xxiii, 269).

Art of Writing.

With respect to writing, these explorations show that, in this city and time, it was not in use for ordinary purposes, and was the rare and recondite possession of comparatively a very few. This fact bears a marked parallel to the position of writing in the poems of Homer, from which we infer that it was nearly an unknown art among the mass of the people.

A pleasant time was spent in the National Museum, where Dr. Schliemann generously deposited most of the results of his labors. What glories of art crowned the fourth and fifth centuries B. C. of Athenian history!

The American Athletes.

The city is still talking of the fine impression made by the American athletes during the late Olympic games. Beside carrying off some of the handsome prizes, their striking appearance and their gentlemanly conduct elicited universal praise.

An enthusiastic Grecian living in Alexandria has just given $50,000 for the restoration of the great Stadium, and a bill is to be presented in the Parliament of Greece providing for the exhibition of these games every four years. The next Olympic games

BELLE OF ATHENS.

will be held at Paris in 1900. Speaking of this Parliament reminds me of the parliamentary election of the new Athenian member that took place Sunday afternoon. The streets were full of shouting men and decorated carriages, the four candidates were borne through the city in grand style and the ballots were all deposited in boxes set up before the altars in the different cathedrals. How is this for church and state?

CHAPTER XXIII.

A GEM OF THE SEAS.

I was the French novelist, Paul Bourget, who exclaimed as his steamer was approaching the picturesque island of Corfu: "It is so lovely that one wants to take it in one's arms;" and the great Bonaparte, as he looked upon the old town, with its massive stone houses of creamy color, built upon the irregular slopes of the hills, said to his companion on the deck of the ship: "Here is the most beautiful situation in the world."

As we came in sight of this gem of the seas, the clearness of the atmosphere, the deep blue of the sky, the play of colors upon the mountainous background of the old-fashioned tower, and the varied tint of the surrounding sea, all contributed to make the picture perfect beyond description.

We may well suppose that contending powers fought fiercely during all the ages for the possession of this little paradise.

Under the Maltese Cross.

Corinthians, Athenians, Spartans, Macedonians, Romans, Frenchmen and Englishmen have, in turn, planted their standards here, and now the flag that bears the Maltese cross floats from the great fortress that proudly dominates the island.

Although for years it was under the friendly protectorate of Great Britain this was never quite satisfactory to the Corfiotes, and when the chance was given them, with enthusiasm they voted, "The single and unanimous will of the Ionian people has been and is for their reunion with the Kingdom of Greece."

As this was more than a gentle hint, it was in 1864 that England gracefully withdrew, and since that time Corfu and her sister islands have formed an important part of the Hellenic kingdom.

The King of Greece.

Here, as everywhere among the Hellenes, we found that the King of Greece is very popular, and his democratic manners make him the idol of the common people.

As will be remembered, he was Prince William, of Denmark, the brother of the Czarina of Russia and of the Princess of Wales, and after his election by the National Assembly, in 1863, he took the name of George.

Before his election was finally announced votes were cast for Prince Albert of England, the Duke of Edinburg, Prince Jerome Napoleon, the Prince Imperial, and some in the assembly enthusiastically advocated a republican form of government, but all at last united on the young prince from Denmark, who was as little of an aristocrat as could be found in all Europe.

Indeed, Greece is more of a republic, perhaps, than any other country with a crowned head at its helm. Suffrage is universal; hereditary titles are not known; there are no entailed estates; the press is absolutely free, and the advantages of education are enjoyed by all classes.

The people are passionately patriotic, and they seem to be intensely alive to everything that pertains to the welfare of their loved land.

The City of Corfu.

Our ship had hardly dropped anchor, a few hundred yards from the esplanade of Corfu, when a score of boatmen were clamoring for our patronage, and, accepting the services of an old Corfiote, whose English and French were as dilapidated as were his garments and craft, we were soon on the streets of the city, whose population of about thirty thousand is composed, besides the natives, of Dalmatians, Maltese, Levantines and He-

A MODERN GREEK MAID.

brews. A strange fact came to my knowledge while gathering data about the island and its people. The heirs of a certain George Colochieretry have been maintained in luxury for many years by means of the embalmed body of a saint by the name of Spiridion, who was martyred fifteen hundred years ago.

28

St. Spiro's Body.

The story goes that he was persecuted under Diocletian. His embalmed body was taken to Constantinople, and in the latter half of the fifteenth century Colochieretry, at his own expense, brought it to Corfu, where it reposes in a silver coffin, lit by hanging lamps, under the dome of the Church of St. Spiro.

Persons are seen in great numbers pressing into the church on certain occasions, where they lay their gifts upon and kneel before the sarcophagus of the sainted dead.

A MODERN GREEK.

Every four months the body is lifted from the coffin and borne up and down the streets, followed by the Greek clergy and the officials of the town, and, during these performances, the ignorant masses of the people bring forth their sick and lay them, with gifts, where the shadow of the saint can pass over them.

If the heirs of George Colochieretry, who inherited this remarkable piece of property, were inspired by the enterprising spirit of certain Americans, a stock company would be formed without delay, and live stock would be issued upon this corpse of fifteen hundred years.

The island contains many antiquities of great interest.

Fifty years ago, when one of the old forts was demolished, an ancient Greek cemetery was uncovered, and among the graves was found the tomb of Menekrates, which bears a metrical inscription in Greek, and which makes the statement that he lost his life accidentally by drowning.

This inscription was carved upon this stone two thousand five hundred years ago, before the battles of Salamis and Marathon were fought, and the writing is still perfectly legible.

Here on Corfu one recalls the Odyssey over and over again.

Nausicaa comes to mind, for Corfu is the Scheria of Homer's poem, the home of King Alcinous.

Not far from where we stand we can see the blue waters of a deep bay which receives a stream upon whose bank Ulysses first looked upon the charming maiden, "where were the pools unfailing, and clear and abundant the water."

Classic Isles.

Out in the sparkling bay an island of classic story is seen. It is the ship which was turned into stone by Neptune, whose masts are now trees,

PRISON OF SOCRATES, ATHENS.

whose deck is now a platform of rock, and whose hull rests upon unseen foundations.

Ten miles south of Corfu we pass Paxo, of romantic legend. To the right is Parga, which is associated with the expression of Hobhouse, "Robbers all at Parga." The next island of the Ionian group is Santa Maura, the Leucadia of the ancients, from whence dark Sappho flung herself in her despair.

ACROPOLIS, ATHENS.

Now comes in sight Ithaca, which Ulysses loved, " not because it was broad, but because it was his own," and as we pass Zante the words of our own Poe are recalled:

> "O hyacinthine isle ! O purple Zante !
> Isola d'oro ! Fior di Levante ! "

The sail through these island-dotted seas was only too short, and on the second day we touched the Italian shore. Although some years since we had enjoyed a delightful visit to Naples, Pompeii and Vesuvius, with pleasure we turn our faces again in this direction. Especially we desired to make another study of the live mountain and dead city.

In a Dead City.

With the exception of Constantinople, no city in Europe and Asia is more beautifully situated than Naples. From the northern shores of the bay it looks out upon a picture in water-colors that is world-renowned, and between the city and the chain of the Apennines smoking Vesuvius, with its lower slopes studded with white villages, rises insulated in the plain, with the partly excavated city of Pompeii in the meadow below.

Of this live mountain and dead city I desire specially to speak.

In the cool hours of a delightful spring day I took carriage at Naples, and, driving along the crowded quays of the Marinella, the picturesque old Castle of the Carmine and the Ponte della Maddalena were soon behind us, and we were dashing down the road that runs near the eastern shores of the bay.

Stretched on the fences, hanging from the limbs of trees, twined about the doors and windows of the houses and festooning the tops of the houses were miles and miles of macaroni, and as the carriage passed over the road Italian boys and girls ran in front of the horses, turning somersaults, and exclaiming, " Macaroni," " Macaroni," which corresponds to our beggar's plea for "bread," macaroni being the staff of life.

The exhibition of the manufacture of the stuff, the display of the serpentine thing stretching over everything in sight and the din of the word from the mouths of the army of beggars have, I fear, turned my taste against a dish that has hitherto been quite palatable.

Our road passed through the court-yard of the palace at Portici, at the head of the bay, and immediately afterward we enter the little city of Resina, where more than ten thousand persons have built their houses and enjoy the pleasures of life upon the tufa and lava which cover the noted town of Herculaneum.

Less than two miles out of Resina we reach the Observatory, about 2000 feet above the sea, and close at hand is the Hermitage, from which a magnificent view is taken of the heights of Camaldoli, Posillpo, Misenum, Ischia, with its pyramid-like Monte Epornco standing against the blue Italian sky, and toward the south can be seen the Monte St. Angelo, with Castellammare, Vico, Sorrento and Massa at its foot, and further in the distance loom up the three-peaked Capri.

At the Crater of Vesuvius.

Declining to be aided by a persevering porter, and accompanied only by a single guide, I made the ascension to the crater of Vesuvius on foot. This is an experience of a lifetime and there is no temptation ever to repeat it. For more

CITY OF NAPLES WITH MOUNT VESUVIUS IN THE BACKGROUND.

than two hours I pressed my weary way through loose ashes and fresh lava currents, and when the top of the cone was reached the waves of sulphurous vapor were so trying that I was obliged to hold a handkerchief over my mouth, and turn my face away from the wind to relieve the stifling sensation produced by the impregnated atmosphere. When I reached the extreme top both of the soles of my shoes were nearly burned off, my trousers were scorched in several places, my new Naples hat was broken in, and I looked, I am sure, like a double first cousin to the most disreputable tramp that ever proudly marched in the ranks of Coxey's army. At the circus, when a wild beast bellowed, an enthusiastic Irishman was heard to exclaim: "That's a mighty sound. I'd like to look into the crater's mouth." While the mumblings and groanings of fiery Vesuvius filled my ears I was prompted by as laudable an ambition, and I said to my obliging guide, "This is a terrible noise that comes out of this trembling mountain. I must look into the *crater's mouth!*" Holding his arm, I walked to the crumbling edge of the pit of fire, and as the wind blew the vapor and smoke in the opposite direction I looked down into this flaming lake, which reminded me of certain thrilling descriptions in Dante's "Inferno."

Its Historical Aspect.

Vesuvius, which rises 4000 feet in the midst of the plain of Campania, is about thirty miles in circumference, and on the west it is open to the plain of Naples, and on the south its base is washed by the sea. During the last three hundred years Vesuvius has been the only active crater among the volcanic group of the Bay of Naples, and Stomboli, the most northern of the Lipari Islands, is the only other permanently active vol-

GRECIAN CADET.

cano in Europe, lying about seventy miles north of Ætna and 120 miles southeast of Vesuvius.

Although Strabo describes Vesuvius as a truncated cone, with a barren and ashy aspect, "having cavernous hollows in its cineritious rocks, which look as if they had been acted on by fire," and Seneca writes that in former times it had given out more than its own volume of matter and had furnished the channel, not the food, of the internal fire, it was not until the sixty-third year of our era, during the reign of Nero, that the mountain began for the first time to give indications that the volcanic fire was returning to its former channel. On the second month of this year the surrounding country was shaken by an earthquake, which, as Seneca informs us, threw down a great part of Pompeii and Herculaneum; in

the following year another earthquake occurred, which destroyed a part of Naples, and during the next sixteen years these commotions continued at intervals.

Death of Pliny.

But it was on the twenty-fourth of August, in the year 79, during the reign of Titus, that the first eruption of Vesuvius of which we have any record took place. It was this eruption which destroyed Pompeii and Herculaneum and which caused the death of Pliny, the naturalist.

The younger Pliny, in letters to Tacitus, gives a description of the death of his uncle (vi. 16 and 20); and says that about one in the afternoon his mother informed his uncle, who was stationed with the Roman fleet at Misenum, that a cloud appeared of unusual size and shape. "It was not," he continues, "at that distance discernible from what mountain it arose, but it was found afterward that it was from Vesuvius. I cannot give a more exact description of its figure than by likening it to that of a pine tree, for it shot up a great height in the form

SOLDIER OF ATHENS.

of a trunk, which extended itself at the top into the form of branches, occasioned, I imagine, either by a sudden gust of air, which impelled it, the force of which decreased as it advanced upward, or the cloud itself, being pressed back again by its own weight, expanded in this manner. It appeared sometimes bright and sometimes dark and spotted, as it became more and more impregnated with earth and cinders. This was a surprising phenomenon, and it deserved, in the opinion of the learned man, to be inquired into more carefully. He commanded a Liburnian galley to be prepared for him, and made me an offer of accompanying him, if I desired. I declined, as my studies were more agreeable. He went out of the house with his tablets in his hand.

"The mariners at Retinæ entreated him not to venture upon so hazardous an undertaking. He sailed immediately to places which were abandoned by other people. He now found that the ashes beat into the ships much hotter and in greater quantities, and as he drew nearer, pumice stones, with black flints, burnt and torn up by the flames, broke in upon them, and now the hasty ebb of the sea and ruins tumbling from the mountain, hindered their nearer approach to the shore.

"Pausing a little upon this, whether he should not return back, and, urged to it by the pilot, he cried out: 'Fortune assists the brave; let us make the best of our way to Pomponianus,' who was then at Stabiæ."

Destruction of Pompeii.

During this terrible night he perished.

The younger Pliny, the historian, gives a minute description of the eruption and the devastation it wrought. The crater vomited ashes, red-hot stones, loose fragments of volcanic materials and enormous volumes of vapor, which fell upon the country for miles around in torrents of heated water, charged with the dry, light ashes which were suspended in the air.

Since this first recorded eruption Vesuvius during every century has burst forth in these fearful upheavals, but the most important eruptions, in modern times, occurred in the years 1632, 1793, 1794, 1804, 1822, 1828 and 1872.

It has been noticed that when the crater is nearly filled up or its surface slightly depressed below the rim, and when there is a diminution of the water in the springs and wells on the slopes and at the foot of the mountain, an eruption is near at hand.

A Dead City.

With a copy of Bulwer's "Last Days of Pompeii" in hand, it was with thrilling sensations of pleasure that I passed through the entrance near the Street of the Tombs, and commenced my study of the ruins of a city that was suddenly checked in its life of gaiety and pleasure by the fiery monster on the plain over eighteen hundred years ago.

The destroyed city was itself built upon the volcanic rocks of the Campania, which formed a peninsula, surrounded by a plain extending to the sea on the west and south and bounded on the east by the river Sarno. Although one of the classic writers informs us that it was "a celebrated city," little of its history has come down to us.

At the time of its destruction it was a commercial town of about thirty thousand inhabitants, was a summer resort for wealthy Romans, and in the year A. D. 55 it became a Roman colony under Nero. Cicero had a villa in one of the suburbs of the place and here wrote his "Offices."

It was in Pompeii that Claudius took refuge from the cruelty of Tiberius, here Seneca passed his early youth, and it was in the amphitheatre of the city that occurred a fight between the citizens of Pompeii and the town of Nuceria, which is so vividly described by Tacitus.

ATHENIAN STREET MERCHANT.

While the people of the city were busily engaged in repairing the buildings that had been injured by the earthquakes of A. D. 63 and 64, the eruption of August 24, 79, completely destroyed the city. Showers of ashes and pumice overwhelmed the place, the roofs of the houses were broken in by the stones, and in their residences and on the streets hundreds of persons were killed.

Excavations and Discoveries.

Although the celebrated engineer and architect, Domenico Fontana, in the year 1592, constructed an aqueduct for conveying the water of the Sarno to Torre dell' Annunziata under the city, passing the Forum and three temples, and sinking his air shafts over more than a mile of its surface, it was not until the middle of the eighteenth century that the city was discovered.

While a peasant in the year 1748 was sinking a well, a painted chamber containing statues and other objects of antiquity was unearthed, and immediately under the order of Charles III, the excavations were prosecuted vigorously. A few years later the great amphitheatre was cleared out, and since that time, with more or less activity, the work has been going on.

For some years there was an annual grant of 60,000 frs. ($12,000) by the Italian Parliament for the prosecution of the excavations, but whether this sum is now devoted to the work I am not informed. In shape the town is an irregular oval extending from east to west and surrounded by walls in circumference about two miles.

Streets and Mansions.

The widest streets are not more than eleven feet, not including the raised footway; there were five principal thoroughfares of the city, and the pavements are composed mostly of large polygonal blocks of lava closely fitted together.

It is interesting to trace the Greek and Roman styles of architecture among the ruins of Pompeii. Some of the temples retain the peculiar features of Grecian architecture, but in most cases the principles of Greek art have been corrupted or cast aside altogether. For instance, the Ionic capital, which in Greek architecture was invariably marked by its simplicity, is here loaded with elaborate ornaments.

It is noticeable that some of the handsomest mansions have shops attached to them, showing the commercial character of the city. There is a sameness in the houses.

Structure of Houses.

The outer walls of the ground floor were stuccoed, and generally painted in bright colors; the upper floors alone had windows, and the roof, being flat, was converted into a terrace and planted with vines and flowers, so as to form a pleasant promenade. The vestibule led into the court, where public conferences were held by the proprietor; and the private apartments of the house consisted of a number of rooms decorated according to the rank and circumstances of the occupant.

Within the limits of this chapter it is impossible for me to dwell in detail upon the interesting ruins of Pompeii, but those that attract particular attention are the Forum, the Basilica, the Temples of Venus, Jupiter, Augustus and Neptune, the Houses of Diomed, Sallust, Faun, Castor and Pollux, the Baths, the Gate of Herculaneum, the Amphitheatre and the Street of the Tombs.

Antiquities.

Among the many antiquities found in the city are valuable works of art and many objects which have made familiar to us the religion, the public institutions, the amusements and the domestic life of this people, but it is remarkable that nothing has yet been discovered which throws light on their literature or intellectual pursuits. With the exception of a single papyrus roll and a few lines found

on the walls of the Basilica, and a verse of the Æneid written on the wall of a
private house, no traces of ancient literature, as far as I can learn, have come to
light.

What strange feelings possess one as he listens to his own footsteps upon
pavements that were silent for so many centuries! Thought lifts the veil that
hides from view the dim, distant past.

Lifting the Veil.

Looking upon the blackened forms of men, women and children, whose warm
blood was chilled by a terrible calamity a few years after the Apostle Paul, the
Roman prisoner, passed near by on his way to Rome (and some of whom, perhaps,
saw the chained Christian hero), ages seem to be annihilated, and we are
brought face to face with events that have heretofore been to us only historical.

The gay town is alive with the aristocracy of Rome; the theatres are crowded
with applauding audiences; the narrow streets swarm with the brilliantly costumed, motley, jostling, laughing, quarreling host of humanity, the growing
plants wave under the cool sprays of the playing fountains in the court-yards as
the rich occupants entertain their guests. Suddenly a crape veil is drawn over
the bright face of the sun, the artillery of Vesuvius shoots forth missiles of fire
and death, and the glory of gladness passes into the gloom of the grave.

PRIEST OF THE GREEK CHURCH.

CHAPTER XXIV.

A CITY OF THE CÆSARS—THE FACTS AND FABLES OF ROME.

S in ancient times, so in these modern days, all the roads in Italy lead to Rome; but how different the mode of travel over these highways now and in the times of the Cæsars! A few hours behind a puffing iron horse, and we pass from the beautiful bay to the turbid Tiber. Rome lies chiefly on the eastern side of the Tiber, a deep, rapid, muddy stream, running southward to the Mediterranean Sea. The seven hills (actually ten hills) upon which the ancient city was built are comparatively slight elevations, having been lowered by the cutting down of their summits and the filling in of their valleys.

The modern Rome is built on the debris of the old city, varying from ten to fifty feet in depth. The streets of the city, with two or three exceptions, are short and narrow—many are crooked and filthy, all are paved with small broken stones, rough, sharp and hard as flint, which are a torment to pedestrians.

The houses are built to the edge of the streets, generally large, three to six stories high, fireproof and stuccoed—and nearly every house is occupied by several families on different floors.

The plazas or public squares are numerous, and many of them are adorned with fountains, statues, monuments, obelisks and arches.

The Pincian Garden deserves special notice. It crowns a hill of historic interest, and here was the villa of Lucullus, the conqueror of Mithridates, and the grave of Nero. An ancient parapet wall, 100 feet high, skirts one side, and from the opposite direction can be seen a landscape of surpassing beauty.

The summit has recently been leveled and beautified with drives, walks, trees, shrubs, flowers, grottoes, statues and fountains. This last word brings to mind the fountain of Trévi, one of the most wonderfully fantastic fountains in the world.

As I came down one of the narrow streets of Rome, I was dazzled by sheets of water, which, from a pell-mell of rocks, dominated by a building covered with statues, came tumbling, foaming and sparkling on every side, to be engulfed in cavernous holes. In the midst of rock-work and shell, Neptune emerges with his steed from the basement of a palace to which this enormous construction is fixed. From graceful bas-reliefs, from the upper basins, from the hollow of rocks in which intertwine climbing plants carved on rough stone, innumerable streams of all sizes spout forth on every side; and gathering into a cataract of pure, limpid water, it dashes into a reservoir in which a small ship might float.

From this basin of crystal water let us turn our eyes to a great reservoir, long since left dry, called the Baths of Caracalla.

These immense ruins, with their thick walls, high arches and vast baths lined with mosaics, are located on the banks of the Tiber, and were commenced by Caracalla in A. D. 212.

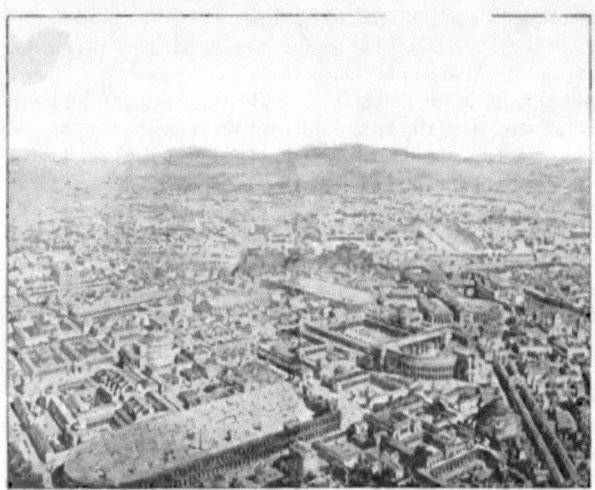

GENERAL VIEW OF ROME.

These baths covered 2,625,000 square yards, nearly a mile square, and could accommodate from ten to thirty thousand bathers.

These and other public baths were the resort of all classes, for pleasure, business and dissipation; and the influence of these gatherings was, doubtless, one of the causes of the degeneracy of the Romans, rendering them an easy prey to the Goths and Vandals.

We must now pass on to the historical spot called the Palatine, round which the seven hills group themselves, and which is the primitive site of Rome. It was just here, according to the legend, that Romulus and Remus, the twin sons of Mars and Sylvia, were suckled by a she wolf, then reared by the shepherd Faustulus; and here it was that the remarkable Romulus harnessed a heifer and a bull to a plow, and traced the sacred enclosure of the city between the rising and going down of the sun.

As we saunter among these thickets of ruins we are borne into the bosom of the classic period of Roman history, and nearly every fragment about us finds its identity guaranteed by a citation from some annalist or poet of antiquity.

ST. PETER'S AND THE VATICAN, ROME.

Here dwelt, besides the chief dictators, the Gracchi, as well as Catuilus, Fiaccus, Hortensius, Catiline and Marcus Tullius.

Just here it was that Cicero referred in those lines to the Tribune Clodius: "I will raise my roof higher, not from contempt for thee, but to veil from thee the view of the city which thou would'st fain have destroyed"

Below the roof, and a little to the right, Julius Cæsar established himself as soon as he was in possession of the pontificate.

Near here Marcus Antonius, Claudius Nero, the father of Tiberius, and Octavius, the father of Augustus, looked from their windows upon the rolling Tiber and formed ambitious and cruel schemes.

During recent excavations a curious and important discovery was made on the Palatine Hill. The pursuit of the excavations brought to light a subterranean passage, round which, in the direction of the ancient palace, were the leaden pipes for the conduct of water. On these pipes we can read, from distance to distance, the words IVLIÆ AVG

INTERIOR OF CHAPEL ON THE SPOT WHERE ST. PETER WAS CRUCIFIED.

(Juliæ Aug.). As the name of the owner is constantly inscribed on pipes of this kind, this inscription is a genuine proof of ownership, and informs that the house in question belonged to the Empress Livia, Julia Augusta, or Livia, widow of Augustus.

This house is decorated in the most brilliant style. One of the panels contains a fanciful landscape, in which trees, terraces adorned with statues, bridges thrown out into space, rookeries and flowing water make up a scene that would delight a Japanese; in the foreground three ducks are coming out of an aquatic grotto, leaving long furrows in the water.

Some of the rooms are enriched by thick garlands of flowers and fruit suc-ceeding one another in festoons and bound with rib-bons; and others contain paintings of rare delicacy, much of the fresh-ness of the coloring being preserved.

But, on the Palatine, nothing interested me more than Nero's Fo-rum, the outline of which has been identified by arch-æologists.   There we see a portion of the wall, there the bench of Council-lors, the imperial judgment seat, and there is the pris-oner's seat.

We know that Paul was tried be-fore Nero.   This was his Forum, and perhaps just here the Apostle to the

ALTAR TO THE UNKNOWN GOD, ROME.

Gentiles stood.   As we cross the Tiber to visit St. Peter's and the Vatican on the western side, we approach the famous castle of St. Angelo, connected with so many outrages and factions that desolated Rome, but most interesting, perhaps, because of the fact that in one of its gloomy cells the beautiful Beatrice de Cenci lingered for many months; and near its massive, frowning walls, on the ninth of September, 1599, she was beheaded.

29

There are 380 Catholic churches in Rome. As the Virgin Mary is the goddess of the Romans, we are not surprised that many of these are dedicated to her; and costly gifts of gold, silver and precious stones are laid on her altars.

The object of universal attraction in Rome is St. Peter's, the largest and most famous church in the world.

That the circus of Nero should be the site of the greatest church in Christendom is a suggestive fact.

As you stand at the opening on the wide plaza and look toward the immense dome, you are struck with the unity of so vast a construction, which was commenced in 1450 and continued over two centuries and a half.

The approach to the church is made through a colonnade, semi-circular in form, composed of 284 columns, set in four rows, and leaving between them a central passage for carriages.

Beautiful fountains and the imposing obelisk of Caligula adorn the centre of the plaza.

The façade or front of the church, 357 feet wide and 144 feet high, is a disappointment. It conceals the fine proportions of the remainder of the building and destroys the effect of the magnificent dome. Let us enter. In Italy they do not shut the churches by a system of small doors. Giving a literal interpretation to the saying: "My Father's house is always open," they are content with a curtain. In passing through the doorway of St. Peter's you push aside a large double leather curtain, with lead at the foot of it.

You enter as if you miraculously made a hole in the wall which instantly and noiselessly closed up.

You are now dazzled with a mass of splendor, as you face the nave, 600 feet long, 100 feet wide and nearly 450 feet to the ceiling of the dome. The floor is paved with marble of various colors; the walls are adorned with pictures in mosaic and statues in full or in bold relief, all of colossal size.

On either side of the nave there are five or six chapels used for ordinary worship, and each is as capacious as one of our good-sized churches.

The Cathedral can contain 60,000 people. Within these walls we can count 44 altars, 748 columns, and a council of 389 statues.

There are three objects of leading interest.

We pass the bronze statue of St. Peter, revered by Roman Catholics more than any statue in the world; and to be convinced of the attention paid it, you need only look at the toe, which has been polished bright by the kisses of the devotees.

At the bottom of the nave the eye is attracted to the front of the master-altar, at the foot of which are the eighty-seven lamps perpetually burning on the circular balustrade of the confessional, where it is said the body of St. Peter lies.

Before the altar over the grave only the Pope says mass.

Above the altar is a most elaborately decorated canopy supported by four twisted columns, ninety feet high, made of bronze, brought from the Pantheon. All Catholics regard it as a great privilege to worship at this confessional. Just beyond, in the midst of a glory, the chair of St. Peter is pointed out to you. It is supported by four colossal figures of bronze and gold, which represent two fathers of the Latin and two of the Greek Church.

The chair that you look upon is only an outside case, containing the curate seat of Egyptian wood faced with ivory, which is said to have been given by the Senator Prudens to his guest, the Apostle Peter. The Vatican (from Vates, a prophet, because here was believed to have been the site of the Etruscan divination) is the palace of the Popes, and is located near St. Peter's.

It is not one building, but a group of buildings, dating from different periods, but as such it is the largest palace in the world, 1151 feet long by

THE VATICAN, ROME.

767 wide, containing, it is said, 11,000 rooms. Just here, we have reason to think, were the gardens of Nero, where, as Tacitus writes, he put to death "an immense multitude" of Christians, on the groundless charge of setting fire to Rome, and in awful mockery nailed them, clad in garments dipped in pitch, upon stakes, and set fire to them. They tell you that St. Peter was crucified here. The apartments occupied by the Pope are very plain. Immediately above them are the rooms of the Cardinal Secretary of State.

The Sistine Chapel, built in 1473, is the most famous of the apartments of the Vatican; doubtless, because of the fact that the ceiling and altar wall were frescoed by Michael Angelo. Upon the ceiling he put his wonderful series of pictures from the Old Testament, extending from the first day of the creation to the prophets; and upon the altar wall is the famous fresco, "The Last Judgment."

The loggia (lodja) and stanza, different parts of the Vatican, are associated with the genius of Raphael, who painted and designed them.

The largest collection of antique statuary in the world is found in the Vatican; and such masterpieces in painting as Raphael's "Transfiguration" and Titian's "Madonna and Saints" may be studied within its walls.

The Vatican Library contains more than 100,000 printed books; but that which raises it above all other collections is the value and number of its manuscripts. Of these, there are over 27,000. Most precious, perhaps, of the treasures of the Vatican is the Codex Vaticanus, designated B. It is written on 759 leaves of very fine vellum (N. T. covers 142 of them) in small uncial letters in three colums of 42 lines each to a page, ten inches by ten inches and a half.

It was carried to France by Napoleon I., but restored after his fall.

Besides this there are 18 Slav manuscripts, 10 from China, 22 from India, 13 from America; 80 in Coptic and 1 from Samaria; 72 from Ethiopia; 590 of Hebrew origin and 459 of Syrian; 64 from Turkey; 787 from Arabia and 65 from Persia, illustrated with fine miniatures. In the great libraries of the world like the Bodleian at Oxford and the library in the British Museum you are overwhelmed by the sight of the great mass of books, which are piled up over your head in endless walls; at the Vatican, on the contrary, you do not see a single volume. The collection is under cover of a multitude of shut and gilded presses.

But we must cross the Tiber again and stand for a moment in a bit of narrow valley, which was, within small compass, the most imposing spot in the universe, perhaps.

Here gathered, during the turning points of Roman history, the brains of the Roman Empire; here dramas have been unfolded, which threw both light and shadow upon more than one empire. The entire history of the most renowned of people worked itself out on the scene of the Roman Forum, the soul and sanctuary of Rome. We know where the Forum was; but only a portion of the place has been exposed by excavations; much of this historic spot is still covered by four and twenty feet of ruins.

It was at the entry of the Forum where we now stand, that the Piso lived whom Agrippina accused of having poisoned Germanicus; and it was there where he was assassinated, Tacitus tells us, at the instigation of Tiberius, who was compromised in the matter.

What wondrous events, on a scene as narrow as that of a play-house, from the days since Brutus showed there the dagger of Lucretia and Virginius bought in the shops north of the Forum, down to the memorable occasion when the curia was burnt before the body of Cæsar. Just here was delivered some of the greatest orations of ancient times; just here were enacted scenes in Roman history that told both upon the rise and fall of the Roman Empire.

EXCAVATIONS OF THE FORUM, ITALY.

Every step brings before you memorials of life and death; every broken monument is an eloquent tongue, telling still the tale of mighty deeds and faded glory; every crumbling wall seems to open before you, and through its black bosom comes forth great spectres of history, that remind us of the decay and death of human honor, hopes and happiness.

Passing along the via Sacra under the celebrated Arch of Titus, leaving the Arch of Constantine on the one hand, and the remains of the pool in which the gladiators washed after their bloody combats, on the other, we reach the

Coliseum, regarded by many as the most august and imposing ruin in the world. Excepting the Pyramids of Egypt, the world agrees in this opinion.

It was commenced by Vespasian in A. D. 72, and completed by Titus after his return from the conquest of Jerusalem. Twelve thousand Jews were employed in its construction. The exterior was adorned by three rows of columns, Doric, Ionic and Corinthian, some of which are in excellent preservation. It is about 620 feet long, 513 feet wide, 157 feet high, 1641 feet in circuit and could accommodate 100,000 persons. There are four stories of different orders of architecture, and it is open at the top. Here it was that Ignatius was martyred: here many early Christians were beheaded, burned and torn to pieces by wild beasts.

THE COLISEUM, ROME.

Another scene of quite a different character is recalled to mind as we look upon this arena, the death-bed of so many Christians.

Beneath the ancient Rome, along the fifteen consular roads which radiated from the capitol as centre, there existed in the early centuries twenty-six great catacombs, which answer to the number of parishes at that time.

Pagan Rome was simply mined by these underground cemeteries, there being 360 miles of winding ways among the ashes and skeletons of the dead.

It is estimated that these leagues of galleries contain no less than six million of the dead.

Passing through a wild garden some two miles from the heart of Rome, we descended some thirty steps, and penetrated a series of narrow corridors, one after another, cut at right angles and intricate like a net-work of lanes. With taper in hand, following an old bent monk, we walked for hours through these strange caverns of the dead.

The use of catacombs as cemeteries long preceded the Christian era. Pliny informs us that the practice of incineration was not very ancient, and that many great families had preserved the custom of burying the dead.

Salust had under his garden catacombs, with chambers for the dead. Moving through these narrow, low and never-ending passages, where the air is made thick by the smoke of torches, the tombs of martyrs and heroes draw one's attention specially. It is easy to make these out, for when the grave-makers closed them, they fastened in the cement by the side of the head a narrow-necked vessel of glass in which the blood of the confessor had been collected. You can see, on nearly every hand, the mark and often the fragments of these vessels. When the martyrs had been drowned, burned or put to death without spilling of blood, then, in sealing up the burial place, the workman with the point of his trowel drew in the fresh mortar a rude sketch of a palm tree, and a number of these are to be seen.

Occasionally we recognize the calcined bones of a martyr burnt alive, and it sometimes happens that the bones are crystallized to such a degree as to shine. In the Catacombs of St. Callistus the paintings are more numerous than in any other. You frequently see the anchor, the dove, the ship, the fish, whose Greek name recalls that of Christ and furnishes the initials of the formula: "Jesus Christ, Son of God, Saviour " (Ἰησοῦς Χριστός Θεοῦ Ὑιὸς Σωτήρ) and many other symbols. Some of the epitaphs are very interesting. One in Greek reads thus: "Here was laid to sleep Gorgónius, whom all loved and who hated none." Here is one in Latin: "Too soon hast thou fallen, Constantia: Admirable for beauty and for her charms, she lived 18 years 6 months and 16 days. Constantia in peace."

Over a picture of a man swinging a pickaxe the following inscription can be traced: " Diogenes the Grave-digger, in Peace."

But we must blow out our tapers and stand in the sunlight before the most perfect ruin in Rome.

The Pantheon, finished by Agrippa just before the birth of Christ, is fronted by a portico, which rests on sixteen enormous monolithic columns of oriental granite, crowned by the finest capitals, which Rome has bequeathed to us. Beneath the magnificent dome the bodies of Raphael and Victor Emmanuel rest. A monument raised at the dawn of the age of Augustus, and at the end of the Republic must be regarded with great interest; but we must hurry on. We have only time to glance at the celebrated Tarpeian Rock, which forms the southern portion of the Capitoline Hill, and from whose rugged height it was customary to hurl persons condemned for treason; and the imposing looking house of Rienzi, the last of the Tribunes, whose crusade recalls to one's mind the Gracchi, the Brutuses and the Scipios, as we make our way toward the most famous highway, spoken of in the profane and sacred history. Appius Claudius, after digging the first aqueduct to direct the waters of Præneste on Rome, opened and paved what is known as the Appian Way, 310 years before our era. This road is broad and very straight, with remains, quite visible, of paths and open spaces in Gothic pavement. The grass is green on the way, but the track of this most splendid of all historical promenades, remains definitely marked with melancholy grandeur, by two avenues of mausoleums in ruins, in every shape and size, which may be counted by thousands. Seneca's tomb is here pointed out. From the last chapter of Acts we have reason to think that on some of the stones of this highway the feet of the Apostle Paul pressed, on his way to Rome and to a martyr's death. The place where the great Apostle was tried, the cell in which he was imprisoned, and the place of his execution are all pointed out by your agreeable and instructive guide.

Before turning from these scenes which recall so many facts and fables that are weaved into the history of Rome, let us mount a noble terrace, near the spot where St. Peter is said to have been crucified, and take a general view of the city and its surroundings. As described by another:

" Rome is only a foreground of the picture, for the view extends toward the north over the plains, reaching as far as the Apennines. Toward the southeast at the foot of the Alban mountains it embraces those plains of the old Latium, where many a heroic battle was fought and won. The sun, ready to set behind us in the Mediterranean Sea, inflamed with its twilight purple the domes, towers, pinnacles, and palaces, as well as the volcanic mounds scattered at the foot of the chains and over the plateaux. Between these two extreme points, the blue-tinged mountains, the city glowing and ruddy in the midst of the bronze zone of its Byzantine walls, lay stretched before us a mixture of verdure and russet outlines, the country crossed by aqueducts, covered by ancient villas, and pierced by long roads of old renown, marked out and lined with tombs.

"The yellow Tiber winds at our feet like a track of sand; going up toward the horizon it melts on one side in the azure of the sky, on the other in the fires of the setting sun.

"We now leave this museum of all ages. It may look with indifferent eye upon our revolutions, upon our institutions of a day; its glory, which has already defied so many ruins, will see new ones, but it has not to dread the fainting memory of men. So long as society stands Rome will remain the Urbs, the city of cities, the native land of arts, the sanctuary of incomparable memories, the home of a people whose character, whose history, whose destiny stand unique through the current of the centuries."

CHAPTER XXV

GENOA AND GIBRALTAR.

S one approaches Genoa by sea he can readily imagine why she was called Genoa la Superba, when she was in the height of her power.

From the deck of your steamer, for miles away, through your marine glasses, you can see the city rising like an amphitheatre, with its two converging moles, its encircling fortifications, its piles of palaces, its promenades and gardens and the verdureless summits of the Apennines and the ice-covered peaks of the Alps in the background.

On closer examination you find that it is one of the best fortified cities of Europe, for not only is the large semicircular harbor defended by moles, but the city is entirely surrounded by a double wall, the smaller encircling the inner city by ramparts, detached forts, redoubts and extensive outworks.

Although I had visited the city some years since, I decided to spend another week within her walls, studying more carefully her people and palaces.

Nearly all of the streets are narrow, irregular and steep, paved with smooth slabs of lava, with a pathway of different material in the centre for beasts of burden: but certain modern streets are wide, well paved and compare favorably with the chief thoroughfares of other commercial cities. Many of the palaces do not retain their former artistic riches, but they all display splendid architectural designs and the internal and external frescoes are well worth studying.

The Palaces of the Doges.

The Palazzo Doria, overlooking the sea, constructed in 1529 by the renowned Doria, prince of Melfi, while it is almost abandoned, retains striking evidences of its past beauty and richness; and the ducal palace restored in 1778 after designs by Simone Carlone, formerly the depository of famous works of art, is elaborately decorated, and gives one a vivid idea of the glory of the reign of the Doges.

As my room was located a short distance from the via Doges, which is lined on both sides with the palaces of these old rulers, my mornings were spent, under the direction of a competent guide, in visiting these magnificent buildings.

You step immediately from the street on the ground floor of the palace, which is composed of a wide, handsomely paved passage-way, with large rooms on either side, and over winding stairways you ascend to a number of floors, where the chambers occupied by the royalty are still in excellent preservation.

One of these palaces is now used as the hall of the town council, where a bust and autograph letters of Columbus, the violin of Paganini and other interesting objects are shown.

Wall paintings and elaborate room decorations were very popular during the reign of the Doges, and some of these that are on exhibition in these palaces on the via Doges cannot be excelled in the world.

The Republic of Genoa.

In legendary traditions the history of Genoa can be traced to a time preceding the foundation of Rome. At the beginning of the second Punic war, Livy men-

PANORAMA OF GENOA.

tions it as having friendly relations with the Romans, and during this war, having been destroyed by a Carthaginian fleet, the Romans rebuilt it, and it afterward became a Roman *municipium*.

Because of its location Genoa has been in all these centuries the centre of the severest struggles on land and by sea. During the rise and fall of the republic its internal commotions, caused by the parties of the plebeians and patricians and the external warfare in which it has been so often engaged with neighboring and distant enemies, have been sources of continual perils and distractions.

Party struggles assumed such a bad shape during the first half of the fourteenth century that the dogate for life was instituted (1339) with the exclusion of both parties. But there were ceaseless quarrels between the Doges and anti-Doges under the Viscontis of Milan and under the rule of France, until, in 1528, the celebrated Admiral Andrea Doria delivered the republic from the French and established a new constitution, which lasted for many years.

This form of government was strictly aristocratic, and the nobility comprised the Grimaldis, Fieschis, Dorias, Spinolas and many others whose names are familiar to the student of Italian history. The Doge was elected for two years, but the power of the State had long since departed and the beginning of the end was fast approaching.

Its Modern History.

The first year of this century Genoa, under Massena, sustained a siege by the Austrians and English, but the Austrians, who held it for a short while, were obliged to relinquish it after the battle of Marengo.

After the coronation of Napoleon Bonaparte at Milan, the last of the Doges, Durazzo, went to that city and expressed the desire of the people for a change in government. The republic was merged in the French Empire and formed the three new departments of Genoa, Montenotte and the Apennines.

This century has witnessed many bloody struggles and many political vicissitudes in the province of Genoa, and the picturesque city on the gulf is associated with one of the most remarkable men of the age.

Reminiscences of Garibaldi.

In 1860, Garibaldi, the Italian patriot, entered Sicily with 1000 volunteers. Palermo and Messina were soon taken, and he became dictator of the island. In his attacks upon Austria he came in collision with his own government, and we find him soon afterward planning his well-known invasion of Rome.

His career in the sixties, his association with Victor Emmanuel and the subsequent change in the Italian government are of too recent occurrence to need special mention.

Perhaps it is not generally known that after his banishment from Sardinia, Garibaldi came to New York in the summer of 1850 and earned a living by making candles in a manufactory on Staten Island until he resumed his occupation of a mariner. Some years later he returned to New York in command of a Peruvian bark, and in 1867, when he was imprisoned during one of his raids in Italy, he protested as an Italian deputy, and it was an American citizen who effected his release.

While he was planning his attack upon Rome, an excited crowd gathered in one of the plazas in Genoa determined to compass his death, and I saw the little shop into which Garibaldi entered, and having exchanged his uniform for the dress of the shopkeeper, passed out through the maddened multitude and made good his escape.

It is a source of great interest and pleasure to leisurely saunter through the narrow, overshadowed streets of old Genoa: to look up the long vista of the lanes and alleys, where the protruding bay windows nearly touch each other; to catch the scent of the numerous roof gardens, where the poorest families have their brilliant flowers and graceful vines, and to drop into an old curio shop here or a studio of a struggling, but gifted artist there, and deal in small barterings or still smaller chat. All Italians are willing to sell, but they are anxious to talk.

Home of Christopher Columbus.

In one of my walks through Genoa I found in a most circuitous little street the house owned for a while by the parents of Christopher Columbus, and where a brief period of the great explorer's boyhood was spent. It is marked appropriately over the door, and while I was translating the Italian sentences, from the neighboring houses a number of well-informed

COLUMBUS MONUMENT, GENOA.

persons saluted me, and within a short time I was the receptacle of a fund of information that I am sure would have been startlingly novel to Christopher himself.

Standing upon the deck of the magnificent German Lloyd steamer "Kaiser Wilhelm II," we waved adieu to our kind friends of Genoa on a beautiful morning, and passing over the calm waters of the gulf, as the crown of the queenly city was lost to view, we turned our course toward Southern Spain.

Strait of Gibraltar.

The Mediterranean was on its best behavior, and, in due time, we were in the swift current of the Strait of Gibraltar, which connects the Atlantic and the Mediterranean and lies between the southernmost part of Spain, from Cape Europa to Cape Trafalgar, and the African coast from Centapoint on the east to Cape Spartel on the west. The extreme length of the strait is about thirty-six miles, and the narrowest point is only nine miles.

It is estimated that the greatest depth of the water is 960 fathoms, and where the two continents are close together there is a strong central current, from three to five miles an hour, setting in constantly from the ocean to the sea. Two smaller currents, one along each shore, ebb and flow with the tide, passing alternately into the Atlantic and the Mediterranean.

Both nature and art have done much to make Gibraltar the most impregnable citadel in the world. The great rock forms a promontory three miles long from north to south, and about seven miles in circumference. It is connected with the mainland of Spain by a flat, sandy isthmus not more than one and a half miles long and three-quarters of a mile wide. Across this strip of land two rows of sentry boxes mark the Spanish and English lines, the "neutral ground" being the space between them.

The Fortress.

The material of the rock is gray primary limestone and marble. Its highest point is between fourteen hundred and fifteen hundred feet above the sea. The north, east and west sides of the rock are so steep as to be nearly inaccessible; and it is perforated by a large number of caverns, many of which cannot be easily entered and show remarkable formations.

The view of Gibraltar from the sea would lead you to infer that it was entirely barren, but upon closer inspection you find that its surface is covered by acacia, fig, orange trees, a large variety of odoriferous plants and numerous wild shrubs. It is said that the only wild monkeys in Europe are found here, and all those seen were of a fawn color and tailless.

The value of Gibraltar as a strategic point caused it to be a bone of contention during many centuries. Under the Spanish crown it was so fortified as to be regarded as impregnable; but in 1704 it was taken by a combined effort of the English and Dutch fleet, and it was confirmed to Great Britain by the treaty of Utrecht.

Since this time besiegers from different nations have brought to bear, both by land and sea, all the resources of war against the rock, but the "Union Jack" has floated victoriously over the crash of the cannonading and the boom of bombardment after bombardment.

A Necessity for England.

To the casual observer it is apparent why England prizes this position. It is the key to the Mediterranean; and as a coaling station, a depot for war material and a port of refuge, it is a necessity for Great Britain in connection with her East Indian possessions.

A garrison of from four to six thousand men, at an annual expense of more than a million of dollars is supported here, and it is quite impossible to tell how

GIBRALTAR.

many thousands of pounds are appropriated every now and then to strengthen this watch tower on her highway to Egypt, Ceylon, Australia and India.

The sides of the gigantic rock are honeycombed with connecting caves, supplied with cannon, commanding every approach by land and sea. Many of the natural caves are used to fortify the place more strongly, but nature is aided by every appliance of military art.

Guns are stationed in secret places, and on certain parts of the rock no one is allowed to go except the officers and regiments in charge.

I was pointed to a beautiful spot, where the verbenas, the heliotrope and blooming heath bedecked the rock, and behind these flowers I was informed there was a screened battery—brazen-throated cannons awaiting to crush the flowers of nations in times of war.

The Town.

There is nothing specially attractive about the town of Gibraltar. It lies on a shelving ledge on the west side of the rock. The main, or Waterport street, is well paved and lighted. The principal buildings are the residences of the governor and lieutenant-governor, the admiralty, naval hospital and storehouses; and during your walk on the chief thoroughfare, as you pass English, Portuguese, Moors, Spaniards, Italians and Maltese, you are impressed by the mixed character of the population.

Among the many caves to be seen St. Michael's is the largest and most interesting. It is more than a thousand feet above the sea level and contains great halls and chambers sixty feet high and two or three hundred feet long.

The Moorish Castle.

But to the student of antiquity nothing on Gibraltar possesses more attraction than the old Moorish castle that is located halfway up the steep precipice on the west side of the rock.

For more than seven hundred years the Moors held sway over Gibraltar; and this old relic of the barbaric ages stands here alone as a grim reminder of their power and prowess.

In girdling the globe, Spain was the last country visited, and after touching some of the picturesque islands washed by the waters of the Atlantic, with inexpressible joy and gratitude, after so many months of peril and pleasure in studying the wonders of the world, I took my course toward the land of my love with the words of De Belloy on my lips and in my heart: "The more I saw of foreign lands, the more I loved my own."